By Sword and Fan

by

Kathleen Buckley

By Sword and Fan

The Wild Rose Press, Inc.
PO Box 708
Adams Basin, NY 14410-0708
Visit us at www.thewildrosepress.com

Publishing History
First Edition, 2023
Trade Paperback ISBN 978-1-5092-5154-4
Digital ISBN 978-1-5092-5155-1

Published in the United States of America

Archbold rode up close beside her and said, "With your leave, mistress, Campbell and I will go first."

"Very well." She had never come this way while he likely knew the thicket well. She did not suppose for a second that there was any danger, but men always thought females needed protection. She loosened the straps on her pouches.

"Gone!" Archbold's low, furious voice left Margaret in no doubt that he would have cursed if he had been alone or only with a man. She rode forward to join him. Two ponies with sidesaddles were loosely tethered in a little clear space between the trees and the foot of the rise. Ackerley's hack was missing.

Campbell said, "I'll be having a look at the road."

The children had been abducted. No one needed to say it aloud.

The Scots groom was back in a trice. "No sign of them. Horses stood a whiles. Sh—droppin's. A few spilt aits."

"Too much to hope for. They'll be away in a carriage."

Margaret said, "They can't be much ahead of us."

Praise for Kathleen Buckley

A Peculiar Enchantment: "The author connects the reader to these authentic characters in a very real way…For historical romance book lovers, this book is definitely worth reading."

~4 Stars, The Historical Fiction Company

Most Secret: Finalist, 2018 OKRWA International Digital Awards, Historical Fiction category; finalist, 2019 Next Generation Indie Book Awards, Romance category.

Captain Easterday's Bargain: Third place in the 2019 OKRWA International Digital Awards, Historical Fiction category.

Also by Kathleen Buckley

Dedication

In memory of the late, great authors who inspired my love of historical fiction: Jane Austen, Sir Walter Scott, Sir Arthur Conan Doyle, Rudyard Kipling, John Dickson Carr, and Jane Aiken Hodge.

Chapter 1

The ride north from Newcastle woke memories of home: the vast sky, the whiff of burning peat, the speech rooted in Lowlands Scots. Alasdair Falstone remembered the spring weather in Northumberland being cool but not as cold as this. The swathes of dog-violet edging the lane had not yet bloomed. Good weather for riding, however.

His first sight of Scot Hall in fifteen years brought a wave of less happy memories surging back. He had not seen it or his brother in nearly half his life, since that overcast afternoon he came home, dreading to tell Sebastian he was leaving. His brother was gone, conferring with a neighbor about some boundary problem. Alasdair collected what he needed and left a letter before riding away for good.

Lord Hawkslowe, it began, *I am off to buy my commission. I wish you joy of your marriage. Alasdair Falstone.* His second craven act was to deviate from the most direct route to Newcastle to a less frequented road, where Sebastian or some minion would not think to pursue him. Probably Sebastian had not made the effort.

Three weeks since, Sebastian's letter had struck like a dagger to his heart. Some undefinable emotion stirred at seeing that familiar hand, recognizable in spite of its shakiness. His brother asked him to come home, adding he had purchased a nearby manor for Alasdair. Remembering Sebastian's high-handed orders that long ago summer, Falstone's first response was anger. To be offered a bribe to return made it worse. The next day or two might find him riding south again.

What did his brother want of him? He had almost decided to refuse until he read the last line, heavily underlined. *The situation here is desperate.* With some misgivings, he requested leave. The visit would determine his next steps.

Judging from the property, either Sebastian was a good landlord or had an excellent steward. The house must be well managed, too, as a groom ran up from the stables before Alasdair dismounted. The house had not altered on the outside. On the inside, change was inevitable.

The door opened to reveal their old butler, who must be on the brink of retiring. "Mr. Alasdair, welcome home. We're glad to see you."

"I'm glad to see you, Graves."

"Peter will bring your valise up to your chamber in a few minutes, sir. Lord Hawkslowe is waiting."

"I should at least wash my hands and face before presenting myself."

"Best not, sir."

At the butler's tone, his heart froze.

"That bad?"

"Ay, sir."

The house was eerily quiet. From his late godfather's letters, he thought he had a nephew who was surely old enough to be away at school. But news from his godfather had ceased with his death. If there were other children, where was the suppressed ferment he recalled from his own youth? Would girls make any noise? Not having had a sister, he could not guess.

"Lady Hawkslowe?"

"She won't trouble you. She is in her sitting room. If you wish, you might see her afterward, Mr. Alasdair. Major Falstone, I should say."

Some of the furnishings were different. The hall in the bedroom wing was carpeted now. To his surprise, Graves led him past the master's suite and down the length of the passage. He tapped on a door at the far end. An unfamiliar manservant admitted him.

The reek of medicine and the sweat of illness greeted him as he entered the bedroom. Sebastian, Lord Hawkslowe, lay propped against several pillows in his bed. Their eyes met for a moment, before the baron doubled over, coughing. His brother was dying. Fifteen years of resentment at their last parting vanished like smoke in a high wind.

Sebastian's sunken eyes were fever bright. "Glad you've...come in time." More coughing. "Left a letter for you...in case you didn't."

"If I'd known, I'd have come sooner." He sank onto a chair by the bed. The fire blazing on the hearth would have been uncomfortable had he not been chilled to the bone.

The manservant held a glass to his brother's lips. After swallowing, he sighed deeply. "Budley. Whisky for the major."

He'd lost the habit of drinking whisky during his years away from Northumberland. Brandy for gentlemen, gin for the poor, and rum for sailors were the spirits of choice in England. But with Scotland's

3

stills so near, their product so easily smuggled and even cheaper than brandy run in from France, usquebaugh was popular with many. Their own family line descended from the Scot who had once owned or at least occupied the property. The cellar held both brandy and whisky. He accepted the offered tumbler.

"None for you?" Falstone hardly knew how to address his brother with the manservant present. Both "Lord Hawkslowe" and "my lord" would sound ridiculous, given they were brothers. Perhaps in some families or in London there were siblings who would address a brother formally. Sebastian and he had used their given names, as there was no secondary title for the heir to use.

Lord Hawkslowe—his brother!—shook his head. "Makes me cough. I'll have barley water."

Budley filled a glass from a jug and presented it with as much ceremony as if it had been the finest brandy. The invalid raised it in a toast. "To our reunited family."

Falstone lifted his tumbler and echoed the sentiment, more in hope than belief.

His brother sipped his soothing drink. Falstone let the usquebaugh linger in his mouth, savoring the strong, peaty flavor most Englishmen found harsh.

"Sorry I didn't apologize years ago, Alasdair. Too proud."

In that moment, Falstone made his decision. "Never mind that now. What can I do for you, Sebastian? You didn't say in your letter."

Hawkslowe said, "Budley, wait in my dressing room. Major Falstone will call if I need you." He needed the respite before the door closed behind the valet to continue.

"I've changed my will to name you guardian and trustee." He paused to catch his breath, and his lips turned up. "Had to scheme with Budley to bring in two unimpeachable witnesses."

Was the situation that bad?

"You'll have to be here to…keep an eye on things. You'll have to live here to…teach my sons to fence and shoot and be gentlemen. I've been…in poor health too long. They ride, at least. I bought Kirkland Grange to give you your own income…so no one can say you're using Scot Hall money for yourself."

"That is generous." If Sebastian was unwilling to appoint a friend guardian, Alasdair was his only choice. Falstone had grown up here, knew the estate and servants and tenants—the ones still living—and Sebastian could trust him to treat them well. As he had no income apart from his officer's pay, he could move here, as some other man, with a property of his own, might not. His brother's good opinion was balm to his soul.

"The boys need a man's presence…but not my wife's brothers." Another fit of coughing.

Alasdair glanced toward the dressing room, then instead rose and held the glass while his brother drank.

When he was able to speak again, he muttered, "Wastrels and rakeshames, both of them. Suppose you can't keep them from visiting Elizabeth, but don't pay their debts. If she wants to give them her pin money, let her. But don't give her additional funds."

They sat in silence while Sebastian's lungs labored.

"I was a fool. When you're the heir, people fawn over you." He gave a gasp of laughter. "Elizabeth's mama wanted a title for her, but her dowry came from her uncle, a Scotch tobacco importer. Will you forgive me? And stay to rear my sons?"

"Ay. I'll sell out."

Looking back, Alasdair half pitied and half despised his younger self for his cowardice and his foolishness. He had thought himself a devil of a fellow and dreamed of military glory. His godfather's tales of his own experiences at the battles of Ramillies and Malplaquet, and his godfather's friendship with men still serving, led Alasdair to choose a career in the dragoons. Besides, the commission cost less than one in a cavalry regiment, for which an officer needed several horses. A dragoon needed only one mount, and that less costly than a cavalry horse. "Sebastian, I should have faced you before running away."

"Alasdair…I was wrong to forbid you to marry that girl. The Bettancourts were good stock. Better than Elizabeth's."

"That's past, now." He had almost ceased to regret his lost chance for marriage.

Hawkslowe drew in a harsh breath. "I know I do not need to ask this, but will you give your promise before God and upon your honor to teach my sons to be decent men and to manage the estate for their benefit?"

Lord Hawkslowe's tone and his request felt oddly ceremonial. "I will."

His brother held out one pallid hand. Alasdair clasped it gently, feeling the bones beneath the skin.

They did not speak much longer before the baron said he was ready to rest for a time.

"I should make my bow to Lady Hawkslowe as soon as I have made myself presentable."

Sebastian sighed. "You must certainly do so, although I fear you will not receive a warm welcome. Please do not tell her you are to be the children's guardian and my executor. I will sleep for a while, if you summon Budley."

The manservant tutted as he gave his master a draught of something from an apothecary's bottle. Laudanum: Alasdair's nose caught the alcohol-tinged bitterness. Budley fluffed the pillows, and his master lay back with a sigh.

Alasdair's hand was upon the door latch when his brother's husky voice stopped him. "Come see me in the morning, Alasdair. There's more to discuss."

On the way to his own old bedchamber to wash and change his clothing, he reflected that keeping the reason for his coming from his sister-in-law did not augur well.

Chapter 2

Lady Hawkslowe eyed his plain, unfashionable garb with distaste. As Alasdair did not aspire to be a beau, her disapproval left him unmoved.

"Be seated," she bade him. She occupied the settee, petticoats spread around her like some exotic flower. He took a side chair. Like all the other furniture in the room (except a red and gilt desk and chair in the Chinese style), it featured curving, elaborately carved legs. Some musky scent permeated her parlor. He hoped he would not sneeze.

"I cannot think why Hawkslowe sent for you when you have been estranged from him forever." The years had sharpened her insipidly pretty features and put fretful lines at the corners of her mouth.

"He wished us to reconcile." He left unspoken "before he dies."

"If only you had married Corinna, you might have been here when he first fell ill."

Rather than say, "I loved another" or "Your sister and I would not have suited," he replied, "I had decided upon a military career. I could not ask any lady to follow the drum," which was true. He quashed a rare smile at the thought of Corinna doing so. But if he had been willing to marry her, he would have lived in town, as she had had as good a dowry as Elizabeth. She certainly would not have agreed to be a soldier's wife.

"I suppose your leave is not long enough to allow you to remain until—" She sniffed and dabbed at her eyes with a dainty handkerchief, though he saw no sign of tears. "I am sure seeing you has been a comfort to Hawkslowe. We cannot ask more of you. My brothers will lend me their support."

"I can stay for a bit." If Sebastian did not want her to know of his being chosen guardian, he would not want her to know about the gift of Kirkland Grange. Wise not to let the cat out of the bag. Doing so might lead to yowling and clawing. "Will I meet my nieces and nephews today?"

"I suppose so, if you wish." Her sour expression implied that an uncle as neglectful as he could hardly be expected to take an interest in the children.

"Sebastian's heir is almost fourteen, I believe?"

"He is."

"And not at school?"

"With Hawkslowe like to be taken from us soon, we thought it best William remain here." The toe of one shoe, just visible under her skirts, began to tap soundlessly on the carpet.

"William? I thought his name was Colin."

Elizabeth Hawkslowe's cheeks reddened. "William is his middle name. Calling him Colin invites confusion with his paternal grandfather."

Confusion, when Colin, Lord Hawkslowe had died before the boy's birth? Alasdair was tolerably sure the lad's maternal grandfather's name had been William. Apparently that did not confuse.

"I believe I can keep the two separate in my mind. When addressing you, I will refer to my brother's oldest son as 'Young Colin.' "

"As you wish, Major."

He heard the unspoken "while you are here." "To return to the question of school, did you bring him home partway through last term, or did he not go back in January?" From something his brother had said, he suspected the latter.

She bridled, which in a younger female might have been coquetry and perhaps attractive, though he preferred it in horses.

"I hardly think William's school attendance relevant or any concern of yours, given our sad state."

As she was not under his command—yet—he said, "I inquired because I don't recall any mention of a tutor. A lengthy break in his education at school would call for lessons at home."

She twisted her handkerchief. "Hawkslowe's health has been declining for months. At Michaelmas term, we decided William should be at home."

This seemed an odd way of putting it. "Do you mean he did not go back to school after Christmas? Or was he not enrolled for Michaelmas term?"

"We felt it best he not be sent away when his papa might expire at any time."

So he had not been sent to school in September where study and friends might have diverted his mind. "This is May. If I understand you, he has been home for two terms and of course last summer. Do I understand he has not been enrolled at school at all?"

"That is correct." She again made play with the bit of mangled linen and lace.

"Did he have a tutor before he was to go away to school?"

"N-no."

"Did my brother agree to Colin, excuse me, Young Colin, not being sent to school?"

"My dear husband has been too ill to take an interest in most things. Though he has managed to speak with his bailiff once or twice a week and to summon you." Which she resented.

"I see. Does the younger boy have a tutor?"

"Everything has been all pell-mell, sir. How could we expect them to attend to their books when their father is dying?"

"Then how do they occupy themselves?"

"Oh…they ride, and I suppose do as boys will."

Her vagueness suggested she had no idea what they did. Mischief, no doubt. Without a tutor, they would be running free.

His lips tightened, a sign his men dreaded. "And your daughters?"

She gazed at him blankly.

"Do they have a governess?"

"They did have one, but she proved to be sadly unsteady and left without so much as giving notice, and I have not been able to replace her, given how distraught I have been over Hawkslowe. I have been trying to keep up their lessons myself."

"I will make my brother's children's acquaintance at the first opportunity." He would not wait for her to arrange an introduction which might be slow in coming.

"There is really no need for you to trouble yourself when you can have no interest in children."

"They are my nephews and nieces. As such, they are very much of concern to me. When I am not with Sebastian, perhaps I can keep them from dwelling upon their fears about their father. I will leave you until

11

supper, my lady."

Small wonder his brother wanted him to watch over his children's welfare. Was Elizabeth Hawkslowe merely unable to deal with the stress of Sebastian's prolonged illness? She had not shilly-shallied in pursuit of her own ends years ago.

He asked Graves where the boys were likely to be.

"If they're out riding, Mr. Alasdair, they might be anywhere. If they aren't riding, they may be in the stable. They like Archbold, who's still the head groom. Or sometimes they visit the gamekeeper, Briggs. He's new since your time. Old Pennyworth died a few years after you left."

"I'll see them when they return, then. The girls?"

"In the nursery or schoolroom with Nurse Sallows."

"Then I'll go up to renew my acquaintance with Sallie and meet my nieces. And Graves? His lordship told me you are in his confidence. Best not to mention I will be staying indefinitely."

"Very good, sir." The butler's thin smile hinted at the state of affairs in the house. Hard to keep much from the servants.

Falstone found his nieces in the nursery with his own old nurse. Sallie was more wrinkled but still energetic and needle-witted.

"Master Alasdair!"

Two girls glanced up at her exclamation, their heads swiveling toward the door. The older one, eleven or twelve, was sitting at a table, sewing a tiny garment of flowered cotton, perhaps a doll gown, while her sister sat on the floor, playing with a doll, mayhap the one for whom her sister was stitching.

"Janet, Isabelle, make your curtsies to your uncle."

Janet set her work down carefully and rose. Isabelle scrambled to her feet, still clutching her toy.

"This is your papa's brother, Major Alasdair Falstone."

This clarification made the girls' faces clear. Janet dipped neatly. Isabelle bobbed and wobbled slightly.

He swept them a formal bow and smiled at them.

"They did not know they had another uncle," Sallie said.

"We didn't," Janet said, then glanced at her nurse out of the corner of her eye.

"I've been away since before you were born, Miss Janet. Do you ever quarrel with Isabelle?"

"Yes, sir, sometimes."

Isabelle nodded vigorously.

"Your father and I quarreled, and because we were already grown, our disagreement lasted longer than yours do. We have made it up now, and I have come to visit."

"Good," Isabelle declared.

Janet's eyes and trembling lower lip suggested she knew her father was dying. She managed a faint smile in spite of it.

"I imagine you miss your old governess, ladies. Perhaps you would walk with me in the garden tomorrow afternoon so that Sallie can have a nap?"

They giggled, and Nurse Sallows tutted. "You're a saucebox, Master Alasdair, and always were. I'm sure my girls will be pleased to show you what Lady Hawkslowe has done to the garden. Janet, you can finish Lady Violet's sacque gown before supper if you tend to your needle. I will make sure your uncle

Alasdair's chamber has everything he requires. Come along with you." This last was addressed to him.

When the nursery door was closed behind them and they were some steps down the passage, she asked, "Have you met the boys yet?"

"I hope to see them in the morning."

"If you don't linger over your port or in the drawing room this evening, you may see them before they go to bed. In the morning, they'll be off like foxes that hear the hounds. Good lads but running wild as gypsies, they are. They need a tutor."

"I'll see they get one. Why did the governess leave?"

"One of her ladyship's brothers tried to take liberties. She'd packed and gone before his nose stopped bleeding."

"Brave of her when governesses are easily dismissed without a reference. Or charged with stealing some trinket."

Sallie uttered, "Ha! The joke was on Mr. Paul Bradnam. Her father is a general and has a friend or two in the court circle."

"Then why was she working?"

"You know the way of it: they have connections but no money. I hope you plan to stop here now."

"Sebastian has asked me to stay, and I'll do so, but I think it's meant to be a secret from Lady Hawkslowe."

"Very likely. She's thick as inkle weavers with her brothers, and my lord's too weary and sick to make them leave when they come to rusticate. Far too often in my opinion," she added acidly.

By the time he met his sister-in-law for supper,

Alasdair had a fair notion of the tactics necessary to subdue the rebel. He refused the port and accompanied Lady Hawkslowe to the drawing room. Elizabeth poured out her woes despite obvious resentment about the inconvenience of having her husband's scapegrace brother thrust upon her without so much as a by-your-leave. He had hoped she would decide in favor of a headache and retire, freeing him to visit the boys before they went to bed. As she did not, he would observe the enemy.

She herself could not quite decide how to view him, it appeared. Since the afternoon, she might have convinced herself that Falstone would be as indulgent as her husband if only he understood how pitiable her existence was, far from town, with an ailing husband, and no society or entertainments worth mentioning. What was the use of a title if one could not figure in society?

At the same time, she must be aware Falstone's sudden appearance would cause her some work as she could not ignore a member of the family. His presence would curtail some of her activities, whatever they might be. Scot Hall was rather isolated, and unless things had changed since his youth, balls, dinners, and assemblies were rare events. Still, he no longer knew the nearest gentry. Mayhap the staid older generation had been replaced by livelier heirs.

In any case, when Elizabeth finally declared she could no longer keep her eyes open and graciously thanked him for bearing her company when he must be tired from his journey, Colin and Matthew would long since have fallen asleep...probably. He would have been less sanguine about their whereabouts had the scattered clouds not covered the sky by supper and commenced to weep a chilling rain. As boys, he and Sebastian had sometimes slipped out to revel in the dark and watch the comings and goings of nocturnal creatures, even when the night was chill and windy. Rain had kept them snug indoors: too hard to explain to Sallie in the morning how their clothes had become sodden and their shoes muddy.

Before he went down to breakfast, Sebastian's valet sought him out in his chamber.

"Budley?"

"Sir, Lord Hawkslowe desires that you come to him at once."

"Is he worse?" Alasdair made an untidy half-knot in his neckcloth, pulled on his waistcoat without buttoning it, and snatched up his coat.

"No, Major, the reverse. He's a bit stronger today. But he wishes to speak with you while the house is still quiet."

Or while Lady Hawkslowe was still in her bed? As he strode toward the door, he turned and raised his eyebrows interrogatively at Budley's peculiar phrasing. Surely the house started the day before the mistress? Budley cleared his throat delicately and spoke very softly. "Some of the servants gossip to her ladyship."

They were in the hall by then; Alasdair merely murmured, "Ah."

Sebastian looked better, or at least less moribund.

"I meant to visit you this morning after meeting your sons," Alasdair began.

His brother waved this aside impatiently. "Good, you'll need to know them. But I have things I must say while I can." Before his strength drained away, he meant. "Budley, the will."

The valet came forward. He was holding two thick packets tied with the sort of narrow red ribbon used by lawyers.

"I dared not entrust it to the post, not if there were a hope of your coming. If you had chosen not to do so, or I waited too long, Budley's instructions were to deliver it to my attorney in Newcastle. It supersedes my earlier will, and Elizabeth doesn't know I have changed it. I have not had the strength to argue about it. I'm sorry to ask you to take it when you have just arrived, but I assumed you would have a trustworthy servant with you who could be sent. One packet goes to my attorney in Newcastle; the other to my attorney in London."

"No matter, Sebastian. I'd already decided I would have to make a quick trip to town and the sooner, the better."

"She hasn't...?" A cough shook him.

Lady Hawkslowe hadn't sent him packing? Annoyed him beyond endurance? "Your children should have a tutor and a governess, not only for their education but to occupy their minds. If you agree, I mean to hire them in London when I go to sell my commission. I will also purchase some books and other amusements for them."

Lord Hawkslowe managed a death's head grin. "Excellent. You rode here...I think? Will you ride to Newcastle to take the coach? I will not tell my wife the reason for your departure. I misdoubt she will ask, unless she discovers your horse remains in the stable."

"I'll ride. I know a reliable inn there where I can have my horse kept at livery while I'm gone. The owner was in my regiment. It will be faster to change mounts than to give Trooper time to rest along the way or go by coach."

Sebastian coughed wetly. "Budley, provide the major with funds for his travel. Money for inns and changes of horse in both directions, for coach fare for the tutor and governess, and for whatever Major Falstone might need in London. And write out a letter for my man of business authorizing him to release additional funds to my brother if requested. There are always unexpected expenses."

"Yes, my lord." Budley bowed and departed through the dressing room door.

Sebastian's voice had grown hoarse. "Best go find my boys now, before they escape for the day. Only, come back soon from your journey. I fear time is of the essence."

To Falstone's surprise, the valet returned in moments and presented a purse heavy with coin. Alasdair nodded his thanks and gripped Sebastian's hand in farewell as Budley measured out a dose of something.

Alasdair found his nephews in the dining room. A few breakfast dishes sat on the sideboard for whatever family member came down to eat. Who would that be apart from himself and the boys, who had apparently been left to forage instead of being served in the nursery? Sallie would make sure the girls ate their meals there. His brother was too ill to leave his chamber, and Alasdair was sure Lady Hawkslowe would have a tray in bed.

The boys were stuffing cold mutton ham into split stottie cakes. They each had a handkerchief laid out to wrap their breakfast before shabbing off for the day. Their heads swiveled as he entered. The older lad cleared his throat.

"Major Falstone? Uncle?"

"I am. You must be Colin."

The older boy made a jerky bow.

"And you must be Matthew."

The younger boy gazed at him speechless until his brother elbowed him, and he croaked, "G'morning," around a half-chewed morsel. He swallowed and made his own bow.

"I've looked forward to meeting you. I see you mean to eat your breakfast in the open air. I want to visit my horse before my meal. Would you care to come to the stable with me?"

No boy could resist a horse. They followed him, munching. Colin was tall for his age and spindly. He possessed his father's brown hair and features. Matthew was still chubby, but his blond hair and square face showed the Bradnam blood. Too early to tell if he would be stocky or slender as he grew.

The older boy commented approvingly on Trooper's conformation and asked about his endurance.

"It's his chief virtue. He's not handsome—most prefer a mount that's all one color or mostly so, rather than a piebald or skewbald like Trooper—nor as fast as some, but he keeps going."

"Doesn't he need to be fast in the charge?" Matthew asked, stroking the brown and white horse's nose.

"I'm a dragoon. We don't charge much. We ride to where we're going, then we usually fight on foot. When the enemy runs, we mount and pursue them."

"I think I'd rather be a cavalryman."

"Not a bad choice. You'll have to wait a few years, however."

They were intelligent, like his brother, if more ignorant of some academic subjects than he liked. Colin read indiscriminately which was preferable to not reading, and he could dredge up a treasure trove of odd bits of information. Matthew, he discovered, was worried that he could not write, having heard from a boy only slightly older that he was making good progress and had even copied out a short poem to give to his mother.

"You are just at the age now to begin learning," Alasdair said. "Do you remember being a small boy and knocking over your blocks when you tried to stack them? Or spilling your milk? Your muscles grow up as you do. When your hands and fingers are cunning enough to handle a quill and not spill your ink, your tutor will begin to teach you."

"But I don't have a tutor."

"You will. Your papa wants me to find one for you."

"Really?"

"Ay."

"Mother felt that Father was too ill to be bothered with a tutor reporting our progress to him. And I was supposed to go away to school last year, but she thought it best I stay here." Colin twisted a button on his coat.

Matthew squirmed. All the children must be worried about their father. Their mother would not be much consolation to them, fretful and selfish as she was. Their Bradnam uncles? Time would tell whether they helped their nephews and nieces deal with Sebastian's coming death. Sebastian's judgment of them suggested they would be of small assistance.

"Nevertheless, he wants you to be instructed, and he is correct. Matthew needs a tutor until he can go to school, and you need one as you are currently not at school. It will work out, and your mama will come around to the idea." She had no choice, and with Alasdair in residence, she would not be able to browbeat Sebastian or dismiss the tutor.

Colin looked down, avoiding eye contact, and mumbled, "Ummm," suggesting he knew his mother's ways.

"I am going to hire a tutor and a governess. Your mother is anxious about your father's illness, but she will not deny you a gentleman's education." Not while he himself was in charge. Then he inquired about Colin and Matthew's mounts and was shown their ponies. Someone had seen to providing Colin with one the right size for his age and height.

"Did your father choose this one, Colin?"

"No, sir. He told our head groom to get one for me. Isabelle is learning to ride my old one. She changed her name to Princess," he added repressively.

"From Juno," Matthew added.

Chapter 3

London, May, 1740

As she always did, Margaret MacGavin glanced up at the sign over the door she was passing. *M. Bettancourt, Salle d'Armes & Fine Weapons* was lettered in green. Underneath, added later in smaller letters, *And Sons* was an afterthought. Aspiring swordsmen who did not know better still assumed the *M.* stood for *Monsieur* and that the fencing master was a Frenchman. Her father had allowed the confusion, as the French and Italians were held to be more skillful with the blade than Englishmen. "The attraction of the exotic," Marcus Bettancourt called it.

Margaret walked briskly past to the well-kept house next door. All the houses on this short street near Golden Square were much alike. Her brother Rupert's home was similar in all respects to the fencing school, except that its door was blue. Her father and Rupert had agreed their house should not appear to be part of the salle d'armes.

She let herself in with her key and hurried along the passage toward the back of the house, hoping not to be stopped by the cook or the maid. In Sybilla's absence (and sometimes when she was present), Margaret was the one they appealed to in any household emergency. In her current melancholy, she wished only to escape to her chamber. At the end of the passage, she lit the extra candle on the side table before unlocking the door in the shared wall between the two houses.

A faint murmur of voices and ringing of blades came from the room where the men fenced. The sound would not carry to the first floor whereas the odor of soiled infant clouts and cooking cabbage, and the children's shrill tones when they were home, penetrated the house next door from lower floor to attic.

She locked the door behind her. The fencing school's back passage was locked so no one except one of her brothers could reach the family's home or the stair to the school's upper floors. She preferred not to think that an intruder would be able to go up one flight to the floor she shared with Adam, her younger brother, if the passage door were left unlocked.

When Margaret was widowed, Rupert's wife had agreed one must take in an almost indigent sister if one could. Margaret repaid her tolerance by assisting with the children and giving them lessons, as Sybilla had not had much education.

Now Margaret's circumstances were about to change yet again. She needed to move if only she could find a way to afford a lodging nearby. The pence and occasional shillings she earned by teaching history, geography, dance, cursive writing, and deportment to daughters of ambitious tradesmen would not stretch far, even with the quarterly pittance from her stepson. She would barely be able to survive.

She had considered applying for a position as a companion or governess, though a post with a girls' school would be best. She would not be dependent upon

Rupert. But she would not be able to teach her nieces and nephews. She might have to leave London.

Taken up with these concerns, her foot was on the bottom step before she heard heavy footfalls coming down. They could not be Adam's; he was wiry and light on his feet, and typically trotted down the steps, but who else would be upstairs in the private part of M. Bettancourt, Fine Weapons & Salle d'Armes?

By the light from the candle and the barred window in the rear wall, she made out a looming figure. It stopped abruptly, seeing her outlined by the same light. Margaret backed away. She would have to unlock either the connecting door or the one leading to the shop, or unbolt and unbar the door out to the tiny yard at the back—"the privy court," her father had called it—to escape. She feared she had time to do none of those things.

Her heart was pounding when she heard Adam's voice.

"Maggie, we thought to find you at home. 'Tis lucky you are returned. An old friend of yours has come to call upon you. Go down, Major."

The man continued down, though more slowly than previously. When he reached the foot of the stairs, he said, "Margaret."

She stepped back as far as she could, then edged sideways to the hall. His suit could not conceal broad shoulders and a deep chest. The unknown man's size and stern features intimidated her. If Adam had not been present, she might have tried to flee, in spite of his claim of acquaintance. She would probably have failed. He could have stopped her with one hand.

"Adam?" Who was this man who felt free to use

her given name?

Her brother descended the last step. "Major Falstone asked about you when he came in to make a purchase. He says you knew each other years ago."

****

1725, Bettancourt Priory, County Durham, fifteen years earlier

When Margaret's grandfather told her Colin, Baron Hawkslowe, was dead, her first thought was of Alasdair Falstone's grief as a strong bond of affection bound Alasdair to his father. She had met Baron Hawkslowe only twice, first at the house party at which she had met Alasdair, and recently when he had visited the Priory. He reminded her of Alasdair: warm-hearted and practical, with a dry wit.

Her second thought was that mourning for Baron Hawkslowe would delay their wedding. There was no formal agreement yet, although a discussion of terms and settlements with her grandfather had been the reason for the baron's visit. Grandpapa had acted as her guardian as long as she could remember, her father having been away on military service for most of his marriage to her mother, and then in London.

Five days after she learned of Hawkslowe's death, Alasdair rode up to Bettancourt Priory on a blown horse. Grandpapa was out with his bailiff, but Margaret had no hesitation in coming to greet Alasdair, who was stalking around the front hall, having refused to be shown to the drawing room.

"Alasdair?"

"Margaret." He came forward to take her hands and press his lips to them.

"I'm sorry about your father. I didn't expect to see

you so soon. Come in and sit. I will send for a tea tray and ask Aunt Rose to join us."

He shook his head. "Will you walk in the garden with me instead, Margaret? I will have to speak with your grandfather too, but I understand he is not here."

She began to give the footman instructions to have a chamber prepared, but Alasdair laid a hand on her arm. "I'll stay at the inn tonight. I start for London in the morning."

She began to fear that his tired eyes and the grim set of his mouth came from something other than his father's death. For that reason, she did not protest and led him out to the garden, not delaying even to fetch a hat. The bench under the crab apple was shady.

He did not sit but walked back and forth, tight-lipped.

"Alasdair?"

"Oh, Margaret," he burst out. "I don't know how to tell you."

Trying to introduce a lighter note, she said, "I suppose it's like confessing a misdeed to one's parents. The sooner done, the sooner the worry is over."

He stopped pacing and gazed down at her. Was that pity in his eyes? "The worry, perhaps, but not the pain. Not this time."

****

London, May, 1740

"Falstone?" To save her soul, she could not have uttered another word. He had never written to her, indeed, could not have written, because they were not engaged. He had not written to her grandfather, either. But then, he had never promised anything at that last meeting.

"I'm not surprised you did not recognize me, after so long," he said. "I was hardly more than a boy when we last met."

His voice sounded deeper than she recalled. He had gained muscle but had appeared taller because he had been above her on the stair. When had his jaw grown so square and his face so harsh?

"I must get back to the shop now, but you'll want to talk about old times," Adam said, oblivious to her turmoil.

Major Falstone glanced at her brother.

Adam paused. "Better use the parlor in the other house, I think. Because, er…"

"A lady and a man cannot be closeted alone. Quite so."

She almost blurted out that they would be alone together there, as Sybilla and the children would not be back for an hour yet, and the maid could not be spared to play propriety. But she wanted to talk with Alasdair again, despite her resentment at his having turned his back on her without a second thought. Besides, no one would assume he had designs upon the virtue of a plain, middle-aged widow.

"Yes, a good idea, Adam. Major?" She was already unlocking the connecting door.

"Your purchases will be ready by the day after tomorrow," her brother assured the visitor as blithely as if he did not know—

Alasdair followed her through the door and stood waiting while she relocked it. She fumbled with the key, almost dropping it, when it occurred to her Adam had been a schoolboy all those years ago. He might never have been aware Falstone had courted her.

The front of the house, the whole floor, in fact, was empty of life. The cook would be busy in the ground floor kitchen, the maid helping her. If anyone knocked on the door, the girl would scurry upstairs to answer it. Margaret did not anticipate any other caller, however. The gentry and the beau monde went visiting; the wives of tradesmen were often too busy.

The contrast between the drawing room at Bettancourt Priory and the parlor here must be startling. However, the floor was polished, the colors of the curtains, upholstery, and cushions were harmonious, and the furniture was old but handsome. The cast-off furnishings of two generations ago had been inexpensive. Margaret had chosen them when she and Adam came to live here, to replace the few rickety pieces that had come with the house and her father had not bothered to replace.

"Please be seated, Major. Forgive me for not offering you tea or other refreshment, but the servants will be busy downstairs." She seated herself and gestured him to a matching high-backed armchair. The upholstery was worn down to the warp in places, and the windows needed washing. After her father died, as Rupert's family grew, the porter/footman/valet had been let go to save money, as a nursery maid had been hired when Margaret was no longer available to help after her marriage. How humiliating that Falstone was seeing their relative poverty.

"I did not come for tea. I thought of your father's shop because I wanted to buy foils for my nephews, and Bettancourt's is well-known to be the best. And of course, I know your family," he added.

As if there had been nothing more between them

than friendship! She almost missed his next words.

"I asked about you and was surprised to find you living with your brothers, Margaret. Mistress MacGavin, I suppose I should call you now. Your brother mentioned you had married and been widowed. I'm sorry for your loss. "

From this dispassionate speech, he had recovered from what must have been only an infatuation on his part. She had not got over her first love so easily. He was no longer the open-hearted young man he had been, but the years had been kinder to him than to her. Alasdair was now a striking figure. The breadth of his shoulders hinted at muscle under his coat and waistcoat. His smoothly fitting breeches and stockings displayed it.

Ignoring the latter part of his statement, she asked, "How old are your brother's sons?"

"Thirteen and near ten. I recall your grandfather saying he had begun your brothers' fencing lessons when they reached ten or eleven. I thought I should do the same. Colin and Matthew need occupation as they are not in school this term and have been without a tutor."

Surely both should have a tutor or attend a local grammar school or take lessons with some educated but purse-pinched gentleman in the neighborhood.

"And you, Margaret—Mistress MacGavin?"

She cut him off to forestall questions about her life. It was not a topic she cared to discuss. "How does your family do?"

He frowned, an expression to make his soldiers' hearts sink. "Not well. Sebastian is in the final stages of phthisis."

"I am sorry. To be losing your only brother must be hard." What else was there to say? He would be grieved, though it had been Lord Hawkslowe who forbade Alasdair to marry her, parting them forever. Obviously his loss of Margaret had weighed but lightly on Alasdair. Major Falstone. "Will your leave be long enough to allow you to remain until…?"

"I have sold out. He asked that I be his children's guardian and manage his property. There was no one else to do it."

"Then with no other family or connections, you had no choice."

"His wife has brothers." He was silent for several heartbeats. "Sebastian does not consider them a good influence. What of you, Margaret? I would not have expected to find you living here."

Why dissimulate? This time she answered. "If my husband and I had had children, things might have been different. As it was, Gideon's son was near grown when we married. When James inherited, he took a wife. It seemed best to remove myself, as a stepmother-in-law would have been an encumbrance." A sister was going to be inconvenient now.

"But you are living above the academy and shop rather than here with your family?"

"I have four nephews and a niece. This house is as full as it can be. I have a pleasant bedroom and parlor next door."

"For you to be all alone in the house at night cannot be comfortable, however. I do not say 'frightening' because you were never timid."

"Adam has rooms there as well."

Another pause. "Is he not to marry soon? Perhaps I

misunderstood."

"He is." Her younger brother talked too much. It did make him an excellent salesman.

"Then will you not soon be in the circumstances that caused you to leave your stepson's home? Or do Adam Bettancourt and his bride mean to live elsewhere?"

If Alasdair Falstone had lost his youthful boyishness, he had retained his quick understanding. She would hate to be questioned about some error or omission under his command. "They intend to live above the school. Rupert and Adam both consider it wise to have someone on the premises at night." She ignored his first question, an evasion he evidently noticed.

"May I inquire what your plans are?"

He had given up the right to ask her such a personal question, but she would reply anyway, lest he think she was without a sensible plan.

"I may move to a lodging house. Or perhaps I will seek a position in a school or as a companion."

His brow creased. Uncertainty rather than a frown, she thought.

As a soldier rather than a tradesman, he would not understand her circumstances, and she would not explain. He would know only that the salle d'armes was thriving, the first choice of any gentleman wishing to perfect his swordsmanship or practice before an affair of honor. Men shot at targets in the basement or purchased firearms as well as swords and knives in a showroom.

Expenses ate much of the profit: the cost of merchandise, none of it cheap, coal and candles and refreshments for the gentlemen after they had shot or fenced. There were the wages of the hired clerk, the porter, and the boy who ran errands and did any other task he was given, the woman who came in to do the chars the porter and the boy didn't do. The summer, when most of their customers went to the country, was a lean time. Nearly all Rupert's money went to support his family. Margaret knew. She had kept the household ledger before his marriage, and Sybilla sometimes still needed help with it. He really could not afford to support his widowed sister. Adam would contribute, for as he pointed out, he lived upstairs for free and had no time to squander his money on wine, women, horses, or gambling. But he was saving for his marriage.

He said deliberately, "I know of a post that would be more suitable and pay better than that of companion."

"Really?" If true, it might solve her problem. Or it might cause another set of difficulties. Margaret hoped he was not offering to make her his mistress. That would be more than she could bear. Widows were generally considered free to indulge themselves with lovers if they were discreet. Perhaps she had failed to acquire London manners, or perhaps it was her north country upbringing. To be offered an illicit connection—with a man whom she had loved and almost married—seemed an insult. Worse, if Rupert or Adam found out, one or the other would challenge him and someone would die. No, she was being foolish. She was hardly likely to attract an offer of that kind at her age. "What sort of work is it?"

"One of the reasons I came to town was to secure a tutor for the boys and a governess for the girls. The tutor is already on his way north. I have ruled out half a dozen women and interviewed as many more who will not suit. Would you consider taking my nieces in hand? The wages are twelve pounds per year."

"What was wrong with the dozen you rejected?"

"Several did not care to relocate to Northumberland, and who can blame them?" he inquired, chuckling. "Two were rather elderly. I did not think they would be able to deal with young girls, especially as I would like them to be taught by someone who will encourage them to be active, and who can ride." He did not continue.

"How did the rest fail to give satisfaction?"

"One felt her most important duty was to teach deportment, fine needlework, and the, hmmm, 'genteel lady's accomplishments, as gentlemen do not care for an over-educated lady.' Another was a great believer in disciplining her charges into submission. Her aim was to instill good manners, obedience, and silence. The other four were too timorous."

"Are your nieces so fierce?"

"No, they're good children. Our old nurse, Mistress Sallows, saw to that."

"Were your candidates fearful of riding or ladies' sports?"

His lips thinned, his reluctance to speak visible. Finally, "I can't ask you to go into battle without warning you of the terrain. My brother summoned me home when he knew he was dying because Lady Hawkslowe is not particularly sensible. With a careful guardian in place, that would not matter. However, when they married, Sebastian named her oldest brother their guardian in the event of his death. You did know we were estranged?"

"No. I know your godfather bought you a commission, and I—my family—heard nothing more. You never wrote." Margaret wished she had not uttered the last three words. They sounded like a reproach.

"As I could not offer you marriage without means to support you as you had a right to expect, I thought it best to withdraw from the lists. I knew you could take your pick from more eligible suitors."

The notion was so far removed from reality that she could not repress a rather derisive laugh. In response to his evident bewilderment, she said, "Thank you for the compliment! You are the first to think my attractions irresistible."

"You must have been sought after, unless you held your admirers at arm's length to discourage courtship. You did marry eventually."

"I did, several years after we left County Durham. My husband was a friend of my father and brothers."

MacGavin was a Scot of pleasant appearance and manner, a gunsmith nearing forty years of age and a widower. The offer took her by surprise. MacGavin had never shown any sign she recognized as romantic interest, talking and bantering with her as he did with her brothers and her father. She had given no thought to marriage after Alasdair, too busy to worry about her future or brood over the past, which was a blessing.

When she had stared at MacGavin, he remarked drolly, "I never thought to see you dumbstruck, lass."

She stammered, "I had no idea…"

"No need to answer now. You'll be wanting to speak with your father and brothers. I asked the colonel's permission, of course, but as you're of age, it's your choice, and no hard feelings if you refuse."

Major Alasdair Falstone was staring at her, awaiting her response. She managed to say, "You were explaining the situation at Scot Hall."

"Until Sebastian wrote me recently, I had not seen or heard from him since I took up my commission. To be fair, I had not written to him, either."

"You have reconciled, then. I'm glad. You would regret the estrangement once he is no more."

"Ay." The bald agreement was not accompanied by a sigh or any visible sorrow or remark about the transitory nature of man's existence.

A stray thought flitted through her brain. Had he schooled himself to show an impassive face to the world? Or, despite the reconciliation, did he still harbor anger against his brother?

He went on, " 'Twas not until he knew he could not live that he began to worry about a guardian for the children and a trustee for the estate. He could not think of any acceptable candidate except several of our father's friends who are old and unlikely to outlive him by many years. His brothers-in-law are libertines and gamesters. So he tells me, and he must know. Sebastian fears if one of them were left in control of Scot Hall's income, he would loot it. Nor are they a good example for the children. On accepting his death was to come sooner rather than later, he wrote to end our breach." He cleared his throat.

"I understand."

"The Bradnam brothers need not worry you. It's Elizabeth, Lady Hawkslowe, you would have to deal with. Though I don't think she will necessarily interfere with your decisions about the girls. I was at Scot Hall for three days and never observed that she spent much time with them or thinking about them."

"The kind of lady who is content to see her offspring for half an hour a day and to mention them occasionally in cloying tones to her friends?"

Merriment lightened his face, bringing back the young man she had known. "Exactly so. She is also petulant and puffed up with her own consequence. Will you consider taking the situation? You need not make a hasty decision. I will be in town another two days at least and will escort you north, if you are willing to take on the challenge."

He considered that adequate time to make her decision, inform her students, and pack?

"May I call on you to learn—"

The front door opened, followed by children's voices, the nursery maid's admonition to hush, and Sybilla's sharper rebuke.

"It's later than I thought. My sister-in-law and the children are home," she said.

Chapter 4

Rupert's wife appeared in the doorway, her head turned to address the servant. "Joan, take them upstairs."

Sybilla entered the parlor, raising her eyebrows at the sight of Falstone. "Margaret. Pray introduce your guest."

She complied, explaining that Major Falstone was an old family friend. "I beg your pardon for borrowing your drawing room, Sybilla, but I thought you would not mind, under the circumstances." Those being that it would be indecent to invite a male visitor up to her sitting room.

"I quite understand, Margaret." How odd that a round, snub-nosed face could look ill-humored when usually it was placidly cheerful.

Sybilla proceeded to address inanities to Falstone, interspersed with probing questions about his family and his relationship to the Bettancourts. "I do not recall my husband or my brother-in-law mentioning your name," she remarked by way of justifying her interrogation.

Alasdair's replies were civil and uninformative without being evasive. His father and the late Colonel Bettancourt's father had been friends with an interest in agriculture and stock breeding. He himself had lived an unsettled life as a dragoon, sent wherever his regiment was needed. Not abroad; they had been employed to put down disturbances here in England and at times to prevent smuggling, all of which was news to Margaret. So much for her earlier supposition that he had been sent abroad to some distant land where he might have died or that, if he had written, the letters had been lost.

He took his leave after a few minutes of Sybilla's company, expressing his pleasure at meeting her. Margaret walked to the door with him. He paused on the steps and lowered his voice.

"Mistress MacGavin, I have another purchase to make from your brothers, for which I will be in the day after tomorrow. May I speak with you that morning?"

"Certainly, if you are here before ten o'clock." Ten was the time she left on her rounds of her students' homes. Equally important, Sybilla would still be involved in the nursery then.

As soon as he was gone, Sybilla went upstairs without another word to Margaret. She did not usually pout or fume; as a rule, she was good-humored if inclined to be imperious. Margaret rather hoped her annoyance did not result from the moodiness of pregnancy. Breeding women were kittle-cattle, and Sybilla more than most. And whatever would they do with another child? When Sybilla had borne the fifth, the bedchamber Margaret had occupied for almost two years was needed for the oldest boy unless Margaret shared her room with the only girl, giving up what little privacy she had.

To her surprise, Sybilla chose to speak of Falstone at supper with all four adults and the two children old enough to eat decorously present. The three youngest ate in the nursery, supervised by the nursery maid.

"Rupert, I came home today to find your sister entertaining a man in the parlor."

"Did you?"

Adam, having swallowed a mouthful of stewed carp, said, "Ay, 'twas a Major Alasdair Falstone who knew Grandfather and asked after Margaret."

"Falstone? I remember him. I was sorry when his courtship came to nothing, Margaret." Rupert leaned over to whisper to Nathan, seven, "Don't lick your fingers."

"Courtship?"

"Ay, Sybilla, years ago. Father told me about it."

"I didn't know about that," Adam remarked.

"You were only interested in climbing trees, fishing, and riding your pony. The betrothal was almost a settled thing, and then Falstone's brother inherited— Baron Hawkslowe of Scot Hall, not far from Morpeth—and forbade the banns on pain of ending Falstone's allowance as his heir presumptive. Between Hawkslowe's opposition and Falstone's decision to enter the army, it was thought best to break it off."

"Family friend or not, for Margaret to be alone with a man for who knows how long is not decent, and his having been a suitor makes it worse, not better."

Both her brothers stared at the lady of the house in perplexity.

Adam recovered first. "I'd think it made it much better, Syb."

"Is he renewing his suit, Margaret?" Rupert asked.

"No." She discarded the idea of explaining he had offered her work as a governess. She had not decided whether to accept. Living at Scot Hall might be awkward if he were living there.

"I hope you will not invite him or any other man into my house again, Margaret. Anything might have happened in the absence of a chaperon. To be making our family scandalous is not to be borne."

Rupert turned the subject by inquiring about the shop's sales for the day. Later, catching her alone for a moment, he said, "I'll speak to Sybilla. I don't know what brought on that tirade. It was uncalled for. And, er, if Major Falstone is interested in you, I have no objection at all. Not that I think my opinion should weigh with you." He gave her shoulder a brotherly pat before she stepped through the door to go up to her rooms.

She sat up for some time, thinking about Major Falstone's offer, which might be the answer to her dilemma, if only she dared to work for the man she had once loved.

Adam had occupied two chambers on the first floor above the fencing academy since Rupert's marriage, and Margaret had moved into the other two before Sybilla and Rupert's fifth child arrived. Living above the school was no sacrifice: after it closed, the house was quiet and she had more privacy than had been possible in Rupert's home.

Now Adam was to marry in four months. Margaret rejoiced for him: his betrothed was intelligent and cheerful and even had a small dowry. But the marriage meant a change in their living arrangements. They would hire a maid of all work who would sleep off the currently unused basement kitchen, as Adam and his bride would not join Rupert's family for meals as Adam and Margaret did. Had either of her brothers considered that two rooms on a floor shared with a sister would not be ideal for the couple? Four rooms would make a satisfactory home for her younger brother and his bride.

Finally, she brought out the box in which she kept her few trinkets: the pearl necklace she had received when she was seventeen, the aquamarine necklet and earbobs, a brooch, and a carnelian bracelet, which had belonged to her mother, and a few other bits she treasured. Beneath them was a much-creased letter. Not from Alasdair, who had never written to her.

From Col. Marcus Bettancourt to his daughter:

My dear Margaret,

I regret practical considerations prevented me from traveling north to meet Alasdair Falstone three months ago. I would have had no hesitation in agreeing to your marriage. However, given that neither he nor I can see any alternative to his going into the army, we are agreed that he will not offer for you as I would reluctantly refuse my permission.

After I described my own marriage, he conceded it would be a mistake to wed. Your mother's health could not endure a life of following the drum, which made it necessary that she return to live with your grandparents, for it must have failed entirely if she had not. She grew up in her papa's vicarage, and while she had some experience of nursing the sick and of some of the more unpleasant aspects of life, nothing prepared her for the squalor and brutality of traveling in the tail of an army. Nor did I understand what it would be like.

The common soldiers' women endure it, but they are accustomed to hard lives even here. At best, following the drum, they work hard under terrible conditions and trudge great distances in the heat, rain, or cold according to the season, in order to avoid being left behind in England to starve, go into the workhouse, or sell their bodies on the street. They perform useful work as laundresses and in nursing the sick or wounded and in cooking, but they are subject to military discipline for any infraction. After a battle, they search for their men. I cannot imagine the feelings of a woman who must make her way among the suffering wounded and the maimed corpses, some unidentifiable, to find the man, wounded or dead, on whom she depends for her support. For the most part, the woman takes another man again almost at once on being widowed. Officers' wives are spared many of these horrors, but to be with child or to rear children in these conditions is not a good life, and that is apart from the actual danger to them. Once I knew what it was like, I could not in conscience continue to subject your mama to it.

But spending the greater part of one's married life living separately, though more comfortable for the wife, is not a happy choice, either. I do not absolutely forbid your marriage to Falstone, but I do require you to wait until you are of age.

Your loving father,

Marcus Bettancourt

Margaret lived on the hope offered by that last sentence for two years and more. At last, like an unwatered flower, her expectations withered and vanished.

Chapter 5

Still undecided about Alasdair's offer, Margaret neared the dining room the next morning, only to halt outside the room. Her brother and sister-in-law were quarrelling. Adam, as usual, would already have departed. The shop opened earlier than the fencing school and shooting gallery.

"…not encourage her to marry?"

"I can't do without her help with the children," Sybilla shrilled.

"When Adam marries, he and his bride will need the entire floor eventually, if not immediately. Marriage is a better choice for her than living in a lodging house."

Rupert had thought of the problem.

"There is a room in the attic here, or space could be made in the attic next door."

"My sister is not to be treated as a servant, an unpaid one at that."

"She lives at our expense, Rupert."

"Margaret helps you with the children and teaches them. Sending them to school would cost more than her keep, and I will not have our children grow up ignorant. No, Sybilla, if she has a chance to marry again, she should. Falstone would be a good choice as they must have been fond of each other if they were considering marriage. I will not have you try to discourage her for your own convenience."

"She can hardly expect her old beau to wish to marry a tradesman's widow. Mark my words, he will want a girl from the gentry."

"If they do not marry, I will contrive somehow to pay for her lodging elsewhere."

Which he could ill afford. The fencing school was profitable, but he had children and a wife to provide for, Adam's share of the profits, the employees' wages, and the cost of the merchandise and candles, coal, a dozen other necessities. He should not have to support a sister who was capable of earning her living.

Sybilla burst into noisy tears.

"Control yourself before she comes, or perhaps you had best go upstairs until you have regained your countenance."

Margaret tiptoed away, to inform the kitchen she was not feeling well and would make do with a slice of bread and butter and a cup of tea, which she would take up to her chamber, asking the maid to make her excuses to her brother and his wife.

At nineteen, she had wanted desperately to marry Alasdair. At four-and-twenty, she had wanted her own home and children. At four-and-thirty, she merely wanted to be independent. How one's desires moderated with age! At her half-century mark, would her greatest aspiration be to die an easy death, without lengthy suffering? She put aside these unpleasant reflections in favor of dealing with what she could control.

The suggestion Alasdair might be courting her again she dismissed as ridiculous. Her choices were to let Rupert pay for her lodging, reducing his profit and over Sybilla's objections, or to take paid employment. Both were fraught with drawbacks. If she remained in London, the little she earned giving lessons as she did at present would mean a hand-to-mouth existence, with any illness a disaster, and nothing saved for her old age. What would become of her if Rupert died or the business failed?

If she found a post in a school, her life and movements would likely be as restricted as those of a maidservant. The conditions of a companion varied by employer, and while one might attend entertainments and travel, some ladies treated their hired chaperons like servants. Either might lead to genteel starvation when she could no longer work.

But if she accepted Alasdair Falstone's offer, she would be in the country, and although she had not lived in Northumberland, it was not unfamiliar. She had visited Scot Hall those many years ago, where she and Alasdair met. She might be employed until the youngest girl was seventeen or eighteen and perhaps remain afterward as a companion. At twelve pounds a year and no living expenses, she could save enough to get by when she could no longer work. Even if she did not stay after they were grown, she would have experience and a reference to enable her to find another position.

She suffered a moment's qualm, realizing she was seriously considering the post of governess to Lord Hawkslowe's daughters. Accepting it would be a major (ha! Major indeed!) disruption of her life. She would miss her brothers and the children, whom she might not see again for many years, if ever. But the same would hold true if she found a position in a school or as a companion, unless she were lucky enough to find one in London.

A governess's position, even with the drawback of Alasdair's presence, would suit her very well, if only he did not change his mind. She would be on tenterhooks until tomorrow.

Sybilla was civil, if rather tight-lipped, in the wake of the breakfast table quarrel. Margaret preferred not to think how she would react when she found out her resented but useful sister-in-law was leaving. Visiting her pupils the day after Falstone's visit, she informed their parents she was considering a position as a governess and expected to leave almost at once.

"I see you went shopping," Sybilla greeted her as Margaret removed her hat and gloves after setting her package on the hall table. "I had hoped to do so, but it's getting too late now." Her lips compressed peevishly.

"I'm sorry. I didn't know you meant to go out."

Most of the time had been taken up with her students' farewells and their mamas' questions, but she had stopped to buy a new nightgown so the Scot Hall laundry maid would not scorn her old, mended ones and four pairs of common gray wool stockings knitted by the grandmother of one of her pupils. The old lady made a business of it, not liking to be completely dependent upon her son. As she often said, she would knit anyway, so why not earn a few pence from it?

The mother of another child, a mercer's wife, made her a gift of enough wool twill in a pretty dark green to make a gown. Northumberland would be chilly. The woman dismissed her stammered thanks, saying, "You've made my Sophie so genteel she caught the eye of a young solicitor at the last assembly. I've hopes he'll be making an offer."

Fourteen years before she had brought two trunks from Bettancourt Priory. The one with her better gowns she had stored in the attic next door. How fortunate she had brought them when she moved to her rooms over the school. The second was still packed with all but one or two of her best gowns, worn on the infrequent occasions when she accompanied her family to Vauxhall Gardens or an assembly. She packed her ordinary clothing, except for what she would wear until she left, with no one the wiser. In the family home, the maid of all work might have noticed and spoken of it. The fencing academy maid came in for only half a day and had no one on the premises to gossip with. Margaret tucked her purchases and the cloth into the first chest.

In the evening after supper, she would try to find a moment to tell Rupert of her decision. Or perhaps it would be better to wait until he left for the shop in the morning. Her last actions before setting out should be to bid the children farewell. Their tears, protests, and objections would be harder to face than her sister-in-law's and would bring on a fit of the vapors in Sybilla.

That evening at supper and in the parlor afterward, Sybilla fretted about how quickly the children were growing and how hard-worn their clothing was, scarcely good enough to pass on to the younger ones.

"Margaret, I think we must make at least one new set for all of them but the baby, perhaps. I vow I'm ashamed for them to be seen at church. We can work in your sitting room as you do not use it much. There's no room here, and we would not be interrupted by the children."

Rupert, looking up from a copy of *The Gentleman's Magazine*, said, "Perhaps it would be easier to purchase their new clothing, except for shirts, which I know you could stitch up in a trice."

Her sister-in-law was threading her embroidery needle. Rupert gave Margaret a faint smile and nod. The action seemed to signify more than sympathy at his wife's attempt to load her with additional work. Did he already know of Alasdair's offer?

****

Falstone left the Bettancourts' home with a good deal to think about. Some casual word Margaret had spoken seemed significant. Something about the husband's death? Both remark and its context were lost to him at the moment. He might recall it later when he was not pursuing the memory.

He drew in a long breath, remembering his meeting with Margaret, and immediately regretted it. London's sooty air, the smell of rotting garbage, horse droppings, and urine in the streets, and untended privies was bad enough in decent neighborhoods. More and worse reeks fouled the poorest parts of town. He would be glad to go back to Northumberland where—the thought was lost in a lightning bolt flash of memory. Ay, Margaret had said she had married four or five years after leaving County Durham.

And Bettancourt mentioned his sister had come back to live with them after being widowed. Margaret had lived with them before her marriage. How had that happened? Surely she had married from Bettancourt Priory? Perhaps he would find out when he went to pick up the boys' foils and receive Margaret's decision. He pondered the matter all the way back to his inn in

Holborn, then distracted himself by making a number of preparations.

He arrived early at the shop two days later, hoping to pry more information out of Adam before seeing Margaret, only to find the showroom was already busy.

Adam Bettancourt was helping an indecisive fellow who had come in search of a pistol for his son's birthday. The other clerk was writing up an order and might be done soon, but he would be useless for Falstone's purpose. To give Bettancourt time to finish, Falstone studied the display of smallswords. He should purchase one while he was here. He had put away his basket-hilt dragoon saber with his uniform. Good riddance to both. He frowned at the half circle of blades mounted on the wall, though not because he was trying to reach a decision. He knew exactly what he wanted.

The gentleman engaging Adam Bettancourt's attention inquired about the possibility of commissioning a pistol with the family's coat of arms, motto, and his son's name on the decorative plate on the butt.

Alasdair's mind wandered. Colin and Matthew would be surprised when he came home with their first swords, and Matthew would bear close watching. Best to keep the foils locked up except when he was giving them lessons.

His thoughts circled back to the question niggling at him since his last visit. He had had no news of the family since his godfather died in '28. A year or two after Falstone began his military career, his godfather had mentioned Sir Percival Bettancourt's death. His brow furrowed. Margaret's father had not been the baronet's heir. He was only a second son, like Alasdair himself and was already fixed in London, as was his older son. Adam might have joined them on Sir Percival's death, but Margaret should surely have continued to live at Bettancourt Priory until she married.

Her marriage came as no surprise. Riding away all those years ago, he had known she would be courted by some sprig of the local gentry. At worst, she might have wed a gentleman successful in some profession; Newcastle was not far distant, and Sir Percival had friends there.

Yet if she had, she would have gone from the Bettancourt manor to her husband's home. Her brother would have said she had come to live with them on being widowed, wouldn't he? Or had Bettancourt spoken loosely, meaning only she was once again living with her family?

However it had come to pass, she was now living as her brothers' dependent. From hearing her speak of Rupert and Adam, he thought they were close, and living with them should have been the best alternative if she did not care to remain with her late husband's family. On the other hand, he could not quite like her residence over a fencing school. She would hardly meet a suitable second husband there. Even so, it might be better than many situations for a dependent widow if 'twere not for her sister-in-law's shrewishness and that Margaret might soon lose her place there. Accepting his offer would be far better for her than finding work as a governess or teacher in a girls' seminary. He hoped for his nieces' sake she would agree. For himself, too. He knew her, so there would be no unfortunate surprises like a discovered dislike of Northumberland's climate or lack of society near Scot Hall.

Rupert Bettancourt emerged from the room behind the shop. His long jaw and aquiline nose echoed his father's and to a lesser degree, Adam's, though the younger man's were less pronounced. His coat did not sit perfectly smooth. He must just have finished giving a lesson. He checked, then approached Falstone.

"Major Falstone? Rupert Bettancourt at your service. I regret we never met before. Will you take a glass of claret with me?"

"With pleasure, Mr. Bettancourt." Here was a chance to get answers to some of his questions.

The office was tiny, with a desk and chair, a pair of armchairs, and, oddly, an armoire. Bettancourt opened it to remove a decanter and two glasses which shared the space with ledgers, files, and a few books, no doubt treatises on arms. His host offered one of the glasses to Falstone.

The ruby red wine's complex flavor lingered on his tongue. "An excellent vintage," he remarked. Perhaps it had been smuggled. He found he did not greatly care. They sat silent, savoring it.

"You've sold out, Major?"

He agreed and explained why. He would not have spoken of it to a casual acquaintance, but Rupert Bettancourt was Margaret's older brother and might well be concerned about her welfare in Baron Hawkslowe's home.

To Falstone's surprise, instead he ventured, "The situation in which you and my sister found yourselves years ago was difficult. My father was sorry to withhold his blessing on your match. I don't know if he explained why he did so. Mayhap his refusal seemed strange, considering he had no objection to your suit originally and had been a military man himself."

"He did, and Sir Percival had warned me he would have reservations. My feelings for your sister did not change, although my circumstances had. I understood his concerns." He had spoken to no one else about his blighted courtship and found he now wanted to explain. "My brother and I did not talk much after Sebastian returned from London when our father fell ill. One or the other of us remained by his bed at all times. I did not think to mention to Sebastian my courtship was all but settled. Nor did I realize my brother had brought home London notions my father and I did not share. In Northumberland, most would not consider Colonel Bettancourt's salle d'armes an ungentlemanly connection to trade."

"Whereas in London, most would, though not usually the men my father instructed. His rank and the presence of serving officers and their sons among his clients insured he was regarded as a gentleman."

"I suppose Margaret met a gentleman through your business."

Bettancourt shook his head. "Our clients considered my father a gentleman, even if fallen on hard times. The case was otherwise with us. After Margaret and Adam came, she entered the *salle* once with an urgent message for Father. She wasn't aware a fencing academy is no place for any female. I am sorry to say she received disrespectful looks and comments. Our father called the men to order with 'Gentlemen, this is my daughter. If you cannot show a decent lady respect, you are free to find another salle d'armes. It may teach swordsmanship of a sort.' I doubt many of the apologies were sincere, but I suppose one could hardly expect it. Adam and I are unquestionably tradesmen even if we are respected for our skill and our merchandise."

Anger surged in a way he had not experienced in years. Had he been present—but he had not. "But she eventually married."

"We met Gideon MacGavin when we added guns to the showroom. The quality of his pistols and muskets made them our most popular firearms, and he became a family friend. My sister had no other suitors. Don't all women want a husband and children and their own home?" He gave a short laugh. "There are not many vocations open to females. Not the marriage she might have expected, I know, Major."

"If she had remained at Bettancourt Priory…"

"She might have married a man of her own class? Hardly. Our uncle Simon denied knowing of Grandfather's intention to dower Margaret. The proposed match between you was recent and had not been put in writing. Uncle Simon may really not have known. He and Sir Percival did not deal well together, and Grandfather did not expect to die suddenly. Well, no one does," he added wryly.

"Still, could she not have continued to live there?"

"As a poor relation—if she had been able to do so? Sir Simon and his wife had half a dozen children, and the Priory is only of middling size. He paid Margaret and Adam's stage fare and expenses, the very least he could do."

"What a curst devilish thing."

"Margaret and MacGavin had a good marriage. The pity was he died. Margaret probably wished they'd had children."

Falstone did not speak, suspecting the man had more to say.

After a moment, Bettancourt admitted, "It may be fortunate they did not. She did not feel she could continue living in MacGavin's house when his son inherited it. And her living arrangements here are not what I'd like for her. My wife takes advantage of her good nature but…" He shrugged.

But a poor relation living with family feels obligated. She might have a little money from MacGavin, though he doubted it, given that she could not afford to live in lodgings. Had Margaret told her people of his own offer? Rupert Bettancourt had been more frank than one would expect to a man he did not know. If he were aware of Falstone's suggestion, he would surely have spoken of it.

"Bettancourt, my nieces need a governess. Two days ago, I asked if Margaret—Mistress MacGavin— would be interested in the post. She will give me her answer today."

His listener's eyes drilled into Falstone. After an endless interval, Bettancourt said, "I'll have your word as a gentleman you will not dishonor my sister."

Falstone expected to hear an objection to Margaret moving so far from her family or to working for the family which had stolen their chance to marry or even to her taking work that would make her hardly better than an upper servant; ay, he could understand those. For the fellow to imply he might debauch Margaret was the last thing he had anticipated.

"What do you take me for, Bettancourt?"

"A gentleman. My father and grandfather approved

of you, but I don't know you well. Gentlemen often assume widows are available. I don't want my sister's heart broken again."

"I like and respect Margaret, but even if we were strangers, I would never engage in an affair with my nieces' governess. That would not be the behavior of a gentleman. You have my word on it."

"Good. I don't know what my sister may have decided, but I have no doubt such a move would be the best thing for her if she wishes to make it." He rose. "You came in for the swords for your nephews, I think?"

"Yes, and a smallsword for me. Though as the shop seems busy, perhaps I should call upon Margaret first, then return."

"A very good notion," Margaret's brother said.

****

At breakfast, Rupert asked if she were well. He had noticed the shadows under her eyes.

"I kept waking and could not easily get back to sleep." True enough. She could not help but fear Falstone would reconsider or not come today. In the deepest part of the night, that had seemed a real possibility. Alasdair had been honorable as a young man. She was sure that had not changed, no matter how stern he had become. Did one's basic character ever really change? She feared it could. Men became drunkards or turned dishonest in their dealings. Females who had been innocent and kind grew bitter.

What if Lady Hawkslowe dismissed her or Falstone's presence made it impossible to remain? Could she bear to stay when he married, as eventually he would? An odd thought, when she had long ago recovered from his loss. Nevertheless, the latter worry remained after the others faded with the dawn.

Sybilla went out to do her shopping immediately after breakfast, saying, "I had best go early so I can be home before you leave to teach those shopkeepers' brats."

On most days she would have spent her time after breakfast tidying her chambers and Adam's as the fencing academy maid did little more than clean their grates and empty the chamber pots. Today she alternately sat by the window in the parlor darning a hole in one of Adam's stockings and raising her eyes to glance out at the street. The overworked maid should not have to come running to admit the visitor.

Margaret admitted to herself with some chagrin that while she would miss her brothers and the children, she would not miss Sybilla. She possessed admirable qualities: she was practical, thrifty, a good mother, and generally even-tempered…except when breeding, which she probably was. Although marriage to Rupert had given her some pretensions, Margaret's education and confidence reminded her of Margaret's (and Rupert's) baronet grandfather and her own tradesman father.

She also disapproved of Margaret working to earn a little money even though she tried to contribute some to the household expenses. Not a great deal and she had to do it surreptitiously as Rupert refused to let her pay what she could to defray her share of the food and coal. Instead she bought a little of Sybilla's favorite tea or perhaps the rose-scented soap she liked. Sybilla enjoyed those little luxuries and thanked her sincerely, but at the same time, they proved Rupert's family was not as prosperous as she would like. Probably she blamed Margaret for that, in spite of depending on her for helping with the children and giving them lessons, which proved one could hold two utterly contradictory opinions at once.

Margaret sympathized with Sybilla's feelings but was glad she would be out when Falstone came. Her sister-in-law would soon discover that Margaret's absence removed an irritation.

Before her nerves frayed more, she looked up and saw Falstone striding toward the door.

"You're here," she murmured, opening the door before his foot was upon the step.

"Didn't you expect me?"

As she couldn't say she feared he would not come, she replied, "Something might have come up to delay you or change your plans."

"Had that been the case, I would have sent word." He had taken off his tricorne but remained standing, although she indicated a chair as she moved to seat herself.

"Have you an answer for me, M—Mistress MacGavin?"

"Yes." In case he mistook her meaning, she continued, "I accept your offer." Leaving London for the country and independence from Rupert and Sybilla (especially Sybilla!) beckoned like the promise of heaven.

He gave an almost imperceptible sigh that sounded like relief. "Good. How soon can you be ready to leave?"

"My trunks are packed but for a few things I'll need until I can discover what days the coach leaves and from what coaching inn."

"Go by stagecoach? Hardly! I've reserved a coach. It will set out when I give the order. Do you think you could be ready to depart tomorrow? Given my brother's failing health, I do not want to be away longer than necessary."

"Oh!" She had expected to travel on a public coach, the same way she had reached London years ago. "I can finish packing within a quarter hour." Then a problem occurred to her. "But surely if I travel with you—even if you mean to ride beside the coach rather than in it—Lady Hawkslowe will turn me off at once. And if you rode ahead to make better speed and did not stay at the same inns, for a female to be traveling and staying at an inn alone—" She need not spell out the difficulty a lone female faced in arranging for lodging at an inn, dealing with coachmen, and the danger of predatory men. She hoped this objection did not anger him. Nevertheless, she must point out the undeniable impropriety.

His brows rose slightly. "Lady Hawkslowe has nothing to say in the matter, having shown she would let the children grow up unschooled and without supervision. However, I have hired a nursery maid to assist our old family nurse, and the girl will also be in the coach and will share your chamber at night. She is waiting at my inn, ready to leave as soon as may be."

"Can you take me away now? In, say, twenty minutes?"

"That would be the most convenient use of my time. But would you not need to remain here overnight to say your goodbyes to your family?"

"No, Major. I need only tell Rupert and Adam and

say goodbye to them. And leave a note for Sybilla, I suppose," she added tardily. "I love the children, but they are likely to set up a wailing and commotion. Rupert and Adam will understand. If you will excuse me, I'll finish packing and scribble my letter. Will you wait for me in the shop?"

"May I explain to your brothers to save some time?"

"Yes, and ask for a hackney to be sent for and have someone bring down my trunks."

Chapter 6

Her heartbeat finally slowed in the hackney carriage on the way to Falstone's inn. While she had not truly expected Sybilla to come home so soon from her shopping, Margaret could not help feeling this time would be the exception. Instead, nothing occurred to prevent her departure. She had stuffed her last few possessions into the trunk, gone back to the house to tell the cook and maid she was going away, and left the letter for Sybilla on the hall table. In the fencing academy passage, she opened the door into M. Bettancourt. The shop was not yet busy. Adam was assisting a customer whose back was to the passage. Rupert and Falstone were standing at the counter, mighty serious. Her older brother's head snapped toward her at the sound of the inner door opening. He jerked his chin toward it in a silent message to the major, who followed him into the passage and closed the connecting door.

"Margaret." The single word and Rupert's slight nod affirmed that he did not oppose her going, even in such a furtive way. His half smile said he understood. "We will miss you, but I think this is the right decision. And, of course, you will always be welcome in our home. Now I'll fetch your trunks, then send Adam in to say goodbye."

She could only manage a nod of her own and a

misty smile. She would miss her family.

****

Days spent in a coach might have been tedious if Margaret had been accustomed to such journeys. Not having been out of London since her arrival so many years ago, she enjoyed seeing the countryside. The weather was pleasant, neither too hot nor cold, and there was no rain. The dust was troublesome, but they kept the windows shut tight. The nursery maid, who had never been out of London, gazed first out of one window then out of the other, speaking only to exclaim at any new sight: a pretty village, ostlers changing a stage coach's team faster than seemed possible at a busy posting inn, some picturesque vista.

Margaret tried to read, but in many places the jolting of the carriage made it impossible to focus on the words. She had plenty to think of anyway, remembering other journeys, like the one that carried her to the house party at Scot Hall.

Her grandfather's chance meeting at a horse fair with Alasdair's father had led to an invitation to Sir Percival, Margaret, and Aunt Rose to a house party at Scot Hall. Aunt Rose, laid low with a spasm in her back, had not gone with them.

In the absence of a chaperon and other young people, she and Alasdair spent a great deal of time together. Alasdair made the visit to Scot Hall magical.

Two weeks of bliss ended in the pain of parting from Alasdair. She shivered at the memory of her grandfather's coach rumbling away from the Hawkslowe estate. The distance between their homes made it unlikely they would see each other often or perhaps ever again. She had thrust her head out the window to gaze back at him, standing by the steps. Aunt Rose would have called her a hoyden. Sir Percival's eyes twinkled in quiet amusement.

She would never see Alasdair again, or not for a very long time. They would both marry other people. He would wed some girl from a titled family who would treat him coldly and perhaps betray her vows. Her own husband would be harsh and unloving, and on her deathbed far too young, her last thoughts would be of Alasdair.

Yet despite the miles between Scot Hall and Bettancourt Priory, a week later Alasdair happened to be close enough to stop in. Surprisingly often over the following year, he had business in Newcastle or farther south in County Durham and came by to deliver a letter from his father to Sir Percival. Once he was on his way to a horse breeder near the city of Durham. The trip that had been so slow in their lumbering old coach was far shorter by horseback.

The fourth or fifth time, Margaret began to wonder whether Alasdair had more reasons for his visits than merely being within a few miles of their home. Visions of wedded life with him replaced tragic fantasies. She had been a foolish eighteen when she met Alasdair Falstone. Such daydreams were the stuff of extreme youth and naivete. After he rode away that last time, she was a lifetime older.

Spilt milk! Her father had sometimes quoted a line of French poetry: *Mais où sont les neiges d'antan?* Where are the snows of yesteryear?

The lengthening days of May meant some fifteen hours of daylight with brief stops to change horses and for the midday meal. Although she and the maid fell into bed exhausted each night, Margaret could not fault the major's desire to travel as fast as they could. He feared for his brother.

His bearing and manner, as well as his ability to pay, insured good horses, or at least the best available, quickly served meals, and comfortable bedchambers when they put up as twilight failed. 'Twas like being a gentlewoman again and almost as young as she had been on that long ago journey with Adam from Bettancourt to London to join their father.

But that coach had been full and the stops so short that eating and using the necessary were occasions for anxiety rather than comfort. Those traveling in their own carriages rather than in the common stagecoach naturally fared better, but her uncle had seen no need to incur the additional expense.

By the time the journey ended in London, they were both gray with dust and exhaustion. Adam claimed he was hungry unto perishing. Margaret had possessed just enough endurance to secure them a hack.

Now she sipped a glass of wine while Falstone gave crisp orders for their supper. On meeting him in London, she had noted only his outward changes from a slender, sunny youth to a muscular, stern-faced man. The greater alteration had been internal. He had gained confidence and made his life what he wanted it to be. Until he offered her the position of governess, she had never had control of her own destiny, except for the few years of her marriage to Gideon, when she had been a valued partner rather than a dependent.

In some indefinable way, Alasdair Falstone reminded her of her late husband. Melancholy washed over her.

Gideon MacGavin had been fourteen years older, an unremarkable difference when girls fresh out of the schoolroom might wed men as old as their fathers. His being a tradesman rather than a gentleman did not bother her greatly, given that her brothers were accounted tradesman despite their birth. Gideon was well-spoken and well-read and possessed a dry humor she had enjoyed. They had been at ease with each other: friends as well as husband and wife. He asked her opinions, while the young men she had known, except for Alasdair and Rupert, seldom cared for a female's thoughts on any subject. Mayhap young men secretly unsure of themselves were jealous of their dignity. She missed Gideon and marriage. Remembering their bed awakened longings that could not now be fulfilled.

Because of this lack she found herself noticing Falstone's broad shoulders and the strong thighs and steady hands with which he controlled his mount. The thought made her cheeks heat. Fortunately, as she was sitting near the hearth, no one need think she was blushing.

Then he took his seat at the table with a tankard of ale and asked whether her chamber was satisfactory. The balance of their conversation remained just as impersonal. She would have enjoyed talking about matters other than their accommodations and the state of the roads. His views on politics and recent news would have told her how much he had changed. During their meetings at Scot Hall and Bettancourt Priory, they had touched on those topics as often as on books and on their dreams. Alasdair had expected to manage his brother's estate and hoped to buy a small manor of his own eventually. She had expected to marry, have a family, and perhaps start a cheese-making endeavor to add to their income. She had learned the craft from her mother as they always had more milk than they needed. She could train a woman or girl to help her; there was always a demand for paying work for widows or young women who could not get positions in service. Neither she nor Alasdair had achieved all or even most of their ambitions.

Now she was content to be independent. Was he satisfied to be returning to Scot Hall to oversee the estate, or had he agreed reluctantly? A military career had agreed with him, and officers were always attractive to ladies. Margaret could imagine the languishing glances he would receive from impressionable girls and the veiled invitations from young widows. Why had he not married? Or had he done so and lost his wife to childbirth or disease? He had not mentioned a wife, but then he had not spoken much about himself except as related to his brother's illness and need for Alasdair's presence.

Chapter 7

He wondered what she was thinking. When he had called upon Margaret MacGavin to receive her answer, she had been ready to leave immediately. When he assured her she might have more time if she needed to make arrangements and bid her family farewell, she had said, "Thank you, but I think it best not to linger after they know I am leaving."

"Will your brothers disapprove?" Rupert had given him to understand he had no objection to Margaret's accepting the position, and surely the younger Bettancourt had nothing to say on the subject.

"I hardly think so. My sister-in-law is another matter. She is given to irritation of the nerves." Her composed reply suggested she would not be unduly upset by Elizabeth Hawkslowe's fits of petulance.

Alasdair breathed a sigh of relief at the sight of Scot Hall in the early evening of the eighth day. No difficulties had slowed them, not even Sunday. He had refused to spend the Sabbath at the inn where they passed Saturday night; he was too anxious to get back to his brother, and there might be any number of mischances on the way. As it fell out, none of the horses went lame, the roads continued dry, and the traveling coach thumped along without a broken wheel or axle.

The only complication Falstone encountered in

arranging the journey had been Margaret. He had intended to send the tutor and governess by coach with their trunks and with the possessions he had left in London. On failing to find a lady to take charge of the little girls as easily as he had found a tutor, he'd sent the fellow ahead by stage with enough money to reach Scot Hall from the nearest coaching inn. When he found a governess, he would ride beside the coach, and at inns, one of the maids could share her chamber. Governesses expected to travel on their own. As the lady was Margaret, he must protect her reputation.

In the one full day between asking Margaret to take the post and their departure, he hired a nursery maid in the expectation she would agree. Nurse Sallows was making do with whichever of the maids could be spared, the former nursery maid having left to marry. Lady Hawkslowe had been too busy to hire another. Falstone would have hired a girl from near Scot Hall, but the need for a chaperon for Margaret took precedence. The young woman he found had no objection to leaving London to work for a baron.

When he rode up to Scot Hall in advance of the coach, the absence of a hatchment over the door relieved his worry that he would arrive to a house in mourning. One of the younger footmen emerged to take his horse with cheerful "Welcome, sir!"

Graves met him at the top of the steps. By then, the coach had appeared around the stand of trees at the end of the lane.

"I've hired a governess and a nursery maid, Graves. Have the housekeeper get them settled. I'm going up to see Lord Hawkslowe, if he's able to receive a visitor."

"Unless he chances to be sleeping, I venture to say he'll make himself able. Budley says he's been fretting since you went. If he is asleep, Budley will be able to put him in better heart as soon as he wakes, knowing you've returned."

As he started up the stairs, Falstone paused. "I've brought some amusements for the children. Send them to my chamber for the moment. Most of the things are safe enough, but I don't want the boys getting hold of the foils until I've given them some instruction. I'll see Lady Hawkslowe after my brother and the children after that."

"Very good, Major Falstone."

Too much to expect the servants would give up using his former rank; they did love titles.

"Thank God" were Sebastian's first words when his servant ushered Falstone in. Hawkslowe was sitting in a wing chair by the fire today. "I feared for you. The world's chancy. Footpads, sickness, a toss from a horse, an encounter with highwaymen on the road…"

"I'm here now, and all you asked is accomplished. I brought a governess with me. Have you met Dorring, the tutor?"

Sebastian nodded. "A good choice. He brought the boys to see me the day after he arrived. Elizabeth hadn't let them visit me. Afraid of infection."

"I didn't know. I'm sorry I didn't think of it."

"You were here and gone again, as I needed you to be. Dorring kept them at a distance, for their safety."

Falstone sketched the plans he had made for the boys' informal education and entertainment when not at their studies.

"And Janet and Isabelle?"

With a sudden misgiving, Falstone remembered who was to teach the girls. "She is well educated and will not scruple to instruct them in more than female accomplishments. She will ride with them, but I don't know what other plans she may have for their recreation. I am sure they will like her."

"If she is as good as Dorring, I need worry no more about my little ladies, then."

"I hope you will not mind, Sebastian, but Mistress MacGavin is the former Margaret Bettancourt."

Sebastian's forehead creased. "Bettancourt? Zounds, the girl you wanted to marry? Alasdair…" He coughed wetly into his handkerchief. When the paroxysm ended and he had caught his breath again, he mumbled, "I do not know how I can face her, when I wronged both of you."

"I do not think she holds any grudge, as she agreed to come here." Why had he not considered how peculiar and awkward Margaret's presence might be? Yet even if he had thought of it, he would have done the same. She had been giving lessons to tradesmen's daughters for a few pence, and she was soon to lose her refuge over the fencing school. He found he could not blame her late husband overmuch. Even a successful tradesman would be hard put to provide for a widow. "After all, it's fifteen years in the past, and her marriage was happy." Rupert had thought so, anyway. Margaret had not spoken of it. "None of the other applicants were suitable."

He entertained his brother with a brief account of how impossible the others were, which made Sebastian laugh hoarsely. Still, when he assisted the invalid back to his bed, Hawkslowe's thoughtful expression revealed a desire to say more on the subject.

Probably "All that time and you never married." Had his brother spoken it, he would have replied that he did not care to subject a lady to the uncertain world of a soldier's wife. Colonel Bettancourt had blamed his wife's early death on the hardships she suffered during the few years she followed the drum. As Sebastian had not voiced the observation, he must be left to speculate.

Falstone expected Elizabeth Hawkslowe to be sulking over the arrival of the tutor, as Sebastian had coolly informed him before he left that there was no need for her to know in advance. "Alasdair, I must choose my battles. Though once you return, you may fight them for me," he ended with a faint smile.

Falstone hoped to speak with her before she discovered he had come back, bringing with him a governess and another servant. When he presented himself, someone had already informed her. Lady Hawkslowe's cheeks flew red flags of anger.

"I am sure I had no idea you meant to return, Falstone. And by what right do you saddle us with a governess and another maid? My daughters are in too much distress to be bothered with lessons, and the nursery is adequately served already. I was appalled when some threadbare fellow arrived, all horrid carroty hair and freckles, claiming he had been hired to instruct my sons. When I asked my husband, he said he had given authority for it. When I tried to reason with him, his man insisted I leave."

"Lord Hawkslowe charged me with engaging a governess and tutor, and it was obvious that the nursery maid who left months ago must be replaced. My brother does not want his children to grow up as ignorant as beggars' brats. Lessons will occupy their mornings, and the boys' unsupervised roaming will be curtailed. The girls will enjoy some exercise each day."

"How dare you give orders in my house? My daughters at least should be under my control."

Her snappish retort proved he had affronted her. He did not regret it in the least. The time for diplomacy was past.

" 'Tis their father who decides all matters regarding his children. You, madam, have failed to carry out his repeated requests, and he has been too ill to enforce his wishes. He sent for me to make sure they are taught and overseen as they ought to be." He would begin now as he meant to go on. The woman's intractability was not to be borne.

Elizabeth Hawkslowe's lips compressed as she visibly struggled to control herself. Good; she responded to a firm hand on the bridle. Sebastian had too long given her free rein, the result of his infatuation with the woman at first and then of his failing health. Love made fools of men as Circe turned Odysseus's crew into swine.

She was not quite ready to surrender, however. "What right have you to judge me, when you abandoned your brother? You might have been here to support him all these years instead of running off."

Perhaps his expression alarmed her, for after a struggle to mask her ire, she continued, "I beg your pardon, Major. I have had to take responsibility for everything since Hawkslowe fell ill. You cannot imagine the stress of shouldering burdens for which no lady is prepared. No doubt you are correct that the children would be the better for more supervision. I have had little time to devote to my darlings. In any event, 'tis done now. What can you tell me of the woman, and how did you find her?"

If Elizabeth was of a mind to be conciliating, he would oblige her. "She is a widow of mature years, some five-and-thirty, I believe. She is the sister of an acquaintance of mine in London and was in need of a position."

"What references has she?"

"Mistress MacGavin has not previously held a formal post as a governess. Since her husband's death, she has lived with her brother's family and taught his children and also given lessons in deportment and the like to some of the girls in their circle."

As his sister-in-law did not appear impressed, he added, "She is the granddaughter of a baronet and received an excellent education herself."

He expected mention of her connection to a baronet would be well received. Instinct did not fail him.

"Oh, I need not worry that she is not genteel, then. Thank you, Major Falstone. I suppose once you have rested for a few days, you will be returning to London?"

"I am able to remain to lend you my support in this trying time and to be with my brother while I can."

"Then I wonder you went away to London when you had only just arrived," she observed acerbically.

"He wanted a tutor and governess as soon as possible. Engaging them would not easily be done by letter." A deceptive reply though not untrue.

"Major Falstone, I hardly like to have to mention this, considering you are my dear husband's only brother, but with his illness and now the presence of Dorring and MacGavin and the new nursery maid in the house, the servants have a great deal of additional work to do. A guest is yet one more burden."

This might be the first time ever she had thought of the servants' convenience. "Pray, do not consider me a guest. I am a member of the family. Under the circumstances, my place is here. The older retainers know I will add little to their duties. I am used to seeing to my own needs."

"My brothers will be coming to support me."

Which would make more trouble for the servants, if he were any judge of the Bradnams.

"If necessary, a few temporary workers can be taken on, my lady."

She sniffed. "At the estate's expense."

"Surely Scot Hall's revenues will bear it." They would have done, fifteen years ago. The tenant farms he had seen appeared prosperous, which should mean Hawkslowe's finances were healthy. Two or even three lower servants hired for several months would cost little. A maid earned as little as two or three pounds a year.

"I do not like to incur costs unnecessarily."

He had schooled his face to impassivity long ago and trusted it did not betray him at this mendacious claim. Doubtless she considered her thriftless purchases to be essential. "My brother wishes me to stay, and I will stay for as long as I am needed."

"It is my home, sir."

"In fact, it is Lord Hawkslowe's, madam."

She turned on her heel, petticoats swirling, and stormed out of the room. He made his way to the servants' stair and took the steps two at a time. Arriving in Sebastian's bedchamber, he nodded to Budley, greeted his brother, and warned, " 'Ware squalls, she knows I'm staying," a moment before Lady Hawkslowe entered precipitately without the courtesy of a knock. She halted, mouth open, seeing Alasdair already present. After taking a deep breath presaging an outburst, she gasped and pulled a scented handkerchief from her pocket to cover her nose. Had she been in the habit of spending any time with her husband, she would have grown accustomed to the sickroom smells.

With an effort which must have cost him dearly, Sebastian grated, "Elizabeth, I should have taken you in hand years ago. I have indulged you long enough. Alasdair is here at my invitation. I trust him to do what is right for you and the children, and you will obey his instructions as if they were mine. Better! You have too often failed to heed my own. He will enforce them in whatever way you make necessary. Do you understand?" By then, his voice was failing him, only an effort of will sustaining him.

Elizabeth stood speechless, flushed, her plump bosom heaving. At last she muttered, "Well! If it is by your will, my lord, I must of course obey. If you will excuse me?"

When the door closed behind her, the fit of coughing he had held in check overtook Sebastian. When it ended, the handkerchief Budley had pressed into his hand was thickly spotted with blood. He was gray-faced.

"Major Falstone," Budley began.

"If she…makes difficulties…dismiss her creatures. Budley and Graves…know who they are. See me…later this evening."

Budley walked to the door with him. "Mrs. Stukeley, the housekeeper, knows who's in her confidence as well. And her ladyship wrote to her brothers as soon as you left for town."

Falstone looked forward to this campaign.

His visit to the schoolroom went better. Daniel Dorring's good humor had already endeared him to Colin and Matthew. Somehow he managed to teach them both at the same time and yet adjust the difficulty of the lesson to each. When Falstone entered the schoolroom, Dorring was explaining to Matthew the value of geometry in building fortifications and for artillerymen. "Eventually you will be able to prove, as Colin can, that if two sides of the triangle are the same length, the angles opposite them will be equal." The younger boy was frowning over that concept as the tutor looked up and saw Alasdair.

"Major Falstone, welcome."

His nephews scrambled to their feet, Colin making his bow, and Matthew exclaiming, "Uncle Alasdair! You're back!" before he remembered his manners.

"I apologize for interrupting your lesson. I wanted to let Mr. Dorring know I brought some educational materials from London, which I'll unpack tomorrow. I will talk to you both then. Now I will borrow your tutor for a few minutes. Dorring?"

The young man was pleased to hear he would have the benefit of a terrestrial globe for teaching geography and of a number of useful books. On being asked whether he fenced or shot, he admitted he did not, apart from having gone out with a musket a few times to shoot birds with a neighbor. He would be happy to impress upon his students the importance of care in handling both foil and pistol.

Learning that Lady Hawkslowe had gone to her chamber with a megrim and would not be down for supper, Alasdair sent a message up to Dorring and the girls' schoolroom to request that the tutor, Margaret, Janet, and Colin take their meal in the dining room, leaving Nurse Sallows and the new maid to supervise the younger children's supper. For him to eat alone in the dining room would be ridiculous, and both Margaret—Mistress MacGavin—and Dorring were gentry. Besides, to be freed from the nursery and schoolroom occasionally would benefit the two older children, who had little contact with adults other than servants.

The evening meal was the first time since turning her over to Graves and Mrs. Stukeley that he had seen Margaret.

She said, "I regret that I have not yet met Lady Hawkslowe."

Janet filled the awkward lapse in conversation while Falstone tried to think of a tactful answer.

"Mama often has headaches. The country air does not agree with her, and she has not visited London for some time."

Indeed, had not been permitted to go to London in the last few years.

"London always makes her feel better for a while," his niece concluded.

"I don't understand it, myself. There's so much to do in the country," Colin said. "Riding, fishing, and looking for birds' nests, and, er…"

"Snaring rabbits, climbing trees, and helping the

farrier shoe horses," Alasdair continued. "Just as your father and I did."

"Did you, sir?"

"Ay. What do you do when you aren't studying, Janet?"

"I like to read. Sometimes I make baskets. The grandmother of one of our tenants taught me how. If I make a big one, I give it to our parson's wife, for when she makes up bundles for the poor. But I make little ones, too, and stuff them with a wool-filled cushion, for pin pillows, to give as gifts."

"Do you like to ride?"

"I did, before our governess left. We rode almost every day."

"You could ride with me if you don't mind a gallop," her brother offered.

"Mama said I wasn't to go out without a groom and a female companion. She says it's dangerous."

"Hah," he muttered.

"What was that comment, Master Colin?" Dorring asked.

"I beg your pardon, sir. It was rude. But it should be unnecessary for my sister to be accompanied by both a groom and a companion," he added.

"While I may agree with the sentiment, to snort or mumble under your breath like a menial does not befit a gentleman. Don't do it again."

Colin caught the amusement in the tutor's tone and grinned.

"Have I been misinformed, Janet? Are there still wolves or Scottish raiders here?"

Even Janet, a serious girl, smiled, and the rest laughed.

"No, Mistress MacGavin. But there's riffraff and poachers and vagabonds and mayhap gypsies."

"Northumberland is clearly a more dangerous place than I guessed. Well, perhaps you can ride with your uncle."

"And with you, M-Mistress MacGavin," he said, catching himself in time before he called her by her given name. Wonderful! He sounded as if he had developed a stammer. Apart from that one "Alasdair!" she had addressed him formally. Now that he considered it, she was right to distance herself from him. He had brought her here as his nieces' teacher. Any sign of familiarity on his part would reflect upon her, and Elizabeth Hawkslowe would pounce upon it and accuse him of bringing his mistress into the household. He could imagine her screeching.

"It has been years since I rode, Major Falstone. So long that I do not own a habit or boots." She did not meet his eyes.

Did she fear he would be angry that she had not confessed her lack of a riding habit? He had not considered the matter, or he would have known she would hardly have either habit or riding boots when she could not have been riding in town.

"As the girls must learn to ride well, and my sister-in-law does not care for the exercise, a riding habit and boots will be ordered for you."

She was clearly contemplating a polite refusal.

"It is a schoolroom expense, as books are, or a dancing master. One of the maids has served guests who failed to bring their own ladies' maids. She will take your measurements, and I am sure a serviceable habit can be made up in Newcastle without much delay."

She could not counter his argument. "Thank you. It will be good exercise for Janet and Isabelle, which I think would benefit them. I will enjoy it, too."

She had been a splendid rider, fearless but sensible, with an excellent seat. Spirited but not a romp. She had changed from that girl into a composed woman who had been married and widowed. He had met older women who never matured, a troubling spectacle. His sister-in-law, for one. Years, trouble, and hardship sat easily upon Margaret. She had been a pretty girl. Now her face reflected her character.

He had changed, too, from the young man who had courted her. He had cast off his only remaining relation and lost his chance to marry. Soon his only family would be his brother's children. His dragoons thought him a grim man, and they were correct. Yet recently the world sometimes felt less dark.

Chapter 8

Lady Hawkslowe sent for her the following afternoon. When the maid admitted her, Margaret found her sitting by a good fire and holding a book, though she appeared to be sunk in thought rather than reading. The poor woman must be beside herself with worry for her husband. The baroness looked up when the maid announced her. After inspecting Margaret from head to foot, she said irritably, "You may sit."

On being asked about her experience, Margaret admitted she had not previously been employed as a governess, though she had taught her brother's children and had given lessons to girls in their neighborhood. This seemed not to surprise her ladyship. Of course it would not; she must have already questioned Falstone about her suitability. Her ladyship had intended to fluster her.

Lady Hawkslowe tested her on her knowledge of titles and forms of address, though not on whether she knew anything of arithmetick or history or geography. Could she sing or play the harpsichord? Dance? How had she learned these accomplishments?

"My mother and a very good governess taught me."

After she answered a number of questions about her family connections, Elizabeth Hawkslowe circled back to the beginning. "You are in straitened circumstances, but you are only now taking employment?"

She meant to keep things as simple as possible without lying. "My husband's will was made some years before we married. He was in excellent health, and so I suppose he thought he had time left to see to it. A roof tile blown loose in a gale killed him."

"Husbands!" her new employer uttered. "We trust them, and all too often we are disappointed."

Margaret confined herself to a sympathetic "Mmmm."

Instead of pursuing the original subject, Lady Hawkslowe confided, "I am perfectly sure it was understood between Hawkslowe and me that we would live in London except for a month or two in the summer, when we would invite friends to stay. Yet no sooner were we married than he insisted on living in this dreary place. We did remove to London for the parliamentary term for a few years, but then he ceased attending. I protested, but he claimed he had a duty to the estate. What did he have a bailiff for, if not to oversee it?"

Margaret's grandfather would never have left all responsibility for Bettancourt Priory in the hands of his bailiff. "A lazy owner makes a bad landlord and bad tenants," Sir Percival said. She could hardly say as much without giving offense. Fortunately, Lady Hawkslowe continued before she could think of some acceptable comment.

"In any case, Alasdair Falstone was to act as steward, but he abandoned his duty and his brother and went off with no notice, and so we could make no wedding visits to our friends. We went almost direct from the church door to the Great North Road. Falstone was courting my sister at the time, too, which would have been an excellent marriage for him and a satisfactory one for her, though not as good as she could have expected. We believed it all but decided they would make a match, then she was bereft, poor girl. Falstone has been a bad brother and an unreliable suitor, and I am out of charity with him. Though his jilting of Corinna was all for the best in the end as she is now a viscountess."

The discontent in her voice must issue from her sister's superior title.

"How very disappointing you could not have your wedding trip. I am happy for your sister, however." Clearly Lady Hawkslowe was either misinformed or guilty of some self-deception. Alasdair had left to buy his commission after Lord Hawkslowe dashed his hopes of their marrying. A wonderfully romantic gesture it had seemed, even though she grieved for the loss of their immediate happiness and worried for his safety. And yet, he had abandoned her as thoroughly as if he had died.

After a few years, she came to feel Alasdair really was dead, making it easier to surrender her romantickal notions and banish her resentment of his desertion. Knowing he had survived and reconciled with his brother gave her a moment's satisfaction, confirming she had recovered from her anger. Most of it. Good! She was pleased for him. Even better, no last seed of hope remained. She had uprooted from her heart the last of the longing. Still, she did sometimes wonder what their lives would have been if they had married.

That Falstone had not healed the breach earlier did

strike her as strange. During their journey to Scot Hall, she had inquired about his service. Surely it could not be considered prying when anyone would have asked the same of a new acquaintance, if only to make conversation. As the daughter of a soldier, she could not help being interested. Her father, her grandfather, and their military friends had reminisced about army life. The major had brushed her question aside, not quite brusquely. She might have learned whether he had ever married. If so, his wife must have died for he could hardly have sold out and moved to Scot Hall without mentioning a living wife.

His lack of openness was proof of how much he had changed, if she had had any doubts. Just as well they had not wed in defiance of his brother and her father and grandfather.

"Of course, once Hawkslowe's health failed, he gave up going to London entirely, for which I cannot blame him because the journey is exhausting and tiresome if one is in good health. Still, that was no reason I could not have gone to visit my sister and brothers, see the latest fashions, and take part in society. Instead, he required me to remain here. I suppose he wanted to cling to me in his illness."

These revelations should have been shared only with a family member or a close friend. Perhaps Lady Hawkslowe had no friend in the neighborhood and so needed a pair of ears to provide sympathy. Margaret could understand the impulse. Since Gideon's death, she had had no one to whom she could speak her mind freely. Before his marriage, she might have spoken to Rupert. After, either he would feel he must tell Sybilla or else he would feel uneasy about keeping his sister's confidences. She could not have subjected him to such a choice.

"So selfish of him. Brothers are often more satisfactory. Why is your brother not supporting you? Or some other relative?"

"My older brother took me into his home when my husband died. But his house is not large, and he and his wife have five children now." *Soon to be six, I fear.* "I decided I could not impose longer. My younger brother will be marrying soon, and I doubt his bride will wish to share their home with his sister. I have no other connections I can impose upon. My uncle inherited the manor. He and my father were not close." Uncle Simon had inherited a scant year after Alasdair's departure. Like Lord Hawkslowe, Simon Bettancourt did not view his younger brother's venture into trade with tolerance. Having Margaret and Adam in his house would have invited questions about their father's whereabouts and activities. Not wishing to hear any chaff from his friends about his brother, the fencing master, Sir Simon proposed they should join Papa in London.

Her charges' mother rattled on. "London houses are annoyingly small. That is the one benefit of a country house, I find. But there is no society here and little company. How did Falstone become acquainted with your family? They do not live nearby."

If she admitted her family's connection to trade, would Lady Hawkslowe turn her off? She did not care to chance it. "He met my grandfather in connection with Sir Percival's interest in horse breeding, my lady."

This seemed to satisfy Lady Hawkslowe. "You will do well enough, I suppose. I feared Falstone had brought back a young female, which always makes difficulties where there are young gentlemen or male guests. As that is not the case, I need worry no more about my daughters."

Over the following week, her ladyship demonstrated no great concern with the girls' education when they were not in her presence. When they were, good manners, a graceful curtsy, and erect posture were enough to satisfy her. Margaret decided that was a good thing, as she suspected her ladyship's presence would be disruptive in the nursery or schoolroom. Nor did she ask about their other lessons or progress. On balance, Margaret was relieved. She could not feel that deportment, the ability to embroider, and paint tolerable watercolors was more important than speaking French fluently, being able to add and subtract, and being generally aware of where France, Italy, India, and China were located. The terrestrial globe had spurred a good deal of interest in geography.

Chapter 9

Major Falstone's presence was a little disconcerting. Any embers of feeling between them had died, leaving them two people who had once been acquainted and were now employer and employed. She expected to see little of him and had steeled herself to endure unavoidable meetings. But by evening of her third day in the house, she knew the household needed his presence. With the baron so ill, Scot Hall was a ship with no rudder.

And he was very good with the boys. Alasdair visited the schoolroom occasionally, which Dorring remarked always put them on their mettle, and spent time with them when they were not at their lessons. He gave Colin and Matthew fencing lessons on some afternoons (and how Margaret wished she might have observed!). He showed Matthew how to care for and train a young dog that mysteriously appeared in the stable, Sebastian's two or three dogs having somehow disappeared in the last several months.

"…since his lordship's kept to the house and then to his room," the blank-faced head groom, Archbold, muttered to Major Falstone. Margaret heard the snippet as she made her way to the house after a walk, the girls having run on ahead. They had seen Matthew and the collie in the stable and spent a few minutes petting and crooning over the little fellow.

"He won't go away, too, will he?" Isabelle whispered to Matthew, who looked worried but did not answer.

"Not if no one talks about him," Janet's words were spoken softly, but Margaret still heard them although she had not entered the stall herself. Her brothers claimed she possessed the ears of a cat.

Matthew's response was not quite as low-pitched. "Uncle Alasdair's here now, too."

Uncharitable of Margaret to assume Archbold's remark implied something about the previous dogs' absence, but the thought was unavoidable. There had been dogs—what farm or manor did not have a dog or two?—and now there were not, and it seemed to have happened since Lord Hawkslowe had become an invalid. The exchange was revealing if one knew Lady Hawkslowe disliked animals. Encountering the kitchen cat in the passage outside the drawing room, she had demanded shrilly how it had come there and sent a message by her maid to berate the cook for its escape.

Margaret saw Janet and Isabelle off for rides with one of the grooms before her own habit and boots were ready. Elizabeth Hawkslowe rode with the girls on one occasion. She had not brought a treat for her mount and neither stroked her nor spoke to her. Margaret conceded the baroness's behavior might result from a fear of horses as she displayed the signs of a timid rider. She did not honor them with her escort a second time. Just as well, since even before they rode away from the house, her frequent, unnecessary admonitions made her daughters and their ponies nervous.

Archbold, the head groom, had taught all four children the essentials of horsemanship, but the girls needed practice. Falstone escorted them several times a week, sometimes riding with his nieces and sometimes with his nephews. Once she was booted and habited, Margaret would take the girls out each day.

Would she be able to remember how to ride when she had not been on a horse in fourteen years? The doubt struck as she met Janet and Isabelle in the hall for their first ride together and found the major waiting with them. What if she fell off? Her humiliation before Alasdair Falstone who had known her when she had been a notable rider would near kill her. *If the fall doesn't.*

The ponies were led up, followed by his unhandsome skewbald. Last came Lady Hawkslowe's bay, a mare with a pretty face and good conformation, though sadly overweight.

"I apologize for your mount. Lady Hawkslowe's is the only one in the stable trained to sidesaddle, apart from the ponies."

"Oh! Do I have her permission to ride her?"

Falstone's brows contracted. "None is necessary. The mare was not a gift to her ladyship. My brother merely provided her for her use. You'll be doing her, the horse, I mean, a favor. She gets too little exercise."

The necessary balance and use of hands, voice, and whip came back to her with no thought on her part, as if those long years had never been. Her heart soared. As they cantered, the girls between them, Falstone said, "I will allow myself the pleasure of escorting you ladies once or twice a week if you permit, Mistress MacGavin?"

What could she say but "You would be very welcome, sir."

He was patient with his nieces and nephews, a surprise, given his demeanor was often stern. Whatever else had changed, she sometimes glimpsed a flash of the man she had known. The boys needed to learn how to be gentlemen, and with their father unable to provide his guidance, who better to teach them than Falstone? Their maternal uncles lived in London.

Margaret hoped she might be as excellent an influence on her charges as Major Falstone, though of course she did not hold his position of power. She witnessed his skirmish with Lady Hawkslowe when he mentioned that Janet and Colin would be dining with them beginning the following day.

"You cannot mean it!" Lady Hawkslowe's exclamation came near to being a bleat. "Children have no place among adults until they are fit to be presented to society."

"A beau monde dining room would certainly exclude them, but this is not London nor is it a house party, where they would be uncomfortable. However, they will be better able to conduct themselves in society if they are already accustomed to dining with us."

Elizabeth Hawkslowe's effort to recreate London elegance was doomed to fail when the only other adults at her table were Falstone, Dorring, and Margaret. She continued to complain, but the result was that the major indulged her six days a week but insisted that all the children should eat dinner in the dining room on Sunday as part of their social training. Lady Hawkslowe grudgingly accepted that as a compromise. Margaret suspected Falstone had never intended Colin and Janet to attend meals in the dining room more than once or twice a week. While she thought dining en famille occasionally would be good for the children, Margaret could not approve of his treatment of Lady Hawkslowe in some of their exchanges. No wonder she resented the major's manner. Silly and vain as the baroness might be, she was suffering.

Yet Margaret admired Falstone's behavior with the rest of the household. In addition to reacquainting himself with the property and tenants and spending time with the children, Falstone sat every day with Lord Hawkslowe. Her ladyship did not, evidently finding his condition too distressing, but Margaret would not have known she did not visit her husband if the baron had been occupying the rooms connecting with his wife's chambers. He had moved to a guest chamber some distance away at the far end of the wing, past the one she herself had been assigned. Major Falstone had moved from the one he had occupied as a young man to the bedroom closest to his brother's.

There were several explanations for Hawkslowe's removal from his own suite: that he did not wish to risk infecting Lady Hawkslowe or disturbing her rest with his coughing. Another was that his new bedchamber was next to the servants' stair, making it faster to bring up food and hot drinks or barley water from the kitchen. Also, unlike the other guest chambers, it possessed a dressing room where his manservant could sleep. The servants did not approve of the change, despite making it easier to care for the invalid, although no one said as much directly. But she overheard Graves say to the housekeeper, "Every baron since the first, barring only the one the Roundheads killed, has died in the baron's bedchamber. I wish his lordship might do the same."

When he had asked her to be the girls' governess,

Falstone had hinted that the household was troubled, as well it might be, with its lord dying. A month at Scot Hall convinced her the problems went deeper than Hawkslowe's illness or Lady Hawkslowe being overset by stress. There was nothing she herself could do about it except to keep Janet and Isabelle busy and educate them to be ladies who understood a household ledger and could discuss a book or play in addition to possessing the usual accomplishments. If possible, they should meet adversity with calm.

Their rides with or without their brothers and Falstone were the most enjoyable part of the day. By a chance remark, she deduced that their mother's anxiety over Janet's and Isabelle's riding had less to do with gypsies or vagabonds than with her fear they would have accidents which would cripple or scar them and thus make them unmarriageable. What a pack of nonsense!

Fortunately, the stables were out of sight of her ladyship's rooms and the front of the house, and as Lady Hawkslowe's trusted servants did not have much reason to consort with the grooms and stable lads, she did not learn that Margaret and the girls rode almost every day. No one mentioned the chestnut mare newly arrived in the stable. One day when Margaret went out with the girls, the mare was standing saddled with the ponies. Margaret did not for a moment think Athena could belong to the major. She was too dainty and was trained to carry a sidesaddle, which would be remarkable in a dragoon's horse. She did not comment upon it, however, having ridden Lady Hawkslowe's fat, timid mare before the chestnut appeared.

They were approaching Scot Hall after one jaunt

when they saw a carriage rattling away and a footman carrying a pair of valises into the house. While she wondered about it, Janet and Isabelle ceased their chatter. The footman trotted out again to take their horses, harried manner signaling trouble, while the butler held the door for them. Portmanteaus and trunks littered the floor. They heard Lady Hawkslowe's twittering soprano from the drawing room.

"...have been the most miserable woman in England. I am so glad you have come to support my spirits, though you should have come sooner. Hawkslowe's brother is here to be in at the death, as I suppose"—the butler and Margaret exchanged glances, and the sisters moved closer together—"and he is a perfect tyrant. I vow and declare—"

Graves opened the concealed door in the paneling that led to the servants' passage and stair and whispered, "Through there, madam." Margaret gave Janet a little push toward the door, thanked him with a smile and nod, and herded Isabelle before her. The door closed softly behind them. They ascended two flights of stairs to emerge in the nursery wing.

"Wash your face and hands, make yourselves tidy, and change your clothing. Don't dally over it." She did not want to be put to the blush if Lady Hawkslowe sent for her children to be introduced to her guest.

Janet, whose ability to guess one's thoughts was sometimes disconcerting, remarked, "It's Uncle Harry. Probably Uncle Paul, too. We will most likely be summoned to the drawing room before our supper."

The nursery supper was taken about an hour before that served in the dining room. Lady Hawkslowe would wish to dress for supper with a guest in the house, not that she ever dressed like a country lady who was not expecting company. The two youngest children would become fidgety if they had to attend their mother for more than a quarter hour. They would not be on display long. Margaret turned them over to Nurse Sallows to be prepared rather as their mounts were now being combed and brushed by the grooms. She herself put on one of her old gowns suitable for an evening in her brothers' and Gideon's circle and thus unremarkable for a governess.

They received her ladyship's summons and slipped into the drawing room behind Dorring and the boys, who were standing just inside the door. The reason for their immobility became clear at Falstone's harsh "…under any circumstances."

"Surely I may be allowed to furnish my home as I see fit." The waspish feminine tones returned fire.

The younger of the two blond men glimpsed over Colin's shoulder muttered apologetically, "I am heartily sorry I mentioned the matter." His eyes and the shape of his face resembled Matthew's.

"Did Hawkslowe give you permission to purchase new furniture for the baron's chamber?"

"How could I bother him with trivial household details when he is so ill?"

"Then he did not know or agree to it."

"But he will when he knows! That nasty old bed and the other old rubbish must be a source of contagion. No one can occupy the rooms until everything has been removed, the walls and floor thoroughly cleaned, and new furniture brought in. Besides, it's past time the rooms were made fashionable."

"That 'rubbish,' as you call it, is as old as the

barony. It will not be replaced. Nor is there any need to do so. The bed and other furnishings can be carried outside to be washed with vinegar and exposed to the sunlight. It's reasonable to get a new mattress"— Falstone smiled thinly—"as it's not of an age with the bed. Nor are the curtains and bedcover, which I recall my mother ordered when Hawkslowe and I were boys. I'm sure he will have no objection to your changing those, which I doubt could be washed successfully."

Unnoticed, Margaret and the girls waited like rabbits hiding from a fox. She put an arm around each, and they huddled against her, motionless.

"But when Colin succeeds to his papa's title and honors—"

The blond man who had spoken whispered to the other, "In a month or less, I'll be bound, Harry."

The older Bradnam brother was taller, broader, and less handsome. The faint vertical lines between his brows hinted at annoyance.

The major's lips thinned dangerously. "He will not be using those rooms until he is eighteen. While he is still in the schoolroom, he will continue on the nursery floor. In September, he will leave for school in any case."

Harry Bradnam turned his head toward his brother to make some soft comment, and his eyes widened, catching sight of their frozen little group. He said brightly, "Here's Dorring and our nephews, and I warrant that's Janet and little Isabelle with their governess right on their heels."

Her attention diverted, Lady Hawkslowe looked over her shoulder, her face a study in chagrin. "Dorring, MacGavin, what are you doing here? Why did you not say something to announce your presence?"

"You sent for them. I expect they could not get a word in to advise you of their arrival."

Her face flamed at Falstone's dry statement. "Take my children back to the schoolroom."

Dorring, Colin, and Matthew bowed to the company in general and retreated while Margaret, Janet, and Isabelle curtsied before whisking out the door on the boys' heels.

At the first landing, Dorring sent the boys ahead of him, and the girls followed, willy-nilly. The tutor spoke quietly. "An unpleasant scene. We arrived as Mr. Paul Bradnam informed Lady Hawkslowe the carrier expected to deliver the new furniture in two or three days. Major Falstone inquired, what furniture? And the fat was in the fire."

"Horrid. I am sorry the children saw their mother and their uncle Falstone brangling like children, and in the presence of others." She could understand Falstone had been upset at the idea of replacing the furniture in the baron's chambers when he was not yet dead, and the more so as the furnishings had historic value. Still, he should have confronted her in private.

"We are like to witness more of the same and worse." Dorring went on meditatively. "From one or two of Colin's remarks, he and Janet at least have a fair notion of their mother's ways. But the worst of it was that they should overhear Paul Bradnam's prediction of their papa's death. I don't believe anyone has explained to them how very grave is his condition. The older ones may have guessed it."

Chapter 10

The morning after the arrival of the furniture, Budley asked for a quiet word with Falstone.

"Mr. Graves came to me when her ladyship's new furniture was delivered, as the carriers needed to be paid off and there wasn't enough in the household account that's in his charge. I went to the office to get the money and made a note of it in the ledger." He paused, biting his lip.

"Go on." There was nothing very odd about a trusted valet being able to access his master's funds as required.

"Looking at it, I saw something was amiss. The amount in the box was short."

"You were able to tell that by sight?"

"I couldn't believe it, not without I looked at the ledger careful and talked to Twissell, the bailiff. I didn't have time to study on the matter then, what with the house still in a ferment"—the Bradnams had brought chaos in their wake, with their demands and luggage and finickal ways—"but I went back an hour ago to see if I could figure what was wrong, his lordship being settled for a nap with a footman watching him. If I knew how much the amount was off, I reckoned 'twould help to know how the problem came about. I haven't talked to Twissell yet."

Alasdair was not surprised the accounts had been

neglected. Sebastian had explained he had been less and less able to manage estate matters. He had never employed a steward to do so, and his bailiff only dealt with the tenants and collected the rents and payments for wool and sheep or other stock sold. Before Alasdair had left for London on his brother's business, Sebastian had summoned Twissell to his chamber and instructed him to take his orders and make his reports to Falstone. Since his return, Alasdair had made a point of visiting the tenants with Twissell and studying the rents and wool prices over the last half dozen years but had not inspected the ledgers yet.

"No doubt Twissell forgot to note some expenditure and no real harm done."

Budley almost wrung his hands. "I don't think it can be as simple as that, now I've studied the ledger."

"Why? How much was the difference?"

"Sir, it was twenty pounds exactly!"

"That much." No wonder Sebastian's man was nervous. It might be a year's rent for a cottage with a stable and a few acres. A cottage by itself or with only a couple of acres could rent for less than ten pounds. "I'll talk to Twissell. He must have failed to record several payments."

"Twissell doesn't have a key for the strongbox nor yet the drawer, Major Falstone."

Falstone sighed. "Have you a supposition as to the cause of the problem, then, Budley?"

"The amount left in the box before I took out what was needed to pay the carter was what it should have been after the last entry before Lady Day." He gave a short nod, as if this statement should be meaningful to Falstone.

"How is that significant?" Alasdair asked when no further comment was forthcoming.

"Why, because there should have been another twenty pound in the box from the Lady Day rents, sir."

He needed to understand Sebastian's rent collection procedures. "In my father's day, the tenants came here to pay in their rent. Is that still the case?"

"Ay."

"Who takes the money in and records it? I suppose Lord Hawkslowe was not well enough three months ago to take part?"

"No, not then. December was the last time my lord received the tenants, though his lordship himself admitted he wasn't well enough to take the deposit to the bank in Newcastle. He was already shivering with the chills when he locked the money in the box and told Twissell to get the key from me and take the money and deposit record to the bank the first day after Christmas it wasn't mortal cold or snowing. Lord Hawkslowe showed me where to write entries in the ledger if I needed to pay out money, in case he should be indisposed when it was needed."

From what Falstone had gathered a word or two at a time, that illness began Sebastian's final decline.

"He must have known he was in for a bad spell, sir, for any epidemic cold laid him low. My lord said Twissell was to deliver all but twenty pound to the bank, as usual, so the box would contain whatever was left over from the three months just ended plus the twenty from the new rents. He told me to note the deposit to the box when Twissell made it. If he needed money for estate expenses during the quarter, he was to come to me, and I was to note those, too. When

Twissell came back, he brought the deposit book with the rent deposit shown, just as it should be. So before December quarter day rent there was sixteen pounds, five shillings, sixpence in the box, and after the quarter day, there was six-and-thirty pounds, five shillings, sixpence, because twenty pounds had been kept back from the deposit to the bank for ready rhino."

"You've been keeping the accounts since December?"

"Ay, Major. When Lord Hawkslowe was mortal bad after Christmas, we thought we'd lose him. Thank the Lord, he recovered. But going down to the estate office was too much for him. I brought the ledger up to him when he'd improved—" The valet hesitated, not voicing the thought that came to Falstone's mind: *as much as he could.* "Even sitting up in his chamber with the ledger exhausted him." The valet hesitated. " 'Twas after that my lord wrote to you, Major."

He could understand his brother involving Budley, as the man was in his confidence, having been his valet a dozen years or more. He must have trusted Twissell, too, to have him deposit the rents.

"Anyhow, the ledger showed nine-and-twenty pounds, two shillings, ha'penny before the Lady Day rents, and the entries accounted for the difference."

"I see. How was the rent collected at Lady Day?"

"Lord Hawkslowe told Twissell and me to do it. We were both at the desk in the estate office with the rent book, and the men gave their money to Twissell, he counted it and passed it to me, and I counted it, too. Then I wrote it in the rent ledger and put the coin in the bag to be taken to the bank, and that went into the box."

In warm, dry weather, Alasdair's father and his

bailiff sat at a table in the shade to receive the money and note it in the ledger, and there would be tables of food and barrels of ale. When it was wet, the rent collection would be held in the home farm's barn. In winter when it was too cold, they made use of the ballroom. Falstone hoped the poor devils of tenants hadn't been expected to wait outside in March to be admitted to the estate office.

Budley went on, breaking into Alasdair's reflections. "Twissell couldn't take it to Newcastle immediately. There was terrible cold and snow here. After a week, the weather warmed, but that only meant the road was deep in mud and no one was traveling unless they'd no choice. I think it was another two weeks or more before the roads improved enough. The rents were safe here until he could get to the bank.

"With one thing and another, I forgot it until the carrier wanted his pay, and Graves asked me to pay out of the estate money, and there wasn't near as much in the box as there should have been."

"You said you entered the deposit in the rent ledger. Is it entered in the estate ledger?"

"No, sir." Budley swallowed convulsively.

"Was the deposit not made? Is that why it isn't in the ledger? "

"I don't rightly know, sir."

Falstone stared grimly at his brother's valet. He had questioned dragoons who had stolen sheep or army supplies, or committed assaults; he was familiar with the need to drag answers out one at a time. In this instance, he did not think Budley was lying. "You will please explain that statement, Budley. Did Twissell make the deposit and not tell you he'd done so?"

"No, he did. I mean, I knew he was going, and he had some other estate business there as well. I gave him the keys for the desk and the strongbox. I didn't go down to the office with him. His lordship had got up to use the close stool when I was gone to the kitchen for a few minutes to get him a posset. I found him on the floor when I came back. He'd fallen, and we were afraid he'd broke something. With sending for the doctor and having to arrange for someone to be with Lord Hawkslowe all the time, that was all I could think of. I sat up with his lordship all night and forgot the deposit and Twissell and all."

Falstone acknowledged this with a brusque nod. They must all have known then that he could not live much longer.

"So Twissell made the deposit, but you forgot to enter it? I suppose he forgot to keep out the twenty pounds. It's only a matter of entering the deposit in the ledger, and I'll send someone to the bank to withdraw twenty pounds so there's enough on hand."

"No, sir." He blurted out, "I can't confirm it was deposited."

Falstone scrambled to get his bearings. "Because?" Questioning dragoons over some cork-brained action was easy by comparison.

"I can't find the bank deposit book."

"Have you asked Twissell about it?"

"He's been visiting some of the outlying tenants and not like to be home before evening."

"Twissell has a cottage in the village, doesn't he? Send a groom to leave a message with his wife that he's to report here as soon as he returns. No, on second thought, the morning will do. A day will make no difference. I won't keep him from his supper."

An annoying incident, but with Hawkslowe an invalid and no supervision, mistakes would happen.

Falstone was finishing his breakfast the next day when Graves informed him Twissell was waiting in the estate office. After the last bite of ham and a last swallow of ale, Falstone took himself off to interview the bailiff.

He began by asking Twissell about the last rent collection. His account tallied with Budley's.

"I'm told it was a hard winter here. Harder than our ordinary winter," Falstone added with faint humor. "I suppose it was a difficult ride to Newcastle to deposit the rents."

"Not so bad. A-course, the cold and snow didn't last more nor a week, then there was the flooding, but that passed quick. I went and returned in one day, though we was late getting back."

The story came out bit by bit. Twissell hoped to get an early start as he needed to talk to the blacksmith about a plow design and he wanted to get home before nightfall; you never knew what might befall in the dark.

"Very wise. Were you able to do so?"

"Nay, for her ladyship told me she'd heard I was going and begged me to wait for her to send for the coach, as she meant to go into town, too, and would feel safer with a man riding beside, and would I bring a pistol with me in case of highwaymen. Highwaymen, ha! In these parts? But she'd made the effort to be up early, and she was pretty quick, and she's her ladyship, after all. Her brother could as well have rid along of the coach instead of inside, and that'd have saved me from having to wait for them and the coach to be ready.

Belike he didn't want to get his fine clothes muddy, and her ladyship felt safer with two men."

"Her brother was visiting, was he? Which one?"

"The younger one, Mr. Paul Bradnam. One or the other or both have come to stay this time and that, as long as I've been here."

From his tone, he had the northerner's scorn for delicate London folk. Alasdair concealed his own irritation at the thought of the Bradnam brothers running tame at Scot Hall. One meeting with them had been enough to form his own conclusions.

"You reached Newcastle without being robbed by a highwayman, I surmise, and deposited the money."

"Ay, Major Falstone."

"Was this the first time you had made a deposit for Lord Hawkslowe?" As well to verify what he'd heard from Budley.

"Nay. I made the one in January, as his lordship had the lung fever. Used to be he took it in himself. His lady would go along to receive her pin money for the quarter, you see, and she'd shop, as well. I recollect his lordship laughing over it once or twice."

"I suppose that explains her desire to visit Newcastle, then."

"Ay, Major. She did say as she wanted her pin money and to buy some embroidery silks and other things."

Another question arose. "Did the banker not return Lord Hawkslowe's bank deposit book to you?"

"No, sir."

"No? Did he not return it to you when you made the previous rent deposit?"

"He did, and I took it back to Budley."

"Do you know what he did with it?"

"I watched him put it in the money box."

"Then what became of it? It's not in the box now."

"I don't rightly know, sir." But suddenly the bailiff's voice was a shade uncertain.

"But you did take it with you when you made the last deposit?"

"Ay, Major."

"And the banker did not return it to you? Did you not ask him for it?" Falstone had previously found the taciturn northern manner efficient. He was rather sparing of words himself. He began to reconsider his opinion.

"Well, no, he couldn't, could he?"

"Why could he not have given it to you?" Falstone inquired sharply.

"He'd-a given it to Lady Hawkslowe."

Mayhap he noticed Falstone's expression. The bailiff scratched the back of his head, at a nonplus, before explaining. "See you, when her ladyship told me to wait for her, she said she'd fetch the rents from the estate office whilst I ordered the team put to the coach."

Falstone stared at the fellow broodingly. Twissell was a competent bailiff and agreed by all to be honest. "Did you give her the keys to the desk and the box?"

"No, Major Falstone. Her ladyship said she had a set of keys, being the lady of the house, and all. I made bold to mention I'd need the deposit book as well. She said as she would bring everything along in her work bag, for if we was robbed, the pad wouldn't think to look there."

Elizabeth Hawkslowe had keys to the money box and desk? Given what he had learned of her from

Sebastian, that seemed strange, unless he had trusted her with them early in their marriage and never taken them back. "I see. And what happened when you arrived at the bank?"

"When we drew up to Fitchett's Bank, she offered to take the money in, as she had to go in herself anyway, and that'd free me to go about my business with the smith and we'd get back to Scot Hall the sooner. And she went right in with her brother."

Falstone closed his lips tightly on a pithy comment or two. "And when she came out?"

"When I was done at the smithy, I met her ladyship and Mr. Paul at the inn as agreed, and we set out directly to get back before dark if we could."

"What of the keys Budley had given you?"

"I gave them back soon as I could, though I had to go to his lordship's chamber to do it, Budley being there to sit up with him. Near as gray as the master, Budley was, as tired as if he'd ridden to Newcastle and back."

That explained the manservant's failure to make any inquiry about the deposit. Understandable.

"I'll get the deposit record from Lady Hawkslowe, then."

The bailiff might be as honest as Budley and Sebastian believed, but he was too trusting by half. He should have insisted on making the deposit himself or watching to see that Elizabeth did.

He did not look forward to his next action, but he would not put it off, if he could find Elizabeth alone. He had gone into action against smugglers and rioters without a qualm. Yet he knew soldiers who went on tiptoe around their women rather than bring on a storm of tears or reproaches.

Lady Hawkslowe was in her private parlor, sighing over some novel, her brothers having gone out riding. Her expression turned censorious on seeing him.

"You might have changed before calling on me, Falstone."

"I have not yet been out this morning, and my riding clothes were well brushed and aired, so I can hardly smell of horse." Indeed, if he did, she would not be able to detect it, with the medley of scents present in her parlor: scented soap, whatever cosmetic preparations she used, and probably the lavender- or spice-filled sweet bags kept in the clothes press. The handkerchief she clutched reeked of some musky perfume. "However, I beg your pardon for appearing before you in riding clothes, though this is the country, where ladies must often endure such informality. I wished to speak with you about something which has come to my attention, and I do not care to put it off."

"I hope you do not mean to go about all day like an uncouth countryman."

He ignored this petulant remark. "I need the deposit book from the last quarter day's bank deposit. Also the keys for the desk and the money box."

The volume she had been holding in one languid hand fell to the floor. "Deposit book?"

"Some time after the last quarter day, you and your brother Paul went into Newcastle with Twissell. You asked him to accompany you as an outrider in case of highwaymen. He had two errands: to visit a blacksmith and to take the Lady Day rents to the bank. You offered to make the deposit for him as you needed your pin money. A deposit or withdrawal would be recorded in the depositor's bank account book, which is now missing. Where is it?"

Falstone knew the moment she decided to lie.

"I-I really have no idea." Her gaze darted around the chamber as if seeking it. "I'm sure Twissell—the bailiff?—never gave me anything to deposit or anything else."

"He says he didn't give them to you, that you said you would fetch the money and bank record, as you had keys."

"H-he did?" Elizabeth Hawkslowe almost speechless was a pleasing sight.

He waited several long, satisfying moments, enjoying her discomfiture. "Do I take it you deny having had the money and having keys to the desk and the box?"

"Certainly I deny it. I have nothing to do with the estate business and never have."

He made a leg and thanked her for her time. She managed a nod without meeting his eyes.

As the door shut behind him, a slither and rustle of taffeta petticoats suggested Elizabeth had abandoned in a flurry of energy the daybed on which she had been lolling. His questions had startled her. If she—or her brother—had diverted the rents to their own use, they should have considered the possibility of discovery. Elizabeth was a stupid woman, but could Paul Bradnam be equally cork-brained? He would have known— Falstone uttered an oath. *I'm a looby. Elizabeth and her brothers did not know Sebastian had sent for me.* Harry Bradnam was to be Sebastian's executor and the children's guardian. Sebastian had turned over the accounting to Budley and Twissell. Who would notice if someone played fast and loose with the bank account? If the valet and bailiff spoke out, who would the authorities believe? Not the servants.

Before dinner, he would accomplish one urgent duty, and perhaps a second. He asked Graves to send a reliable footman—not one of the Bradnams' creatures—to the estate office and went there directly himself. In no more than a quarter hour, he sat down to write to his brother's banker. He would send it by a trusted groom in the morning.

Chapter 11

He hated to tell Sebastian about the problem, more because of his frail health than because he feared it would grieve him. Alasdair did not ask how he felt. The imminence of his death was all too plain. He chose to begin at the end and work his way to the heart of the issue.

"Sebastian, I believe your desk is not secure. I have moved your current records and the strongbox to a safer location."

"Good. Should have…suggested it myself once I was no longer able to go downstairs."

Sebastian had not asked for his reason. Mayhap he did not want to know. Alasdair wished he could spare him, and yet he was owed honesty. From certain of his remarks, that was why he had asked Alasdair to return.

"Budley brought a mystery to my attention."

"Budley is a trusty Trojan." The phrase they had often used in their boyhood brought a faint smile to Sebastian's colorless lips.

"He is. You have loyal servants."

"All the old ones, anyway." A spasm of coughing racked him. When he caught his breath, he said, "A mystery, you say."

"One. Mayhap two, though I do not have confirmation of the second yet. Twissell has been responsible for making the last two rent deposits, I understand."

"Ay. In December, I knew I could not make the trip to the bank myself. Budley has been handling the estate ledger since then, with Twissell taking the money to Newcastle." Hawkslowe's lips twisted. "There was no one else I could trust but Budley and Twissell. Or Archbold, of course, but I've felt his hard head and fist were best employed here."

"Budley brought to my attention that, since the last time Twissell took the rents to Newcastle, the bank book is missing."

"Missing? Not merely misplaced?"

Alasdair summarized what he had learned from Twissell.

His brother's eyes focused on his cairngorm signet ring. Sebastian had lost considerable weight: the signet would have dropped from his finger if 'twere not for the string wound around the shank. "I see." He sighed. "Twissell is very good at dealing with the tenants, and there isn't much he doesn't know about farm animals and crops. Outside of those things, he's not a deep thinker. And…" Eventually he was able to go on. "I have preferred to conceal my wife's faults…as much as possible." A long pause. "Am I to conclude the rent monies have disappeared, Alasdair?"

"That is not yet certain. I am looking for confirmation of the deposit after Lady Day as we have no proof it was made, in the absence of the bank book."

"Did you ask Elizabeth what she did with it?"

"I did." He was bitterly sorry to have to say more. "She denied knowing anything about it."

"Oh…Hades." His brother had bitten back a stronger oath.

"Sebastian, would the bank pay out money to Lady Hawkslowe if she brought in the bank book?"

"No." Hawkslowe sighed again, slumping back against his pillows.

"I've written to Fitchett's to request a new bank book and a copy of their entries since the last date in your previous bank book. A good thing you gave the bank instructions to deal with me, but I'd have you sign it. You are still able to manage your affairs." He passed the sheet to Sebastian, who read it and nodded. He was having one of his better days. No need to spell out the implications. Budley was tidying the vials and bottles on the bedside table, imitating a servant who neither sees nor hears anything he should not notice.

"Bring me my lap desk from the table, if you will."

The shaky scrawl was not the bold signature Alasdair remembered, but it was unmistakably Sebastian's. From boyhood, his capital *S* had been distinctive. It resembled a snake, if one looked carefully, a reference to the adder which, with a stooping hawk, was featured on the family's coat of arms.

"You'll let me know as soon as the ledger copy comes?"

"I will."

"I'm glad you're the one untangling the mess, Alasdair."

"I'll let you rest now." If their suspicions were correct and Sebastian wished to confront his wife, Falstone would make sure to be present. Lady Hawkslowe's vapors were hard enough for a healthy man to endure.

As he reached the door, Sebastian said,

"Midsummer quarter day is coming up. I want you to make the deposit. You'll take a reliable groom. Archbold will send Campbell with you."

****

Lady Hawkslowe had been sulking in her rooms for the past two days. This affected only her maid, leaving the rest of the household unscathed. Or relieved by her absence, Margaret conceded to herself. Harry and Paul Bradnam spent a good deal of time with her in her over-ornate parlor.

"Got her tail in a knot, right enough," the cook muttered when the delicacies sent up for her dinner were sent back almost uneaten, with a complaint.

A footman bringing in a bucket of coal said, "Ay, and not even the younger brother can coax her out of the dismals. The older one was fratchin' at them both."

Margaret overheard the exchange when she went to the kitchen to beg a treat of biscuits for the children. She repressed her curiosity. Whatever had roiled the waters was no business of hers.

Another day of tranquility passed, except that the cook made her annoyance known at being expected to produce an orange cream on short notice and with no oranges. Colin related that tidbit. The boys often passed through the kitchen on their way to or from the stable yard or the freedom of the park. On the way they usually managed to get some caraway comfits or prawlins.

"Cook wanted to know if Mother thought she was in London."

"Why?" his younger brother asked.

"I suppose because she has spent a great deal of time there, where there are so many more things to buy, she forgets it's different here."

"Oh."

The children had been rather subdued for as long as Margaret had been in the house, judged by the behavior of her own nieces and nephews. Now they were withdrawn, and from her reddened eyes and blotchy face, Janet had been crying. Isabelle took to slipping away to hide. She could sometimes be found in the linen closet on the nursery floor, sitting in the dark with her arms around her knees. On another occasion after a panicky search, one of the maids discovered her in a corner of the attic used for storage of things seldom used or outdated but too good to dispose of. Isabelle had made herself a nest behind a carved chest under the slope of the roof, furnished with a blanket and pillow. Margaret did not allow Nurse to scold her, choosing instead to explain how worried they had been, and how grieved her papa would be if they had not been able to find her. The child would not promise not to hide again, for which Margaret could not blame her. She herself had often longed for a truly private retreat when she lived in Rupert's home.

Dorring said Matthew tended to be sullen. Margaret thought she read misery in his eyes when he was not occupied with some interesting activity. Colin's worry showed itself in a certain inattention to the people around him in spite of his seeming composure. Hawkslowe's heir was behaving like an English gentleman three times his age, a laudable feat but one he should not be expected to perform when his father was dying. Having a tutor was helpful, but what they needed was a father. In a pinch, a fond uncle would do. When Alasdair was present, they relaxed. Margaret would have liked to speak to Alasdair about the girls and to suggest he talk to Dorring about the boys.

She could not seek him out, in part because of the awkwardness between them. In addition, however, it took no great insight to realize that any familiarity between them would give Lady Hawkslowe a reason to insist she be dismissed. If she complained to her friends that the governess was angling for a husband and her prey was Falstone, or worse, hinted she was his mistress, she would be believed. Besides, now that Alasdair had taken over his brother's responsibilities, his time was fully occupied, making it impossible to encounter him accidentally in private long enough to disclose her concerns. While it was understandable the children were unhappy and anxious, she thought some part of their distress was caused by the tension between Falstone and their mother.

Margaret wished the Bradnams' influence on their sister was more calming. They entertained her with gossip and games of chance played for farthings but did nothing to persuade their sister her complaints were unreasonable. Perhaps one could not expect it; impossible not to hear the servants' opinion that Harry and Paul Bradnam ventured so far from London as much to avoid their creditors as out of affection for their sister. Surely if they did not support her whims, she and Alasdair might contrive to get along. And she ought to spend less time with the Bradnams and more with her children. Yet her dealings with them gave little comfort. Janet and Colin were courteous but showed no pleasure in their mother's presence, and she made Isabelle nervous. Only Matthew looked forward to spending time in her presence, possibly because she treated him as a pet.

To give Harry and Paul Bradnam their due, they brought gifts for the children. Paul gave dolls to Isabelle and Janet, who would probably have preferred a book, and pocket knives to the boys. His judgement was faulty here, too. The bone-handled knife was not a bad choice for Colin, but Margaret was not sanguine Matthew would confine his use of it to outside the house. Falstone had best speak to him about its use. Harry's selections were more appropriate: a silver-mounted riding crop for Colin, and two little books, *The Gigantick History of the Two Famous Giants* and *A Description of Three Hundred Animals*, certain to appeal to the unbookish Matthew. Janet received a fan painted with an Oriental scene. Isabelle's gift, accepted with squeals, was a set of bedroom furniture for her partially furnished dollhouse, built by the estate carpenter.

Harry Bradnam also made an effort to entertain the children. He took the boys on an expedition to hunt for bird's nests on one occasion and to fish in the nearest stream on another, from which Matthew returned wet and laughing, having fallen in.

He played fox and geese, Pope Joan, quoits, and marbles with all four children. Even the girls could not resist marbles, as the little balls were made of different colors of stone and were, as Isabelle pointed out, pretty. He also knew a great many riddles and amusing rhymes and often succeeded in making his nieces and nephews laugh. Sometimes Paul joined in their games.

Although Margaret was grateful for their efforts, she could not forget Paul's remark about Lord Hawkslowe's imminent death. Admittedly, he had not known the children could hear him. On the other hand, the comment should never have been made at all. Nor was she the only one with reservations about the younger Bradnam brother. He had led the children on an expedition to the attics and located several sets of bows, from a size Isabelle could manage to one for Colin, and quivers of arrows as well. Margaret and Dorring supervised the lesson, as the thought of four armed youngsters with a single adult was not one either of them enjoyed.

Bradnam's admonitions about being careful to avoid hitting livestock, horses, or yokels, or to think of the target as being someone the archer wanted to slay struck Margaret as inappropriately playful. Matthew piped, "Like the English longbowmen at the battle of Crecy or Poitiers? Good sport!"

Afterward, Isabelle and Matthew went down to the kitchen to beg for biscuits and lemonade, and Dorring and Colin excused themselves to find a book in the library. Janet sat contemplating a piece of embroidery thoughtfully although Margaret suspected she was not seeing her needlework.

"Is something troubling you?"

The girl sighed and looked up. "I should not say so or even think it…"

"If there is something on your mind, voicing it to one discreet person may help."

Janet gave a sober nod. "Mistress MacGavin, I know one should respect one's elders and love one's family, but what if one doesn't? I've prayed about it, but it doesn't help."

She had not expected such a difficult question. She would not respond with pious pap, when she knew

116

exactly how Janet felt. "There are many things one should do, Janet, but sometimes one can't. Some people are difficult to love or impossible to respect. All you can do is be civil and not tell them or anyone else how you feel. Unless that person needs to know for a reason. For example, it's perfectly acceptable to tell me in private, because a trouble shared is a trouble halved," she added. "Is it some particular relative?"

"Uncle Paul is very pleasant to us..." Janet's hands twisted together in her lap.

Margaret waited.

"But there's just something about him. Mayhap he is not as comfortable with children as you and Mr. Dorring are. I did ask Colin if he liked Uncle Paul, but he didn't really answer. Which makes me think he agrees with me. But it's lowering to remember the presents he brought us and not be able to be really grateful for them."

"Especially if you didn't like them?"

Janet turned lobster red. "I'm too old to play with dolls. Except to amuse Isabelle, I mean."

"That does make it uncomfortable." She herself had rejoiced to inform James MacGavin she no longer needed his grudging payment of pin money when she accepted the post of governess to the Falstones. "Nevertheless, you thanked him prettily and you are never rude to him, which is as much as can be expected if you do not feel warmly toward him. Do you like Mr. Harry Bradnam better?"

"Yes, because he talks to Colin and me as if we were adults and doesn't treat Isabelle and Matthew as if they are babies. And he does amuse Matthew and Colin." For the first time her lips curled up in a smile.

"I don't know what he thought I'd do with the fan he gave me for the next four or five years. But I'd rather be thought grown up than a child."

Later, Margaret wondered whether Janet's unease about her uncle Paul resulted from the same source as her own distrust of both Bradnam brothers. Paul was light-minded and insincere, and while Harry appeared honest, something about him—a wariness in his eyes, perhaps, and the way he pandered to his sister's caprices—made her uncomfortable.

Chapter 12

When she did finally rejoin them, Elizabeth Hawkslowe was still in a pet over Alasdair's accusation, which only added to her ire at his rejection of her plans for redecorating. Her anger did not fade with time. Conversation at dinner and supper was restrained, most of it initiated by the Bradnam brothers. Falstone replied civilly but briefly to comments addressed to him. The Bradnams paid little attention to Dorring, a mere "tutor fellow," after all, although Harry addressed a few common civilities to him and asked Margaret about her family. Paul made an occasional spritely comment to her, which Falstone supposed was merely habit with any lady, young or old, beautiful or plain. So much the better; if one of them pestered Margaret, he would have to take measures to prevent it happening a second time. He would enjoy doing so, but such action would lead to a bout of hysterics by Elizabeth, complaints to Sebastian, and a further disruption of the household.

He did not attempt to include Margaret by more than an impersonal greeting and smile. Drawing attention to her would be a mistake. He could not help glancing covertly at her, however. When Elizabeth rose and Margaret followed her out, Alasdair was able to relax.

The respite proved only temporary. Paul Bradnam

cleared his throat. "I must apologize for causing the misunderstanding about the furniture. Elizabeth wrote, asking me to choose some furnishings for a gentleman's chamber. I assumed she meant them for Hawkslowe's sickroom. If I had had any idea she intended to replace family heirlooms, I would certainly have dissuaded her in the liveliest terms."

"As I would," Harry added. "Hawkslowe's illness has unsettled her, and her distress comes out in volatility and ill-considered decisions."

"I see." He had not liked her fifteen years ago. His opinion now had been formed by his brother's letter and his recent meetings with her, and by what Sebastian had not said, as much as what he had put into words.

"Well, then, I trust we can put the matter behind us. Now I confess I am all agog to hear about your military career. I would have liked to buy a commission, but my mother was adamant that I must be the man of the house. Thus I missed my chance at military adventure and glory." Harry Bradnam smiled wryly.

"There may be glory during a war—" Though Falstone doubted it: more likely blood, pain, and death resulting in little or no victory. "My own service has been spent on English soil. Arresting smugglers and putting down riots is useful work, but there's not much fame or honor involved."

"Yet you attained the rank of major. Unless—"

"I did not purchase the rank. I was successful in my assignments and received preferment." He had not disliked the orderliness of the military, though the stupidity and arrogance of some of the officers infuriated him. Preserving civil tranquility and upholding the law were necessary, but it offended

Alasdair to his soul that rioters were sometimes hanged. They could instead have been sentenced to transportation to the American colonies to be indentured servants. Who could blame hungry men and women for rioting, when food was too dear to purchase and the government ignored their distress? Nor did he think that would be the end of the unrest. He had been glad to sell out.

"I meant no slight, Falstone. How long is your leave?"

"I am able to remain as long as necessary."

Harry Bradnam did not pursue the topic. To revive the flagging conversation, Paul Bradnam inquired whether he had often enjoyed leave in London. "There's always amusement to be had in London. Provincial towns…" He shrugged.

"Not often. As a rule, I have been posted too far from London to make traveling there convenient." He had lost touch with most of his Northumberland acquaintance for the same reason. No. He had severed those ties of friendship as he had cut those of family and of love. They would have gone on with their lives: married, had children, inherited or purchased a property. He had preferred not to know. When he took leave, he idled his way through parts of the country where he was unlikely to meet anyone he knew, having no desire to be drawn into society at any level. Bad enough that he was a target for hopeful young women in his postings.

The younger Bradnam babbled on about theaters, masquerades at the Haymarket opera house, discreet gaming establishments, the best brothels, Vauxhall Gardens—music, dancing, fireworks, fair nymphs in the shrubbery—

Harry interrupted this spate with a repressive, "Of course, only chubs and fools gamble to excess or conduct themselves in a manner unsuited to gentlemen."

"Just so," Alasdair agreed. The brothers must be hoping to win him over, though Paul had bridled at his brother's remark. Harry had more brains, Paul more charm, if one liked libertines. He would trust neither of them with a half-crown, given something learned from his brother.

Sebastian had reluctantly confided he had long declined to let his wife go to town unless he accompanied her. She had no thought for economy and had run up bills he considered excessive. Or alleged bills and debts, he added as an afterthought.

"She fell into the habit of gambling too much and losing, or claimed she did. When a friend remarked on her brothers' surprising ability to avoid debtor's prison, I began to suspect she was giving them money. Even now, I believe she lines their pockets somehow. That new furniture?" He managed a hoarse laugh that ended in coughing. "She delegated the choosing of it to her brother Paul, who fancies himself knowledgeable in all matters of fashion. I have no doubt the price was inflated for the Bradnams' benefit."

After a good deal of experience with impecunious young officers, Alasdair could easily believe Harry and Paul overspent their income, whatever it was. But they were too old to be playing the fool. Paul was a year or two younger than Elizabeth, though his frivolity made him seem more boyish still, and Harry was several years her senior.

Thank God no one had mentioned to Sebastian that the furniture in question had been meant for the baron's chambers. Instead, it had gone to furbish up various guest bedrooms.

****

The ledger copy came. Falstone breathed a sigh of relief. The mischief had begun and ended with the deposit Lady Hawkslowe had gulled from Twissell. The Hawkslowe estate's account was lower by the amount of the rents than it should be but not looted. All payments out were supported by Sebastian's and Budley's ledger entries for normal expenses—hay, oats, wine and spirits, coal, and the other normal household expenses—and were consistent with expenses for previous years. This was good news for Sebastian.

He would eventually audit the account of the London bank the baron used. Very likely there would be no mischief to find, as it had been years since Hawkslowe or his lady had been to London. Falstone had heard Lady Hawkslowe bemoan the fact often enough.

Relieved of one concern, Falstone turned his attention to how Elizabeth had got into the locked drawer and the strongbox. Twissell said she claimed to have keys. The ledger had been correct to the farthing up to the March rent collection. Perhaps the money box had not been worth raiding until then or not safe to raid while Sebastian was overseeing the accounts. Given that his brother had known for years how coin ran through Lady Hawkslowe's fingers, was it likely he had let her keep the keys? Falstone had neglected to ask.

He could see no way of avoiding the question now.

The air in the sickroom was unexpectedly fresh,

and a hint of breeze stirred the bed-curtains. The casements stood open. Alasdair glanced at Budley, eyebrows raised.

His brother, sitting in a wing chair by one of the windows, answered. "What use is keeping out the drafts when the patient cannot recover? Besides, the day is warm, and I am glad to breathe fresh air. I want to enjoy the sight of the Cheviots. Come, sit down."

With a heart weighted with grief to come, Alasdair took the other chair. To the west, the hills rose. To the east, the land gradually dropped away toward the coast.

"Go away, Budley. I won't need you for a while. You've spent too much time shut up here with me."

The valet bowed and departed without argument, and Falstone swallowed a lump in his throat. "Sebastian, I apologize for leaving you with no more than a curst rude note. I should have waited for your return to take my leave of you."

"I was furious when I read it. But if we had met then, we might have come to blows. After I'd cooled, I came to regret your absence, though it took some time before I began to see I'd been wrong." A spell of coughing. "Even then, I was too stubborn to try to mend the breach. I don't know if I could have found you without knowing your regiment, your godfather having died."

"But you did find me."

"When I knew the worst, I asked my Newcastle attorney to find your godfather's heir or heirs. There was only his daughter who lives with her husband in Glasgow. I wrote to inquire if she might know how to find you. She sent back her reply—'Why, the —th Dragoons, of course! My father's old regiment'—with a packet of the letters you had written to him. I wrote to army headquarters."

They sat in silence for a few minutes, watching high clouds scud over the Cheviots. At last, Falstone ventured, "Sebastian, how many sets of keys are there to the estate office desk and the strongbox?"

"Three. Mine, which you now have, Budley's, and the spare set."

"The spare set," Alasdair repeated.

"Ay. All the household and stable keys in case Graves, Mistress Stukeley, Budley, Archbold, or I misplace ours. Not to be able to get into the cellar to replenish the brandy decanter would be inconvenient." A faint, ironic grin.

"Where is it kept?"

"I should have told you, though Budley knows, of course. The key chain is in the last slot of the letter box on the estate office desk. Use the paper knife to fish it out." His brother studied his face, a frown wrinkling his brow. "May I ask why you inquired?"

Do you really want to know? But Sebastian already knew about his wife's diversion of the last rents. "Lady Hawkslowe was the one to retrieve the rents from the office the day the deposit was to be made. Twissell would have hesitated to lend her his keys, but she said she had a set. Would she have known where to find the spare keys?"

His gaze fixed on the clouds' shadows sliding across field and moorland, Sebastian spoke at last. "I would have said no, as she has almost never set foot in the estate office. But it's not kept locked. She or anyone else could have gone in, and as it's tucked away near the side door, the chances of anyone noticing would be slight." His voice weakened. His brother was tiring.

"I think it's time I left you to rest. I'll send Budley up."

Sebastian nodded wearily. "Thank you, Alasdair."

The mahogany box with its ivory marquetry stood on the left side of the desk. Vertical divisions inside held correspondence not yet answered. The last one contained no letters or documents. The key ring at the bottom would be invisible even to someone peering into the cavity, unless they held a candle over it. He lit a candle and did so. Making out something at the bottom, Falstone poked the paper knife in. The slots were fourteen or fifteen inches deep, but as he moved the knife back and forth, the blade rang on metal. It was a moment's work to hook the tip of the opener through something and bring it up.

The chain held a dozen keys, aligned by size from largest to smallest. Anyone who searched the office carefully could have found them. Elizabeth was unlikely to have gone to so much effort. The next to smallest opened the desk drawer, and the littlest one the strongbox.

He studied the two keys searching for signs of wax. Whoever had found them could have had them copied the day Elizabeth, Paul, and Twissell went to Newcastle. There would not have been time to wait while the duplicate keys were forged, so the locksmith would have had to make impressions in wax. Then someone, presumably Paul Bradnam, would have had to pick them up another day. Finding no wax on the keys nor any sign they'd been cleaned, Falstone dismissed the notion. Bradnam or Elizabeth might have feared Twissell would discover he had visited the locksmith or that the locksmith would question him about his possession of the keys or simply been too lazy to make the long trip again. Or they thought they would have easy access to the keys any time they chose to raid the drawer, so why spend money on copies? Even if they possessed another set of keys, they would do Bradnam and his sister no good now, with the strongbox safely concealed in Falstone's chamber.

Chapter 13

Lady Hawkslowe wandered into the schoolroom while the girls were engaged in monogramming handkerchiefs and Margaret read excerpts from a travel book to them. She inquired briefly about their studies and inspected their embroidery, approving of Janet's and remarking irritably about the size of Isabelle's stitches.

"It does take practice," Margaret pointed out. "Isabelle's next effort will be better."

"I'm sure I hope so." She picked up an oversized but thin volume lying on the table and leafed through the first few pages. At one, she paused.

Margaret could not see which it was; perhaps the title page, though there was nothing to wonder at in a book of harpsichord music. "The pieces are a little advanced for students who are only beginning to play," she said.

"Oh…no doubt." Elizabeth closed the book and replaced it. "I believe I heard you playing a few days ago. You play quite well."

"When I was refreshing my skill? I have seldom had access to a harpsichord for some years. It's my hope that hearing good music may spur the girls to master the exercises and simple pieces for beginners. Also I have been thinking Janet and, er, William should have dancing lessons, with your permission, of course, my lady. Mr. Dorring plays the harpsichord and admits he did so for his sisters' lessons."

Her ladyship smiled, a rare sign of approval. "That is a very good notion. I did not have lessons until the year before I was released from the schoolroom. I admit to being almost overset when I made my first appearance at a dance, fearing I would forget the steps." She tittered. "And the first time I danced with Hawkslowe, though he was only the heir then, was so romantic I thought I would swoon. My mantua and petticoat were of the palest blue brocade. Blue always becomes a lady, or so men think." She sighed at the happy memory.

Margaret sighed, too. She had never danced with Alasdair. Her suitor's visits had not coincided with any entertainment in their neighborhood.

"How will you show the movements of several couples without having a partner?"

"I thought I would begin by teaching the movements of a simple dance like The Dumps or Prince George's Birthday. Once they are comfortable in their part, they will find it easy to adapt to the presence of other couples." And where was she to find even one other couple?

"Then when they have reached that stage, you must call upon my brothers to assist you, and I will assist as well so you will have two experienced couples."

"Thank you, my lady. The children will look forward to it." Though she hoped she would not have to face dancing with one of the Bradnams too soon. She would rather demonstrate with Alasdair Falstone, which would be impossible, if only for her peace of mind.

With a few words to her daughters to pay attention

to their lessons and the promise of an unspecified treat at some time in the future, Lady Hawkslowe drifted out of the nursery parlor. She was restless, and no wonder. The house, servants included, held its breath each morning until word went around that Budley had fetched Lord Hawkslowe's chocolate. The overdone cheerfulness that greeted the news was almost as bad as the strain of waiting to hear that Hawkslowe had awakened. Remembering how Lord Hawkslowe had arbitrarily forbidden Alasdair to marry her, Margaret concluded he must have changed, as the servants' evident liking for the baron told her all she needed to know. Why should he not have altered as much as she and Alasdair had?

When the hour ended and the girls were released to Nurse Sallows, Margaret returned *A Voyage Round the World by Way of the Great South Sea* to the bookcase. She picked up the music book and held it for a moment.

She had brought Rambeau's *Pièces de clavecin* to Scot Hall with her few pieces of jewelry, her mother's old lace, and everything she could not bear to lose. Fortunately, it all fitted in her two trunks. Rupert would have promised to keep her things for her and meant it. But if Sybilla decided Margaret's things took up too much space or could be better employed than by being stored, they would be lost to Margaret. She had unpacked it, meaning to attempt one or two of the compositions later. Opening the book, she turned over the first pages as Lady Hawkslowe had done.

Margaret—In the hope it may give you pleasure— Alasdair 1725

How could she have forgotten the inscription? Heat rushed through her body as she flushed with shock and embarrassment. This must be why Lady Hawkslowe's gaze had lingered on the page. What had she made of it? What could she have made of it except that her daughters' governess had known Falstone years ago, they had been on such terms that he had given her the book and used her first name, and neither of them had informed Elizabeth Hawkslowe of their prior acquaintance. She sat clutching the volume and wondering how soon she would be summoned to be told to pack her belongings and leave. Whatever Alasdair claimed, she could not stay if Lady Hawkslowe were her enemy.

But Lady Hawkslowe did not speak of the book's inscription when she and Margaret sat in the drawing room after supper. She picked up a book of sermons rather than work at her embroidery or air her complaints about life in the wilds of Northumberland, as she usually did. Her choice of reading material was understandable. Shortly before the meal Budley had sent a message to the doctor to come at his earliest convenience. The sermon could not have been of much consolation or even distraction, as minutes passed before she turned a page.

Margaret picked up a copy of *The Gentleman's Magazine* and tried to read about the causes of the many recent riots. Her attention being divided between the essay, Lady Hawkslowe, and her contemplation of her own future, she got no farther than the first column before the gentlemen entered. Gentlemen. What an inexact term. With the first amusement she had felt since Lady Hawkslowe's visit to the schoolroom, she thought, *Major Falstone and Dorring certainly are*.

She put aside the magazine and prepared to make

polite conversation if necessary. Later she would ask Falstone his opinion of the rioting resulting from the high cost of grain. Gideon would have quoted, "Thou shalt not muzzle the mouth of the ox that treadeth out the corn." She had best reserve her question for an occasion when Alasdair came riding with the children. Such a controversial topic would be out of place in the drawing room.

After warm smiles and greetings for her brothers and a few stilted exchanges with her brother-in-law, Elizabeth Hawkslowe excused herself. Paul Bradnam took the seat nearest Margaret and began with an inquiry about her day and how her charges did. Then he slid into the sort of questions she would have asked a new pupil if the child were shy. Had her family always lived in London? How had her family been willing to let her go so far from them? Before he could ask anything she was not willing to answer, she excused herself to look over the lesson she had planned for tomorrow. Margaret hoped Paul Bradnam practiced his wiles on any female and had not singled her out for some reason.

She went to bed wondering if this attempt to draw her out came at Lady Hawkslowe's request. As she began to drift into sleep, another thought roused her. She must warn Major Falstone before his sister-in-law could tax him with their prior acquaintance.

****

Margaret was not the only one to find Midsummer Day the most memorable feature of June. Early that morning, a table was set up on the lawn some distance from the house, where trees provided some shade. The bailiff and Falstone collected and wrote down the rents, with Colin sitting beside the major by Sebastian Hawkslowe's order. No one needed to ask why. Colin Hawkslowe would be the next Lord Hawkslowe. Lady Hawkslowe was not pleased, even pointing out he would miss a day's lessons and sniffing when Alasdair retorted that this was a lesson, too. That was not the sole point of disagreement. She also protested about the tables of food and drink set out for the tenants, and the amusements for those waiting and their families: in fact, a sort of festival or holiday. She would have forbidden the girls and Matthew from being present even briefly to "rub shoulders with country louts." Supported by Falstone, Sebastian had overruled her.

Margaret, Dorring, and the children had been summoned to his lordship's chamber to be assured that he wished them all to be present. As his heir, Colin must be present. The other three should also attend for at least part of the day.

"In ten or twenty years, the tenants' children will be serving ours. They need to know and like our family. That's what builds loyalty," he ended raspily. So the family, except for Elizabeth, talked with the tenants and took part in some of the games. The younger children were beside themselves with glee to have playmates, while Janet conducted herself like a pleasant young lady who could converse with anyone without condescension. At the makeshift desk, Colin spoke with each man and displayed a knowledge of each and of agriculture which surprised Margaret, until it occurred to her that the boys had spent months running loose on the estate without supervision.

Even the Bradnam brothers made an appearance, though they kept to the outskirts of the gathering, observing rather than taking part, like enemy scouts. Where had that notion come from? Yet it felt too apt for Margaret to dismiss. Perhaps it arose from awareness that Alasdair would rather the Bradnams went back to London, or to the antipodes or to Hell, though the latter was perhaps a bit extreme.

She still worried about her past connection to Alasdair, or rather, about Lady Hawkslowe's knowledge of it. A fortnight had passed since the incident with the book without a word spoken and almost as long since she had informed him that her ladyship might have seen the inscription. His impassive face told her nothing. He merely said there was no point in worrying until Elizabeth broached the subject, but in any event, Margaret would not be dismissed. Mayhap she had been looking at a different page in the book or had supposed it to be some other Alasdair, though the name was not common this side of the border. Perhaps it was only Margaret's conscience pricking her for lying by omission.

At the end of the day, the rents paid, Falstone took the money to his chamber and the ledger to the estate office. He did not think the Bradnams would force the lock on his door, search his room, and break into the padlocked chest which had accompanied him to his postings. If they did, they would find only the strongbox, not the rents. Looking ahead to this quarter day, Falstone had pried up a floorboard under the washstand to make a hiding place. The bag now rested there. Diverting the Lady Day rents had been easy. Robbing his room would be harder and far more dangerous.

From the office window, he watched the last of the

tenants departing with their exhausted children still nibbling pieces of parkin or seed cake, and the servants clearing away the remaining food and tables before setting out a simple supper in the dining room. He suspected his nieces and nephews would have little appetite and would go to bed early with no encouragement needed.

Colin appeared in the doorway. "May I speak to you, sir? It's rather important. It's not something I can discuss before anyone else."

"Certainly. Shut the door, sit down, and tell me what concerns you." What worries had troubled him at Colin's age? The prospect of going away to school or when he could expect to change his pony for a horse? Something related to puberty? No, from the way the boy's lips were compressed, a more serious issue: unsurprising, given that his father was dying.

He began hesitantly. "The tenants all know, don't they? No one came right out with it, but there wasn't the usual joking and chat. One of them said he was sorry not to see my father today. That he was a good man and a good landlord."

"Your father's condition is no secret. Many of your servants are related to tenants or have friends among them. All of them take an interest because he's well liked and they are understandably concerned."

"I hope they'll find me worthy, when—when I'm of age and take over the management."

"I believe they will."

Colin frowned, searching for the right words, Falstone thought. "Someone wondered when you would be returning to duty. Which made me wonder, too."

One of the Bradnams, probably. They would be

anxious to see his back.

"I sold out. When your father asked me to be your guardian, there was no choice."

"Oh…I'm s-sorry. I-I—" The boy stuttered to a halt.

"No need. I'm not. I was glad our estrangement ended, though the reason for our healing the breach saddens me. Was that your only worry?"

"Yes…that is, not entirely. I mean, someone has to manage the estate, and I don't know how because my father has been too ill to continue teaching me, and even if he hadn't, no one will listen to a boy anyway, once he's…" He took a deep breath. "Twissell knows the land and our people, but even the best bailiff needs to be given instructions."

"That's part of the reason your father asked me to sell out. That, and he felt you and Matthew would need a man here once he was gone. I can't replace him, but I can teach you the things he would have. I grew up here and learned a good deal about how the property is managed. What I don't know, I'll learn with you."

"Good. My other uncles would not wish to live here most of the year," Colin remarked. "Even if Father trusted them."

"Know that, do you?" He might have guessed Colin would have formed his own opinion of his Bradnam uncles. The lad was observant and had brains.

"Even if he thought one of them capable of managing the estate, they'd probably leave for London as soon as you returned to duty. As you mean to stay, all's well."

Alasdair's lips twitched. "You'd counsel me to let them know I'm not going, then?"

"We would all feel better, knowing."

"Nevertheless, Colin, I would like to keep it our secret for the moment."

"So we can ambush Uncle Harry and Uncle Paul?"

"It would be best to take them by surprise," he allowed. "And far better not to let them know I'm to be your guardian. I wouldn't let the younger children know, but you may tell Janet if you think it will reassure her. But swear her to secrecy."

Sebastian's heir grinned.

Chapter 14

A pall lay over the house. The servants were silent, even in the kitchen when Margaret went downstairs to ask for a posset to soothe Isabelle, who was fretful. She had scarcely seen Alasdair except at meals. She seldom saw Lady Hawkslowe's brothers before supper, if then, as they rose late and breakfasted in their bedchambers to the annoyance of the servants for whom it made more work. Then Paul left the house until the evening and sat up playing cards with his brother, who spent much of the day with Elizabeth Hawkslowe. Presumably they were avoiding Falstone, who had made it clear he would not tolerate their loose talk where the children might hear.

Lady Hawkslowe was inclined to sulk in Falstone's presence and to carp at Margaret and Dorring for keeping the children at lessons or at some form of exercise most of the day. She complained that they seldom saw their maternal uncles and mourned the loss of her children's company to the schoolroom, though she did not avail herself of it on Sunday when they were at liberty after church. She preferred to spend the afternoon in her sitting room, reading from a book with a beautifully embroidered cover that might conceal any sort of volume at all, even a novel. Which one should not be reading on Sunday if one were particular in religious matters. Margaret herself and Dorring, too, saw no harm in the children playing games or amusing themselves in whatever way they could, as long as they were quiet and out of their mother's sight.

Graves had discreetly readied the black armbands for the servants and the hatchment to mount over the door. The cook had been preparing a supply of almond Portugal cakes because they kept well and of potted meats and various pickles. They would be needed for the gathering after the burial. Lady Hawkslowe had less discreetly paid a visit to her Newcastle mantua-maker to choose black fabrics, lace, and patterns for her mourning attire.

A young footman interrupted their lesson at midmorning. "Begging your pardon, ma'am," he muttered, Adam's apple bobbing. "His lordship would like to see his daughters. Mr. Dorring has took the lads down."

Isabelle clung to her hand, not letting go even when Hawkslowe beckoned them to come closer. They were still six feet away when he held up his hand to stop them. The boys and the tutor stood equally distant on the other side of the bed. Margaret blinked back tears, throat aching with the effort. Later, all she could remember of Hawkslowe's faint words was the promise that their uncle Alasdair would take care of them and his pained smile as he gasped, "Best leave now."

Falstone made a minute gesture toward the valet, who ushered Margaret and her charges toward the door. Dorring herded the boys out after them. The tutor spoke softly, saying, "I think we might all sit in the schoolroom parlor. I will ask the kitchen to send up lemonade and cakes."

Margaret kept a hand on Isabelle's shoulder as she

escorted the children upstairs. The little girl sniffled. Her older sister was wooden-faced. Was the shock of a sudden death, like Gideon's, worse than this drawn-out suffering? They had all known the baron was dying and had had time to prepare. On one occasion, Janet had confided to her in a burst of candor that every morning when she woke up, she wondered if her papa had died in the night.

"I know someone sits up with him, in case he should need medicine or a drink of water, ma'am, so they would tell Uncle Alasdair. But I don't think they would wake us."

Perhaps waiting for a loved one's end accustomed the family to the coming loss, leaving them numb or even relieved when it finally came to pass. Her husband's unexpected death, his body carried home on a door, had felt like a mortal blow. A strong gust of wind still gave her a moment's terror lest trees or roof tiles fall and kill someone.

Margaret and Dorring kept the children together in the cozy nursery parlor, playing silly games. Sallows suggested they ask the kitchen to send up a lighter dinner than usual, only the dishes the children particularly liked, and the nursery maid was dispatched for this purpose.

If the meal consisted only of ham, bread and butter, some very good cheese, strawberries, an almond cream, and cheese cakes, the children managed to eat enough to keep body and soul together, as Nurse put it. The maid informed them the dinner meant for the dining room was not much more elaborate, the kitchen being stood all on its head, and scarcely anyone to eat it at the table like decent folk, except her ladyship's brothers.

The major had had a bite of meat, cheese, and bread in his lordship's chambers, with a mug of ale, and her ladyship had ordered a tray in her parlor.

Not long before the nursery supper, the footman who had been sent for them earlier came to tell them that Major Falstone would call upon them shortly. He bowed himself out, without saying more and without meeting their eyes. The waiting was over. The girls turned to her but asked no question. None was necessary. Matthew stared down at the table where he had been drawing pictures of cannon, largely from his imagination as a search of both the schoolroom library and his lordship's library had yielded no examples to copy. Colin put aside Defoe's novel *Captain Singleton*, in which he had been absorbed, despite having read it before. There was consolation in rereading a favorite book when one was low in spirit. He sat staring at his clasped hands.

Janet had begun a sewing project for Isabelle's new doll: shift, night-rail, petticoats, mantua, and cape. The sewing room had yielded ample scraps of all kinds. Now she secured her stitch, trimmed the thread, and set the little taffeta petticoat in her work basket before placing her needle in the pin-pillow, blinking as tears welled. Isabelle, chin trembling, clutched her doll.

They looked up as the door opened again. The lines at the corners of Falstone's mouth were deeper than Margaret remembered, and there were dark smudges under his eyes. He had sat up all night with his brother and stayed with him all this day. He looked at each of his nieces and nephews in turn without speaking, though he gave a minuscule nod to Colin.

Janet swallowed hard and held her handkerchief to

her eyes briefly. Matthew crossed his arms on his chest, hunching a little, and Isabelle rocked back and forth where she sat.

"Would you like to join Sallie in her sitting room?" Alasdair asked. "She was your papa's nurse, you know, and is grieving, too."

Oh, well done. They would need a more familiar and comforting presence than a recent governess could provide, and his suggestion gave them something to do.

"Yes," Janet gulped. She took her sister's free hand and led her out.

"Matthew, Colin?"

Matthew gave a short nod and followed the girls. Colin raised his chin. "Sir. I think I should take supper downstairs. It's not our usual day to do so, but…"

"I think you should. You have time to wash your hands and face and make yourself ready. You might also wish to visit Nurse Sallows briefly. If you change your mind, I will understand."

****

The gathering in the drawing room was strained. Margaret and Dorring sat silent, listening to the Bradnam men chaffing their sister over her fine new mourning attire while her ladyship complained about the vast number of inconveniences a death caused. Falstone and Colin had not yet appeared. On Graves coming to inquire whether the meal should be held back, Lady Hawkslowe said sharply, "No. Falstone knows at what time we sup. If all is ready, let us go in."

Paul Bradnam escorted Elizabeth Hawkslowe to her seat at the foot of the table, and Harry Bradnam had reached its head when Colin entered, followed by Alasdair.

"What are you doing here, William? You should be upstairs with your brother and sisters."

His face flushed at his mother's rebuke. Nevertheless, he replied calmly, "Under the circumstances, I felt it right to be present."

"And I agree." Falstone added, "As a general rule, you may wish to continue to take most meals upstairs, as your younger siblings still need you and also because you must still rise early for your lessons."

Colin smiled faintly at that. "I thought I would not be able to escape logic and Latin so easily. My place, I think, Uncle Harry," the boy said, marching forward. "If you will sit on my left, and my uncle Alasdair on my right, and Uncle Paul on my mother's right, with Mr. Dorring on her left, and Mistress MacGavin on Mr. Dorring's left, we will be sorted out."

Colin had contrived to put her between Dorring and Alasdair. Had he noticed she avoided the male Bradnams? Or had Alasdair suggested the seating?

"You should sit by your mama, boy. I have some claim to this seat, being your elder uncle and your guardian."

"His elder, certainly, but as Baron Hawkslowe, Colin is entitled to that seat." Alasdair Falstone's voice came like a thunderclap, crackling with an officer's authority.

Harry Bradnam's lips tightened, but he moved to take the seat to the left. "Elizabeth, I will send a man to Newcastle to notify his attorney of Hawkslowe's death."

"No need, Bradnam. I've already dispatched a groom to him." Alasdair pulled out Margaret's chair for her.

But for Harry's swift glance at his sister, Margaret would have missed seeing his suppressed amusement and their brother Paul's lips twitch.

Most of the family would have done better to sup in their chambers. They certainly were not banding together for comfort or lending each other strength. Paul Bradnam supported Lady Hawkslowe's spirits by sallies of wit hardly becoming in a house of mourning. Harry Bradnam reproved him once, then limited himself to unexceptionable comments and brief replies when asked a question. Their sister dabbed her eyes with her handkerchief at intervals between bemoaning her widowhood and responding to Paul's banter. Colin displayed a self-control and dignity they might have emulated.

They were eating the apple dumplings which had likely been meant for the dinner so few had eaten. The cook had supplied a custard sauce to pour over them in place of the usual butter and sugar, hoping to make them tempting, as they were no longer hot from the boiling. The Bradnam brothers ate with good appetites.

Lady Hawkslowe only nibbled, criticizing the food. The kitchen had done its best, but with the servants grieving Lord Hawkslowe's death (more than the widow did, Margaret suspected), the selection of supper dishes had largely depended on the food left over from dinner.

"Falstone, you will no doubt wish to stay for the funeral." She did not sound as though the prospect pleased her.

"I shall."

"I suppose you will depart the following day. We should not take up more of your leave."

"It was no sacrifice, my lady. I was glad to be able to spend time with my brother."

****

Two days later, as the adult family members and Colin prepared to enter the carriages to attend the funeral, Attorney Obadiah Jelliffe arrived from Newcastle. A thin man in his fifth decade with an air of chronic dyspepsia, he was courteous without being deferential. Margaret wondered he had not come earlier until it occurred to her he might have planned his late arrival.

"Lady Hawkslowe, my condolences upon your loss. I had the greatest respect for the late Lord Hawkslowe." He turned to Colin. "My lord, I am sorry you have lost your father. However, he has left you in good hands. Mr. Falstone, Mr. Bradnam, Mr. Paul Bradnam, good day. After the service and the gathering, the day will be far advanced. I will read the will in the morning, if that is acceptable."

Lady Hawkslowe's eyebrows drew together in annoyance. Some silent communication passed from Harry Bradnam to the baroness. She kept almost all the acid from her voice when she replied, "That is thoughtful of you, Mr. Jelliffe. I know I will be prostrated after those who attend the funeral depart. The morning would be better."

"Will nine of the clock be too early?"

"Perhaps ten? To allow us to eat breakfast comfortably?"

"Very well. The long gallery at ten."

Ten in the morning would be sacrificial for Elizabeth Hawkslowe, but no doubt she would be anxious to be done with it.

Margaret was with the girls in the nursery parlor the next day, reading aloud to them while Janet embroidered a border on a doll's petticoat—more interesting than a handkerchief—and Isabelle toiled over a pocket, an excellent practice piece as, being worn under one's petticoat, its imperfections would be out of sight. The arrival of a footman to relay Mr. Jelliffe's request that she bring the girls to the gallery for the reading of the will took her aback. Surely it was unnecessary to subject them to obscure legal terms they could not understand? But she could not spare them the ordeal. Instructing them to use the close stools in their rooms before she took them downstairs, she hurried to her own chamber to make sure she was tidy.

The widow and her brothers sat in the first row of chairs before the small table provided for Jelliffe and his documents. A row of servants stood at the back of the room. They would be the ones who had served the family for some time and were to receive bequests. Two seats remained in the first row. Should Janet and Isabelle sit there? It might be necessary for one or both to go out if the experience should prove too much for their self-control—or if Isabelle needed a close stool again.

As she hesitated, Falstone, in the second row, turned his head and made a gesture toward the chairs beside him. Beside Dorring, Matthew was sitting in the chair on the aisle. She whispered to Janet to sit beside the major, took the next seat herself and drew Isabelle to the outer chair. If anyone needed to leave the proceeding before its end, the most likely candidates were Isabelle and Matthew.

Having been present for the reading of both her

father's and her husband's wills, Margaret prepared for tedium. She was not disappointed. Finally, they were past the standard language about the testator's soundness of mind, the payment of his just debts, varying amounts left to long-time servants, and Lady Hawkslowe's jointure.

"I name as guardian of my children who have not yet reached the age of one-and-twenty, their uncle, Alasdair James Falstone—"

"What?" Elizabeth Hawkslowe exclaimed.

Paul Bradnam turned to stare at Falstone.

"There is some mistake," Harry Bradnam said. "I was named as guardian in Hawkslowe's will at the time of my sister's marriage."

"Lord Hawkslowe executed this will on the fourth day of May this year."

"He cannot have done so! He said nothing about a new will. Of course Harry is their guardian," Lady Hawkslowe snapped. "He is my older brother and the natural choice for the children's guardian."

Jelliffe fixed gimlet eyes upon her. "Major Falstone, or Mr. Falstone as I should now call him, is the late Lord Hawkslowe's brother and therefore the more appropriate guardian, particularly as Lord Hawkslowe chose to appoint him as such."

"He must have been wandering in his wits, Jelliffe. It was always understood my brother Harry would be their guardian."

The attorney's exasperated sigh was audible in the second row. "The witnesses will affirm that Lord Hawkslowe was of sound mind and knew what he was about, my lady."

"Faugh! Servants, I suppose, who would swear to

whatever they were told to say."

"The will was witnessed by Dr. Milford, who attended him regularly for the last several years, and Sir Hugh Montgomery, a magistrate near Rochester, who has known him for some twelve years. Further, his lordship's written instructions to me were clear and well-reasoned and written in his own hand. I will now continue with the reading."

Harry Bradnam nudged his brother and turned to speak into his ear. Either the attorney had acute hearing or he had experience of disgruntled heirs. Jelliffe harrumphed.

"I should add that this most recent will was executed in duplicate, with the other copy delivered to Mr. Jelliffe, my father, of the firm of Harrison and Jelliffe, the late Lord Hawkslowe's legal representative in London. He will be dealing with all matters which may arise there and the legalities regarding transfer of the title."

The servants had been dismissed after hearing their bequests, thank goodness. Janet had managed to press herself against Falstone's shoulder as Isabelle had shrunk against Margaret, who put an arm around her.

Falstone was also executor of the will. When Jelliffe finally finished reading, the Bradnam men began to rise. Lady Hawkslowe continued to sit as if paralyzed.

"There is one more item, though it is not part of the will. Mr. Falstone is to reside at Scot Hall. I have here a letter for Lady Hawkslowe, setting forth his reasons both for appointing Falstone executor and guardian and for specifying he live here." He rose and passed the letter to her.

She pulled the flap free so violently that bits of the broken seal went flying. There was a single sheet. The late Lord Hawkslowe must have been blunt as well as brief, for only moments passed before she demanded, "How dare he?"

Harry bent and murmured in her ear. She stood up abruptly and left the room clinging to his arm.

Alasdair whispered something to Janet that made the tension drain from her face before leaving his chair to talk to Jelliffe as he packed his papers away in his green lawyer's bag.

"Mother is monstrous angry."

At Janet's quiet observation, Margaret replied, "She was surprised." She could not in honesty deny Elizabeth Hawkslowe's anger. "I am sure she will get over it."

"I know she will, Mistress MacGavin. 'Tis uncomfortable while she is in a fury, but it never lasts long. Only just now…"

Margaret hugged her, wishing she could say something helpful. In her own experience, grief was like a grave injury for which one could not take laudanum: nothing eased the pain except time. 'Twould be charitable to ascribe Lady Hawkslowe's ill temper to grief. Margaret found herself unable to spin such a tale to Janet.

The attorney departed after speaking with Alasdair. He took his leave of the new Lord Hawkslowe, saying, "My lord, you have inherited the title earlier than your parents or I would have liked. However, you have a trustworthy guardian and need not take on all the responsibilities that come with your title until you reach your majority. Bear them in mind, but know you need not leave your boyhood behind yet." He bowed to Colin and less deeply to Alasdair, Margaret, and Dorring, spoke kindly to the younger children, and took his leave of them.

Margaret and the girls left the gallery in time to see Jelliffe address a few cool words to Paul Bradnam, who was lingering by the stairs. The brothers had encroaching ways. That much had been obvious to her almost from their arrival. Jelliffe had taken their measure as well. Gideon would have called the lawyer a canny man. Falstone would put a stop to the brothers' habit of acting as if they were the masters here.

By the time they returned to the nursery parlor, the attorney's hired coach was rattling away from the door. Margaret guessed he had not sought out Lady Hawkslowe to bid her farewell, or else she had refused to see him. Whatever was in Sebastian Hawkslowe's letter to his wife had thrown her into a rage.

Chapter 15

One expected a house in mourning to be subdued, but an odd sense of currents below the surface kept Margaret on edge. Lady Hawkslowe seldom emerged from her chambers. When she did, she strolled with her brothers in the garden. If she came down to dinner, she sat between them and ignored Falstone. The Bradnams and Lady Hawkslowe often conferred in her ladyship's parlor.

She would have liked to speak with Alasdair about it if he had not been busy with estate affairs. When he was not meeting with Twissell, he was with the children. She would wait for some innocent occasion when she could have a few words with him unheard by others. Seeking him out privately would cause talk. Lady Hawkslowe might not be able to discharge her, but she would surely complain if she suspected Margaret of any personal interest in Alasdair. She could make Margaret's position so uncomfortable that giving notice would be her only choice. Not that Margaret had any interest in Falstone, of course. She kept out of sight as much as possible, staying close to the nursery wing except when taking the girls outside to ride or walk. She breakfasted early, before the Bradnams rose, though Falstone ate even earlier and was in the estate office or riding around to the tenant holdings before she came down. He did insist she eat dinner and supper in the dining room as Dorring did, pointing out that the children needed some relief from their instructors.

Elizabeth Hawkslowe's withholding of her company, ostensibly because of her grief, was not a bad thing. The children were unaccustomed to spending much time with their mother and thus did not really miss her presence. In her resentment, she could hardly be a consolation to them.

Dorring agreed that keeping them busy was the best plan. Between them, they arranged activities like collecting specimens of wild flowers or leaves to press, rides to various parts of the estate with bottles of lemonade and biscuits or little cakes or gingerbread for refreshment, and conversations in French among the children. Combining the girls' and boys' lessons as much as possible helped. Matthew enjoyed assisting Isabelle with her numbers and was pleased to receive drawing lessons, which had not previously been part of the boys' studies. Dorring was now able to teach Colin basic accounting, a necessity for a landowner. The tutor suggested having the children write little essays about their own interests. If they had a shilling to spend, what would they buy? What was their favorite farm animal and why?

Under Margaret's tutelage, Isabelle was learning to print using a pencil. She already read well, and thus, although her letters were ill-formed, she was able to participate. Matthew began to learn the use of a quill to write cursive. His attempts were not much better and were accompanied by ink blots both on his paper and on his clothing.

Falstone approved their altered teaching methods. "Their education has been neglected. I am in favor of anything which aids in making up for the lost time, as Colin will be going to school Michaelmas term. Now, I plan to visit the tenants regularly. As regularly as the weather permits, at least. I would like Colin to accompany me as the new Lord Hawkslowe. I see no reason not to include the other children."

All the children, including Isabelle, were wild for the treat. Margaret could see no way of avoiding it as the girls should have a female with them. Dorring begged off, citing his unreliable horsemanship. Little Isabelle and her pony would put him to shame.

"All the tenants?" Colin asked.

"Those nearby for now. The more distant farms would be too long a ride for the ponies."

Matthew and Isabelle did not notice the major's wink in response to Colin's look of surprise. The lad blinked. "Too long a ride for the ponies. Oh, quite. It was foolish of me not to think of it, sir."

Isabelle, giggling, demanded to know what the ponies rode.

"Prince would carry me as far as Newcastle, even," Matthew protested.

"The distance around Scot Hall land is twice as far as to Newcastle. The poor little fellow would be worn out, perhaps even lame."

This argument persuaded Matthew to surrender his desire to tour the whole estate until he should be old enough to ride a larger pony, which convinced Isabelle that she would also prefer to wait. Colin's and Janet's eyes slid to Margaret. They too had noticed the flaw in Falstone's misleading explanation. The farthest tenant holdings would not be at the outer edges of the property, and certainly he did not mean to visit all the tenants in one day. Margaret was hard put not to smile, grateful he had so easily discouraged Matthew and Isabelle from the longer excursions. They would soon have been exhausted and complaining.

Alasdair began sometimes to take his breakfast in the nursery with the children, asking them about their studies and their previous day's activities. Margaret wished she might do the same. To suddenly avoid breakfasting downstairs might be perceived as setting her cap for Falstone. She was glad not to see more of him. Of course she was. His presence stirred memories both happy and unhappy. If he had not given her up without a second thought, they might have had children.

****

The house came to a boil suddenly, the result of a passing comment by a friend of Lady Hawkslowe who had come to pay a call, ignoring the convention that discouraged calls to those in the first stages of mourning. She was the wife of a baronet and pleased to be counted among a baroness's circle. Company of any sort was thin in the neighborhood, making a baronet's family preferable to mere gentry. Even better, Lady Ralston was the daughter of a viscount, a connection which might be useful to Lady Hawkeslowe when visiting London.

Janet was sure she would do so once her year of mourning ended. The girl's clear-eyed judgement of her mother disconcerted Margaret. But would it really be better if the child were ignorant of her parent's ways?

The ladies and the Bradnam brothers were in the drawing room. As the footman opened the door for Margaret and the girls, who had been summoned for display, Lady Ralston was saying, "…hoped to get

Kirkland Grange as a dowry for our daughter, but Lord Hawkslowe bought it. Your late lord, that was," she clarified, lest anyone should think Colin had been purchasing real estate.

Margaret shepherded Janet and Isabelle into the room, but before they were noticed and could make their curtsies, Harry Bradnam spoke. "Hawkslowe bought it? I had not heard it is part of the Hawkslowe property. Elizabeth, did you know of this?"

"No." Her fair coloring advertised her sentiments, almost certainly anger rather than embarrassment.

The children edged closer to Margaret.

"I expect that's because he did not keep it," Lady Ralston said, satisfied she had borne news unknown to the hearer. "Ralston heard he had transferred it to Major Falstone."

Paul Bradnam gave a short laugh.

Now Lady Hawkslowe noticed them. "Why are you standing there? Make your curtsies to Lady Ralston. Yes, very good, Janet. Isabelle, you need more practice. MacGavin, take them back to the schoolroom, and make sure the next time I see them Isabelle is able to curtsy more gracefully."

The pot was still simmering days later.

Janet and Colin had taken supper with the adults. At its end, Elizabeth Hawkslowe and her brothers went to the drawing room, and Margaret and Dorring took their charges upstairs to spend the rest of the evening in the nursery parlor. Had Falstone not gone to discuss with the bailiff how the late sowing of the barley might affect the harvest, he would have expected them to join the others in the drawing room. In his absence, it was a relief not to have to remain. The Bradnams were better behaved when Falstone was present. Margaret found their wit embarrassing, and Lady Hawkslowe's petulance made her want to box her ladyship's ears as if she were a spoiled child. What a pity no one had done so when she was growing up.

Colin and Dorring settled in the nursery parlor with Dorring's chess board. Margaret visited Nurse Sallows to be sure Matthew and Isabelle were with her and found them listening wide-eyed to stories of their papa's childhood.

When she returned to the parlor, Janet was still present. She admitted she was not at all sleepy and apologized for having lied. "But I would rather be here where it's comfortable than sitting mumchance in the drawing room." She opened her ivory-inlaid sewing box, a gift from her father, and one hand stole to her throat to touch the necklet she had worn at supper. The chain and pendant were gone.

"My necklace," Janet uttered. "Papa gave it to me on my last birthday." She often wore it, an enameled pendant in the form of a yellow pansy surrounded by its leaves, with a tear-drop pearl hanging from it. "Mistress MacGavin, may we go downstairs to search for it?"

It was her most cherished possession, as dear to her as her pony. Janet might not know that the pansy stood for remembrance, but when he gave it to her, Hawkslowe must already have known he would not live to see Janet a year older.

When the footman opened the door at their approach, Margaret heard Lady Hawkslowe's voice. "…cannot think why Hawkslowe would buy a property to give to Falstone, without so much as a word to me."

As they entered, three heads turned toward the

door. Elizabeth jabbed her needle savagely into her embroidery and frowned at them. Margaret begged her pardon for the intrusion and explained their errand. They had already tried the dining room without finding the necklet nor had the servants.

"Oh, very well, then. But be quick about it. Surely 'tis time for you to go to bed, as tired as you were earlier."

"You cannot expect Janet to sleep before she finds her necklace, Lizzie," Harry said with a grin, "any more than you would if you misplaced your rubies."

" 'Tis hardly the same," she sniffed and made an impatient gesture to her daughter to get on with her search.

Paul Bradnam gave a covert glance toward Margaret, which she noticed anyway. She had become sensitive to everything about the Bradnam brothers: the meaningful looks that passed between them and their sister, their tones of voice, Paul's attempts to befriend the children.

Paul Bradnam tried too hard. Alasdair's manner was natural, and they responded to it, while Paul's felt insincere. From experience with her own brothers, Margaret suspected Colin of concealing annoyance. Janet was polite but wore a grown lady's social mask. Matthew and Isabelle laughed at their youngest uncle's jokes and accepted the treats and gifts he brought them, but they did not talk as freely with him as they did with Falstone. She thought she recognized their response. Her father had introduced her to a business connection of his, met by chance at an assembly before her marriage. The Irishman was a handsome fellow with an easy manner but too full of a practiced charm she did not trust.

Harry Bradnam's casual friendliness was more successful with his nieces and nephews. Margaret did not know whether to find that reassuring or not. Mayhap 'twas only that both Bradnams were thick as inkle weavers with their sister which made her suspicious of them.

Janet went to the chair where she had sat briefly while the family waited to be summoned to the dining room, and Margaret glanced around the floor. They were both forgotten.

"At least it was not a great burden on the estate, Elizabeth." Harry took a pinch of snuff from a pretty gold and enamel snuffbox. "The place must have gone cheap. I am sure it needed work, having been unoccupied for several years."

"I heard the repairs were made at the estate's expense." Paul declined his brother's offer of snuff.

Harry shrugged. "Just so, but mostly by that property's workers and men employed here."

"Oh, I do not give a rap for that, though 'tis horridly vexing Hawkslowe should do such a thing, but I am bored almost to screaming. I have been a prisoner here for years, and now there is a year of mourning to be got through."

Harry pursed his lips. "Northumberland is notably lacking in company. As even visits from neighbors are not really acceptable so soon after a bereavement, I understand you have little to occupy you."

Particularly as Lady Hawkslowe spent no more than half an hour a day with her children, and sometimes not that, and left all household matters to the housekeeper and butler.

Paul added, "I misdoubt the Ralston female would have made the effort if she were not so eager to curry favor."

"Oh, here it is, under the side table!" Janet popped up, clutching her treasure. She curtsied to her mother and uncles. "Good night again, Mama, Uncle Harry, Uncle Paul."

As Elizabeth Hawkslowe opened her mouth, Paul said, "Mistress MacGavin, I don't believe I have seen little Matthew and Isabelle in two days. Will you accompany me to the nursery floor? I should like to wish them good night. They are always busy during the day, now they have a governess and a tutor."

"Certainly, sir." Margaret could not refuse. She heard, "Harry, I want you to ask—"

Paul Bradnam pulled the door shut behind them before the footman could, cutting off the end of the sentence.

Chapter 16

The Bradnams lingered at Scot Hall. Either their pockets were to let, or they knew their creditors were unlikely to pursue them to Northumberland. To be charitable, they might really wish to be of assistance to their sister. As much as Falstone distrusted them, they did seem fond of Elizabeth. Mayhap their continued presence was a blend of all three motives. However, they kept out of his way for the most part, as did Elizabeth, which suited him. Although they were on their best behavior at dinner and supper, they watched him covertly.

Alasdair looked up from the tenant lease he had been pondering when Elizabeth Hawkslowe swept into the estate office without bothering to knock. He only half rose to greet her. Churlish, but his mood was not conciliatory.

"How is it I learned from a neighbor that Hawkslowe gave you Kirkland Grange?"

"He chose not to tell you because he did not want to be subjected to your vapors and fits of spleen. Do sit down, Elizabeth."

She continued to stand. "To waste the estate's money in such a way without a word to me, I vow I do not comprehend. Confess you were ashamed to admit you extorted it from him as your price for returning."

Sebastian must have had the patience of a saint.

"My brother bought and transferred the property to me before I received his letter asking me to come home." He added, "I can prove it by the date on the documents, the date on the letter he sent, and I am sure my colonel will provide a statement as to the date I requested leave to visit my brother. In court you would lose."

Ignoring this, she raged on. "How could my husband insult me by replacing Harry as both executor and guardian of my children without informing me?"

Although it was clearly a rhetorical question, he answered it anyway. "He did not confide in you for the same reason he did not tell you about Kirkland Grange or that I was returning: because he was too ill to deal with your reproaches. Sebastian named me guardian and executor because he knew your brothers are wastrels and did not trust them not to plunder the estate, to the detriment of the children's future. How correct he was in his decision was proven by your stealing the Lady Day rents."

"Are you back to that? I know nothing of the matter."

"And I do not believe you. The bank has provided a transcript of their ledger for the estate account. There is no record of the last quarterly deposit."

Her lips moved without sound. At length she forced a bitter laugh. "Then that proves the fellow—Twissell?—embezzled the money. Or there is some mistake. Perhaps the teller did not record it and embezzled it himself."

"The mistake was yours, my lady, or yours and your brother Paul's. In my letter, I also asked whether anyone recalled the transaction. As it happened, the clerk remembered your coming in to withdraw your pin money, because he was surprised at the end of the day that the quarterly deposit had not been made. He remarked upon it to the head clerk, who mentioned it to the banker. He decided not to inquire of Hawkslowe, knowing my brother was gravely ill and the account still held a respectable amount. He concluded Twissell had not been able to bring the deposit in for some reason. Then he put it out of his mind."

She fidgeted like a child caught in mischief. "I know nothing of the matter except that I did go into the bank to get my pin money. If Twissell did not take the deposit in, 'tis no fault of mine. If the money truly is missing, the bailiff must have taken it. He should be turned over to the magistrate."

"Have done lying, Elizabeth. There is no question in my mind Twissell and the clerk are truthful. Twissell has been employed here for a number of years, and no one has ever accused him of dishonesty. I believe his account of that day. Further, the probabilities are against you. The most likely explanation is that you pocketed the payments. Sebastian suspected that the money you claimed you had lost at cards you gave to Harry or Paul to support their spendthrift ways."

He waited to see if she would deny the charge. Perhaps she was too surprised that Sebastian had guessed her stratagem to form a rebuttal.

"I am satisfied in my own mind that either you or your brothers benefited from a quarter's rents belonging to the estate. I choose not to bring a case at law and cannot deduct money from your jointure to reimburse the estate. Instead I will give you this warning: incur no debt you cannot pay out of your jointure. The barony will not cover it. You are now a *feme sole* and responsible for your own debts. Do not believe any embarrassment at my brother's widow being pursued by bailiffs or thrown into debtor's prison will persuade me to rescue you. That responsibility rests with your brothers."

As soon as he spoke the words, he knew he had erred. He had learned to tamp down his emotions over the years, earning a reputation for coldness which had served him well. Civilian life was proving more challenging to his temper than military life had.

She whirled and flung out of the office.

****

"Mama is in a temper," Janet remarked as she and Margaret walked in the herb garden. Margaret had begun to devote an hour or two every day to each girl outside of their lesson time. She treasured the memory of spending time alone with her mother and being able to speak of matters she would not have discussed in the presence of a third person. Would she have made an exception if she had had a sister? Perhaps not. Certainly not, if the sister were younger. Lady Hawkslowe was scarcely involved in her daughters' lives. Seeing Alasdair Falstone attempt to fill some of the gaps left by the death of the boys' father spurred her to do the same with Janet and Isabelle.

"Oh?" She would not prompt the girl. Neither would she chide her for the comment as she clearly wished to talk about it.

"I wanted to make a pencil sketch of Papa's portrait. To make a watercolor of him as a gift for Isabelle," she explained, "and another for myself. But when I approached the door, I heard Mama talking with my Bradnam uncles about that manor that Papa gave to

Uncle Alasdair. She was angry because my father had not asked her opinion. Uncle Paul laughed and said, 'I apprehend he knew what answer you'd give, Lizzie.' Uncle Harry told her it would have been better if he had left it to him in his will. Mama said she did not see what difference it made. Then I heard them moving, I think toward the chairs at the end of the gallery near the door and thought I should leave."

"That was very sensible, Janet. One would not wish to be caught overhearing a private conversation."

"Mistress MacGavin, do you know what difference it would have made? Father putting the manor in his will instead of just giving it to Uncle Alasdair?"

How could she reply without offending? "I am no expert in these matters, but I have heard it is sometimes possible to challenge a will." Someone had suggested to her own father that he attempt to overturn Sir Percival's will based on his promise to provide Margaret a dowry. He had refused on the ground that going to law was expensive and uncertain. "It is not wise to rely on an inheritance."

Janet broke a twig off the rosemary bush. "Uncle Paul said something about it being a bribe." She searched Margaret's face.

"I do not think 'bribe' is the right word. But Lord Hawkslowe may have believed that Major Falstone could not abandon his profession to be your guardian. As a second son, he would not necessarily have inherited much, if anything, from his father. Most sons who are not heirs to a property must pursue some employment."

"Oh. I see." After a pause, she said, "Sallie says distilled water of lovage takes away freckles. Do you think I could try it, Mistress MacGavin?"

"If someone here knows how to distill it, I'm sure you may. Although wearing a hat when you are out in the sun would prevent them."

The confidences seemed to be at an end. Then Janet observed, "My Bradnam uncles are out much of the day now and even overnight."

She was correct. Margaret knew the Bradnams had been in the habit of riding out on any pleasant day. They had friends in the neighborhood, she understood, as they had been regular guests at Scot Hall ever since their sister's marriage to Hawkslowe. Presumably they called on them or perhaps met them in inns to raise a few glasses. Mistress Stukeley had made an acerbic remark about the Bradnams being looked up to by the young men in the area as examples of the London beau. But lately their expeditions came oftener and kept one or both out far longer, though Margaret had not given their habits a thought until Janet pointed it out. She certainly had not known they had been away overnight as she did not miss their presence in the drawing room after supper or indeed at any other time. Elizabeth Hawkslowe had not commented upon their absences, which did seem out of character as she and her brothers were so close. She might have been expected to be nettled by their abandonment.

During the girls' French lesson a few days later, Margaret received a summons to take tea with Lady Hawkslowe in her parlor. Dorring had set Colin to write out one of Aesop's fables in Latin and Matthew to copy out in his best hand a set of several paragraphs on the importance of discipline in an army ("For I don't see him going into the church or the law," the tutor whispered to Margaret). He suggested Janet might write an essay in French on the importance of something she was being taught. Her thoughtful expression suggested that her composition might be amusing to read. For Isabelle, he produced a chapbook with simple illustrations of everyday objects with their names and a descriptive sentence or two in French.

"What a useful thing, Mr. Dorring. Wherever did you get it?"

"My cousin is a printer. He prints them in French, Latin, and German. I wish they might make his fortune for him. I've found them very useful."

She would order a set for the girls, assuming Lady Hawkslowe did not order her to pack her trunk and depart. In spite of Major Falstone's claim that no one but he had the authority to dismiss her, it would be difficult to remain if her ladyship wanted her gone.

As it happened, Lady Hawkslowe greeted her warmly and waved her to a chair at the pretty round table in her parlor as her maid brought in a tray laden with the tea service. A perfunctory question about the girls' studies as she measured out the tea leaves implied their mother had some other reason for wishing to see Margaret.

Elizabeth Hawkslowe sighed heavily. "You cannot imagine how I miss my dear husband"—Margaret could indeed imagine it, if her hostess had been as fond of Sebastian Hawkslowe as she herself had been of Gideon—"and 'tis the worse for being trapped here with no friends to pay calls and not even the few entertainments appropriate for a lady in mourning." She chose to ignore Lady Ralston's recent visit.

This early in full mourning, Margaret could not

think of any amusement which would be deemed suitable. Only women of the lower classes could ignore strict mourning because they had no choice. They must continue to work if they were employed or go out to do the marketing if they were not. "The support of friends is helpful, my lady." She would have added, "and family," except that she could not forget overhearing Paul Bradnam's words that day she and Dorring had returned with the children. Nor had that been the only occasion when the Bradnam brothers' manner struck her as unbefitting anyone claiming to be a gentleman. Or indeed, any decent human being down to the most ragged crossing sweeper.

"Our nearest neighbors are very little comfort in my bereavement. They have few pretensions to gentility, much less the beau monde, and can speak of nothing but parish matters, cattle, sheep, and the best way to treat colic in horses and children. I do not enjoy country life. The people I care to visit live too far away, and the roads are bad. There are no shops worth the name nearer than Newcastle, and those have little enough to tempt one. I can tolerate the weather in the summer, I suppose, but it is horrid in the winter, and I fear I shall languish here until next summer." Lady Hawkslowe pouted: not an attractive expression for a woman of three- or four-and-thirty. "My brothers tell me I could attend concerts or any sedate event in Bath or even London." Meditatively: "No one spends the summer in London, of course. Bath would be the place to visit in the warm weather. Or some friend's estate."

Was Major Falstone really insisting on a full year of mourning? Considering that he could scarcely conceal his impatience with his sister-in-law, she would have thought he would be glad to rid the house of her.

"Perhaps you might invite a female relative or friend to stay? Someone with similar interests who could enter into your feelings?"

"The most vexatious thing! I wrote to my sister to suggest it, but her husband forbids her to go because she is breeding. He wants another son and fears the coach's jolting may bring on a miscarriage. Corinna does have difficulty carrying to term," she conceded. "Then I wrote my cousin Eleanora who lives with her married sister. She would have been delighted to get away from Martha's unruly brood, but three of them have come down with the measles, and Eleanora is needed to nurse them. I am sure my aunt would come because she would think it her duty, but I will not ask her. She is full of piety and good works, which is not at all cheering."

Impossible not to feel some sympathy for her charges' mother. Having grown in the rich social loam of London, she was wilting in the thin soil of Northumberland. That metaphor proved Margaret was no more genteel than Lady Hawkslowe's neighbors. The gardener improved his ground by spading in well-aged horse droppings, implying London's beau monde—Her voice was slightly unsteady when she agreed, "How true!"

Taken for sympathy, her agreement won a faint smile from Elizabeth and elevated Margaret to a confidant.

"You cannot imagine how difficult my life has been, Mistress MacGavin. My marriage was all that I could hope for, but it never occurred to me when I accepted Hawkslowe that he would decide to live here and seldom take me to London. The last few years when his health was failing, it was understandable, though I might have gone…"

If he had permitted it, which evidently he had not, presumably for good cause. Margaret's original resentment had faded and then turned to respect for his concern that his children, even the girls, be educated, and his unmistakable love when he summoned them to his deathbed. He might have made a mistake in forbidding Alasdair's marriage, but who did not err on occasion?

"I thought I might pass my mourning with my sister, Corinna. My brother Harry would have raised no objection to my doing so. He was to have been my children's guardian and trustee"—as if Margaret had not witnessed the indecorous scene at the reading of the will!—"and we could all have been comfortable. I near swooned away when I found Hawkslowe had changed his will without my consent."

"No one would have wondered at it, I am sure, my lady." Let her take that remark as she would!

"To put me and my darlings in the power of that despot! Such a blow when I was almost prostrated by my husband's death." Dabbing at her eyes with her handkerchief, she went on. "You have seen how harsh he is to the children. I have no doubt he will pillage the estate and leave us all penniless."

Now that, Margaret did not believe. His years as a soldier had given Alasdair a stern demeanor. While he might seem severe to his spoiled sister-in-law, his devotion to his nieces and nephews was beyond question and disproved her complaints.

"At least I can be thankful dear Corinna did not

marry him. Falstone courted her and only went into the army when she rejected him. We both had excellent dowries, and he coveted hers. She had the sense to accept the viscount and thus got a title for her money and a far more agreeable husband. Though he is rather old. Still, she could not refuse a title and a manor."

After a few more peevish remarks about Alasdair, Lady Hawkslowe subjected her to an interrogation about the latest London fashions and gossip. About the former she knew almost nothing. She was able to dredge up some scandal from satirical engravings displayed in printers' shops. Then Lady Hawkslowe dismissed her, remarking upon what a good listener she was.

****

Elizabeth avoided Falstone for several days, taking her meals in her parlor on the excuse of suffering a megrim. At supper the second night, Paul Bradnam jovially explained (as if he might not have noticed) that his sister fell into fits of the sullens when unhappy or bored. Harry intimated that he and his brother would be bringing their stay to a close.

"I am sure Lady Hawkslowe is grateful you came to lend your support during her husband's last days and the first of her mourning." Diplomacy was needed in civilian life, where one could not simply order one's guests to go home or to stay in other parts of the country with friends.

His respite from her company came to an end when his sister-in-law sent him a note by her maid, begging the favor of a word with him. *If only it may be limited to one word.*

She rose from the sofa on which she had been

drooping as her maid admitted him to her parlor and greeted him, shoulders back, chin up: a persecuted heroine.

"Falstone, I wish to speak with you."

"So I understood, my lady."

She dismissed the maid with a flick of one soft white hand before sinking back onto the divan and invited him to be seated on an armchair. She smoothed her petticoat before beginning. "I know you cannot begin to imagine my grief at Hawkslowe's death after years of watching his health fail."

"No," he agreed. He could not imagine her grieving.

"I remained at his side continually, with no more than an occasional visit to Newcastle for shopping in the past two years. Or to stay overnight with our more distant neighbors who held some entertainment, when it was not possible to return the same day." She stared down at her lap while he waited. If "by his side" she meant in the same house, he believed her claim.

"I cannot endure Northumberland for another year, and in mourning, too. Paul and Harry mean to leave in a day or two. I want to go with them. They will take me to stay with our sister, Corinna." She stole a glance at him from under her eyelashes.

She did not know him well enough to recognize the impassive face that had often reduced soldiers under his command to stammered explanations. Nevertheless, it and his failure to reply at once caused her to hurry on. "You met her once, before you took up your commission. Her husband is a viscount with a manor in Kent."

The implication was *So she did better than you for*

a husband. Falstone did not feel insulted. No matter how large the dowry, marriage to Corinna Bradnam would have been unthinkable when he loved Margaret.

"While I would not attend any social gathering, I would at least have her company and she would have mine." She hem'd. "She is in a delicate condition just now."

"Are you requesting my permission to take the children with you?"

His sister-in-law's lips turned down at the reminder he was their guardian.

"Yes. The girls at least should be with their mama. They have not seen their aunt, either, since she visited several years ago. I suppose you would wish the boys' tutor to accompany them, and Corinna's home does not have rooms enough to accommodate all the children. The nursery would be stretched past its limits. The boys and their tutor can stay here, and the girls would not require MacGavin's presence. Corinna and I would oversee their instruction."

"Have they visited their aunt before?" He believed not, from something Colin had said about never having been outside Northumberland.

"No," she admitted reluctantly. "When they were younger, the length of the journey would have been exhausting for them and then too in the weather when coach journeys are possible, she often had house parties. Adding several children, myself, my maid, a nursery maid, and perhaps Hawkslowe would have been impracticable."

"Is she not holding a house party this year?"

"No." Primly she added, "The viscount prefers she remain quietly at home under the circumstances. She knows how overset I am, and she needs her sister's company during her confinement."

"Then I think we should not tax her hospitality by sending the children, my lady."

"You would deprive me of my daughters?"

"By no means. However, a visit would interrupt their lessons, and their aunt may not find their presence restful."

"You are cruel to a widow in her first mourning. Must I miss my children as well as my husband?"

In a more conciliatory tone, he went on, "I cannot imagine Isabelle enjoying so long a coach journey. I think also my nieces will be better in familiar surroundings with their usual pastimes and studies, though I am sure you will be glad of your sister's company. I do think you should delay your departure for several days, to allow the coach to be prepared. It must be inspected to make sure it will not delay you on your way, and I will arrange for outriders. You should be able to set out four days from now, if that is agreeable."

She preened a little, accepting the suggestions as proof she had swayed him. Perhaps she had never expected him to let her take the children with her. "Thank you. The outriders will be welcome as a discouragement to highwaymen, although my brothers will accompany me in the coach as they did not bring their own horses."

If they owned any: keeping a mount in town was expensive. The Bradnam brothers probably made do with hacks hired from a livery.

"I'm sure that will make the journey more enjoyable." Though her brothers were unlikely to be much use if they were accosted by a knight of the road.

"Thank you, Falstone. I will not need to take much, only my widow's weeds as I shall be living quietly." The last statement was doubtless uttered in case Sebastian had told him about her frivolity and expensive habits in London.

Lady Hawkslowe then begged his pardon for taking his time and thanked him again almost warmly before excusing herself to tend to household matters. Sending a footman up to the attic for her trunks and valises, most likely.

He betook himself to the nursery.

"Mistress MacGavin, may I have a word with you?" He gave a slight jerk of his head toward the passage. By her slight nod, she took his meaning: a word in private.

"Certainly, sir. Janet, compose a letter in French, as if it were to one of your friends. Isabelle, be prepared to translate the passage on page ten of your French storybook."

He led her to the far end of the passage where a window overlooked the kitchen garden.

"I made an error, and I need your help," he said.

"If I can help, I will."

"You may not wish to, once you hear what it is. I won't hold you to your agreement if you cannot like the project. What I plan is perhaps ungentlemanly. You may not like to assist me."

"We won't know until you tell me what it is."

"Through mischance and the misplaced trust of the bailiff, Elizabeth managed to embezzle the rents paid in March." From her creased forehead, he guessed what she was thinking. He had loved Margaret for her wit and liveliness, but even then he had admired her judgement and ability to see both sides of any question. "There is no doubt about it: I don't believe Twissell and the teller and the head clerk are all lying. I lost my temper and made the mistake of telling her she must live within her means as I will not pay her debts out of the estate. I wouldn't, even had she not diverted those funds, but given that she had…well, I was angry and spoke without thinking."

"I should think you would be angry! I would have been furious. What kind of mother steals from her children's livelihood?"

"One who cares more for rescuing her brothers from their financial embarrassments than for her children's future. That was my brother's belief and why he stopped her visiting London without him. And he stopped going himself when he realized he could not watch her continually." His lips tightened. "Just now she told me she wants to visit her sister in Kent as her brothers intend to leave and they will escort her."

Margaret tilted her head, considering the matter.

"I suppose it's not surprising," she said finally. "She doesn't like Northumberland, and in her sister's home, there would probably be neighbors paying calls. She may not have seen her sister for some time, either, and may long for her company. She is very attached to her brothers."

"All of those points may be true, Margaret. Mistress MacGavin, I should say. However, there's one aspect to take into account. They will pass through London on their way."

"Well, they'd have to, wouldn't they, to cross the river?"

"They would. They might even break their journey there for a day or two."

"And you think Lady Hawkslowe might indulge herself with some shopping?"

"Possibly a great deal of shopping. As soon as I warned her she must live on her jointure, it occurred to me she might incur substantial expenses and tell the merchants to send the bill here, believing I would pay rather than let our name suffer embarrassment. I couldn't in good conscience not pay, not to avoid humiliation but because it would be unfair to the tradesmen. A few gowns and trinkets would be one thing. It might be a great deal more, if she thought to line her brothers' pockets for the next few months, as I expect she did with the rent money. Paul Bradnam was a party to it."

"How could she enrich them at the estate's expense?"

He found himself grinning. "You are too honest, Margaret. She could order suits for her brothers, charging them to the estate. Again, annoying but not a serious matter. She could buy a carriage, horses, and jewelry, then let her brothers re-sell them. If she thinks to do so, she has not yet got my measure."

"How do you plan to prevent it?"

"I mean to write to the merchants she has bought from in the past, advising that she is responsible for her own debts, that the estate will not pay her bills. I must also inform our men of business and our bankers in Newcastle and London not to pay them or advance her any funds." He smiled coldly. "I doubt the bank in Newcastle would give her a farthing now, as the banker knows she is a widow and likely guessed what happened from my letter. However, it's best to put it in writing. I need to make a list of the merchants from the estate accounts, which will not be quick. I will write out some of the letters and sign them all, of course, but the work will go faster with two people. I will also place an announcement in the *London Gazette*. I want to send the letters to town by messenger within the next two days to be sure they arrive before she does. If you do not feel you can assist me, I will understand. It must seem vindictive."

"Of course I will help. Actions have consequences. To have so little regard for the health of the property her own son will inherit and the source of the girls' dowries strikes me as showing little maternal regard."

"Thank you, Margaret. I'll begin by composing the letter, then."

"I wonder—"

"Ay?"

" 'Tis something I thought odd at the time. Now it begins to seem significant." She described a scene in the drawing room and Paul's sudden urgent desire to say good night to the children. "I had no reason before to consider Lady Hawkslowe anything more than an inattentive mother. I wonder now if they were making plans they thought it best I not hear."

"Something beyond discussing Lady Hawkslowe's travel arrangements." No need to make it a question; he would have suspected the same.

As soon as the girls' lessons ended for the day, he provided her with a copy of his letter, a list of merchants, and a supply of paper. "When you've finished, I'll sign and seal them."

Margaret wrote a good commercial hand, not the

delicate, fussy script favored by ladies. His letter had been short, but even so, she finished more quickly than he expected. The number of tradesmen from whom Lady Hawkslowe had purchased proved to be shocking: not only mantua-makers, milliners, glovers, cobblers, and haberdashers, but jewelers, furniture makers, bookshops, sellers of Chinese porcelain and Turkish carpets, and others. No wonder Sebastian had forced her to rusticate! She had been prodigious expensive to maintain in town.

Four days later, the great traveling coach rolled away, laden with valises, bandboxes, trunks, Lady Hawkslowe, her maid, and her brothers. It was accompanied by a pair of outriders. Scot Hall almost audibly sighed with relief.

Chapter 17

Margaret woke early to a stripe of sunlight falling across her bed. The nights were cool, but she seldom drew the window and bed-curtains completely closed as she had in London. There it was necessary for privacy, as one would hardly want someone in the house across the street to be able to stare into one's chamber. Necessary, too, to dull the city's incessant noise, to which she had never become deaf.

She lay gazing up at the faded canopy, contemplating the day stretching before her. In the bustle and confusion of getting Lady Hawkslowe on the road, she had made no plans. Lessons, of course. A ride perhaps. An al fresco luncheon? This was the first day since coming to Scot Hall she had wakened looking forward to the day, rather than wondering about its challenges. She felt as carefree as she had in her youth for the first time in…months? Years? She was back in the north country, among gentry, familiar foods, and familiar accents, able to ride when she chose, not dependent on her brothers' charity or her sister-in-law's tolerance.

This was also the first full day of Lady Hawkslowe's and her brothers' absence. Margaret was glad to be free of their habit of turning up unexpectedly to disconcert her. Their speculative stares made her uncomfortable, particularly as they could not be dismissed as the kind of glances men gave pretty young women. As an unremarkable female in her fourth decade, she should have been invisible. She would be able to converse and ride with Falstone without incurring Elizabeth Hawkslowe's suspicion. The thought gave her a moment's pause. Her intention had been to maintain a proper distance from him.

She must speak to Falstone about the children occasionally, of course, and he did join in some activities with the children. So did Dorring, and his presence did not make her uneasy. Perhaps because he was eight or ten years younger than she? No, her qualms about increased familiarity with Alasdair Falstone had to do with their prior relationship.

Which was troubling, as it suggested she had not got over her youthful infatuation. Surely it was only a habit: both of them had changed. She was no longer young and light-hearted, expecting the best of life, and he had grown hard, boyhood left behind. She acquitted him of being unnecessarily harsh to Lady Hawkslowe: a foolish, frivolous woman, shockingly expensive, and worse, a careless mother. Dishonest, too, if she had stolen the rents. She might have done so only on her brother's persuasion, but one owed more to one's husband and children than to a brother, however dear.

She and Alasdair Falstone would be alone in the house, apart from the children, Dorring, and the servants. That was disquieting. A gentlewoman should not be living in the same house as a man to whom she was not related, with no female companion, a thought which had not occurred to her until now. Neither her own age nor the children's and servants' presence did much to lessen the impropriety. Except mayhap the rules were different for governesses who were only upper servants in the minds of most.

Perhaps Falstone would remove to Kirkland Grange now his sister-in-law and her brothers were gone. But his presence was good for the children, and he needed to attend to estate matters here as well. His staying at Scot Hall would be more convenient for everyone. *More enjoyable, too*, her heart added. *For the children*, her brain replied. The children's needs must rule although Alasdair's removal to the manor would be better for her own peace of mind.

The children were present at breakfast. Margaret and her brothers had not been confined to the nursery as much as children in London seemed to be, manners in the north being freer. They had benefited from the contact with their grandfather and with their father on his infrequent leaves. With the Hawkslowe children's mother and maternal uncles away, permitting them to take breakfast en famille would offend no one and cause them no anxiety. Colin and Janet would take their dinner with Falstone, Margaret, and Dorring every day, not merely Sundays. The younger ones would continue to take dinner and supper in the nursery. Nurse Sallows did not hold with children eating as soon before their bedtimes as supping with the adults would entail. Margaret did not envy Alasdair the task of explaining the new rule to Lady Hawkslowe on her return.

Falstone served himself a slice of ham, toast, and porridge. Margaret passed him the quince marmalade without being asked. He smiled his thanks and said, "I thought I might ride over to Kirkland to inspect the house. Sebastian had repairs made, but the furnishings are as they were when it was last occupied. Mistress

MacGavin, would Janet and Isabelle like to come along? And you, too, needless to say? Colin and Matthew, I am sure you would enjoy the expedition. Dorring, you are welcome, as well, unless you would like to have a holiday from these rapscallions. I believe I can manage them for few hours."

"If I could leave them to you, I do have some letters to write and errands in the village. Thank you, sir."

"I'm sure we would all enjoy it. Perhaps I should ask Cook to pack something to eat? Your house will not be prepared to make even a simple meal without notice, I suppose."

"A very good idea, ma'am. You are an excellent quartermaster. Quartermistress."

She felt like a girl again.

They could not indulge in a good gallop, of course, not with children on ponies, and their conversation was often interrupted by questions or comments from one of the four, or by some instruction or remonstrance to Matthew or Isabelle. It was like being part of a family. She had not felt this sort of connection since before Rupert married Sybilla. If they had had children, she and Gideon might have been a family. Instead, they had merely been friends, partners, and lovers. Theirs had been a good marriage, compared to many, though it had lacked some essential ingredient. Her late husband had been deserving of love, yet she had not loved him, or not the way she had loved Alasdair. Of course, she had not been a girl anymore. She did miss him, however.

Was it only the absence of children? Gideon had been sensible without being dull, possessed a dry wit, was kind, and best of all, he did not regard women as childish and weak. Neither had her brothers treated her thus, but they were unusual in that respect. Rupert behaved differently with Sybilla, but then, he loved her.

Kirkland Grange, built of rough blocks of stone, while smaller than the Bettancourt family seat, was more than a cottage or even a substantial farmhouse. It appeared well-kept until one crossed the threshold.

Falstone had to rap on the door repeatedly before a flustered elderly woman opened it. When he identified himself and asked if she were the housekeeper, she confessed she was indeed Mistress Polk and hurried into apology both for the delay and for the state of the house. Her gaze stole to Margaret and the children.

While free of dust and cobwebs and not smelling of mildew, the wood surfaces were dull and the plaster was an odd light brown, very depressing to the spirits.

"I'm right sorry 'tis not looking better, Major Falstone. I was housekeeper years ago when a family lived here, before the last owner. I think it a pretty house, but it does need freshening. The gentleman as bought the Grange after the family preferred town life and never stayed long. Without the servants to keep it up, I haven't been able to polish all the furniture and paneling." She indicated the walls. "When I came to work here near fifty years ago, the walls were the color of rich cream. 'Tis the smoke from the fires that's darkened them." Mistress Polk gave a helpless shrug.

Colin and Matthew were immediately drawn to a monstrous ugly painting of some mythic battle while Janet and Isabelle studied the entryway dubiously. To the right, a stair led up. Straight ahead, a dim passage led deeper into the house. Then Isabelle's eyes fixed upon the post at the end of the stair's balustrade. A carved lion capped it, the pupils of its ivory eyes staring back at them. She squeaked and went to peer at it, transfixed, followed by Janet.

Margaret took the opportunity to peek into the room on the left. A parlor, the term *drawing room* being too formal for what probably served as both a place to entertain guests and for the family to congregate. She wandered in.

Behind her the housekeeper said, "Lord Hawkslowe that was ordered repairs, and the chimneys don't smoke now, the windows fit tight, and there's no leaks. I guess he'd-a given orders about the inside, too, if his lordship's health wasn't failing. I've done my best, but with only a girl to help me, and she without all her wits, and Hobbs for the heavy work and the garden..." She added, "Things should be under holland covers, but I took 'em off when I heard you was expected at Scot Hall, and I kept thinking you'd be here any day, and never got 'em back on."

"I meant to visit the house sooner, but I thought I'd best look Scot Hall's land over first and call upon the tenants. I suppose the furniture will need to be replaced." His lack of enthusiasm was apparent.

The furniture was handsome, though old and heavier than the current fashion. The wood could do with a good polishing to make it glow. Margaret sat on one of the armchairs and found it solid though the upholstery was in tatters. A settee was in similar condition. The green wool velvet curtains had once been fine but were now moth-eaten. No rugs covered the floor: rolled up and stored away, if Falstone was lucky.

Over her shoulder, Margaret said, "Major, if the

rest of the furnishings are no worse and you do not insist on being fashionable, I think you need only have the upholstered pieces re-covered."

He joined her in the parlor. "I don't care a straw for fashion. All I ask is comfort." The warmth in his voice and his eyes when she looked up at him made her heart give a skip.

Colin and Janet had taken their younger siblings by the hand to keep them from escaping, as both were wild to explore. Falstone consented (with suitable admonitions) and asked Margaret to inspect the rest of the house with him.

"Would you make a list of colors for paint and fabrics for each room?" Alasdair asked.

"What colors do you favor?" To plan the refurbishing of a house of her own would be bliss.

"I don't know. Nothing too à la mode, I think, as this is the country. Just something comfortable, that suits the house."

"But as you will be living here eventually—"

He shook his head. "There can be no question of my moving to the Grange until Colin is of age. Likely not immediately then as he may still need my assistance with the younger children."

Of course not. Young Lord Hawkslowe might still need a bulwark against his mother and uncles.

"Once the house is fit to be lived in, I'll lease it out."

The prospect of redecorating it for Alasdair suddenly seemed more enjoyable.

They completed their tour, retrieved the dusty and cobwebby younger members of the party, and ate their midday meal in the untidy garden. The hollyhocks in particular had escaped their bed to riot in others. Between bites, the children described their adventures with the enthusiasm of explorers. Margaret listened with half an ear. Alasdair's request for her help had flattered her while making her heart ache at the same time. She had not changed anything in Gideon's house, the home he had shared with his first wife, whom he had loved dearly. To destroy the physical signs of her existence had seemed wrong.

****

Falstone wrote to Newcastle for samples of fabric and paint in the colors she recommended and hired several women from the nearest village to wash walls and polish the floors and furniture.

Margaret visited the manor with Janet and Isabelle, accompanied by a groom, to take measurements for the material needed for curtains and upholstery in each room. She permitted the girls to see if they could find anything useful in the attic and provided Janet with paper and a pencil for notes. Rummaging there entertained them while Margaret and the housekeeper took measurements. Janet confided later that searching for furnishings made her feel she was helping her uncle as well as Margaret. She had found a set of chinaware painted with bright flowers and some exotic bird, and a chest full of bed linens and blankets, most of them usable.

Guiltily, Margaret enjoyed the project. She also felt she was helping Alasdair and without any impropriety. They were never alone together, if one ignored that visit to Kirkland Grange, when the children had gone off to explore. But Mrs. Polk had been around, though not always present. And no one knew of that, and they never discussed anything not related to the children's education or the work on Falstone's house. While the latter had nothing to do with her role as governess, the subject was as impersonal as a conversation with the curate about some parish charity project.

Years ago, she and Alasdair had talked about everything: books they had read, amusing incidents, the failure of law and social customs to reflect the Bible's teachings, life. She missed those conversations and wished she had anyone to talk with about more than day-to-day matters. It could not be Alasdair. The major. Conversing as if they were friends would be a breach of their respective positions. She yearned to speak of her marriage as his one or two references to it suggested he did not understand how it had come about. Unsurprisingly: men seldom asked, *Why?* They were concerned solely with *what?* and *how?* as a rule. Whatever Rupert and Adam had told Alasdair probably misled him. But she could not tell Alasdair why she had married five years after he had left her behind. They were no longer on terms that allowed such personal disclosures as he had made clear when he turned aside her one tentative query about his military career. Renewal of their former relationship was not possible.

She could take meals with Falstone, the children, and Dorring and not outrage the conventions governing unmarried women. Discussing the latest news or of some facet of England's history was some compensation for the loss of their former ease. If she were not employed in the Hawkslowe household, they could once again be friends or even something closer. Widows were freer than unmarried girls; some took lovers. She sighed. Whatever might be acceptable in town, her own principles would prevent an illicit connection.

But somehow their friendship was coming to life again, like the shoots of some plant that had vanished over the winter. While he was busy with Scot Hall's affairs and his new property, he still made time to ride with the children and Margaret, as they were doing this morning a week or two after their inspection of the Grange. Margaret reveled in the sun's warmth, Athena's smooth paces, and the gorse blossoms' odd, sweet scent. It was almost at the end of its flowering, delayed by the late spring.

The major had not spoken much, except to answer several of Janet's and Colin's questions about the Romans' presence in Northumberland. Falstone had mentioned the traces of a Roman fort at Rochester several miles from Scot Hall. He promised they would visit the site some time while the weather was still favorable.

"And there's one sign of Rome's occupation even closer to Scot Hall. Their road runs by the eastern edge of your estate, Colin, all the way up to near Edinburgh."

Colin said, "That makes Latin lessons more interesting. More as if they're about real people."

Alasdair's smile was the one Margaret recalled from their youth.

The children rode a little ahead, the older two speculating about what life had been like in those distant days, Matthew full of questions. After lengthy meditation, Isabelle had only one: "Did the little girls have dolls and ponies? And almond pudding?"

While the four debated this point, Alasdair began, "Margaret…"

"Yes...?" She had almost called him Major Falstone, which seemed ridiculous when he had addressed her familiarly. But she could not use his given name, as he should not use hers.

"Archbold, the head groom, told me something troubling this morning. A groom who has kin in Bellingham visited them the other day. His mother asked if it were true that we had been acquainted years ago."

She glanced at him, stricken. "Oh, no."

"Oh, yes, I fear. We have not noised about our earlier relationship"—his voice spoke the word gingerly—"although I did confess to my brother that you were once Margaret Bettancourt. Budley might have heard, but if so, he would not have told anyone. It's not impossible Sebastian mentioned it to Elizabeth when they first married or shortly thereafter, perhaps to explain why I left home. I am surprised she recalled it, however."

"When she saw the inscription in Rambeau's *Pièces de clavecin*, I feared she would want to dismiss me, but she never even asked me about it." She hesitated. "Lady Hawkslowe has sometimes treated me as a confidante. Not long after I came here, she confided to me things she had better left unsaid to a virtual stranger. She may have thought any female would be sympathetic when she complained of her brother-in-law. I admit at first I did think you treated her rather harshly when I believed she was no worse than a silly, frivolous woman. I'm sorry I trusted her word and doubted you, Major."

"I am a major no more. You might call me 'Alasdair' when we are alone, as you used to do."

"And you might call me 'Margaret'?"

"As I have just done. I hope we can resume our friendship."

But not their love. They were both older, wiser, and that youthful blaze had been extinguished. "So do I, Alasdair."

Ahead, Matthew and Colin squabbled amicably. A few words drifted back.

"…army is good but nothing to compare to the Roman legions. They built roads and forts as they went…"

"I asked Archbold if he had heard any rumors about us. He had not, but as he pointed out, he might not. Anyone who knew him would know he'd not tolerate gossip concerning our family. He's set another of the grooms, Duncan Campbell, to pick up any talk in the ale house in the village. If Elizabeth mentioned the inscription to Harry Bradnam, he might remember hearing of our courtship. He's as sly and clever as a weasel, and either he or Paul might speak of it to make mischief during one of their jaunts."

"I wonder where they went and what they did on their rides. They're town beaux at heart, not country gentlemen. They could hardly have been visiting friends on all those occasions. I did not think about it until Janet told me the brothers were sometimes away overnight."

"Were they? I didn't know that," he said. "As I'm in the guest wing, I wouldn't hear them come in. I suppose they might have been visiting, er, female acquaintances, if I may suggest such a thing."

Margaret snorted in a thoroughly unladylike way. "You may. Alasdair, what are we to do about the gossip, if it spreads?"

Alasdair blew out a breath. "There is nothing we can do. Except to continue to 'be as strange and as well-bred as if'—well, as if we had never met before."

He was paraphrasing part of a speech from Congreve's popular play. They had read *The Way of the World* aloud once for her grandfather's amusement. Margaret remembered the quotation. The line ended "as if we were not married at all": inappropriate here.

Chapter 18

The writer of the letter had prudently included a return address on the outside, presumably in the hope a careless recipient would not toss it in the fire unread. Why would Attorney Isaiah Jelliffe of Harrison and Jelliffe, London, be writing now? Alasdair had met him when he delivered the duplicate of his brother's will and letter of instructions. That brief acquaintance told him that the man was busy and wasted no time on trivialities. After Sebastian's death, he had written a proper letter of condolence to Lady Hawkslowe and a separate letter, much warmer in tone, to Colin, assuring him of his continued service to the barony. He had added that Colin, Lord Hawkslowe, could trust his uncle Alastair, not because he was Colin's uncle, but because his own inquiries about Falstone showed him to be intelligent and honorable. Colin had let Alasdair read it, halfway between laughter and embarrassment.

"Perhaps he should not have investigated you, sir, but I believe he is devoted to our family's interests. And as his opinion is complimentary, I thought I would share it."

Alasdair laughed. "I think the better of him for doing so."

Colin's answering smile was rueful. "So do I." Colin had formed his own idea of his uncle Harry's qualifications to be guardian.

A letter from the baron's London attorney could not be good news. On breaking the seal and reading it—concise and mercifully lacking in legal jargon—he swore in a way which would have got him fined for profanity if it had come to a magistrate's attention.

At the estate office door, he shouted for a footman. When the man skidded to a halt in the passage, wide-eyed at the abrupt summons, Falstone issued curt orders.

"Have my valise packed. I will leave tomorrow morning. I'll be riding. Send a message to Twissell to attend me this afternoon. Ask Mistress MacGavin to see me at her earliest convenience." A fit horse should be able to make the journey in little more than six days. Trooper could do it, but Falstone would not push him to make it. Better to change horses along the way. In all, he should be gone about two weeks plus however long the legal business took. Not more than a day or two, he hoped.

****

Isaiah Jelliffe strongly recommended Falstone consult Gustav Miller and had even spoken with the man to ensure he would make time for Falstone immediately. Alasdair had been glad to take his advice.

The day following his arrival in town, after a quick visit to Jelliffe, he found himself ushered into Miller's office with no nonsense about needing an appointment. The attorney greeted him, waved him to an armchair, and grinned alarmingly. He had rather long, yellowing, almost equine teeth and a long, narrow face to match. In the heat of the office, he had removed his wig and tossed it onto a side table, revealing gray stubble. "This is what comes of the ignorant hiring the least expensive attorney they can find."

" 'This' being…?"

"Ah, I have leapt into the middle of things, Major Falstone. I understand Jelliffe informed you of Lady Hawkslowe's attempt to gain control of the children. This may sound more alarming than it is in reality. 'Tis one thing to be familiar with the law relating to land, conveyancing, tenancies, and inheritance, and quite another to understand the intricacies of other areas of law." He chuckled, holding up the notice of which Jelliffe had informed Falstone before dropping it on his cluttered desk as if it were dead vermin. "As you saw, Lady Hawkslowe's infant attorney has requested a writ of habeas corpus from the court of common pleas to have the children given into her care. I will submit our answer, but you need not worry."

Falstone had never found that phrase reassuring. "I rejoice that you are confident, sir, but I wish you will tell me why. While not lacking in courage, I hope, the prospect of any legal action is daunting to a layman."

Leaning back in his chair, Miller steepled his fingers, as happy as a mouse in a grain bin. "You must not be aware of the Tenures Abolition Act of 1660, which gave the father of minor children the right to appoint a guardian for them in the event of his own death."

"I suppose I had assumed he had a right to do so as I cannot imagine Obadiah Jelliffe would have written a will which was defective."

The lawyer inclined his head in acknowledgment. "Certainly not. You are therefore the testamentary guardian of the children. Now, if the mother had the children in her possession without your approval, you could file for a writ of habeas corpus and they would be returned to you in a trice because you are their guardian. But a court of common law cannot change the children's guardian, d'ye see?"

"So the court will not order them given to Elizabeth?"

"In a word, no. I believe the matter will end when the court rules that all they can do is confirm you are their guardian."

"There would be nothing more she could do?"

"She can petition the Court of Chancery, which has jurisdiction to change guardianship, if there is cause. However, from what you have told me, I doubt she and her family could afford to do so. Chancery is a court of equity, and equity, alas, does not come cheap. Still, it's well to be prepared for it. If she does take her case there, you will have to answer, which I will do if you wish me to serve the barony in this matter. Or I can refer you to a different solicitor if you prefer. I can recommend Seth Brigginshaw. He knows what he is about."

"As Jelliffe has sent me to you and I trust his judgement, I would prefer to retain you, Mr. Miller."

"Very good. Now, I have Lord Hawkslowe's will. I suggest you make your deposition now and assemble any other proof you have as to your brother's intentions. If we are ready, you may be spared having to visit London a second time."

"Will I not need to return for the proceedings?"

" 'Tis not a trial. All is done by documents. You will have to provide whatever evidence you have that he was of sound mind and meant you to be his children's custodian as well as their guardian."

"I have the letter he wrote asking me to sell out and come home. I can get statements from his doctor and Sir Hugh Montgomery, who witnessed to his will, as to Sebastian's competency."

"The doctor, excellent. Is Sir Hugh a credible witness?"

"He knew my brother for some years and has been a magistrate for almost as long."

"Excellent, indeed. They must both make their depositions. As a magistrate, he will know how it is to be done. Now, as there is no question that Lord Hawkslowe intended you to be their guardian, it seems to me that Lady Hawkslowe's best chance is to prove you unfit. There has come to be a sort of feeling that the best interests of the children should be given some weight. What can she allege of you to convince Chancery to transfer the guardianship?"

"I don't know," Alasdair said after some reflection. "This is unknown terrain for me."

"Come, come, Major. I suspect you know if only you think about it. Jelliffe instructed Lord Hawkslowe to write memorializing his reasons for appointing you. He did so, and Jelliffe sent me a copy knowing I would need it. It provides good support for your guardianship and spells out why the other uncles are unsuitable. I understand from Jelliffe his client left a copy to be given to Lady Hawkslowe after his death, which of itself was not a bad notion. But to have it given her at the reading of the will led to a painful scene, I understand."

"It did," Falstone agreed.

"Well, that's neither here nor there. Is there any proof of the brothers Bradnams' unfitness?"

Falstone explained the missing rent money.

"Excellent. You'll add that to your deposition, and we'll want a copy of the bank's letter. What can you allege you have done thus far in managing the estate? Have you engaged a tutor and governess for your nieces and nephews?"

"I have. Dorring tutored the young cousin of a fellow officer until the boy was ready to be sent to school. The lad liked him, and his father was pleased with his academic progress."

"You have a written reference for him?"

"Yes."

"It should be entered as evidence with the rest, assuming you do find yourself in the Court of Chancery. And the governess?"

"Mistress MacGavin is a widow of four-and-thirty."

"Over the age of being thought a temptation, then. Good. Her references?"

"I do not have one. She was not previously employed, having been married."

"Then what qualifications does she possess for the post?"

"She is a gentlewoman and is both sensible and well-educated."

Miller waited, shaggy gray eyebrows lifting inquiringly.

"I have known Mistress MacGavin for some years. Her grandfather and my father were friends." A sense that more was required caused Alasdair to add, "They both had an interest in stock breeding. Mistress Margaret Bettancourt, as she was then, and I met on a number of occasions before I bought my commission."

"Do I understand you have maintained this acquaintance ever since?"

"No." Explaining began to seem awkward. "I met her again by accident when I went to her brothers' fencing school to make a purchase."

"In trade," Miller muttered. "How did you come to hire her?"

"She had been instructing her older brother's children and some girls in the neighborhood, teaching both academic subjects and deportment, so she was not without experience."

"I wonder she would leave her family's home to take a position in Northumberland."

Alasdair's slight hesitation made the attorney's eyes sharpen. "Why did she?"

"Her older brother has several children. There was not really room for her." He saw at once that his evasion had been noted.

"Was she living with her family, Major? Or not?"

"The brother's family lives in the house adjoining the family business. Mistress MacGavin's younger brother lives above it, and so she moved to rooms there, too."

"Hrmpf! But she was willing to leave London for Northumberland?" The gray brows met over the bridge of the lawyer's nose. "A case in Chancery may seem unlikely, but if it does come to that, Lady Hawkslowe will have the right to pose you written questions, to, er, probe your defenses, as it were. I do not like to be ambushed."

"Mistress MacGavin's younger brother intends to marry soon, and Margaret, Mistress MacGavin, that is, felt that he and his bride would need the entire floor for their home. I gather there was some discussion of helping her pay for a lodging. Mistress MacGavin was qualified to be a governess, would need to move anyway, had grown up in County Durham not far from Newcastle, and I had not been able to find a suitable candidate. The other ladies I interviewed were too young and pretty"—not that Margaret was not—"or too timid or too severe. Some were better able to teach ladylike accomplishments than academic subjects. Hiring Margaret seemed an ideal solution."

Miller frowned over this explanation. "I see. Have you formed an opinion as to how she and the children are getting along?"

"From what I have observed, the arrangement is working very well. Janet and Isabelle like her and enjoy their lessons."

"Then your choice may scrape by, Falstone, particularly as she is an older female."

As if that unquestionably made her undesirable? Perhaps it was as well the attorney thought so.

Chapter 19

The day was perfect for a ride: clear, not too windy, and neither too warm nor too cold. Janet and Isabelle would already be downstairs: they loved their morning rides. The boys often rode in the afternoon.

Margaret had not known how much she had missed riding and the country until she came to Scot Hall. In town she had been so busy keeping house for her father and brothers that her previous life was only a fading dream. By the time she married, the joy of riding was forgotten. What a pity anyone had to live in London all year.

She pulled the casement shut and washed her face and hands in the water still remaining in the jug from last night rather than wait for warm water to be brought up. She would wait only to drink a cup of chocolate before dressing. Janet and Isabelle were sure to be ready before she was.

But the maid who brought her chocolate also brought news of a disaster. The kitchen maid who rose early to make up the fire found the flour barrel open and a mouse inside. She timidly woke the cook. Margaret's maid described Cook as being "in a taking," almost certainly an understatement.

"The dough that was left to rise overnight is baking now, and there will be porridge and eggs and ham, but maybe not very soon, as she's behind in her work because of it. But there won't no more fresh bread or rolls nor anything made with flour until fresh flour can be fetched from the village, and until the barrel's scrubbed and dry," the girl explained. "Tomorrow there'll be toast or French toast from today's bread."

"She hasn't simply scooped out the top layer?"

"No, ma'am. She's that particular, she won't abide vermin of any kind, no matter if it does cost to buy new. And she's told Mistress Stukeley and Mr. Graves the one who opened the barrel must be found and turned off, for it was shut tight when she went to bed."

Who would have thought their hard-bitten cook would have such a horror of mice?

"And Mr. Graves wants to speak with you about it as maybe you'll be able to settle her mind."

She scrambled into a sacque-back gown to speak first with the butler, then with Cook, who had to be coaxed out of her ire. The kitchen maid, thank goodness, had boiled eggs and made porridge and sent them up to the nursery.

And so by the time Margaret sat down to eat a hard-boiled egg and porridge, she was later than she should be and had had only one cup of tea. She would have to dress quickly.

Where was the maid? Her habit and shirt were on the bed, and the boots should have been on the floor. Could the girl have taken them to the scullery to be cleaned? She might be behind in her duties because of the "storm in a cream bowl" or more precisely, the furor in the flour bin. Margaret was hurrying toward the back stair, the quickest way of getting to the kitchen and servants' areas when she met Nan, coming from that direction.

"Ma'am, begging your pardon for being late, but I can't find your riding boots. I went down to see if they'd been taken for cleaning, though why anyone would, I don't know, when they were cleaned and polished up after your last ride and put away like always."

Margaret turned back. "They must be somewhere. Come, with two of us searching, we must be able to find them. I suppose the children hid them for a prank, not stopping to think it would delay their own ride."

"I never thought of that, mistress. Would they do such a thing?"

"Do you have no brothers and sisters, Nan?"

"I've a brother, but he was out in service when I was learning to walk. He's first footman to a rich merchant in Bristol now and means to be a butler someday."

"He's done well for himself. As you had no one to tease you as a child, I think we will find my boots under the bed."

"They're not here," the maid, on hands and knees, almost wailed a few minutes later. As she scrambled to her feet, she gave the coverlet's scalloped edge a twitch where it did not hang quite straight. "Mayhap they hid them in the nursery? We should look in their rooms and the school room and the nursery parlor. Then there's that big oak chest under the window at the end of the passage. After that—"

Margaret stopped listening as she stared at the expanse of quilt. Was it quite flat? She ran a hand over it. Then she flipped the bed cover up and groped under the mattress, pulling out a pair of boots.

"However did you think of looking there, ma'am?"

"The bed looked lumpy. Quick, I must change. The girls will regret having to wait, but it will teach them a lesson."

Nan lifted the gown over Margaret's head. She chewed her lower lip. "It mayn't have been the young misses, ma'am."

"What? Who, then? Surely not Colin or Matthew."

"When I come up to lay out your things, I saw Bessie turning the corner to the other wing. She's got no reason to be in this part of the house."

"Mayhap she was on some errand. You know things are all upside down because of the problem in the kitchen."

"Not she, ma'am. She's always been a sneaking, lazy, tale-bearing thing. I wish Lady Hawkslowe had taken her back to London."

"Did Bessie come from there?"

"Ay. She'd been with her ladyship's own family, I think."

Why would Elizabeth Hawkslowe bring a maid with her from her family's home, apart from her lady's maid? Surely a London maid would hesitate to remove from familiar surroundings. Nor was there a shortage of local young women to work as domestics. But Margaret had heard mutterings from Mistress Stukeley and Graves that Lady Hawkslowe had brought several servants with her on her marriage.

Nan had been thrown into confusion by the prank; she was all thumbs, taking twice as long as usual to help Margaret into her habit and boots.

"My crop and hat, and hurry. I don't want to keep the girls' horses standing any longer."

The footman on duty in the hall opened the door

for her, and she whisked through it to stop abruptly. Neither the girls nor their ponies were waiting. Neither was her horse. Her first thought was that they were now giggling in the stable yard. Could they have convinced the groom to aid and abet them and take her horse back to the stable as well?

"Edward, where are Miss Janet and Miss Isabelle?"

"They went riding with the groom, ma'am, seeing as you weren't to go."

"Who told you that?" A lump of foreboding grew in her stomach.

"Ackerley, ma'am."

"Ackerley? Which one is he?"

"He's the tall, burly one. Square face, don't talk much. You mayn't have seen him often. Before her ladyship and her brothers left, he was mostly their groom. Lady Hawkslowe asked to take him on several years ago. He'd worked in town for the Bradnams, but he hadn't enough to do there."

"Has he gone out with the girls much? Before I came?"

"Ay. Her ladyship trusted him, o'course, being as he'd worked for her family so long."

She stood frowning. "Did the girls like him? They weren't reluctant to go with him?" If her charges had been boys, she would have suspected they were playing a trick to escape her stricter supervision.

"He said you'd had Cook pack bottles of lemonade and some cakes and fruit, to make up for you not being able to go. He'd a pair of canvas bags behind his saddle." Edward's brows contracted, and his gaze turned inward. "Now I think on it, it's strange she'd pack food in sacks that were none too clean. And her all in a pother over the mouse, too."

"Do you know where they meant to ride?"

"They went off toward that rise to the east. I did hear Ackerley say something about a pleasant view. Which there would be from there, leastwise."

"Have my horse saddled as fast as you can, and tell Archbold I'll need a dependable groom with me. Two would be better. I'll be ready in five minutes. As fast as you can!" she snapped again when he gaped at her. Without waiting for him to reply, she ran up the stairs to her chamber.

When she came pelting down, joined leather pouches over her arm, her mount was waiting, with the head groom Archbold and a raw-boned Scot who had sometimes ridden with her and the girls.

"Young Edward says the girls went off with Ackerley, who claimed you weren't to go, having some ailment," Archbold said without greeting her.

"My boots were hidden. That's why I was late coming down. I may be wrong, but I suspect Ackerley of luring them away. Ackerley was Lady Hawkslowe's groom, wasn't he?" She asked this over her shoulder as she hastened to her mount.

"Howts!" Archbold exclaimed. "Ay, he was. I wondered he didn't go with her." He watched her curiously as she arranged the pouches over the pommel and strapped them in place.

He assisted her into the saddle, and he and Campbell mounted their own hacks.

"Edward overheard him mention riding east, to some rise. Do you know it?"

He nodded. "It has a view of the River Rede. It's by the old Roman road. Dere Street, it's called."

The road that ran by the estate's eastern edge. He read her expression.

"You'll be thinking Ackerley is up to mischief." It was not a question.

"What else can it be, when my boots were hidden? And there's the matter of the flour bin and the mouse. No one would admit to leaving it open, but why open it at all except to make trouble in the kitchen, which also made me later than I should have been in meeting the girls. Ackerley could not have hidden my riding boots because he'd have no excuse for being in any part of the house but the kitchen and servants' hall. He could not have escaped notice by another servant and would not know which room was mine. He must have had an accomplice. Nan saw Bessie near my chamber and says she is another of Lady Hawkslowe's servants."

"That way, is it? Ay, it would make sense. But what could they mean to do with the girls?"

"Major Falstone went to London because Lady Hawkslowe has gone to court to get custody of the children. She may have thought having the girls would strengthen her case."

Archbold grunted. "Campbell says you're a 'braw leddy for riding.' They won't go fast because of the little misses. We can catch them up."

For answer, Margaret spurred her horse. The others wouldn't be going above a trot. Janet was already a skilled horsewoman—horsegirl!—but Isabelle was not.

Trotting or cantering, they wound between the low hills that sloped down to meadows bordering the Rede east of Scot Hall. They did not speak. Margaret tried to guess how long Ackerley and the girls had been gone before the pursuers set out. She had not thought to look at the clock in the drawing room: anything from half an hour to an hour, she guessed.

"How far is the rise from Scot Hall?"

"A matter of three mile, or a bit less. We're near it. See the trees all along? 'Tis because of the river."

She would not have taken Isabelle on a ride of three miles and said so.

"Miss Isabelle's slow but a hardy rider all the same. Be as good as Miss Janet when she's older." He scowled. "She'd be a bit tired, but after food and a rest, she'd be ready to ride back. But I'd not expect she could go much farther."

Margaret considered this and recalled that she could have ridden for an hour or more when she was six and often had when she tagged along after her brothers. "Should we not be close to the hill, then?"

"Ay, and there it is." He jerked his head toward a tree-bordered knoll to their left. The rise itself was almost bare. There was no sign of the girls and the groom.

"Archbold, could they be on the other side?"

"They might be in the grove, as the sun's warm today, having a snap of food."

All three spurred their horses until they came near, then they slowed to a walk. Archbold rode up close beside her and said, "With your leave, mistress, Campbell and I will go first."

"Very well." She had never come this way while he likely knew the thicket well. She did not suppose for a second that there was any danger, but men always thought females needed protection. She loosened the straps on her pouches.

Chapter 20

Miller had been correct in his judgement that the court of common pleas would not change guardianship, but he did not advise assuming the matter would end there. Alasdair would arrange for the depositions of Montgomery and the doctor, and perhaps think of others whose affidavits might be useful. Nurse Sallows would probably have something to say about Elizabeth Hawkslowe's lack of care for her children. Ay, that was a thought. He would deal with all those details. As Miller said, "Best to be prepared." Falstone agreed.

He remained for the hearing and was relieved that the Bradnams and his sister-in-law were absent, their case presented only by their attorney. As soon after the judge's ruling as he could hire a mount, he rode north, feeling he had been away from Scot Hall too long. He made good speed on the first leg of the journey, though he had not left town until midafternoon.

The following days he rode steadily but without pushing himself or his hack too hard. He stopped briefly for meals and to rest his horse but put up for the night by eight or nine, allowing time for supper, a stroll to stretch his muscles and relax, and an early bed. He was eager to get home, but he had no need to ride until the end of twilight, nor did the hired horses have Trooper's endurance. Between riding and relief, he slept soundly at night.

He looked forward to the gathering of evidence and to seeing how Margaret and the children went on in his absence. Should he remove to Kirkland Grange to prevent any gossip, now that Elizabeth and her brothers were gone? The thought was unwelcome. He should be at Scot Hall for his nieces and nephews. But Attorney Miller's opinion of his living in the same house with Margaret was clear: she was a widow Alasdair had known for years and hired as a governess with no references. Anyone, said Miller, would assume the worst. Viewing the matter as a stranger would, Falstone conceded the point but remained reluctant to leave them with no man in the house but servants. Graves, Budley, and the footmen did not count.

Miller advised him to marry, to provide the children with an aunt, which would make it acceptable for him to live at Scot Hall.

"See if you can think of a suitable wife. You're of an age to need one, after all, and it would be best for the children."

Falstone wished he could turn back time.

In late morning of the seventh day, his heart lifted at the sight of Scot Hall. He was saddle-sore, but a hot meal and a hot bath would put him right. He wanted to see Margaret, though perhaps not until he had bathed, shaved, and put on fresh clothing. Few ladies would appreciate two days' growth of beard, not if the possessor of the beard kissed them. Was he thinking of kissing her? His brain stuttered. Anything between them had ended years ago. She had married, happily, by her brother Rupert's account. There was no going back. And now she was widowed.

He gave himself a shake. He was tired, he ached,

and he was hungry. He could not think about Margaret until he'd dealt with those things. Mayhap he could fit in a tankard of ale and perhaps a bun to eat with it while bathing. Tomorrow he would call upon Sir Hugh and the doctor to inform them that their depositions would be necessary. Once he had taken care of that business, he could approach Margaret and try to get a sense of her feelings. If he must marry—

His pleasant musings came to an abrupt end as he reached the house, meaning to go directly to the stable yard. Graves burst out of the door in a most unbutler-like manner, exclaiming, "Thank God you are returned, Major! Mistress MacGavin's gone after the little misses—"

Alasdair snapped, "Report!"

Graves took a deep breath. "She came downstairs for their morning ride, and they were gone with Ackerley. She suspected some plot because her boots had been hidden and went after them with Archbold and Campbell. Edward thought Ackerley, that was her ladyship's groom, meant to ride toward the rise by the old road."

Alasdair had gone to Hawkslowe House in London to reconnoiter, ostensibly to make sure the house was being well maintained. The knocker was absent from the door, so Lady Hawkslowe and her brothers were presumably not in residence. They would not have needed to be in town to bring their case to court; Elizabeth's sister did not live so very far from London, after all.

The butler, a longtime retainer of the Hawkslowes, showed no sign that he knew the true state of affairs between Lady Hawkslowe and the late Lord

Hawkslowe's brother and executor. "Mr. Harry Bradnam arrived unexpectedly, but I understand her ladyship had already gone on to Viscount Bagshot's seat. We had no notice of the family coming, or the house would have been prepared. The letter must have gone astray in the post," the butler opined. "But Mr. Bradnam departed yesterday morning before going on to a house party."

The Bradnam men did spend their summers visiting one or another of their friends with country homes to escape their lodgings in town, except when they came for a long stay at Scot Hall. London tended to be hot, dusty, and smelly in the warmer months. More comfortable to sponge on their relatives and acquaintances. Cheaper, too.

"What of Mr. Paul Bradnam?"

"I believe Mr. Paul escorted Lady Hawkslowe to the viscount's estate."

Alasdair had not attached much importance to the male Bradnams' nonappearance at the hearing, though he was surprised Elizabeth had not been present in court to try to wring sympathy from the judge. Now that he knew of Ackerley luring the girls away, the brothers' absence took on significance. She and Paul must be together and likely not with Lady Bagshot.

Did they think to get possession of the girls, then convince the Court of Chancery that she, rather than a bachelor uncle they hardly knew, should be their guardian? Elizabeth could then milk the estate for as many expenses for them as possible without actually incurring them.

Dismissing those speculations, he demanded of Graves, "How long since?"

"Mayhap two hours, sir."

So long and they had not returned.

"Does Dorring know?"

"Yes, sir. He is not a strong rider, however. Lord Hawkslowe, Colin, Lord Hawkslowe, that is, wanted to go in search of the young ladies, but Mr. Dorring would not let him. He said we must trust Archbold and Campbell and of course Mistress MacGavin to find them. Though I meant to have the other grooms go out to look if they were not back soon. We did not know what else to do for the best."

"I'll take a fresh horse and go after them. Send a note to the magistrate near Otterburn to inform him the children may have been abducted. He won't be able to do anything until we find them, but he should be prepared." He signaled Trooper to trot and made for the stable.

He had finished saddling and bridling Sebastian's roan gelding before a groom came running to perform the task Falstone had done thousands of times during his military service.

Chapter 21

"Gone!" Archbold's low, furious voice left Margaret in no doubt that he would have cursed if he had been alone or only with a man. She rode forward to join him. Two ponies with sidesaddles were loosely tethered in a little clear space between the trees and the foot of the rise. Ackerley's hack was missing.

Campbell said, "I'll be having a look at the road."

The children had been abducted. No one needed to say it aloud.

The Scots groom was back in a trice. "No sign of them. Horses stood a whiles. Sh—droppin's. A few spilt aits."

"Too much to hope for. They'll be away in a carriage."

Margaret said, "They can't be much ahead of us." When Alasdair had brought her to Scot Hall, their course from the Great North Road had been roundabout. Northumberland was not well provided with roads as understood farther south. "Route" would more nearly describe the way they had come. Some sections might have been drovers' roads. They had left the Great North Road at Newcastle, turning west. By then she had been too weary and travel sore to pay much attention. At Corbridge, they had turned north again on the old Roman road that continued north past Otterburn to Scot Hall's eastern boundary, whence their way led west by a less traveled track along the southern edge of the Scot Hall lands.

"Riding, we'll catch them easy." Archbold turned his horse toward the road. Campbell and Margaret followed. Emerging from the trees and undergrowth, the head groom turned his horse's head south and said, "Mistress MacGavin, will you send word to Squire Hart, the magistrate? The stable lad knows where he lives a bit out of Otterburn. I reckon we'll bring Ackerley there within a few hours. Built a fine road, the Romans did. Even so, they wouldn't make much better time than on most English roads, seeing as how the Romans aren't keeping it up. They might make four miles an hour."

"I will. But are you sure they would go south?"

"They'd be going to London, surely? I'd change teams in Corbridge. Then I'd be on my way to Newcastle, if I was them, to pick up the Great North Road. Myself, I might go straight south toward York instead of going east. But they'd have to know the way."

"There's no chance they went north?"

"Nothing much to the north and west but Scotland. Not much of anything along the way, neither, after Rochester. A few holdings and more sheep and cattle than people."

South was the most likely, then. "Ackerley would know I'd be coming after them, and that we'd guess they'd go to Newcastle, however."

The head groom shook his head. "Ackerley don't know you well, ma'am. Might have judged you by other ladies. Most would sit and dither. Maybe have a fit of the vapors. Mr. Dorring's a good fellow, but I don't know as he'd do much except to send to the magistrate."

"A good enough dominie, they say," Campbell interjected, "but not a braw lad. No disrespect intended," he added tardily.

"So with the major not here, they might have got as far as Corbridge or even Newcastle before anyone did anything to the point." She bit her lip. "Campbell can go to the magistrate while you and I follow them, Archbold."

Archbold cleared his throat. "Mayhap you should go to Squire Hart with one of the grooms. Magistrate would put more faith in what you could tell him, belike." Seeing her expression, he said, "Or it might be well if one of us, as it might be you, ma'am, went north a ways to make sure they aren't playing some trick on us. Most like they've gone south, and either Campbell and I can get the lasses back or I can send him for the nearest magistrate."

Men. They would try to protect a lady. Still, they could not waste more time discussing it. "Very well."

"If you don't mind me saying, Mistress MacGavin, go canny. You don't want to come up upon them of a sudden, if they did go north. They can't be far ahead of us. The road would shake the coach apart if they went faster than a walk. When you've gone three or four miles, best you turn back and let them know at Scot Hall what's toward. Have the stable boy take the ponies back."

"I will." She was off on a wild goose chase. "Archbold, are you armed?"

"Ay, ma'am. So's Campbell. It seemed best."

"I quite agree." It would be useless to caution them

or give them advice, and indeed Margaret did not know what she could advise. "Be careful."

"Ay." With a quick bob of each head, the men rode south.

She urged the mare to canter. If she did catch sight of a coach in the distance, she would follow more slowly.

The road ran arrow-straight between fields with occasional groves or lines of trees as windbreaks. If she had come upon anyone else, she would have asked if they'd seen a coach passing. Once or twice she saw someone in a field or by a cottage too far off to make it worthwhile to leave the road to question them.

The road angled east to meet the River Rede. Hoofprints of horses and cattle and wheel marks proved it was easily forded. The water did not come as high as her stirrup.

She had hoped to pass a village where she might find someone to ask if they had seen a coach go by, but Horsley, the first village after the ford, was too far off the road. The Roman road drew away from the Rede again before Rochester as well and left behind most of the signs of civilization. The road ran parallel to a stream at a little distance, though the water was visible between the low, rolling hills.

She walked Athena between stretches of trotting or cantering. How far had she come? By the sun's position, it was midmorning, though she had not taken note of the time when they set out. She might have been gone an hour and certainly had ridden more than five miles. She should turn back. Ackerley taking the girls to Newcastle or south anyway made sense. Taking them north didn't. Yet the obvious route was where they'd be pursued. If the plan was to hold them for ransom, where would they be most in danger of being found: in a more densely populated area or up here where farms and villages were few?

Overhead, the sky went on forever. She watered the mare when she could. Even when the road parted from the river for a time, a spring or burn was never far away.

The way passed a grove, which grew up close beside the road. Had it been there when the Roman army marched along it? One would think it would lead to ambush by unfriendly locals. Had she been a Roman commander, she would have cleared the trees away. But then, the Romans had been gone a long time; the wood might have grown up since. She reached the edge and saw farm buildings. Then the road made a turn eastward at one of the few curves in the old track. No more than a quarter mile away, a coach pulled by four horses lumbered on at a walk, with another horse tethered behind.

Two men sat on the box. It might not be the one bearing Janet, Isabelle, and their abductor. But who else could it be when carriages were far more rare in this sparsely settled countryside than carts or wagons? She reined in her own mount to let them get farther ahead. To the right, the ground rose, utterly bare. To the left, the ground was flat and empty. She would be visible if anyone glanced back after she left the wood's shelter.

She watched, grateful for the trees' shade from the noonday sun, as the coach dwindled in the distance and the road turned north once more. No cover there, either, as far as she could see. Would they be looking for pursuit? Mayhap not. They might assume they'd be expected to go south as indeed Archbold had. She pushed her mare to a canter until she came to the turn. She could still see the carriage ahead and dropped back to a trot. If she kept some distance behind them, she might escape notice.

The hills closed in on either side. This was not the almost feminine undulating country found farther south. The road stretched on, moorland and rough slopes and ridges. Were Janet and Isabelle frightened? Getting tired and fidgety? Had Ackerley or his confederates really provided food and drink? She estimated they had traveled about ten miles. Difficult to be certain how long ago she had parted from Archbold and Campbell: two hours or more? They should have returned to Scot Hall long since unless they had pressed on, as she had.

How much farther would the coach go? More important, how long could she follow them? They must have some stopping place in mind, but it was difficult to imagine where in this bleak land. The occasional scatterings of trees were behind them. The moorland with its gorse and grass stretched on like a lumpy ocean, continuing until a range of higher hills rose before her on either side of the road.

Following the coach presented no challenge. It bumped along no faster than a horse could walk. She need only keep it in sight. The coachman and the other man on the box were unlikely to look back. Even if one of them did, what could they do, given she was out of range of whatever weapon they might have?

On sighting the coach, her first thought had been to follow it. The question now was, what could she do to rescue Isabelle and Janet? She had somehow assumed one or the other of the grooms would come after her when they found no trace of the abductors on the road to Newcastle. If they had searched for an hour, which should have given them enough time to catch up with a slow-moving vehicle, it would yet have taken them an hour to ride back to the rise. Had she been in charge, at that point, she would have sent Campbell to take the road north.

The groom would be at least two hours behind her and on a horse which had already been ridden fast. Thank goodness, the late baron had kept a number of mounts and had not sold them when his illness made it impossible for him to ride. But even if Campbell or Archbold broke off pursuit at the earliest time and returned to Scot Hall for a fresh horse, he would still be far behind her and would still have to cover the distance she had come. The groom would be faster if he knew the road. As she did not, she would not have attempted a gallop even on the long straight stretches.

Now she had found the coach, she prayed Archbold or Campbell was on his way, and that quickly. She would need assistance to rescue the girls. The thought of holding up the coach like a highwayman made her smile. Unfortunately, that was the idea's sole value. In reality such a daring attempt would not go well, with two men on the box and another in the coach, one or more likely to be armed. Someone must be riding inside because Margaret could not imagine Janet would allow herself and her little sister to be taken away unless they were under guard. With the carriage moving slowly, she would have been out the door with Isabelle at the first opportunity. Unless they were bound? That did not bear thinking of.

The question was, what could she do? All

depended on what the abductors did: whether they stopped at some holding or continued on. She had seen no indication of current habitation since they passed the farm by the wood. A few piles of stones here or there might be the ruins of a hut, and once in the distance she saw one still standing, though it appeared to be derelict.

They could push on another six or eight hours or more, until the light failed, with stops to water, feed, and rest the horses. They were sure to come to some town or village in that time, weren't they? Granted, Northumberland was less populated than County Durham, but it wasn't the end of the world. Not quite.

If they did keep going and she continued to follow them—there was no "if" about that—when they finally halted, how would she get Janet and Isabelle away? She might find a magistrate who would intervene, but she could not count on it.

She could make no plan until they stopped, as they would have to do, for their team would tire eventually, even at a walk. Her mount was still fresh, but her own situation presented some problems. She was many miles from Scot Hall and unaccompanied and might be as much an object of suspicion as the coach with its burden of two little girls in the charge of a rough-looking groom.

Well, if she were on her own, she would take whatever action seemed to be required.

Chapter 22

The roan was fresh and eager for a gallop. Alasdair had ridden Pasha on some of his estate errands, but during his stay in London, the horse had been exercised by grooms, who had the other horses to exercise also. It was a pity Pasha had not been trained to sidesaddle; Margaret would have been able to ride him.

He had more urgent things to think of. If he were abducting the children, he would not do so without a coach. Take them away on their ponies? Impossible. Janet was sensible for her age and would refuse to go. Certainly, it would be impossible for them to ride as far as Newcastle. From what Graves had told him, Margaret and the grooms could not be far behind Ackerley and the children. They would travel faster on horseback. But if they had prevented the kidnapping, they should be on their way back to Scot Hall by now, and he would encounter them. If they had failed...where were they?

The rise by the Roman road was in sight. It was lucky that the Bradnams had to carry out this piece of villainy in Northumberland rather than in the south, where more towns, highways, and posting inns would have made escape easier. In some parts of the country, zigzagging on lanes and byways to avoid the main route might be a clever way of eluding pursuit for someone on horseback and if time were no object. Doing so

221

here? Falstone smiled grimly. Northumberland's scant population meant fewer roads. Off the post road, it would be hard or impossible to change horses and difficult to find lodging, particularly with children reluctant to be taken away. They might happen upon a cottage where they could buy bread and cheese.

The Great North Road was about thirty miles away. In theory, if the coach could travel at five miles an hour, they could reach it in six hours. On some roads in the south, this would be a reasonable calculation. In Northumberland, such a pace was unlikely. Where were Archbold, Campbell, and Margaret now?

He approached the rise from the south and circled to the road to look for traces of a coach. No sign of one except a pile of droppings and wheel marks of something other than a wagon in the grass edging the road. Archbold and Campbell should have caught up with them by now. They would take the children up before them to bring them back. Margaret was with them. Her presence would be reassuring to the girls, especially Isabelle. She should be safe enough with Archbold. Falstone did not believe the head groom would have set out without a pistol. But in any exchange of fire, someone might be wounded or killed. If 'twere Margaret—

He could not think of that terrifying possibility now. Where were they? Ackerley would have at least one accomplice, the coachman. Could the pursuers have been captured? Or murdered if Ackerley lost his head? Falstone swore. The idea was ridiculous: Ackerley might not hesitate to kill the grooms (and Margaret if she were with them), but would the coachman be willing to help? Unlikely. One man needing to reload between shots could hardly prevail against two men, one of them armed, and a woman. Archbold would see to it Margaret stayed well back from any confrontation so she at least would escape. At worst, coach and grooms were at a stand. He could remedy that dilemma. He turned Pasha's head to the south.

If he could rely on the butler's estimates of when Ackerley had ridden off with the girls and when Margaret and the others had followed, the coach could hardly have been more than a few miles down the road when they caught up with the abductors.

Hoofbeats on the road interrupted his contemplation of alternatives and all the things that might have gone wrong. The approaching horse slowed to a canter before Alasdair recognized the red-haired groom.

"Campbell!"

"Major, it's glad I am to see you come back. You'll have heard the lasses are taken?"

"Ay. Where's Mistress MacGavin? And Archbold?"

"Archbold sent me to tell Mistress MacGavin and Mr. Graves there was no sign of a coach, though we went near ten mile. They can't have gone so far. Archbold is riding to Magistrate Hart for advice, though Hart's as useless as an udder on a bull. Thank the Lord you've come."

"Mistress MacGavin's not at Scot Hall, unless she arrived after I left. Was she with you and Archbold?"

"Not after we reached the road, sir. Archbold thought she should not be with us when we caught the coach. He said she should ride north a bit in case they'd gone that way. No danger for her there, o' course,

223

because why would they? Then she'd go back to the Hall."

Falstone saw his own thought reflected in Campbell's face the same moment it occurred.

If Ackerley and the coach were not on the road to the south, they must be going north. There were drovers' roads, but could a coach get to them from here? In his youth, he had always ridden, and besides, he'd been gone for years, so he was not as familiar with the tracks a carriage could travel. Perhaps the coach had gone north a short distance on the Roman road to the Rede's ford, then traveled south to Otterburn. From there they could—probably—make their way to Elsdon, where they could take to a drove road. "Otterburn," he began.

"I stoppit in there to ask after a coach, them being rare in these parts, while Mr. Archbold went on farther south. Nae sign of them."

It would have been too easy. "Go to the house. I'll ride after Mistress MacGavin. Very likely she's gone farther than she meant to."

"And if she's returned, sir?"

"Take a fresh mount and come after me. And if she hasn't…" The roan was dancing with impatience. So, though not visibly, was Falstone. "…if she hasn't, the same."

Archbold and Campbell's assumption the abductors had taken the road south had made sense. At Corbridge, Dere Street crossed the Stanegate, the east-west Roman road that followed Hadrian's Wall west to Carlisle. At Corbridge, the abductors could get a fresh team at the Angel Inn and continue south on Dere Street to York, or go west to Carlisle where they could take another Roman road south, or east to Newcastle and the Great North Road.

He might have chosen to go to Carlisle, where pursuit was less likely. But if they'd gone north, there had been a reason. He wished he knew what it was.

He had ridden Dere Street in his youth. It wasn't likely to have changed in fifteen years when it had already existed for over a thousand. At a gallop, Pasha's long stride ate up the first mile and a half. Crossing the Rede, Falstone kept Pasha to a sedate walk for a mile before going to a trot.

He grudged the necessity to let Pasha stand or walk, but he would not risk injury to the animal. Margaret was a sensible woman, the daughter of a soldier, raised by her grandfather, as long-headed a man as Alasdair had ever met. If she was following the coach, she would stay out of sight. Unless she had come upon them unexpectedly and been captured. Or she might now be lying dead in a ditch, something he could not bear to think of.

Chapter 23

The road rose gently to a long ridge, and the carriage disappeared over the crest. For the first time, Margaret hesitated. If they had stopped on the other side to rest the horses, her sudden appearance would be disastrous. In this desolate place far from any manor, a gentlewoman's presence would be inexplicable. But she could not remain where she was, like a rabbit cowering in its burrow. If she were a man, she could dismount and creep up through the gorse to peer over the ridge. Being a female, if she dismounted, she would have to take the time to lengthen the stirrup as far as it would go, use it to remount, then shorten the stirrup leather once she was in the saddle, an awkward business. If she rode up just far enough to see over the crest, they were unlikely to notice her. If they had pulled up for some reason, she would back her horse.

The coach had not halted. Not far down the hill, it was disappearing around a curve. She followed slowly. Out here, she could scarcely lose them. From where she was, she could not see the road again until it met a little stream at a right angle to the ridge. They would be wise to water the horses and let them rest before starting up the hill on the other side. She approached the curve cautiously. If they did stop at the stream and one of them happened to look back, he would see her once she rounded the bend. Yet she had to take the chance. The only real risk was that Ackerley would pursue her on his horse, in which case she would turn and flee. She was willing to gamble on his hack not being a match for Athena. His mount had not been moving as fast as hers, tethered as it was to the back of the coach, but Ackerley was big and would ride heavy. However, she did not want to alert them to pursuit as seeing her would. If she rode only as far as the curve without rounding it, they might not notice her. She edged Athena forward...

...in time to see them enter the ford. The carriage came to a shuddering halt in the narrow, steep-banked channel, spanning the little burn at its bottom, the horses on the uphill side, the front wheels still in the water. The driver cracked his whip, causing the team to strain forward without moving the coach an inch. The breeze blew the men's raised voices to her, although she was unable to make out the words, and probably just as well. She saw the coachman shrug and shake his head. The other man, on the side away from her, clambered down from the box. As he went to the lead horses' heads to encourage them to pull, she saw how big the fellow was. Ackerley, for a certainty. Then were Isabelle and Janet tied up or dosed with laudanum to keep them from struggling to escape?

A man's head emerged from the window on the side toward her and called something up to the coachman. It might be Paul or Harry Bradnam: impossible to be sure from this distance and angle. Margaret raised her hands and pulled back on the reins gently to urge Athena to back before the man turned to respond. He might be unlikely to glance up the hill, but she would take no chance. She rode back up to the ridge. With only her horse's head and neck showing above the crest, she hoped not to be conspicuous if one of the men did look their way.

In the distance, she heard shouting again, and smiled. The coachman left his seat to assist Ackerley. Margaret did not rate their chances of success highly. A stagecoach would have its passengers get out to lighten the load. Here the weight of the two girls would scarcely make a difference. The bank rose too sharply from the stream. The coach would not be moving soon. Perhaps with a team of six horses they might have made it or perhaps not.

More shouting. Whyever had they thought a carriage could travel this way? From certain signs, she suspected it was most often used by drovers. The loud voices died away.

They would have to send someone for a team of draft horses. No doubt the messenger would be Ackerley. If he rode south to the farm two or three miles back, he could not fail to see her. The hillocky moorland behind her lacked a rise high enough to conceal her.

Heart pounding, she took a deep breath of the heather and gorse-scented air. How fortunate Falstone had remembered she was a skilled rider and provided her a horse that was fast as well as reliable. That thoughtfulness was like his younger self. When Ackerley started up the track, she would turn and gallop for the farm by the wood to ask them for help.

Ackerley abandoned his effort to encourage the team. Margaret imagined he was uttering a sulfurous oath or two. He stalked back to the coach and was hidden behind it. The man inside emerged, jumping down into the shallow water, probably cursing the ruin of his boots. He paused to speak to someone within. The girls? When he stamped to the near bank, Ackerley appeared from the far side of the coach and followed him.

The inside passenger's over-elaborate clothing convinced her he was Paul Bradnam, and who else was likely to be with Ackerley, if not one of the brothers? The men stood talking, Bradnam increasingly agitated judging by his gestures, Ackerley stolid. The latter jerked his head toward the other side of the ford. Bradnam paced back and forth on the bank, pausing occasionally to say something to the groom. At last he returned to Ackerley's side. A quick exchange and a nod from Bradnam followed. Ackerley untethered his horse and mounted.

She would easily outdistance the groom, who would hardly attempt a gallop up the slope from the coach anyway. She would reach the farm with enough time to explain matters to the people there. She stroked Athena's neck, murmuring, "We must ride like the wind, I fear."

And the farm might not have a pair of cart horses or oxen, or their animals might not be immediately available, or the farmer might be persuaded to delay providing them. If they could not or would not help her, she could ride to Rochester to summon aid. Assuming the farm did have draft animals, it would take time to get them back to the coach and harnessed.

Margaret commenced backing Athena again, hoping to be out of sight before Ackerley turned toward the ridge. But before the crest cut off her sight of him, he nudged his horse into the burn, paused to let it drink, then rode across. Once up the bank, the way was less steep.

Margaret heaved a sigh of relief. She had not wanted to let the coach and the children in it out of her sight. She could not rescue them by herself, but at least she could be nearby. How far would Ackerley have to ride to get help? A good, long way if she were lucky. One of the Scot Hall grooms must catch up soon.

Bradnam stood on the bank, watching Ackerley's progress up the hill. His attention snapped back to the coach when a face appeared in the window. Janet! Margaret knew that pale oval face despite the distance. Then her sight of the child was blocked as Paul Bradnam strode to the carriage. His rigid posture hinted at some tense exchange, which evidently displeased him. Then he pulled the door open, took Isabelle in his arms, and carried her to the near bank. Before he could turn back to assist Janet, the girl hopped down and splashed through the water, holding her petticoat up to keep it dry.

Janet did not care to accept help from her captor. Margaret guessed what one or both of the girls needed and filled in the dialogue for herself as the little drama played out before her eyes.

"I need the necessary," Isabelle would have wailed.

"You should have asked sooner."

"It is not something one cares to mention to a gentleman, Uncle Paul." Margaret knew the tone Janet would use.

"Why didn't you take advantage of our last stop?"

Isabelle, sulkily: "I didn't need to then."

Janet held out her hand. "Come, Izzy. There are bushes."

"They're too short."

"We'll go up the hill a little way to those clumps of gorse. See, it is almost as tall as you and quite dense. Aren't the flowers pretty? If they weren't all spiny, we could gather some."

Bradnam's stance and gestures betokened the desperation of a man unused to dealing with children's problems. Margaret had never seen him with his nieces when they weren't on their best behavior in a setting with someone else available to deal with their needs.

No doubt he agreed. "Yes, yes, if you insist. Don't go any farther, and don't be long. If I have to chase you, I'll be angry."

"It will take whatever time it takes, sir, if you know what I mean." Janet would be speaking in her prim governess voice.

The coachman, now sitting on the bank, took his pipe from his mouth and turned his head to look at Bradnam. "Not as if there's anywhere for 'em to go, sir," Margaret imagined him saying.

Janet took Isabelle's hand and led her away from the coach as fast as the younger girl could trot. In a few more steps they were lost to sight behind the curve of the hill. Would Bradnam pursue them if they went beyond the nearest brush? He watched them for a moment before returning to the bank. They might already have stopped. If they had shown any sign of following the road up the hill, he would surely have stopped them by shouting or by running after them. Would they attempt to escape if he were inattentive to their actions? She might ride down as far as the curve to see if she could espy them.

Bradnam prowled back and forth, casting glances in the direction the girls had gone, perhaps watching their progress. Reassured by whatever he saw, his gaze roved over the hill across the brook. Pulling a flask from his pocket, he drank. If the girls took their time and he drank more, dare she attempt a rescue? With Ackerley and his mount gone, what could Paul do to stop them? If she could get to the children before Paul Bradnam, she could snatch them away. The men could not pursue on foot, and it would take time to unhitch one of the horses, which would be difficult for Bradnam to ride without a saddle if he had never lived in the country. He might not ever have ridden bareback.

She could take Isabelle on what passed for her lap. Getting Janet up behind her would be more challenging. Unless Margaret removed her foot from the stirrup so the girl could use it and swing herself up behind with a hand from Margaret? Janet was tall for her age and strong. But if she couldn't…

For the hundredth time, she looked back the way she had come, knowing she would see nothing but a narrow road running almost straight through the moor.

She blinked at the roan horse cantering toward the ridge. It looked like the one Alasdair sometimes rode, but he was in London. Archbold or Campbell? Either would do. Margaret waved her arm over her head and gestured toward the north. The rider saw her and spurred his mount.

Alasdair!

Chapter 24

He knew he was on the scent. A few miles back, at Featherwood, he had met a girl on the road and questioned her. Earlier, when she had been concealed in the grove, eating pilfered biscuits, she had seen a coach go by, then a lady on a horse.

"I never seen the like," she said. "The lady, she stops where the road turns and waits a bit afore going on." She wasn't as clear about how long ago it had been. She'd finished her biscuits and sat for a while wondering why a coach and a lady would be going this way. Then she'd done a char or two: turned the cheeses aging on their shelf and put away the churn that had been drying in the sun. Alasdair estimated he had the advantage. Pasha was still fresh, and the coach would be traveling slowly. But where the devil were they going? As he recalled, the old road led only to the border with Scotland.

The way ran level for a distance before it passed between ranges of hills. The track rose and fell gently. Ahead a steeper hill led to a ridge—

Where a mounted figure was waving wildly. Margaret! Pasha leapt forward at a touch of his heels. He slowed to a trot at the base of the hill, and she rode down to meet him partway.

She was already speaking when she came up to him. "The coach is at a standstill in a stream. The team

233

can't pull it up the hill on the other side. The girls are out of the coach or were when I saw you coming."

An excellent, concise report. "How many?"

"The coachman and Paul Bradnam. I'm sure it's he. Ackerley rode across the stream and up the hill, to get help, I assume."

He gave Pasha the office to move on. They paused before the ridge. "Where were the men?"

"The driver was sitting by the stream, and Bradnam was standing nearby. He's probably looking up the hill—not in our direction," she added. "There's a turn to the left down to the ford. The girls were walking up behind the coach. I suspect they needed some gorse bushes on the hillside. If I know Janet, she and Isabelle won't go back to the coach in a hurry."

Alasdair spared a smile for that remark, sure Margaret was correct. Janet would be a handful when she was older.

"I'll go down and tell them to come to you. You may keep watch from the crest."

At the top, they reined in. He saw no sign of the girls or Bradnam, but the coachman was puffing on his pipe, staring at the water. He blew a meditative cloud of smoke, very much at his ease. The watercourse was the beginning of the River Coquet, if Falstone recalled his local geography. Ah, and Bradnam was getting into the coach. Afraid to sit on the bank and get his coat and breeches dirty.

He gave Margaret a nod. "Wait here. I expect Campbell in a while, but I don't want to risk Ackerley coming back before we have the children."

"I hope you don't intend to confront Bradnam, Alasdair."

"That would be foolish. I'll reconnoiter and send the girls up to you."

She hesitated, frowning a little, then said, "Be careful."

"I don't apprehend much danger from a coachman and Bradnam." He started Pasha down the track.

Margaret calculated. If he went no farther than the curve which cut off her view of where the girls went, he should be safe. The coachman had left his musket on the coach. Would Bradnam have a pistol? That bend might be within range of a pistol shot. Not necessarily within effective range, however. And all depended upon whether a man on the low ground happened to look up the road, how good his weapon was, his skill, and the size of the ball. He would be firing uphill, which would also affect accuracy.

Impossible to know what the hypothetical pistol was like. A well-crafted pistol with a rifled barrel could hit the mark at greater range than the common smooth bore flintlocks. At a guess, Bradnam would not be experienced with a pistol: enough skill to hit a highwayman from a few feet away, mayhap. A shot at a greater distance would call for practice.

The road below meandered its way to the curve where Alasdair would halt. He was as safe as anyone could be in a world where a falling roof tile could be fatal. If the girls saw him, they would run to him for rescue. That might attract Bradnam's attention, but Alasdair and his nieces need only retreat around the bend. On foot, Bradnam and the driver could do nothing. By the time they gained the higher ground, Janet would be mounted behind her, Alasdair could take Isabelle up, and they could trot away, with no danger to anyone.

Down by the stream, Paul Bradnam jumped down from the coach, pistol in hand, and strode toward the rear.

How could he have seen Alasdair at the top of the rise? Thinking a curse she had heard occasionally from her brothers, Margaret shifted the reins to her left hand as cavalrymen rode and loosened the strap on the right saddle bag before her. She urged Athena to a canter.

Chapter 25

Alasdair held his horse to a walk. He had ridden this way once or twice many years ago, before he met Margaret and County Durham had become more alluring than Scotland. The men below were unlikely to hear his approach, with the wind against him, and he might frighten the children, coming upon them suddenly.

This was no longer the Romans' typical arrow-like road but wandered slightly, though if he looked back, he would still be able to see Margaret at the top. He resisted the impulse. The track straightened. Not far ahead, it angled slightly to the left and rounded the bulge in the hillside Margaret had mentioned. Once there, he might perhaps see the girls.

At the bend, he paused to study the terrain. The coachman was still on the bank, wisps of pipe smoke rising to be shredded by the breeze. The coach would not be easy to pull out even with the help of draft horses or oxen, given the steepness of the bank. Not his problem, thank God.

Past the bulge, the road ran down to twist to the left just above the approach to the ford. The girls might be hidden among the clumps of gorse. Falstone's head swiveled toward a flash of color glimpsed out of the corner of his eye, to see Paul Bradnam striding toward the slope by the road's turn down to the stream.

Bradnam scanned the hillside, uttering a sharp "Janet! Isabelle! Come out at once or I'll come—" breaking off as he saw Falstone. He raised the pistol he had been holding by his side.

Alastair ducked, grabbing for his own weapon as the horse shied in alarm at his sudden movement. Trooper would have stood like a statue. At least Pasha had not bolted, he reflected grimly as he drew the pistol from its holster on the horse's off side.

The report came from behind and to his left, echoed almost at the same moment by a second, more distant, one. Pasha reared, coming down as Falstone raised his pistol. A fraction of Alasdair's brain acknowledged he had not been hit by either ball even as he took note that Bradnam was lying motionless down the road.

Impossible to tell how badly injured he was: his claret-red coat might conceal a wound. Campbell or Archbold must have pushed his horse hard to be so close on his heels. When Falstone turned his head to thank the groom, he saw a sight that would be etched in his memory to his dying day. Margaret sat her horse, arm still outstretched, pistol in hand. The familiar sharp reek of burnt powder carried to him on the drifting smoke from the muzzle.

By the stream, the coachman had jumped up, stood stock-still for a moment, then ran stumbling for the coach. "Halt!" Falstone shouted, in a voice he'd used to good effect on smugglers, rioters, and his own men. Whether he had been heard or would have been obeyed they might never know, for the man tripped on the brushy ground and did not move.

Margaret, white-faced, lowered her arm.

"Margaret? Are you well?"

"Yes, thank you." Her voice was higher than usual.

"I think you should withdraw around the shoulder of the hill," he said. She had not broken yet, but he had seen a new recruit do so the first time he had killed his man. In a crowd, where someone else could have fired the fatal shot, one might escape the shock or guilt. Margaret had courage and fortitude in excess, but he would not be surprised if she were overcome at having shot a man she knew, dead or not. "You might reholster your weapon now."

The coachman was still down and almost visibly cringing. Alasdair stole another look at Margaret. She was still holding the pistol.

"I prefer to keep it by me for the moment, Alasdair. In case of further trouble, you know."

She spoke as calmly as if she were saying, I prefer to have a few coins in my pocket so I can buy a posy or a piece of gingerbread.

She must have been more unnerved than she appeared. "But now that you have discharged it, it's useless until reloaded."

Margaret said, "No, it isn't. It fires three shots."

She transferred the pistol to her left hand, still holding the reins, and deftly rotated the next barrel into position.

Falstone had heard of pistols with more than one barrel but had never seen an example. This one was about the size of a pocket pistol. "I would like to take a better look at that when we have more time. At the moment, I must see how badly Bradnam is wounded. Do you think the girls will reveal themselves if you call them?"

"Yes. They will need comforting. As for Bradnam, I think he is likely dead. I will ride down with you. You will want to tie up the coachman or at least take charge of any weapons he has."

Falstone rather thought she needed comfort, too, even if she were not aware of it, but he believed she would not give way until later. He hoped she would not have nightmares. He did not return his own weapon to its holster, not sure how he felt to have been a bystander rather than a combatant.

Margaret began calling as they walked their horses down toward Bradnam.

Nearly to where Bradnam lay (and it was strange he should not have moved at all, unless he had fainted), two heads popped up out of the gorse. Then Janet and Isabelle pelted toward them, crying, "Uncle Alasdair! Mistress MacGavin!"

She was off her mare before Alasdair could dismount. Margaret crouched as they reached her and enfolded them in her arms despite the pistol still in her hand. Isabelle began to sob. Janet, her arms around Margaret and her little sister, looked up at him. "Our uncle Paul said he was taking us to Mama. We didn't want to go, but Ackerley tossed Isabelle into the coach, and Uncle Paul said she would be frightened without me if I didn't go. And I thought if I did, we could escape."

"I understand. I will want to hear about it, but right now, I must deal with Mr. Bradnam and the coachman. Will you stay here with M—Mistress MacGavin while I do so?"

"Yes, sir." She did not look down the road toward Bradnam.

He and Margaret traded glances, hers inquiring, which he interpreted as meaning *Are you sure you can manage the coachman on your own?* Her doubt was not quite flattering, but on the other hand, she had saved his life or at the very least, prevented his being wounded. His own said, *I was a dragoon.* She gave a minuscule smile and nodded, agreeing her place was with the children now.

As he rode down the hill, Janet was speaking earnestly to Margaret, with brief interruptions from Isabelle. His nieces needed to spill out the story to someone immediately. He would ask them to repeat it later.

A glance at the coachman assured Falstone the fellow was still hugging the ground. Bradnam did not move. His pistol lay under his hand, discharged. Falstone dismounted and approached slowly. The shot had taken him almost in the center of the chest, and the wound was not bleeding. Dead as salt cod. He nudged the pistol out from under the flaccid hand.

The *crack!* of a shot from behind took him unawares. Falstone spun and crouched, raising his pistol. Pasha had jumped sideways but had not bolted. Up the road, his eyes met nothing but Margaret and the children. Margaret was waving her left arm over her head. She gestured in the direction of the coach.

On the ground, nearer the coach than he had been, the coachman was clutching his thigh. Falstone stared back at Margaret before starting down the hill. He had not seen so much combat since that fight with the smugglers down in Kent. "Seen" was certainly the correct word here when he had yet to get off a shot. Damme, Margaret was a veritable Amazon or

Boadicea.

The end of any action consisted of rounding up the prisoners and dealing with the wounded and dead. He used the coachman's neckcloth to bandage his wound, which was not likely to be fatal unless it mortified, the ball having gone through the muscle without hitting either bone or artery. "Should you feel like attempting escape," he told the man, "know that the lady has another ball ready to fire."

The coachman groaned. "I'll not chance it, sir. Lost my head for a moment, I did, not being used to such doings."

Nevertheless, Falstone climbed up to the box to remove the musket before turning his attention to Paul Bradnam's carcass. A minute of action, an hour of aftermath: very like his military service.

Margaret had taken the children far enough around the bend that they could not see Bradnam or the driver or the necessary preparations. Alasdair found rope among the carriage's hoard of useful tools and equipment.

The question was, how to transport Bradnam and their prisoner. Unhitch two of the coach horses, one to carry the body, the other for the coachman. Getting the burly coachman onto the horse would be difficult unless the coach step could serve as a mounting block.

A shout from the top of the ridge, a Scots-burred "Major!" hailed him. Duncan Campbell had come.

They lashed Bradnam's mortal remains over a coach horse. Falstone gave silent thanks for the groom's arrival: hoisting the driver onto the horse without help would have been challenging. The fellow could scarcely walk, even after a generous swallow of brandy from the coach, but thought he could ride. Without Campbell, Falstone might have had to leave the driver until he could return with a cart. In the same circumstances, he himself would choose to wait for a wagon in the hope Ackerley would return before it came, or with the idea that as soon as Falstone and the rest were out of sight, he could limp over to the horses, unhitch one, and make his escape.

What was the penalty for a servant who participated in an abduction at his master's bidding? He would say he did not know it was kidnapping; he had been told they were to take the girls to their mama. The counterargument would be that Ackerley had brought them to a point well away from the house, they had no governess or maid with them, and not even a change of clothing. But perhaps he would be willing to testify against the Bradnam brothers, which might earn him a lighter sentence.

But first they had to find a magistrate. Featherwood lay about three miles back. Falstone would inquire there, hoping Sir Hugh would be the nearest. They needed food and drink as well.

Isabelle was leaning against him, asleep, before they reached the farm. Even Janet, who was riding behind Margaret with her arms wound tight around her waist, looked wan. Margaret...looked like her dear self, though with a hint of tension around her eyes. Campbell led the drooping coachman's horse and the one bearing Bradnam by halters improvised from rope. The other two coach horses must await Ackerley or someone sent from Featherwood or dispatched by the magistrate. There was little hope of returning with men in time to capture Ackerley, alack.

He and Margaret needed to talk, but they would require privacy for that discussion. Perhaps it would be best to wait until Margaret had recovered from the shock of having killed a man though she appeared unmoved now. Not the behavior one expected of a gently bred female. Yet if she had not disabled the driver, he might have reached his musket. While he was relieved to be alive, of course, he did not know how he felt about owing his life to a woman, even Margaret. Maybe particularly Margaret. Alasdair put that thought aside for the moment. Definitely their conversation must wait until he had had time to sort out his thoughts.

Chapter 26

As Alasdair helped Janet down, Margaret steeled herself to dismount, hoping her knees would not fold. Take her foot from the stirrup, free her right leg from the pommel, and spring to the ground. Before she could complete the last maneuver, he reached up to her waist and lifted her off the saddle, surprising her with his strength. Alasdair was broad-shouldered, but she was no sprite. He did not release her at once, for which she was grateful. Her suspicion had been correct; her knees felt no more substantial than syllabub. Isabelle stared around with eyes as big as guineas. Campbell helped the coachman off his mount to stand leaning white-faced against the horse.

A small crowd had already collected, murmuring like bees: a pair of young boys, a maidservant, a lanky fellow with a scythe, an old man who had left his place on a bench by the door to stare at them as at a Punch and Judy show. Where had all these people been when she rode past earlier? The farmer's wife came out, wiping her hands on her apron. How were they to explain who they were and what they were doing with a wounded man and a corpse?

"Mistress, I am Major Alasdair Falstone. My nephew is Lord Hawkslowe of Scot Hall, near Otterburn."

Her eyes opened wide to think of a lord's kin not

six feet from her.

"My nieces were abducted this morning, and their governess, a groom, and I went in pursuit. As you see, we have retrieved them"—all eyes went to the coach horse with its burden and the driver with a stained neckcloth around his thigh—"and we now need to find the closest magistrate. Do you know if that's Sir Hugh Montgomery, near Rochester?"

"Likely you need food and drink first," she retorted, with a nod toward the girls. "Joe, fetch the master."

The scytheman ducked his head, laid down his tool, and took off at a run.

"Dick and Billy, take the horses to the stable and see to them. And mind you don't meddle with what's on them." The younger boy took the rope lead of the unburdened coach horse while the older lad hesitated briefly at the one bearing Paul Bradnam's remains before taking its rope. The old man grunted something and took the reins of Pasha, Athena, and Campbell's hack.

"Come along inside now. There's ale and barley water or tea for the ladies, and bread and butter and cheese…"

Margaret lost the thread of what the woman was saying as she led them inside. She only began to revive when she was sipping tea at the long table in the kitchen after seeing Janet and Isabelle served with barley water sweetened with honey. Campbell and the coachman were drinking ale on the bench outside the kitchen door.

"Lizzie, close your gob. You've seen gentry afore. Go help your sister weed the neeps." The young girl who had been sitting on a stool scrambled down and trudged to the door, though she cast a wistful look in their direction.

When the grizzled farmer arrived, they had to repeat their story.

"Ay, you'll want Sir Hugh Montgomery, a mite south of Rochester. Being from the north yourself, you'll ken magistrates are not thick on the ground." The farmer thought a moment and said, "I'll send one o' my men and a wagon with you. Your prisoner and t'other can ride in the back, and Miss Janet could ride on the bench with Charlie. 'Twould be easier than riding behind the lady." They were glad to accept the offer.

Margaret dreaded remounting, but when Alasdair laced his hands to make a step for her and she rested her hand on his hard shoulder to steady herself, her heart thrilled to the touch. She only wished she were not so tired in mind and body. Any other time, she would have reveled in the sensation.

The excitement when they reached Montgomery's manor rivaled that at Featherwood. Sir Hugh was a few years older than Alasdair, neither heavy nor lean, with a sharp-eyed, humorous face. From his sun-browned complexion, he spent a great deal of time outdoors. After speaking with Alasdair, he gave terse instructions to his butler before going to arrange for the removal of Bradnam's body and the coachman's detention.

They followed the butler into the house, where the housekeeper attempted to take Margaret, Janet, and Isabelle to a bedchamber to be plied with tea and lemonade and to lie down to compose their nerves.

Falstone said, "Mistress MacGavin should stay. She is made of sterner stuff than most ladies and has a backbone of iron. She played a major part in the pursuit and rescue. And I think Janet's testimony would also be helpful."

Margaret suggested that Isabelle needed a nap but perhaps should not be left alone. The child made a mute appeal to her which Margaret could not have refused, had the housekeeper not enticed Isabelle with the promise of kittens to play with in the kitchen, and milk and singing hinnies. Whether it was the prospect of kittens or the cakes, the child went happily.

The butler settled them in the magistrate's study to wait. Sitting with Janet on a well-padded settee in the room's comfortable warmth, Margaret's tension began to ebb. The only words spoken were Alasdair's "All will be well."

Montgomery returned, followed by the butler carrying a tea tray and a maid bearing a second tray with a jug and mugs.

"Ma'am, would you pour for yourself and Miss Janet? We men will drink ale."

The latter statement apparently included Campbell, standing by the door like a proper servant.

"Certainly, Sir Hugh." Best to be sedate and governess-like. Margaret had had no qualms at the time about shooting Paul Bradnam, and there was no way to conceal her actions, but they would be sure to outrage the magistrate's male sentiments. She couldn't even be sure how Alasdair felt, in spite of the warmth in his eyes when he helped her dismount.

"Very well, then. Now, Major Falstone, would you describe the crime?"

"You'll understand that the Bradnams were not pleased by the change in guardianship."

The magistrate's suppressed snort indicated he knew enough of the Bradnams and the late Lord Hawkslowe's reasons for the alteration to understand.

Falstone began by summing up the Bradnams' attempt to change the guardianship, which might have been only a ruse to lure him away. "On returning, I learned the girls had been taken. Mistress MacGavin should describe for you how the abduction was managed."

"Ma'am?"

Margaret explained the trick that allowed Ackerley to take the girls riding, and how she and the Scot Hall grooms had gone in search of them. "I think Janet should tell you her part of the story, sir."

"If you think it not too painful for the child, Mistress MacGavin, and her guardian has no objections."

"Janet, do you think you can tell how you and Isabelle came to be taken away from Scot Hall?" Margaret had heard a confused account of the children's abduction. Falstone had not.

The girl was still pale but straightened her back. "Yes, Uncle Alasdair." She slid a glance at Margaret, who nodded encouragingly.

"Young lady, please proceed."

Janet's voice did not falter, beginning with how the maid Bessie told them Margaret could not accompany them that day, but Ackerley would. "My sister and I do not like Ackerley, and if we had not already been dressed for riding and our ponies saddled and at the door, we might have refused to go without our governess. But Ackerley said Mistress MacGavin would follow if she felt better soon."

"The road is Dere Street," Falstone interpolated.

"I know it well."

"We rode to the rise, but instead of going up, Ackerley said we should go into the grove at its foot. Isabelle wanted to see from the top of the hill at once, and I thought it would be chilly because the trees and brush are thick and we would be out of the sun. Ackerley said we'd go up the hill next, but he was sure we'd want to see a hedgehog that has her den in the thicket, and her babies."

In other circumstances Margaret might have been amused to imagine Ackerley's attempt to wheedle the children. He had seemed like a dour man and could not have had much experience with little ones.

"Isabelle wanted to see the hedgehog babies. There was no discouraging her, though I said we mustn't stay long in the shade as she tends to catch colds. He led us in farther than I expected, almost to the other side of the spinney. I told him Mama and Papa never let us ride close to the road."

Janet's hands had been clasped in her lap. Now she began to pick at the skin at the edges of her fingernails. Margaret reached over and covered her hands with one of her own.

Janet gave her a slight, troubled smile. "Ackerley took hold of Isabelle's reins and led her right out of the grove onto the road. I had to follow. I didn't know what else to do. There was a coach and Uncle Paul. He came toward us and told us to come along because our mother had sent for us. I said we had been told nothing of this, and why wouldn't he have brought the coach to the house. Mama would not have sent for us without having Nurse pack our clothing, which we would need if we were to travel all the way to Kent.

"Uncle Paul told me not to argue. Ackerley opened the door and lifted Isabelle in. Uncle Paul told me to dismount and get in. I didn't know what to do. I knew we shouldn't be taken away without Uncle Alasdair agreeing, but Isabelle was in the coach and crying. I thought if I went with her, I could get her away as soon as we stopped."

"Janet, you did well, and there is nothing to fear now." An empty reassurance, Margaret knew, when the girl's uncle had abducted the children and they had witnessed their governess shoot Paul Bradnam. The world must seem a very unsafe place.

Falstone spoke. "If you hadn't gone willingly, Ackerley would have tossed you in. You did the only thing you could in the circumstances, and if you had got away yourself, Isabelle would have been terrified to be alone. Fortunately, Mistress MacGavin and I and Campbell were close behind you."

Janet gave a little nod. "Ackerley took our ponies back into the wood. After that, we only stopped twice to water the horses, but there was no chance to run away with Uncle Paul in the coach. Then we came to that brook the coach couldn't ford."

"The Coquet, I think," Falstone explained.

"By then, Isabelle needed a—a privy. I was trying to think of how to slip away with Isabelle, but there weren't enough gorse bushes to hide us while we escaped. And we stayed away such a time that Uncle Paul called us and then walked up the hill to find us. And Mistress MacGavin and Uncle Alasdair came."

Falstone took up the tale. "Neither Bradnam nor the driver was aware of our presence up the road.

Neither of us could see the girls, though Mistress MacGavin had seen them leave the coach. I came around a curve in the road hoping to send them up to her and instead found Bradnam with his pistol in his hand." Alasdair paused.

He would be thinking how to explain Bradnam's death.

"You did not see Bradnam start up the hill after your nieces?"

"No. A bend cut off my view. When I rounded it, I was no more than five-and-twenty paces from him."

"Major, I find myself baffled," Sir Hugh began.

Janet said, "He wanted us to come down. I think he believed the gun would frighten us into obeying."

"Thank you, Miss Janet."

"Then he must have heard my approach or caught sight of me out of the corner of his eye. He turned and raised his weapon."

"You had drawn yours before riding down the hill, Major?"

Margaret heard chagrin in Alasdair's voice when he admitted, "I had not. I did not expect private life to be as dangerous as army life."

"And yet you were able to shoot him and suffered no injury yourself. Well done, Major."

Falstone shook his head. "I cannot take credit. Mistress MacGavin saw Bradnam walk up the road and came after me. Her shot saved me, as I could not draw my own pistol in time."

As Sir Hugh was momentarily speechless, Margaret hurried to speak. "I could see Mr. Bradnam leave the coach with a pistol because I had a clear line of sight from the crest. I rode down to join Major

Falstone and was already holding my pistol when I saw Mr. Bradnam take aim at the major."

Montgomery studied her for an endless moment before transferring his gaze to the major. At last, he turned back to Margaret.

" 'Twas very brave, ma'am. I hope any governess I employed would do as much. If I had a daughter." He paused. "If I were married and had a daughter."

The stress of the day must be affecting her, for she found herself replying, "I hope you would employ a governess for your daughter whether you were married or not."

For a moment, Sir Hugh appeared to have swallowed a frog. He cleared his throat. "Ah. Yes. Just so."

She stole a glance at Alasdair. His face was impassive, but his eyes glinted with amusement. Had she really spoken of the magistrate having a hypothetical illegitimate daughter? She had. Perhaps he assumed she meant if he were a widower? That stunned expression suggested otherwise. Perhaps that was a good thing, if it distracted him from Alasdair's disclosure that she had shot Bradnam.

Sir Hugh said dryly, "I believe I was unaware that governesses are now accomplished marksmen. Or markswomen."

She was not entirely sure he was joking. "My late husband was a gunsmith, sir, and taught me to shoot."

The magistrate's face cleared. "Ah, that explains how you happened to have a pistol, then, I suppose."

"He made it especially for me as a model for a ladies' pistol. I thought it sensible to bring it when we learned of the abduction."

"I would very much like to see it, ma'am."

"I would be pleased to show it to you. 'Tis in the saddle bag on my horse's off side. The one on the near side holds the flask of powder, pouches for flints and ball, and a few necessary tools."

The magistrate asked Campbell to bring it in.

"A handsome piece," he said, examining it. "Very plain for a lady's weapon."

"My husband said some men wanted ornamentation and he would oblige as a favor, but he preferred weapons stripped to their essential nature: accurate, reliable, comfortable in the hand, and deadly. Some engraving on the metal parts, the butt polished to a sheen, but an efficient tool, not an accessory." Her stepson favored the more elaborate French and Italian style of decoration. Perhaps it was fortunate for the sake of his business, as he was not the gunsmith his father had been.

" 'Tis well balanced, despite the weight of the additional barrels. Three barrels, two shots fired. The barrels are rifled?"

"They are, sir. He thought the grooves greatly improved accuracy, essential when the barrel is shorter than usual."

"Apparently he was correct, for your ball is in Bradnam's heart. At what distance were you when you fired?"

"About fifty feet, I think."

"More like sixty," Falstone said. "Thank God, Bradnam was so intent upon me that he cannot have noticed Margaret come up behind me."

Montgomery listened, asked questions, and took notes. Finally he was satisfied.

The butler reported that the coachman's wound had been cleaned and dressed. "Will you wish to remain while I question the fellow?" Sir Hugh asked Falstone. "You'll want him held for the next assizes, of course."

A long moment passed before Alasdair said, "I believe the driver did no more than what his employers told him to do. Paul Bradnam should certainly have been charged, had he lived, and I would have hoped the coachman would testify against him. I don't particularly care for him to be charged, but it would be helpful if you would have him make a sworn statement of all he knows of the abduction."

"Certainly. It would be needed for the inquest, as he may not be able to attend. Shall we say, on Thursday at ten in the morning, which makes it three days from now, but it's too late to count today. We'll hold it in the inn at Rochester."

"Can we be sure the coroner will be available?"

"He will." The magistrate grinned like a rogue. "He's my cousin, and he loves inquests."

"Will you also arrange for the coachman's care if I leave funds for the purpose? If he's not to be charged, he'll need money to travel when he's healed. Probably back to London—I assume he's in the Bradnams' employ."

"Ay." Sir Hugh frowned as he pulled out his pocket watch. "Will you stay the night as my guests? 'Tis already near six of the clock."

"Thank you, but I think we must return to Scot Hall as soon as possible. They will be worrying about the children."

"I cannot send a lady and two children off on horseback after such an experience. You, Campbell, tell my butler to have supper set out while my coach readied. As quick as can be, man. Supper will only be cold meats and pickle and bread and butter and mayhap a few kickshaws, and by the time we've eaten it, the coach will be at the door." As the groom hurried out, Sir Hugh pointed out, "With the children, you could not travel faster by horse than by carriage. Will it be convenient for my driver and horses to rest overnight at Scot Hall? 'Twould be full dark before they could return."

"By all means, and thank you for lending them. It would be best for Mistress MacGavin and the children."

Beside her, Janet stirred, annoyed at being lumped with Isabelle, probably. Margaret murmured her thanks. Bless Sir Hugh! She was as wrung out as an old dish clout, and Janet's pallid face told her that the girl was exhausted but too proud to show it.

As the magistrate saw them to his coach, Falstone said, "The only thing that I find bewildering is why Bradnam would choose to go to Scotland with my nieces. Well, that and if he meant to do so, why he did not first find out if a coach could pass that way?"

"As to the latter, it's been my observation that felons are often stupid, or if not, made so uneasy by their crime that they act unwisely. He very nearly succeeded in his aim. The border with Scotland runs along the top of the slope on the other side of the Coquet." He raised his eyebrows at Falstone's perplexed expression. Margaret's own must be equally blank. "You have not spent much time in Scotland, have you, Major?"

"I visited friends there often as a youth. Not since I left home, however."

"Scots law is not English law. If Bradnam went there with his nieces, and better yet with a copy of the will naming him their guardian, he would almost certainly be appointed their guardian. The children would have to remain in Scotland, because this side of the border, your guardianship would be recognized. I don't know how the legal tangle would be resolved."

Would Lady Hawkslowe be willing to live in Scotland? Margaret found it hard to believe.

"Paul Bradnam was not named their guardian in the original will. His older brother Harry was."

"Well, all may become clear when I question the coachman, and I look to see you on Thursday, and you, too, of course, Mistress MacGavin."

Chapter 27

Two tedious hours later, Sir Hugh's old traveling coach rolled into the Scot Hall stable yard, Alasdair and Campbell riding beside it and Athena tethered behind. Archbold out-distanced the undergroom who came running to take their horses. Margaret saw him approach Falstone and speak. But she needed to wake Isabelle who had slept almost the whole way. By the time Sir Hugh's coachman helped them down, Archbold and Campbell had retreated to the stable. Alasdair picked Isabelle up and carried her into the house, adding to Janet, "I would that all my dragoons had your fortitude." His eyes sought out Margaret's, conveying the same message.

The boys had not gone to bed and were in the nursery parlor with Dorring, Graves informed them.

Alasdair paused on his way to the stairs with his burden, who had fallen asleep again in his arms. "If you are not bound straight for your bed, Mistress MacGavin, perhaps you would come to the nursery with me? I imagine Colin and Matthew will not sleep until they know their sisters and you are safe."

She would like nothing better than to fall into her bed and not show herself until morning, but weary as she was in body, her mind was buzzing. She could not stop castigating herself for letting the girls be taken in spite of knowing she could not have prevented it, given the efforts made to delay her. She would not be able to sleep soon or peacefully. Alasdair might have been killed.

"Of course I'll go. They must be terribly worried." She put her arm around Janet. "Do you want to go straight to bed? You must be exhausted."

"I will come see my brothers, too, Mistress MacGavin. I'm not a baby."

"No, you are not. You were very clever to take Isabelle up the hill to get away."

With the first animation she had shown in some time, Janet giggled. "Isabelle really needed to relieve herself. So did I," she whispered.

Falstone left Isabelle in Sallie's charge, the nurse exclaiming and clucking and whispering endearments to the child, who woke enough to mutter, "Is it time to get up?"

As they trudged to the children's parlor, Margaret exclaimed, "Oh! Shouldn't Bessie be detained? If she's still here?"

Alasdair said, "She is. Nan told Graves Bessie had caused your delay, and he gave orders she was not to be allowed to leave. She could hardly escape on foot, anyway. Graves had her locked in her room. She did not share one with another of the maids, I'm told, being Lady Hawkslowe's pet. I'll take her before our local magistrate in the morning. Margaret, will you come to give evidence?"

"Yes, if you wish, but Nan should do so as well. She saw the woman near my chamber, where as I understand it, she had no business to be."

When Falstone opened the door, the boys and Dorring came to their feet like Jacks-in-the-box. Seeing

Janet, they broke into grins.

"I knew you'd save them, as soon as I heard you had come home, Uncle Alasdair." Colin made a belated bow to Margaret. He came forward and gave Janet a gentle buffet on the shoulder. "I wish I'd been with you."

"If you and Matthew had been with us, we would have been home the sooner. Uncle Paul"—her voice faltered on the name—"would have left us by the side of the road after ten minutes of your squabbling."

Matthew said, "I'd have kicked him in the shins."

"Dorring, have the boys had something to eat since supper? The troops sleep better after a meal, and Master Matthew is ready to go to bed."

"No, I'm not." He yawned widely and blinked.

"Ay, Major. They've—we've—had biscuits and chocolate. Lord Hawkslowe and Master Matthew won't starve until breakfast."

"But what happened?" Colin demanded. "Is Isabelle all right?"

"By now, Nurse Sallows has tucked her into bed. Both your sisters did well today. Now it's time for you to retire, too. Explanations can wait until tomorrow."

"Uncle Paul is dead," Janet stated.

Silence followed this bald announcement.

"If he stole you, I'm glad."

"Did you shoot him, Uncle Alasdair?" Matthew demanded, the bloodthirsty little brute.

"Explanations tomorrow. Troops dismissed."

Matthew heaved a sigh, and Colin grinned. "Yes, sir, Major. Come, Matt."

"Dorring, you look half dead. Get your rest tonight. There will be more to deal with in the morning."

When the tutor was gone, Margaret stood looking at Alasdair, too exhausted in body and mind to move.

"Margaret, thank you. There's more to say, but it must await a better time. I own I am too tired to think, and you are drooping with fatigue. Come, I'll walk you to your chamber."

While curious as to what more there might be to discuss, she was glad to leave it for now. She suppressed any tendency to hope.

****

The magistrate nearest Scot Hall, a red-faced, paunchy man whose waistcoat buttons were strained to their utmost, heard their evidence with his left foot propped on a cushioned stool. Alasdair had not expected a different outcome even if the fellow had not been suffering an attack of the gout.

"Hmm. I heard some nonsense about an abduction from Hawkslowe's groom. Sounded like a Banbury story to me, but if you tell me it's true, I must believe you, Falstone. Still, the matter's in Sir Hugh's hands. Don't know what you expect me to do with the wench. Hidin' a pair o' boots is no crime, 'less it's in the course o' stealing them. Makin' a mess in the kitchen? No evidence she did it, and if she did, what's it matter? Gives the scullery maid something to do."

He ignored Margaret and Nan, sitting silent and demure after having related the previous morning's events, and the maid, Bessie, white-faced and trembling by the desk. Falstone suspected Margaret's gaze at her hands clasped in her lap concealed indignation at the man's dismissal of their accounts.

"She was an accomplice in the abduction. I have no doubt the coachman will testify to her involvement. I ask that you keep her in custody until the coachman has given his deposition. And if she chooses to testify against the Bradnams, so much the better."

The magistrate agreed: holding the woman made no work for him, and he disapproved of dishonest servants.

"Or if she is willing to make a deposition regarding her actions and those of her accomplices…"

The maid looked up. "If I was to tell what I know, sir, what good would it do me?" she asked cautiously.

"I want those who instigated the abduction of my nieces punished, one way or another. That is more important than seeing their tools hanged or transported." No jury was likely to find her guilty of doing as her employer ordered, and jurymen were notoriously reluctant to convict for minor offenses. But most people feared the slow, harsh process of the law. While waiting months in custody for the next assizes, a suspect might die of jail fever or some other illness.

"Then I will, sir."

"I've no one to take down a confession at the moment, and the arthritis in my hands makes it impossible for me to write more than my name or a word or two."

Falstone said, "I write a legible hand. If you've paper, ink, and a quill, I will write out what she has to tell us and make a copy, too."

The magistrate snorted. More work for him, and his dinner would be delayed.

****

The whole family and several servants attended the inquest on Paul Bradnam's death. Alasdair Falstone had innocently supposed their party would consist of himself, Margaret, Archbold, Campbell, and Janet. Margaret could have told him he was mistaken.

At supper the evening before the inquest, Colin's casual assumption he would be going brought the matter to the fore.

"There is no need for you to testify," Falstone said, "as you have no independent knowledge of the events."

"Janet and Isabelle are my sisters, and as Lord Hawkslowe, I should be familiar with legal matters like inquests, and who knows when there may be another?"

The major conceded the point. Then Matthew said, "They're my sisters, too." He gazed hopefully at Alasdair, a puppy begging for a treat.

Colin scowled at him. "If you come with us, you'll have to sit and be quiet."

"I can do that."

"And not complain of being tired or bored or hungry."

Matthew drew himself up in his chair. "I'm not a baby."

"Margaret—Mistress MacGavin—?"

"Neither am I," Isabelle interjected.

"I think Matthew might be permitted to attend, but if he does, Mr. Dorring should come in case it's necessary for Matthew to leave the room."

"Agreed."

Colin and Matthew exchanged grins.

"I want to go, too. I was there, Matthew wasn't." Before Margaret could protest that Isabelle was too young and would be tired and out of sorts, Isabelle added, lower lip trembling, "What if you don't come back? I'd never see you again." She sniffled, not very convincingly.

"Isabelle, I fear you are a minx." Falstone's eyes sought Margaret's.

She sighed. "If Isabelle comes, the nursery maid had best come, too."

"The coach will be full with Mistress MacGavin, Dorring, the nursery maid, Isabelle, Matthew, and Janet. Colin, or should I call you Hawkslowe? We will ride."

"Please call me Colin, Uncle. At least when we are informal."

"I will ride, too. To give the passengers more room," Margaret said. Five in a coach and two of them young children, would not make for a peaceful journey. She hugged to herself the understanding twinkle in Alasdair's eyes.

"I will, too," Janet offered. "With four in the coach, it will be easier for Isabelle and Matthew to nap on the way home. If they should be tired," she added kindly.

The girl would prefer not to be squeezed in with her younger siblings who were likely to be excited and fidgety on the outbound journey and probably cross by the end of the inquest. Margaret fully sympathized. Smiling, she arched her eyebrows at Alasdair.

"Very well, but mind, anyone who is not ready will be left behind."

****

Margaret's testimony proved less of an ordeal than she had anticipated, perhaps because Sir Hugh had primed his cousin the coroner beforehand. She had expected surprise and disapproval of her skill with a pistol. However, the coroner's questioning brought out details of how she had assisted her gunsmith husband both in polishing the metal and wood parts of his guns and in testing the small ones intended for ladies. The jury, composed of farmers and men in trade and business, understood a woman helping in her husband's work. It was laudable, by George!

They heard about her pursuit on the less likely route and how she had persisted in spite of possible danger to herself. When they heard she had shot Paul Bradnam before he could shoot Major Falstone, who had not time to draw his own pistol, there were approving nods and an audible mutter of "Served him right."

The coachman, still confined to bed with his wound, had recovered sufficiently to make a statement, which Sir Hugh Montgomery had written out and read at the inquest. His evidence answered several puzzling questions. Sir Hugh had been correct. Taking the children into Scotland was intended to change their guardian without going through the Court of Chancery. Harry and Elizabeth were waiting in Jedburgh, some twenty miles from the border. Or had been waiting, for by now they must be aware their plans had miscarried. The Bradnams had bought a small property near Edinburgh where the girls and their mother and uncles would live. The coachman knew no more than that.

Margaret suspected that once Lady Hawkslowe had the children and money for their maintenance, she and her brothers would be off to London, leaving the children to the care of a governess, nurse, and servants.

The inquest ended with no surprises, and the driver's deposition cleared up one additional point. Paul Bradnam had scouted the coach's route on horseback and had no difficulty fording the stream. He had failed to take into account that a coach, even with four horses, was an entirely different matter, as the coachman pointed out in his statement. He himself had known nothing of their route before he found himself driving it. Margaret intercepted Sir Hugh's cynical glance at Alasdair and had no difficulty interpreting it as *I told you felons were stupid.*

Somehow Margaret had assumed the adjournment of the coroner's court would be the end of the matter. Instead, troublesome details lingered. The coroner and Sir Hugh approached Falstone as the room was emptying of the jury and the merely curious.

Sir Hugh's cousin said, "Major Falstone, will you be taking the body with you today? I am sure the innkeeper would prefer not to have it on the premises or in an outbuilding overnight, even if it would attract more custom."

Sir Hugh offered the use of his wagon and man to transport the body. "I assume you'll want to remove the decedent for burial. There's no sense in my taking it back with me when you'd only have to send a wagon for it tomorrow or the next day."

Margaret, Dorring, and the children hung back, waiting for Falstone to escort them to the inn yard. Then Colin edged forward to stand near his uncle.

"I'd be grateful if your man could deliver Bradnam to Scot Hall—"

"No." The word dropped like a stone. "I don't want him lying with our family," Colin said, his voice breaking slightly. "Not after he abducted my sisters and tried to kill you, Uncle."

The magistrate and the coroner looked to Falstone. After a moment, he said, "Lord Hawkslowe's objection is reasonable. Can you arrange for burial here or nearby?"

"Certainly, Major. No funeral?" Sir Hugh directed the question somewhere between Falstone and Colin.

Alasdair glanced at Colin's tight-lipped frown. "I think not."

Nor was that discussion the end.

"Will you want me to issue an order for the arrest of the other Bradnam and Ackerley? I can send to the sheriffs of Roxburghshire in case they are still in Jedburgh and to Midlothian if they have retreated to the Edinburgh house, though it may or may not be effective. Across the border, you know. Their justices of the peace may or may not be helpful."

"Perhaps Lord Hawkslowe and I should discuss this and let you know."

At long last, they were able to depart.

Chapter 28

"Thank you for not treating me like a child, sir." The formality of Colin's thanks made it plain he had been right to defer to the new Lord Hawkslowe's wishes. Falstone could understand the boy's reluctance to make room in the family burying ground for Bradnam.

Alasdair had intended he and Colin would discuss what to do about Harry Bradnam and Ackerley privately. However, Colin requested that Janet, as one of the victims, join them, and Margaret MacGavin also.

"You do not insist on Isabelle's presence, as she was also taken?"

"She is a child. So is Matthew. But Mistress MacGavin helped rescue my sisters. She is true blue."

He himself would not be averse to hearing Margaret's advice, and so the four met in the estate office the morning after the inquest. The plain room with its dark paneling and massive old table on which deeds, maps, and ledgers could be spread out seemed appropriate for serious discussion. Morning light slanting through the diamond-paned casements illuminated dust motes hanging in the air.

"There is a decision to be made," Falstone began. "Bradnam's coachman and the maid, Bessie, have sworn out their statements about the planning of the abduction. Sir Hugh can issue arrest warrants."

Postponing the discussion until they had had a night's sleep should have allowed them time to weigh the alternatives and the consequences. He waited while Colin frowned and Janet stared at her hands, clutching a handkerchief before her on the table. Margaret's hand stole up to touch her cheek. Ah, they had recognized the problem.

"Lord Hawkslowe?" The title seemed called for. Their meeting was informal but echoed the old times when the lord's power was almost absolute.

"Must we bring charges against all?"

"No. What about Ackerley?"

"He was horrible. He swore at Isabelle for kicking him when he lifted her off her pony and said he would beat her if she didn't stop arguing." Janet's knuckles were white. "She has nightmares about the journey."

"Ackerley should be brought to justice," her brother said. "Could you ask Sir Hugh to inform the Scots sheriffs and also send a warrant to London, in case he's gone to the house there?"

"The Bow Street magistrate, then. It may not be possible to find Ackerley, however," Falstone said. "It's easy to vanish if a man has no ties and is willing to change his name."

Janet spoke. "He might not."

"Why would he not, when he must know we will prosecute him if we find him, Janet?"

She flushed. "Ummm...I should not know this, but once Mama and my uncles were talking when I was present. Either they forgot I was there or else thought I was too young to understand," the girl ended tartly. "I think Ackerley is, ummm, a connection of theirs. Ours."

"You mean he may be our Bradnam grandfather's

son?" Colin asked. "Because he's too old to be Uncle Harry's by-blow."

She nodded.

Falstone and Margaret exchanged wry glances. The topic was unsuitable for children, but a rebuke was impossible when the fact was relevant.

Colin nodded. "That would explain why he was treated better than the other grooms and seemed to have more money to spend. And why he acted like a favorite old family retainer."

"In that case, we may be lucky. I'll write to Sir Hugh today and offer him one of the grooms to carry the warrant to Scotland. The London warrant can go by post. I don't believe your mother and uncle will linger long in Scotland."

"Thank you, Uncle."

"The harder decision is, do you want a warrant issued for your uncle Harry? I do not intend to advise you one way or the other. You may discuss it here or in private and let me know later, if you wish."

"Ladies first, Janet," Colin said with a twisted smile.

"It's hard. If it were only Uncle Harry, I would say he ought to be punished because he probably had the idea to abduct us. He's cleverer than Uncle Paul…was. But there's Mother, too."

"It would not be necessary to bring a case against Lady Hawkslowe," Alasdair said.

"No, but she depends on our uncles. She and our uncles are very close. Our uncle, now."

"That's true," her brother admitted. "Mother would be lost without Uncle Harry to advise her. She's not like Mistress MacGavin." He acknowledged Margaret with a duck of his head. "I think we should not have him arrested. Would it not cause a great deal of talk, Uncle Alasdair?"

"I had considered that. I take it you are both agreed Harry Bradnam should not be prosecuted?"

Colin and Janet locked eyes. She gave a minute nod.

The boy—Lord Hawkslowe—nodded slowly. "I do confess I think it unfair to punish Ackerley and not my uncle, even if he is family. Er, legitimate family, I mean. And what of Bessie?"

"Should we arrange for her to sail for the American colonies? I would rather she not report back to Lady Hawkslowe and your uncle."

Janet agreed, reluctantly. "I did not like Bessie. She sneaked around and tattled on us and on the other servants."

Colin blew out a long breath. "Let her go. In the colonies, she will have a chance to reform."

"In that case, my lad, haven't you a Latin translation to work on?"

"Yes, sir, if you will excuse me." He rose and bowed to Margaret and his sister, who stood up more quickly than gracefully.

Margaret spoke for the first time. "Before you both go, may I ask whether either of you has written to your mother or your uncle?"

This time Janet took the lead. "No, ma'am. Neither of us. We didn't know what to say. Colin thought we should wait until after the inquest, and I don't know what to write, because I am angry at Uncle Paul and Mother and not sorry he is dead."

"Are you not angry at your uncle Harry, too?" The

elder Bradnam must have been the guiding brain. As Janet had observed, Harry was the clever one. Paul Bradnam was feckless.

Janet frowned over the question. "I should be, but somehow I can't feel Uncle Harry could be responsible. If he had arranged our abduction, it would not have been botched."

She had no difficulty believing it of her mother and younger uncle. To be so clear-eyed about a parent struck Falstone as saddening.

"The coachman only mentioned Uncle Paul, not Mother or Uncle Harry," Colin said.

"Sir Hugh, the coroner, and I agreed beforehand the coroner would not read the parts of the coachman and Bessie's statements about Harry Bradnam because they implicated your mother as well. I apologize for not consulting you, Colin, but I felt sure you would not want her name dragged through the mud."

Colin and Janet wore identical expressions of horror.

"Oh, no." The soft objection was Janet's.

"Quite right. I agree with your decision, sir."

They all contemplated the inevitable. While Rochester was far from London, word of Paul Bradnam's death and its circumstances would come to society's ears sooner or later, but damage to the family's reputation would at least be limited.

"Now, Mistress MacGavin was asking about your letters."

"We could write our usual letters. Just what we've been learning and, er…" Colin's reply trailed off.

"What we've been doing when not in the schoolroom?" Janet inquired acerbically.

"No, perhaps not," Colin conceded.

"You should continue to write your mother," Alasdair said. "I would prefer you not mention the abduction or the inquest. Continue to direct your letters to the London house, please. If they have to be re-directed to Edinburgh, so much the better. We only know Lady Hawkslowe and Bradnam have been in Scotland because the coachman told us."

"Because you want to see what they'll do when they don't hear about Uncle Paul?"

Perceptive of Colin to understand that in a flash.

"That's it. Ackerley won't have been able to inform them of your uncle's death. If he returned to the stream before Montgomery sent men and a team to impound the coach, two horses being gone may have led him to think Bradnam and the driver escaped with Janet and Isabelle. Or if he found the coach gone, he might suppose they'd got free on their own and gone back to find a different route. In either case, delay will give my letter and copies of the coachman's and maid's depositions time to reach London. Seeing what Harry Bradnam and your mother do next might be helpful."

Janet dipped a curtsy. "Please excuse me. I should spend some time with Isabelle. She is still uneasy."

Colin lingered. When the door closed behind his sister, he burst out, "I don't wonder Izzy and Matthew are put about. It's as if Mother had died, except that for Janet and me, it's worse. People do die, and there are rules for it." He shrugged helplessly.

Margaret ached for him. "Forms of behavior, you mean?"

He nodded. "Everyone knows how to act. There's mourning, and you grieve or pretend you do, and after a while, you go on with your life. This isn't over, and when will it be? Maybe it's even harder for Izzy and Janet, because girls are closer to their mother. Agatha Butterfield, Squire Butterfield's daughter, missed her mama terribly. She's between Izzy and Janet in age, and she didn't start to get over it until her aunt came to live with them."

What was one to say? Falstone was sure he didn't know. Perhaps Margaret had some words of consolation.

Then his nephew added, "Of course, Agatha spent a good deal of time with Mistress Butterfield, as they didn't have a governess. I expect my sisters miss Father more. Mayhap it's the awkwardness that's the worst of it. Pray excuse me. Janet and I review Isabelle's and Matthew's letters. I will remind her to make sure Isabelle doesn't write about the—the incident."

Colin hurried out, leaving Falstone and Margaret alone.

"I wonder what else they have to confer about," she remarked pensively.

"Do you think that's what they're doing?"

"Probably. I am very glad my monthly letter to her ladyship about the girls is not due yet. In another two weeks, I can limit my report to Janet's ability to converse fluently in simple French and Isabelle's progress in writing and curtsying."

He was taken by surprise when Margaret put a hand on his arm as he began to rise. He settled back into his chair. "What is it, Margaret?"

"Do you think this will end it? If Colin goes to school in September, might they try to take him from there? Having Lord Hawkslowe in her control would be as effective as having her daughters, wouldn't it?"

"I will be writing the school with instructions that he is not to be released to his mother, uncle, or any other person than myself or someone bearing instructions containing a particular phrase." He raised one eyebrow. "I'm not inclined to worry too much, however. Colin would not go docilely, and abducting him would be difficult, I suspect."

"Oh, good. While I agree that bringing a criminal charge would cause scandal, I did wonder if 'twere safe to assume they would give up."

"I share your concern, but unless Bradnam attempts something else, I do not see what I or anyone can do, if we do not bring charges. If Bradnam shows up, I'll haul him before Sir Hugh to be locked up and make it clear any further attempts will result in prosecution. That should dissuade him. He need not know we have already decided not to bring charges because of the potential scandal. However, the children will not ride without a pair of armed grooms or myself."

"Or me?"

He scowled. "I would rather you not form part of the guard. If you were injured, I do not know what I would do." With that, he stood and ushered her out of the room.

****

Later, Colin approached Margaret in the garden where she was cutting flowers. Lady Hawkslowe had valued only roses, which unfortunately did not thrive at Scot Hall. Vases of oxeye daisy, pignut, buttercup, common sorrel, and red fescue improved a room as much and seemed more suited to the country than more formal bouquets.

He paused by a bed of pignuts, head tilted to listen to a tweeting birdsong. "That's a male blackbird calling a female."

She was tolerably certain he had not come to tell her about the mating habits of birds.

"You may have wondered that Janet and I did not want to have Uncle Harry charged."

"You and your sister are old enough to know how damaging gossip can be."

"That was only part of it, for me. He taught us things. He took Matthew and me out foraging for a meal. We dug up some of these"—he nodded toward the pignuts—"and wild garlic, gathered berries, and caught fish and cooked them wrapped in leaves. That was several years ago before my father's health failed."

He did not immediately continue, so she said, "What a treat! My brothers and I were never so ambitious. We did stuff ourselves with berries and apples until we could hardly eat our dinner."

Colin said, "I liked Uncle Harry. Even now I can't dislike him. He's a dab at any sport or game and knows all sorts of interesting things. He taught me to skip stones, shoot a bow, play cricket and golf—that's a Scottish game, you know—and tennis. He told us about the adventures he had on his Grand Tour."

"Did he?" She hardly liked to imagine what sort they might be, judging from the few mentions of such travel she had heard. The stated purpose of traveling on the Continent was to broaden one's mind, visit sites of historical or artistic merit, polish one's French, and form connections with the foreign aristocracy. A prolonged course of drunkenness and debauchery seemed to be more common.

Happily ignorant of this, young Lord Hawkslowe went on. "Ay. The carnival in Venice, the running of the bulls in Spain, his stay in the Alps when his friend broke his ankle on their tour. He spent time with the shepherds as there was little else to do and learned to use a sling, like the one David used to kill Goliath. He showed us once. Uncle Harry gave good advice, too." Colin sighed, adding as an afterthought, "He only talks nonsense when Mother is present. If you know what I mean."

"I think I do, Lord Hawkslowe. Many men speak to ladies as if they were children." And not very intelligent ones at that. So annoying. Though Falstone, like Gideon, was not guilty of it. Mayhap that had been part of the reason she had married MacGavin.

"Mistress MacGavin, please call me by my given name. I know I have to be Lord Hawkslowe sometimes, but other times, I'd rather be Colin, as I used to be."

"Very well, Colin."

"I cannot help remembering sometimes and missing him. He was like a much-older brother rather than a grown man. Not stiff and full of propriety, not that Father was that way, but Harry knew different things. Maybe because he hadn't been brought up to be responsible for an estate. Janet liked him, too, though now she says she must have been mistaken in him."

Chapter 29

Janet and Isabelle, who had been brave during their terrifying abduction, were still showing its effects. Janet was quiet. Isabelle woke with nightmares. The boys were affected also in their different ways. Matthew protested about being forbidden to go off on his own to ramble around the estate, a habit Margaret and Dorring had never liked even when it had seemed safe enough. Colin pressed Alasdair for more lessons in swordsmanship for both himself and Matthew and also requested instruction with a pistol, arguing that letting Matthew watch and promising him lessons when he was older would be a further inducement not to sneak out.

"I am not sure Matthew would be dissuaded merely by the promise of future training, though I will let him attend Colin's. Fortunately, Matthew is too young to handle even a lady's pistol. I was tempted to tell Hawkslowe that if he wanted to learn to shoot, you should be the one to instruct him," Alasdair said, grinning, when he and Margaret had a few minutes' privacy.

Margaret cherished the compliment in that rare lighthearted moment. She was on edge herself, feeling they had survived Act II of a harrowing drama but were waiting for Act III. Did Alasdair also dread the next development? Either he did not or else his years in the military had accustomed him to meet dangers as they came without worrying about them in advance. She tried to believe they could all pretend it had never happened, though she also hoped Lady Hawkslowe would not return.

Still, they waited. When she spoke of this, he said, "It will likely be some time before we hear from the Scots sheriffs or from Bow Street that Ackerley has been apprehended."

"Do you think he will be?"

"I am not confident."

So she remained on tenterhooks.

Midway through the morning about a fortnight after the inquest, Alasdair came to the nursery parlor door.

"Major?"

"Mistress MacGavin, will you attend me briefly?"

She told Janet to help Isabelle with her printing and shut the door behind her. Alasdair took her arm and escorted her along the passage.

"I'd would rather not be overheard if someone should listen at the door. Sir Hugh has written to inform me that a stranger spent two nights at the inn in Rochester a few days ago. He passed the evenings in the common room, listening and asking the kind of questions a traveler might. Montgomery heard of it only last night, or he would have warned me sooner. The fellow can't have been Bradnam or Ackerley as they'd have been recognized. Whoever the visitor may have been, he wasn't a gentleman. Though from what they reported of his dress and speech, Sir Hugh thinks he might be a clerk or bailiff, or perhaps an upper servant of some sort. The publican took a different view. He'd not spoken with him, beyond a greeting and renting him a room, but he's observant. He thought the man was used to doing things his own way rather than taking orders."

"Was he scouting on Mr. Bradnam's behalf, do you think?"

"If he was, he couldn't fail to hear about the incident and the inquest, which must be the most memorable thing to occur in Rochester in the last fifty years. I'd take my oath they'll be talking about it for another half century."

"I wonder what Lady Hawkslowe and her brother will do now."

"If the visitor was Bradnam's intelligencer, we can assume he now knows what happened, or soon will."

"Need we wait to see what he and Lady Hawkslowe do next?"

His sudden rakehelly grin took her by surprise.

"No, my dear, I think we might send out a scout of our own. Presumably they are still in Scotland. I'll dispatch Campbell to learn what he can."

He had called her "my dear." With difficulty, she herded her thoughts back into order like a collie with sheep. "If he's recognized, he might be in danger." And *we*, he had said, as if they were on the same footing as they had been before he left Northumberland.

"Ackerley would be the only one he need worry about. Do you think Bradnam or my sister-in-law pay any attention to servants except for his valet or her maid? And Campbell will be just another red-haired Scot."

Lady Hawkslowe and her brothers hardly knew the names of the Scot Hall servants. Very likely Alasdair was correct about that much. Ackerley was another matter entirely, but the abduction and its aftermath might have made her unnecessarily fearful.

Queasily, she remembered her last view of Paul Bradnam through the standing notch sight. His handsome, startled face, his crimson coat, his arm rising to aim. Sometimes she had nightmares, though they were of Alasdair dying because she had not fired that fatal ball. Probably if she had not fired, Bradnam's shot would have missed or only wounded the major. But even a simple cut could kill if it turned gangrenous. She could not have gambled with Alasdair's life.

"If they've gone back to London, I suppose we can assume they will pursue the matter in the Court of Chancery, and we need not fear another kidnapping attempt, at least."

"I sent Attorney Miller a copy of the coachman's and maid's depositions, attested to by Sir Hugh. If Lady Hawkslowe takes her case to Chancery, those documents will be submitted to the court. Perhaps Campbell will learn something of their plans."

The hard little seed of worry in Margaret's heart diminished if it did not vanish. The memory of Alasdair's endearment and the warmth in his eyes comforted her.

Lessons went on amid the country year's cycle of planting, growth, and harvesting. In the kitchen garden, Dutch cabbage lettuce, radishes, and endives were sown for late crops. Ripe seeds were gathered to dry for use next year. Margaret took Isabelle and Janet outside to see how the fruit, vegetables, and herbs were cultivated and to the kitchen and stillroom to learn something of the making of preserves and pickles. Fifty years ago, any lady would have been expected to know the work of kitchen, stillroom, and dairy. Margaret's aunt Rose had been taught the housewifely arts as a girl and trained her in them. They had stood her in good stead when she found herself keeping house for her father and brothers. Neither of Lord Hawkslowe's sisters might need to do these things, but the knowledge would ensure a well-run household. Elizabeth, Lady Hawkslowe had been utterly negligent in that respect as in so many others. To be fair, she had grown up in London.

A badly spelled letter from Campbell assured Falstone, who reassured Margaret, that he had arrived in Edinburgh and let it be known he would be looking for a position in a stable once he had recovered from a broken leg. He had cut a rough walking stick for himself on the way and put a few dried peas in his left boot to provide a convincing limp. Lady Hawkslowe and Harry Bradnam were still in residence a mile or so from the town. Margaret could almost hear him saying "th'toon." His accent reminded her of Gideon.

Scot Hall enjoyed peace. Isabelle's nightmares came less often and gradually ceased, unless something occurred to upset her. Matthew still fretted at his loss of freedom despite lessons in swordplay. Janet regained her usual calm. Neither Margaret nor Dorring could guess what Colin thought or felt.

Perhaps they might go out to gather bramble berries for preserves and jellies. Given the brambles' tendency to invade, they were not grown in the kitchen garden. In Margaret's youth, berrying had been an occasion for horseplay that ended in scratches and stained clothing, just the thing to take the children's minds off their worries and let them work off their fidgets. As soon as the berries were ripe, she would organize an expedition.

When Alasdair asked her to walk in the flower garden with him, she thought he meant for enjoyment. She did not permit herself to hope he wished to renew their earlier acquaintance. Best not to call it more than that. But the invitation was only to warn her that all excursions by the children must be curtailed. Falstone would accompany them when he could or two of the most reliable grooms, who knew how to shoot, might substitute, with his permission.

"While I would rather not tell the younger children lest they be frightened, you must know. I mean to speak to Lord Hawkslowe and Janet, because he has a right to know and both of them may help you to keep Matthew from wandering."

"Is there news?"

"No, but there are reports of losses of a chicken here, a duck there. I might think it only a fox except that a snare was found. That might be unrelated, only some needy or light-fingered cottager poaching a rabbit for the pot. But one of Hawkslowe's tenants swears her best hens are not producing as many eggs as before. I cannot help but wonder if the 'fox' "—a wry emphasis on the last word—"in question has two legs rather than four. I would be less concerned if not for a sheep dying for no visible reason. That is one coincidence too many. That's why I want the children not to venture beyond the grounds around the house without an escort. And if you ride or wish to visit the village, tell me first. I'll arrange for an escort."

"Do you plan to go out only with a groom to guard

you?"

He laughed. "I was a soldier. I don't need an escort."

****

The waiting was like that before being called into action and yet life went on at Scot Hall. The groom who saddled his horse said, "Mary come back from her folks after her half day with a tale of having heard something as she passed the old bastle house and barn. Ghosts from the reivers' time, she said."

Mary Lumley, that would be, the maid of all work. He was beginning to know the servants who were new since he left Scot Hall. Her afternoon off work would have been the day before yesterday. A hard-working girl but not keen-witted. "In daylight?"

"She was late starting back, her sis having brought the new baby to show the family. Near found herself locked out o' the house, but she pounded on the kitchen door, and the scullery maid let her in, sir."

Then her claim of hearing a ghost was probably a diversion from the lateness of her return. "I don't suppose she saw aught?"

"Nay, but she said she heard a horse snorting and maybe some rustling. Nothing but the wind, most like."

"Do you know if she was nearer the bastle or the barn?"

"Her way'd lie between them."

Falstone had made a habit of riding out before breakfast to look over one part or another of the estate. Instead of riding south today as he had intended, he changed his mind. He would visit the bastle that was the original Scot Hall. The new house had replaced it a century ago.

The old bastle had not been rented out again after the last tenant to live there died before Falstone had left home. Sebastian had intended to have a stone floor installed over the dirt on the lower level and the ventilation openings enlarged as had been done with others. Before he could commence the work, his health had failed, and he lacked the stamina to undertake the project.

"It will survive me by centuries," the late Lord Hawkslowe had remarked with mordant humor. Bastles had walls as much as three feet thick, not surprising when the origin of the term was the old French word for fortress.

The bastle should be put to some better use. Throughout the Borders, bastles were often used as farmhouses now they were no longer needed as refuges during attacks. He should have Sebastian's plans carried out once the present uncertainty was past.

He halted some distance from the abandoned building. Even in sunlight, the bastle was not inviting. A stark rectangle of stone with narrow slots for air, a double door on the side toward the barn through which valuable livestock could be brought in, an upper floor with windows hardly wider than arrow slits, and an outside door reached by a narrow stone stair. From the ground floor, the men who herded the cattle in could reach the upper story by a ladder after they had barred the lower door. Mayhap some vagrant had been sheltering there?

He rode closer, noting that some slates were missing from the roof, the only sign he could see of needed repairs. The barn also looked solid with three sides of stone blocks; the fourth butted up against the low hill behind the little fortress. Its roof, once covered with slates, might need to be replaced. Fifteen years ago, some had been missing. Now it appeared a layer of windblown soil had accumulated on the ones remaining, as heather and gorse were growing there.

Something was wrong. Falstone wheeled his mount and spurred away around the low rise. In spite of having heard talk about "second sight" from superstitious country folk and from Nurse Sallows, too, there was nothing mysterious about it.

He had known these moments a handful of times before. The first time came as he and his detachment would have started across a wooden bridge. Thank God he had paid attention and halted his men. His own horse's hooves were no more than a foot from the planks. With a roar like a peal of thunder, the bridge deck fell away as the wood piles supporting it failed. Perhaps he had heard the timbers creaking in the spate of flood waters.

He must have noticed some sign here without being conscious of it. With the rise between him and the bastle's arrow slits, he need not fear a musket shot. That thinking came from his years as a dragoon, for why would he suspect an ambush? Still, something was amiss. Mary might have felt the same and thought of ghosts. He emptied his mind of speculation and listened, studying the gently rolling moorland. He saw nothing but a windhover suspended in the air as it hunted voles and heard nothing but the breeze in the moorland grass. He took a deep breath.

And smelled a faint odor of something burnt. He dismounted and made his way up the slope, removing his hat and dropping to the ground as he approached the top. He slunk to the edge of the barn's roof, moving gingerly to avoid disturbing the brush growing there. His head should not be too noticeable among the heather and the gorse if someone were in the bastle. The charred wood smell was stronger now. Wafting up through the gaps in the roof, he thought. When no sound came to him from the interior, he risked a peek down through a hole where several of the slates had fallen away or been removed to repair some cottage roof.

Bars of sunlight fell through the narrow windows. Below, he could see a darker circle on the dirt floor and some debris near it. Falstone retreated down the hillock, resumed his hat, and led his horse back to the barn's entrance, keeping his mount between him and the bastle. He grinned at the hasp meant to secure the door by a peg through a metal loop. A cord dangled, intended to keep the rod or stick from being lost. The lower end had been cut through not long since as the fibers were not frayed or as weathered as the rest of the cord.

If he had taken up residence in the barn even briefly, he would also have taken the peg to make sure he could not be trapped inside. He entered, leaving the door standing open for more light. The black circle in the dirt contained charred bits of wood. Against one wall a stoneware bottle lay forgotten, a cork beside it. A sniff revealed it had contained ale.

He also found a few oats and horse droppings no older than a day or two. Someone had been here and warmed himself by a fire or cooked a simple meal. So much for Mary Lumley's ghost!

He could not have made use of the bastle, he

realized. Sebastian had mentioned the bastle's upper door had been padlocked for years as a result of a tenant's children playing lord and reivers in it without anyone's knowledge or permission. No one would have been the wiser, either, if one of the boys had not fallen through the hatch from the upper floor and broken his leg. This incident, impossible to conceal as the lad had to be carried home, led to the doors being secured.

He found no sign of tampering with the padlock. It might be easy to pick but was much corroded. Scratches and traces of dislodged rust would show any attempt to open it. The cattle doors on the lower level were immovable, still barred from within.

He rode directly back to Scot Hall, penned a letter to Sir Hugh requesting he detain the fellow who had been asking questions in Rochester if he should reappear and sent it off by a groom. The thought someone had been lurking on Scot Hall land was worrisome. If he had a company of dragoons…but he didn't.

At dinner, as he pondered, his gaze fell upon Margaret. He would ordinarily have dismissed the thought of sharing his concerns with a woman. But Margaret was an old friend. With a pang, he thought, *much more, once*. She was sensible and might have saved his life, and her ability to shoot was not the only way she differed from other genteel women he had known.

After the children were freed to amuse themselves before resuming their lessons, he invited her to join him in the estate office, where no one would intrude. She listened to his account, leaning forward slightly in her chair.

"That is disquieting," she agreed when he had finished. "I am not surprised Mr. Harry Bradnam would send someone to Rochester to scout the territory when his brother and nieces did not arrive in Jedburgh. But his man must have heard all he needed to know from listening to talk in the public house. Are you sure the intruder in the bank barn is connected to Bradnam?"

"No. Yet I find it hard to believe some wanderer happened upon the barn on our land by chance. The proximity in time to the abduction and to someone making inquiries in Rochester renders it suspicious. Besides, what would a traveler be doing on Scot Hall land, so far from the road?"

"He may have hoped to find someplace to spend the night under cover."

"Finding the barn by luck?"

"Unlikely, I admit."

"The Bradnam brothers spent a great deal of time riding," he said. Seeing Margaret bite her lip and her almost imperceptible shudder, he reached out to pat her hand, meaning only to comfort her, and found himself staring into her golden-brown eyes.

An eternity passed before she lowered her gaze, during which he recalled how much he had loved her all those years ago. His feelings had been real despite their youth. They might have slipped away to Scotland and married. He could have been the one to teach her to shoot. Sunk in these reflections, he hardly noticed how much time passed before she spoke again. His hand still rested on hers. Guiltily, he removed it and straightened.

"If Bradnam sent a spy, how long do you think he's been gone from the barn?"

"The man was certainly there the night before last

when Mary passed and thought she heard a ghost. The ashes were cold when I was there this morning. I imagine he left at first light yesterday."

"So he is on his way back to his employers with whatever intelligence he gathered."

"Ay."

Chapter 30

Alasdair was reviewing accounts by the light of an oil lamp, the rain having made the afternoon twilight dim, when Graves sought him out.

"Sir, Campbell's come back. He's in the kitchen, wet as can be. Where would you wish—"

Excellent news. Falstone put the ledger aside. "I'll see him there." The kitchen, at least, was both warm and dry.

Campbell stood as near the hearth as he could, though Falstone doubted he would catch fire if he stood in the fireplace. He had shed his greatcoat, but his clothing and hair still dripped. Seeing Falstone, the Scot said, "I'm fair drookit."

Mistress Lindsay, the cook, offered him a pewter tankard, saying, "Drink up, lad. A sailor's drink is what you need," and he closed his hands around it with a nod of gratitude.

When she went back to her work table at the other end of the room, Campbell said, "I've a peddler's pack full of news, sir."

"Have another draft of your flip first." A pot of soup was warming over the fire, but most of the preparations for supper had not begun yet. The kitchen maid was beating eggs at one end of the table where the cook had resumed rolling out pastry, far enough not to hear if they kept their voices low.

Campbell took a long drink. "They've been living a bit out of Edinburgh in a wee house, not a cottage, but not a manor, neither. A gentleman's house. Leddy Hawkslowe doesna like the tall, narrow houses and wynds o' the town." His accent was more Scots than usual.

"A hard ride back?"

"Ay, but it didn't come on to rain heavy until the ford o' the Rede, and then I didna want to take shelter because who knows how long it will rain?" Another swig of hot ale, brandy, sugar, and spices.

"What did you learn? I don't need to ask if you were careful, Campbell." Something important, clearly. He had not been absent as long as expected, and he had defied the weather on his way back.

" 'Twas easy, all the servants being Scots, barring the valet. And Mr. Harry, Ackerley, the baroness, and her woman are awa'."

"Back to London?"

Campbell grunted a sardonic laugh. "Her leddyship said she was going to stay with friends, but not who they were or where, which is gey peculiar. She sent her maid to hire a coach. Easy to hide where she was going, her not having coach nor coachman."

"Because John Coachman is still lame with a bad leg at Sir Hugh's, where the coach and horses we took are being housed. What of Bradnam?"

"That's strange, too. The ones I talked to didn't remember exactly when—serving in a household with most days the same as all the ones before—but about three weeks or a month ago, Ackerley came, spoke to the master and the leddy, and then was gone the next morning. Mr. Harry swore something fierce."

Ackerley might well have left to avoid being involved and possibly charged, as the servants at Scot Hall could attest to his having taken the girls away. "In Ackerley's place, after returning to the coach and finding everyone gone, I'd have made for Edinburgh as fast as I could ride to report to my employer. Bradnam must have found a man to listen to the talk at the inn." Would Bradnam know how to find some Captain Sharp to spy for him? "What happened then?"

"The house was all on end for a bit, except when they had guests or went out—"

"What? While my sister-in-law was in mourning for her husband?" Low as his opinion was of Elizabeth Hawkslowe's sense and honesty, he would not have expected her to flout society's expectations completely.

Campbell snorted. "When her leddyship should be in black, weeping her eyes out and reading sermons? Och, never, Major. When Ackerley came, I'm told they could have heard the wailing and cursing all the way to the Canongate. Her maid put it about her mistress was suffering a bad head cold, and the leddy kept her chamber for a week or thereabout. Then she and Mr. Harry went on with attending dinners and routs and the like."

That his brother's widow was more distressed over her brother's death than her husband's angered him so much he could not speak at once. "I suppose she needed the time to compose herself after Paul's death. She and her brothers were close."

Sebastian had not trusted her to safeguard the estate from the Bradnams, but he had never accused her of anything worse than being a spendthrift. Still, one expected a widow to make a pretense of grief even for an unloved husband. Acceptable manners in society required a good deal of hypocrisy. In the army, too, for that matter, where the emphasis on appearance and style often took precedence over common sense. "Did she not know such behavior would be bound to get back to London?"

"From what I was told, they didn't know anyone there until her brothers scraped some acquaintance with local gentlemen. They came to call, and as Leddy Hawkslowe wasn't wearing widow's weeds, they weren't to know her loss was recent. Might be she thought Scotland too far away to matter even if there was talk."

Farewell to the expensive mourning wardrobe her ladyship had ordered.

"After a bit, she and Bradnam fell out, though the folk in the house didn't ken why. They were both snappish for days after. Then a letter came for Bradnam, and he left sudden. A day later, the widow says she'll go stay with friends. At the stable, they gave me the name of the place she was bound for, some house party, they thought. I saddled up as there was no more point in staying."

"You don't believe them, Campbell?"

"Bradnam left his manservant in Edinburgh and only took a valise with him. I wasn't able to talk to the man, who's not one to blether with a groom. The leddy, I'm not sure. But the housemaid told me a gentleman called the day before the lady's maid hired the coach, and 'twasn't the first time, neither."

"Did Bradnam go by coach?"

The groom grinned. "He rode. I couldn't find out where he went. He spoke friendly with the groom and stable boys, but he didn't tell them aught but he had some business to attend to and would be back by and by."

Falstone tallied up days. "Someone may have been poaching near here. One of Towson's sheep died. It wasn't ill so far as he could tell, and there was no wound. That might not have anything to do with the poaching. Mary Lumley thought she heard a ghost by the empty bastle one evening. I found signs somebody had camped in the bank barn. Whoever it was had a horse."

"Not some puir auld body taking shelter, then."

"No. I wonder if 'twas Harry Bradnam."

"A fine London gentleman like him? I can't see him poaching, Major, for how would he cook whatever he caught without a French chef and a kitchen?"

"Far-fetched, I admit, Campbell." And if it were Bradnam, what mischief was he about? He could hardly expect to abduct even one of the children again, when they never went farther than the stable unaccompanied.

****

News of Duncan Campbell's return reached Margaret when a maid brought word the major requested she join him in the estate office. Janet and Isabelle were at liberty to amuse themselves before supper. Her heart thumped.

His summation of the groom's news ended with "The disappearance of both Lady Hawkslowe and her brother from Edinburgh would worry me less if it had occurred immediately after Ackerley reported to them. That would have suggested they had all fled to avoid being charged. I think we will not let down our guard yet. I mean to write Attorney Miller asking him whether they have returned to town. Mayhap they'll attempt to bring a case in the Court of Chancery after all."

"I wish this waiting were over, Alasdair." She had been addressing him as Major Falstone or simply Major. Reverting to familiarity was a blatant bid for…for what, exactly? Not for friendship as they were friends. Use of his given name had been an invitation to resume their old courtship.

"So do I. We cannot make any plans while this unfinished business hangs over us."

"It troubles the children, too. Janet and Colin try not to show it, and I think Isabelle is mostly recovered from her fright now and has not realized the matter did not end with the rescue. Matthew is restless and complains about being a prisoner."

"My sister-in-law was at fault for leaving the boys to their own devices," he said. "Matthew fell into the habit of wandering at large. Now he misses that freedom and is not mature enough to understand why he cannot do so now."

Margaret had wondered what Alasdair had meant when he had called her "my dear" before sending Campbell to Scotland. Had it meant anything at all? Her love had revived, or at least, she had admitted to herself that it never died. Had he discovered those old, tender sentiments still lived in his heart? She tried to banish both thoughts and hope: embarrassing to find she was no more sensible than the most inane heroine in the most vapid novel. Or as her much younger self. He had not repeated the endearment. That he called her by her given name at times signified nothing. They had been on such terms all those years ago. He would surely have spoken by now if he still loved her. Her attachment must have been more lasting than his. Either he had no interest in wedding, or if he did, he would court a younger female with a dowry.

She should resign herself. Unfortunately, hope is hardy and not easily rooted out. At meals or when Alasdair visited the nursery suite or rode with Margaret and the children, it flourished again.

****

Margaret made an appealing picture in the garden against a background of evening primrose. A few tendrils of her hazelnut brown hair had escaped from under her demure cap. Her head turned at his approach, her eyes widening.

"Is something amiss, Alasdair?"

He could tell by the slight tremor in her voice how the strain of the past weeks had affected her. At the same time, her use of his given name warmed him.

"On the contrary. I have received some excellent news in a letter from Lady Hawkslowe. Shall we sit on that bench while you read it and let me know what you think?"

July 17, Brackenridge Court, Annan, Scotland
Major Falstone,

I write to inform you of my marriage to Angus Brackenridge, Earl of Annan. Under ordinary circumstances, I would have apprised you of the happy event beforehand in the hope that my older son and daughter might be able to attend the ceremony. However, Lord Annan has pressing affairs to attend to in London. He will not find it convenient to come north again for some months and therefore solicited my hand, and we were wed the same day, as is possible in Scotland. We set out for London today. My direction so that the children and MacGavin and Dorring can write me will be Brackenridge House, Southampton Square.

I have no objection to the children remaining at Scot Hall for the time being. Lord Annan has many calls upon his time, as will I, and he has pointed out that their presence would be a distraction, in particular as we will be entertaining a good deal and will often have house guests. Besides, the country air is said to be better for children. Perhaps when it is time for Janet to enter society, she may come for a month or two.

I trust they are all in good health.

Elizabeth, Lady Annan

Margaret smothered an unladylike snort.

"That was my own response. I should disapprove of my sister-in-law insulting my brother's memory by marrying in haste. However, in truth, I'm relieved. First, because she makes it clear she has no interest in having the children live with her, so she cannot hope to prevail if she brings a case in Chancery." He had meant to add a second reason, but as it was not germane to the guardianship and was petty, he should not mention it. Margaret might not notice.

"And second?"

She had always been needle-witted. "As it happens, I know something of the earl. Elizabeth may have enthralled him, indeed, must have or why marry her? But he's not a man to tolerate her tricks and vapors. He has two or three sons, and I doubt he'll let her change her mind about trying to get guardianship of the children. You'll note she doesn't even mention having them come to visit at some unspecified future date."

"Except Janet," Margaret said doubtfully.

"By then, assuming Lady Annan remembers to

invite her, we will accompany her and prevent my niece from being pushed into accepting an offer from the wrong kind of suitor."

"Oh. Yes, of course." She smiled at him in a way he had not seen in some time: frank, open, and happy, rather than a social smile that did not reach the eyes.

Was she amenable to a second courtship by him? Although he had spoken of both of them going to London with Janet, that plan was not feasible as things stood. A bachelor and a widow living together—Annan would hardly care to have them as guests—would lead to talk and damage Margaret's reputation and Janet's chances of a good marriage. Unless they employed a chaperon, but even that would not necessarily prevent gossip.

Chapter 31

Margaret was writing an unexpectedly difficult letter to Rupert. She had written not long after coming to Scot Hall. She had described it and its inhabitants, dwelling on the children and several amusing anecdotes but passing lightly over Lord Hawkslowe's failing health and Lady Hawkslowe's disobliging nature. She did not want her brothers to worry about her. In this second account of her doings, there was even more to suppress. Lord Hawkslowe's death took a paragraph, and another went to praise young Lord Hawkslowe's dignity on his elevation to the title. She mentioned the departure of his Bradnam uncles but hesitated to admit the widow had not only gone with them but had now remarried scandalously soon. Safe to leave that out, probably, as while Rupert and Adam would read the newspapers at a coffee house, she doubted they bothered with notices of marriages. Unlike gentlemen of leisure, they would not linger long. Certainly she would not disclose the abduction and her part in it. They would be proud of her but also horrified, and she could only imagine Sybilla's freely expressed opinion of such ungenteel doings. No, best to describe the natural beauty and excellent husbandry practiced on the property. At "husbandry," her pen left a little blot when her mind stuttered over the word.

Alasdair had informed the children of their

mother's marriage. Predictably Isabelle wanted to know when they would visit her. She did not sound eager. Matthew asked when she would return. Janet bit her lip. Colin's face set in stern lines, eyes flinty. Their uncle explained that the former Lady Hawkslowe's plans were uncertain. They would have to wait and see. At least three of the four were clear-sighted about Elizabeth's ways. Matthew was the one most attached to her despite his mama's dislike of noise, fidgets, and dirt and her lack of patience with a little boy composed of those elements.

Nurse Sallows bustled into the library just then. "Ma'am, have you seen Master Matthew?"

"Not since dinner. Is he not with Colin? Or Mr. Dorring?"

"He said he was going to find a quiet place to do a lesson Mr. Dorring assigned him. Now it's near time for the children's supper, and I want to make sure he's not all over muck or dust afore he sits down to table, Mistress MacGavin."

Understandable, as Matthew's person did attract an unseemly amount of dirt and debris, and the contents of his pockets did not bear thinking of. The boy's stated desire for a quiet place was less common. "I'd expect to find him in the stables, if he's not in the house."

"Master Colin searched the stables and the dairy after I couldn't find him in the house. Archbold said he'd been there but hadn't stayed. He asked for a scrap of leather, then went off again."

"Did he take his pony?"

"That he did not. The stable lads and grooms all know he's not to ride alone, and they kept an eye on him."

"Are you certain he isn't in the house?"

"Master Colin and Miss Janet between them searched all the children's hiding-holes, attics to cellar, with the under-footman's help."

"Then as he's not inside, he's on foot, so he can't have gone too far." She said it more to reassure the nurse than because she believed it. Matthew knew he was not to go farther afield than the stables and paddock. That did not mean he would obey the ban.

Matthew had not resigned himself to the limitations on his rambles. The prospect of being abducted was unlikely to worry him. The boy would assume it could not happen to him or else see it as an opportunity to exercise his ingenuity in escaping. "Does Major Falstone know?"

"He's out of the house, mistress, visiting a laborer that's laid up with a bad back."

He might return soon, as he would not sit down to supper smelling of horse, sweat, and stable yard. But dare they wait for him? "I think perhaps we should order the grooms out to search for Matthew."

On her way to the stables, Margaret entered the kitchen to warn Mrs. Lindsay to set supper back a little. She found Colin there, just returned from the ice house.

"It was the only place we hadn't looked yet," he explained. Informed that she meant to dispatch the stable hands, he fell in after her. They were halfway across the yard when the miscreant came around the corner of the stable block. Matthew's cheerful but tuneless whistling broke off when he saw them.

"Where have you been, Matthew?"

"Ummm, for a walk, ma'am."

An obvious lie: he had not expected his absence to

be noticed.

"Where did you go?" Margaret kept her voice calm.

Colin did not. "You pestilent little weasel, didn't you think we would be worried for you? You know you're not to go off alone."

"I wasn't gone for long."

"Colin," Margaret began. A high-handed tone with a younger brother was bound to lead to a squabble.

For once, young Lord Hawkslowe was not listening. "You've been missing almost three hours, since you left the stable. We searched everywhere, and when we didn't find you, Janet began to think you must have broken your neck or your ankle or been snatched by gypsies to be sold to a chimney sweep—"

"Ho!" the wretch jeered.

Margaret said, "He's too well-fed for a sweep's boy. He'd stick in the chimney."

This unimpassioned observation caused Colin to grunt a laugh and Matthew to mutter half-heartedly, "No, I wouldn't." He was still chubby and thin-skinned about it.

"But would you want to be a sweep?"

"Uh…no."

"Well, go along to the nursery and clean up. You, too, Lord Hawkslowe."

Colin grinned and pulled his brother's tail of hair, which was straggling out of its braid and gave him a gentle shove. "Let's go, monkey."

Speaking privately to Falstone after supper, Margaret mentioned his younger nephew's desertion. Alasdair accepted it philosophically.

"He can't see why his freedom should be restricted.

As my sister-in-law has married again and"—his eyes gleamed with amusement—"feels the children should not be torn from their familiar surroundings, there's little reason to worry about further attempts to remove them. 'Tis my hope we will soon hear that she's given up any intention to apply to the Court of Chancery. Lord Annan will not wish to pay for that, however enamored he may be."

"So we only need to concern ourselves with whether Matthew may break his leg or his head while out on one of his jaunts, run away to sea, be spirited away by gypsies, gored by a bull, drown…"

Falstone grinned as she ran out of dire fates Matthew might suffer, looking much as she remembered him from their youth. "All venturesome children run those risks or others. We will do the best we can to keep him safe. He's a restless lad, and I think might do well in the army when he's older, if he learns to be less heedless. I'll tell him so tomorrow."

Somehow she and Falstone had acquired the worries and responsibilities of marriage and parenthood without any of the benefits. Margaret considered this riddle, feeling herself blush at the thought of the advantages those entailed.

Sallows appeared at the door, Colin behind her, before the moment became uncomfortable.

"Sallie? Colin?"

"I'm right sorry to bother you, Major, Mistress MacGavin, but his young lordship said as I shouldn't wait until tomorrow to tell you."

Oh, no. What now?

"When I was emptying Master Matthew's pockets before putting his clothing away, I found something in one o' them."

Colin was containing himself with difficulty, and why had he accompanied her anyway?

"Not knowing rightly what it was, I asked Master Co—Lord Hawkslowe—if he knew." Her apron had pockets like a market woman's. As usual they bulged with things that she might urgently want. Now she pulled out an odd object and held it up, a small rectangle of leather with long cords attached to the sides. Before Margaret could ask what it was, Alasdair took it from the nurse.

"A sling? Boys will play with them. As long as he's not killing anyone's chickens or geese, I don't see the harm. I suppose he got it from one of the stable boys."

Colin burst out, "Uncle Harry Bradnam made one and showed us how far it could throw a stone and how accurate it was. He could line up apples on a wall and hit every one. He told us about a Swiss shepherd killing a wolf with a sling, and I think the Romans used them in battle. That sheep, Uncle Alasdair, Towson's sheep, I think that's what killed it."

"You think your brother killed the sheep?" Falstone asked, brows raised skeptically.

Margaret said, "Matthew asked Archbold for a scrap of leather after dinner. Isn't it possible he only made this—this implement of destruction today and spent the afternoon practicing with it?"

Colin took a deep breath. "I don't think Matt killed the sheep. I expect Mistress MacGavin is correct that he only just made this sling. But I wonder if someone else has a sling."

"When did your uncle demonstrate his sling?"

Margaret asked. She would have been aware if he had spent any significant time with the boys after her arrival.

Colin's eyes focused somewhere beyond the room. "It was late summer or else autumn, because of the apples. It can't have been this past fall, because I'd been looking forward to starting at school, but then Mother said I shouldn't go when my father was in such poor health. And my Bradnam uncles weren't here at the time so it must have been the year before."

"Wasn't Matthew only about eight then? Almost two years is a long time at that age." From her experience with her brother's children, she would have expected him to want to make a sling immediately after learning of it. "Perhaps we should talk to Matthew, Major Falstone."

"The lad is in bed, asleep." Sallows tutted.

"He may be in bed, though I doubt it, but he won't be asleep. He'll be practicing sailors' knots. You have to be able to tie them in the dark. Or as it's still light, he might be playing with his marbles. He doesn't sneak out at night since I threatened to tell you, Uncle Alasdair. Probably," Colin qualified.

The bed hangings were open on the side nearest the door, and judging by Matthew's breathing, he had just scrambled into bed, though his eyes were closed and the covers pulled up to his chin. If more proof were needed, several inches of rope dangled below the bedclothes.

"Master Matthew," Sallows began.

An unconvincing snore.

"You may go, Sallie. Mistress MacGavin and I will discuss the matter with Matthew. And Lord Hawkslowe," he added when Colin cleared his throat.

Alasdair strode to the window and threw back the curtains. "Matthew, we know you're awake. We need to talk to you."

The little wretch sat up and rubbed his eyes before blinking owlishly at them.

"Nurse found your sling."

Falstone let the statement hang in the air, a method Margaret had used successfully with her brother's children. Somehow it compelled them to rush into explanations. Mayhap Major Falstone had found it worked with his men as well.

"Uh…" After a moment, Matthew said plaintively, "I didn't aim at anything."

"What did you aim at, Matthew?"

"Only an old wall, Uncle Alasdair."

"Where is this wall?"

"It's the one on the far side of the orchard, sir." A momentary pause preceded the reply. Margaret wondered if Alasdair had heard it. Her experience with small boys suggested there was something Matthew was not saying. One needn't be a mother or a governess to recognize his unease.

"If I go there, will I find a scatter of stones likely to have been thrown by a sling?" Falstone's bland expression did not deceive Margaret.

"Ay." Plenty of conviction but a certain lack of detail. Her younger brother had always expanded his stories in the belief that the more words, the more believable the tale.

"You'll find them, right enough," his older brother agreed. "That's where Uncle Harry showed us how to use a sling. I don't suppose anyone's picked them up since."

"Where did you go?"

Colin huffed. "I see you smirking, weasel, don't think I don't. Where was it really?"

Matthew darted a glance at Colin that said as clearly as if he had spoken, "If we were alone…"

"I will have an answer from you, boy."

Matthew swallowed convulsively. Margaret would have been intimidated by Falstone's tone. She could not think of him as Alasdair when he spoke like a hardened officer. She might have gone to give the boy a hug and comfort him, but he was in the wrong, and she would not undermine that lesson.

"That's where it was, sir. The stones being there already meant I wouldn't have to gather any."

"You disobeyed my order not to wander about on your own. You knew the reason for the order. I'd have had a dragoon who did the same flogged."

She loved him, but if he had ever spoken to her in that steely tone, she would have quailed.

"…Unless he had a very good explanation for doing so. Do you?"

Matthew swallowed. "No, sir. I was just bored and wanted to be outside."

"Then you are confined to this house until I tell you otherwise. Just the house, mind: not the yard or stables or anywhere outside these walls. Do you understand?"

"Yes, sir."

"Do you promise to obey that order?"

"Yes, sir." Matthew stared at the floor.

"Very well. Consider yourself lucky. If your father or I had committed such an offense, we would have been caned."

Margaret, near as shaken as Matthew, was glad to follow when Falstone left the room. She paused only long enough to tell Colin he should leave his brother to contemplate the error of his ways.

Chapter 32

Alasdair was off with the bailiff early the next morning to decide which fields of wheat must be cut first. Margaret wished he had not gone before she came down. In the middle of the night, something about Matthew's answers and demeanor began to trouble her. She might have spoken to Colin about it, but the boys were with Dorring, and she would not disrupt their routine. Her questions would wait until they were released from lessons. But later in the morning, Matthew wandered into the girls' parlor.

"Why aren't you in the schoolroom?"

"Mr. Dorring is testing Colin's Latin. He thinks everyone should be able to speak it, as if we were going to meet Caesar and need to ask where the bog-house is."

Controlling her impulse to laugh, Margaret said, "And your Latin didn't need the practice?"

"He said I was bothering Colin."

"Because you were bored and couldn't sit still?"

He shrugged. "Mayhap, ma'am."

"Janet, would you get out the sketching paper, pencils, and chalk. I would like you and Isabelle to draw a picture of whatever you like, while I speak with Matthew for a moment. We will go out so we don't distract you. Come along, Matthew."

"I'm sorry I caused you worry yesterday," he

muttered once they were in the passage. "I won't do it again."

"I know. It's very difficult to guess what will upset adults, isn't it?"

He cast a glance at her that wrung her heart. "I knew I shouldn't have gone out. I did disobey. But other times, how can you tell if you're doing the right thing?"

"Learning that is part of growing up. With more age and experience, you learn judgement." Or one hoped one did. A conscientious governess would have questioned him last night, but she had only sensed his discomfort, and that might have been caused by dread of punishment. The suspicion he was lying by omission and withholding something significant had not entered her mind when they were in his room.

"Matthew, how did you come to think of making a sling?"

He looked down at the toes of his shoes. "I remembered how much I liked it when Uncle Harry showed us how far his sling would throw a stone. He let us try, too."

"That was almost two years ago, wasn't it? What called it to mind that you suddenly remembered it yesterday?"

From his startled gaze, Margaret might have been his worst nightmare. Instinct had been correct. Guilt was writ plain on the square little face.

"You've seen your uncle Harry recently, haven't you?"

He froze. "How did you know?" he asked plaintively.

"I am a governess. I know boys the way Archbold

knows horses. Now, when and where did you see your uncle?"

Colin emerged from the schoolroom with a sigh of relief. His remark "I'm done and Mr. Dorring has given us half an hour free, not that you deserve it when you've been idling already" cut across Matthew's "I promised not to tell."

"Not to tell what?" his brother inquired, his attention caught.

"Uh…"

"I think we should talk about this in privacy. Follow me." She led them to a room used to store unneeded nursery furniture. It might have been a bedchamber for either a child or a second nursery maid. When they were inside and the door closed, she explained, "Matthew has admitted he has seen Mr. Harry Bradnam recently."

"You noddy, you should have known there was something wrong if he's skulking around here. And especially if he made you promise not to speak of it." The exasperation in Colin's voice would have made her smile if the matter were not so important.

"Do you know why he asked you to keep his presence secret?"

"He's guarding us, Mistress MacGavin, to make sure Janet and Isabelle aren't stolen away again, so we can catch the bully-ruffins. If I told, they might hear of it and be warned."

"Matt, Uncle Paul abducted our sisters."

"Ay, but he had a gang, and they mean to try again."

"Uncle Harry and Uncle Paul were both involved." Colin grinned without humor. "I imagine Harry planned it. Paul doesn't—didn't—have the wits for it."

"He wouldn't. Uncle Harry is a trusty-trout. Nobody said anything about him at the crowner thing."

Colin took a deep, exasperated breath. Before he could speak, Margaret said, "Matthew, the coroner did not read the parts that spoke of your mother's and Mr. Harry Bradnam's part in the abduction. Your uncle Harry knew about it and gave the driver his orders."

Matthew, for once struck speechless, stared at her. Margaret suspected he would like to deny it could be true but dared not imply she was lying.

"This is what comes of keeping things to ourselves. The major and Sir Hugh thought it best not to make the scandal worse by implicating your mama and other uncle. Your uncle Falstone told your brother about the complete statements. You should have been part of that meeting."

Denial of Bradnam's guilt and pride at the suggestion he should have been included warred in his expression.

"But why would he?" Matthew chewed his lip before going on, "Why would they take my sisters?"

Before she could decide how to explain it, Colin took the matter into his own hands. "Why do you think Janet and Izzy were taken, Matt?"

"So we'd give money to get them back."

"Uncle Paul told Janet Mother wanted the girls with her. You know Uncle Harry and Uncle Paul would do anything to help Mother, the same as we'd do whatever we could if Janet or Izzy asked us."

"Oh." Matthew sat digesting this. "But why would Uncle Harry say it was rum coves if it wasn't?"

"Maybe he thought that sounded more exciting. I'll

warrant you enjoyed the idea. But you shouldn't be using terms like 'rum coves' in a lady's hearing. Or anyone else's, either. They'd take you for a hedge bird." A pause. "A scoundrel, I should have said, ma'am."

Matthew was not deflected by the admonition. "If Mama wanted the girls to live with her, why didn't she ask for them?"

"Your papa wanted you all to live here, rather than in London, as I apprehend Lady Hawkslowe means to do. The countryside is healthier for children." Margaret would have added that they would have more freedom in the country, if they were not forbidden to roam at the moment.

"But what if Janet and Izzy want to live with our mother?"

"Your uncle Falstone is your guardian and must abide by your father's wishes."

Colin's succinct, "Would you?" was a better reply although not one Margaret could have used.

"No. But I'm not a girl."

"Janet and Isabelle took their first chance to escape, Matthew. When I came upon them, they were halfway up a hill from your uncle, hiding in the gorse. They didn't want to go. Wouldn't you miss them if they were gone?"

Matthew said frankly, "Not Izzy, when she acts like a baby."

"She is very young. I think you must forgive her not being as grown up as you are." Margaret gave him a conspiratorial smile.

"I would miss her sometimes, and Janet, too. Why didn't Uncle Harry come to the house? If there aren't any rogues, he'd be more comfortable here."

Margaret sensed Colin's sigh rather than heard it.

"Matt, he would have done so if he were not up to some mischief. Instead, he is hiding and told you to keep mum about seeing him. Mayhap he means to steal one or both of the girls again."

After a frowning moment's reflection, his brother sighed deeply and repeated, "Oh. So it was all a Banbury story, then?"

"Ay. Where did you see our uncle?"

"The ruined cottage."

Margaret raised her eyebrows inquiringly.

"It was burned during one of the raids, I don't know when, and neither did Father. We used to go there to dig for treasure." He caught her look and added, "I know! Not much of value in a hut no bigger than a cowshed. I did find an old Scots penny—"

Matthew interrupted, "I found a dagger!"

"No need to worry, Mistress MacGavin," Colin said. " 'Twas the grip and cross-guard only."

"One night last summer, Uncle Harry went there with us, ma'am, and we cooked our supper and slept there."

Colin grinned at the memory. "You were so tired you didn't even notice how hard the ground was."

"A reiver wouldn't care for that."

"It sounds very uncomfortable."

Both boys gave her a look that said *ladies have no love of adventure*.

"How did you get there yesterday, Matthew? You didn't take your pony."

"It's only about three miles, I think, no walk at all."

"Is—never mind, I've forgotten what I meant to

say. Cook was making jumbles earlier. You should go down and see if she will give you one or two to fend off starvation until dinner."

"Thank you! I'll race you," Matthew tossed the challenge over his shoulder, already moving.

"Not a chance, monkey." Colin had seen Margaret's quick head shake, staying him. "Barons don't run in the house."

The boy clattered down the stair.

"Colin, where is the cottage? Could you draw a map? Major Falstone will want to know."

"Uncle Alasdair grew up here, Mistress MacGavin. I'd wager he played there, too."

"He was gone for more years than you have lived and may have forgotten."

"Then I will take him there."

She drew in a deep breath. "I don't think he will want you to come with him. I did not want to ask Matthew, but did you receive the impression that your uncle might be staying at the cottage?"

"I wondered," he admitted.

"If he is, your uncle Falstone will not want you present, as, mmm, hard words may be spoken."

He searched her face but did not utter what he clearly suspected: that the confrontation might be violent. "I'll do it now. May I use your parlor? In case Mr. Dorring asks what I'm doing?" Since his father's death, Colin had been growing into his title.

****

Colin's map, drawn in a few minutes on a sheet of writing paper, showed the house, stables, a spinney, sheepfold, and two or three other landmarks she knew from riding with Alasdair or the children. Margaret thanked him and sent him off to join his brother and the tutor. Their lessons would have resumed by the time she changed into her riding habit. After asking the second footman to have her horse saddled, Margaret slipped into the study. She was doing the right thing; she was. She was almost certain, but what if she were wrong? She scribbled a note in pencil and left it on the desk, weighted by the pounce pot.

"She's lively today," the groom said, as Archbold emerged from the stable.

"Geordie, you'll go with Mistress MacGavin." To her, he said, "You'll want a groom with you, ma'am."

She definitely did not want one. "It's quite unnecessary. I'm only going to the village."

"The major said you and the children was to take a groom, mistress."

"If the children rode, certainly. He did not mean if I went out by myself." She suspected he had meant she should be accompanied, too, but salved her conscience with the reflection that Alasdair's instructions had not actually said the order applied to her.

Archbold's frown suggested he was torn between insisting or taking her word and letting her go. The latter won out.

"I reckon not much can run-a-reel, between here and the village," he admitted.

She rode out of the stable yard sedately, guiding her mare toward the lane. Out of sight of the house and stables, she turned north to the moorland.

At the spinney, if the map's relative distances were correct, another two miles would bring her to the old cot.

Chapter 33

The bothy might almost have been undamaged, seen from the south, except that it was unroofed. She rode no nearer than a pistol ball's range as she circled the cottage. Its west end was almost intact, too, with only a few of the unmortared stones fallen from the gable-end. A fitful western wind was blowing, potentially carrying her horse's scent and the sound of her hooves. She trusted the stone walls to block both sound and scent.

The north wall had fared badly, with most of the middle fallen into rubble. The door and windows on that side likely weakened it, causing the greater dilapidation. Reining in, she sat, visible to anyone not sheltering in one of the front corners. There was no sign of horse or man in the interior, so far as she could ascertain. But she could not see what might be concealed behind the remaining sections of wall at either end. If she had hidden in such a hut, she would have kept to those sheltering angles.

Urging Athena forward to within shouting distance, Margaret shouted, "Mr. Bradnam!" To shoot, he would have to see her, and no one could mistake a lady riding sidesaddle for a man. Then she waited while the mare stirred restively. Margaret murmured, "There now, that's a fine girl. Nothing to worry about," and hoped she was correct.

A tall brown-clad figure eased into view at the edge of the gap. His right arm hung down at his side, the hand out of sight, holding a pistol, no doubt. His eyes swept the moorland beyond her and to the sides. Would he be wondering whether an attacker or attackers were waiting out of sight? Probably not. Most gentlemen would not expect a mere female to be used as a decoy.

"Mistress MacGavin."

"Mr. Bradnam, may I dismount and approach? I have news you must hear."

"I would prefer you do so if you are not armed, for I hear you are a desperate fine hand with a pistol." He laughed, as at a jest.

Drawing room civility contrasted oddly with their words and raised voices. Bradnam's dispassionate face and voice warred with her previous impression of him as a shallow man about town. Margaret freed her foot from the stirrup and her leg from the pommel and slid to the ground.

When she was near enough they could converse in normal tones, Harry Bradnam spoke again. "I conclude you pried my presence out of Matthew."

"A sling was found in his pocket. As Colin, Lord Hawkslowe, mentioned you had shown them how to use one, I found it odd that Matthew would remember that lesson from years ago. When I questioned him, he let it slip he had seen you recently. He believed there was no real harm in telling me because he believed you were here to protect his sisters."

Bradnam dismissed her ironic remark with a curt, "A necessary deception. You must not have informed Falstone, or he would be here instead of you."

"When men who are out of sympathy with each other meet, the very best outcome one can expect is hot words. I felt it better to resolve the matter in a more rational way. I have news which I trust will make that possible."

He barked a sardonic laugh, quickly cut off. "I hardly know whether to praise your resolve or censure you for lack of female delicacy. I am not sure I approve of you as an example for my nieces. Janet was already too tart in her speech. Though I admit I would not object to Janet and Isabelle possessing some part of your character. A female without good sense is plaguey tiresome. Well! You say you have news. Pray tell me what brought you in search of me and how you believe it can change anything."

"Major Falstone received a letter from Lady Hawkslowe a few days since. She has married."

His thunderstruck silence was all she could have hoped for.

"What?" he demanded.

"Lady Hawkslowe wed Lord Annan, a Scottish earl. She informed—"

"Lord Annan," he repeated, his brows drawing together.

"Yes, do you know him? Lady Hawkslowe, that is, Lady Annan now, wrote she and the earl would be leaving for London. She thinks it best the children remain at Scot Hall."

Bradnam frowned over this disclosure. At last he said, "I don't believe it. This is some trick to keep Elizabeth's children, my nieces and nephews, from her." Maybe 'twas more hope than conviction.

"I have the letter in my pocket." She put her hand

through the slit in her habit's skirt slowly, drew out the letter with equal care, and held it out. He approached and took the letter with his left hand.

He retreated some paces before fumbling it open one-handed to read it with half his attention still on her. He stood scowling, then read it again. "I cannot believe it."

"Is it not Lady Hawkslowe's hand?"

"Ay, but I meant, that she would give the girls up, when she wept and railed over their being required to live at Scot Hall."

His perplexity was unmistakable. The flintlock hung at his side as if he had forgotten its existence. Margaret's horse cropped grass.

"Shall we sit on that bit of wall in the shade, Mr. Bradnam?"

He exhaled sharply and made a polite gesture with the hand holding the letter, inviting her to go before him. The remnant of the house wall was just a little higher than a bench, though not nearly as comfortable. He took his seat to her right. Staring at the paper, he set the pistol down to his right as she had intended. Really, they could not talk if his mind was always wondering if she would try to grab the gun. That would certainly be foolish! He folded the sheet and gave it back to her.

"I did not think she felt so strongly, Mr. Bradnam. Her ladyship seemed composed when she departed for her sister's home."

He flushed. "She thought she would get them back without difficulty."

"But that failed."

"Because of my ignorance of the laws relating to guardianship. We would have pursued her case in the

Court of Chancery, but she was distraught, and there were reasons against it."

"The cost and the length of time to get a decision?"

The tired, rumpled man beside her nodded. "Among other considerations. Apart from the expense, she could not have been happy"—he likely meant without prolonged fits of the vapors and megrims—"until the matter was resolved."

Another reason was perhaps her theft of the Lady Day rent monies. The court might also have disapproved of her failure to provide a tutor and governess for her children.

"I apprehend you took her to Scotland, where she could have claimed custody if she spirited Janet and Isabelle away." She struggled to keep censure out of her voice.

"Girls should be with their mother. Naturally, William—Colin, I should say—has to grow up at Scot Hall, and taking Matthew away from his brother would be wrong. And boys fare better reared in the country. Growing up in town does them no favor." He went on in a non sequitur, "My father moved our family to London when Paul was still in leading strings."

"I'm sorry about your brother."

"It's for Falstone to be sorry for shooting him when no real harm had been done."

"But he didn't shoot him," Margaret said.

"Paul's lying dead in the ground, no doubt of that. If Falstone didn't murder him, who did?"

"I did. He was going to shoot Major Falstone."

"You?" Bradnam stared at her.

"Yes."

Brow furrowed, he said, "The man I sent to

Rochester mentioned some such rumor but thought it nonsense. Rumors! Who ever heard of a female, a staid governess at that, able or willing to shoot a man?"

"My husband was a gunsmith. I tested the firearms meant for ladies."

Bradnam's eyes focused inward in thought or memory. "I seem to recall my sister speaking of your late husband."

Probably that she could not understand how a gentleman's granddaughter could lower herself to marry an artisan.

He nodded slowly. "I suppose Falstone and the magistrate between 'em did what they could to conceal your part in it. Hardly suitable conduct for a female of any sort. In London you'd feature in the satirical prints. Fortunately for you, this is Northumberland, so it may work." Slumping, he no longer looked like a London beau or a man in the prime of life.

"I'm sorry for his death," she said softly. "But not that Major Falstone survived."

"Paul should have given over when he saw there was no hope of getting away with the girls. If they'd been able to turn and go back the only way they could, they'd have met Falstone. Killing him wouldn't have made it possible to escape. If Paul had killed Falstone, likely he'd have hanged."

"I wonder they chose that route, as the rise from the stream was so steep."

" 'Twas the shortest way. Paul did not always think things through before acting. Cattle and horses used the road, therefore a carriage should pass as well. My brother…" He grunted. "I helped him out of a good many predicaments when he was younger. And not so young, neither."

"I know the three of you were close."

The moorland wind whistled around the ruined bothy at their back. Bradnam's voice was not much louder. "We had to be." His gaze roamed over the moorland before them.

Margaret waited while he sat lost in memory.

"In most families, the oldest son at least receives some attention. Our father inherited a manor and a competency, and there was my mother's dowry as well. Most men who fritter away their livelihood do it by cards and dice or living above their means. Our father's interests lay in scholarship, which should be a benign, inexpensive pastime."

She scarcely breathed, not wanting to interrupt him.

"His interest in antiquities far outweighed whatever affection he felt for his wife. By the time I was six or seven, I knew she was unhappy. Eventually I understood she married my father because he was handsome and a member of the landed gentry. He had courted her assiduously for her dowry. She either assumed, or he led her to believe, they would live in London part of the year. He did keep that promise as soon as his father died. He took us to town where there are booksellers and collections of ancient artifacts and ignored the running of the property. He refused to hire a bailiff because that would take money he could spend on old bits looted from some Roman or Druid or Viking site. Books, too, of course. He was contemptuous of society and the entertainments my mother longed for. We seldom visited the manor."

"Colin told me about your Grand Tour," she

ventured.

"He sent me on the 'Grand Tour' "—his tone gave the words a bitter twist—"only because a neighbor who was plump in the pocket asked me to accompany his son. He covered my share of the travel and lodging and paid me a bit besides. I'd have gone into the army afterward, if I could have bought a commission. I might still have been able to do so on my fool of a papa's death. His library and old curios should have brought a considerable amount if he hadn't left them to a museum. Thank God he died before my mother inherited from my uncle, a Scotch tobacco importer. The beau monde scorn money made in trade, but when all's said, 'tis better to have money than to be poor."

How true that is. "Did your mother not…?"

"Buy me a commission? No. I imagine she had been so disappointed in her marriage that she had no tenderness to spare for her children. I was useful, so of course I could not be permitted to abandon her. She was pleased when Elizabeth caught Hawkslowe's eye, and Corinna delighted her by catching a viscount."

"Your brother and sisters were enough younger than you that you acted as their parent."

"How did you guess that, Mistress MacGavin?" He swiveled to fix his attention on her as if seeing her for the first time.

"I served a similar function for my younger brother after my mother died. My father was away in the army or in London once he sold out. My grandfather loved us, but he could not take the place of a mother."

"Ah. Then you understand how it is. I did my best with them. It was not good enough. They were hand in glove, being only a year apart and so like in their natures." His jaw clenched.

"I had hoped Elizabeth would be happily established with Hawkslowe. If he had flattered her and allowed her little indulgences while curbing her greater excesses, all might have been well. Unfortunately, he expected her to be sensible and to behave as if they were no more than landed gentry. Paul only encouraged her. I did keep her from giving Hawkslowe cause to divorce her when she was in London. She was starved for attention and responded to any personable man who gave it. You may be sure I kept her from giving anything back. I had to call one rakehell out to discourage him. Now Paul is dead, and she must have decided to trade her claim to her daughters to be a countess and live in London part of the year."

"And for her new husband's admiration. I gather he is quite rich."

His smile was twisted. "I am not such a hypocrite as to pretend wealth is not important. I confess I may have been at fault in giving in to her desire to go about in company a little. But I do not think I could have persuaded her to observe proper mourning for Hawkslowe."

Was that what he and his sister had argued about shortly before he left Edinburgh? She could not ask without letting him know they had been spied upon. "You did not guess she and Lord Annan were becoming so friendly?"

"We had met him. Elizabeth referred to him several times, but no more than she had spoken of this man or that. I believe she was content until Ackerley returned to tell us of the mishap with the coach and that Paul and the girls and the coachman had disappeared. Afterward, she was in a taking with worry. I was concerned but thought they might have left the ford on the horses to find other transportation. Ackerley dared not make inquiries in case he drew further attention to the ill-fated affair. When they did not arrive, I found a man willing to ferret out what news he could."

She let the silence stretch, broken by the rustling of the grass and a bird's call.

"Apparently some of the coroner's jury findings were garbled by his informants at the public house, as my fellow said Falstone had killed him. The bumpkins may not even have been present at the inquest. When she heard Paul was dead, my sister was thrown into fury and despair, and I do not know which was greater. After the first transports of her grief, Elizabeth insisted on attending whatever entertainments we were invited to, and I gave way. We could hardly turn them down pleading mourning when we had been accepting some invitations as if she were in the last stages of mourning for Hawkslowe. But when she was invited to a house party, I told her she could not attend so newly widowed. 'Twould cause talk and set people's backs up. I also feared that she might be indiscreet. I should have held my tongue. Now I suspect Annan was to be present, and she meant to meet him there." He stared across the rolling moor to distant hills, face stony.

He had confided more than she had expected which made her next step difficult to decide. The note she left had been vague, but her meeting with Bradnam must be finished soon for everyone's good.

Alasdair, I've gone to make some inquiries. If I am not returned by supper, ask Colin. Margaret

A trifle awkward to ask what Bradnam had been

doing, lurking in a ruin on Hawkslowe property or what he meant to do now. Needs must, however. She broke the silence. "Mr. Bradnam, what brings you here?"

He turned to look at her. Meeting his stare, she saw that his eyes were storm cloud gray.

"Why, to kill Falstone."

As she had suspected, which explained why Bradnam was encamped here, and perhaps why he might practice with a sling. His casual admission chilled her nonetheless.

"Your desire for revenge is understandable, but now you know he is not to blame for your brother's death. If you killed him"—*or me*, she reflected—"you would hang, depriving your sister of her remaining brother."

His mirthless laugh gave her more cause for fear than his bald statement of intention had done.

"Madam, your markswomanship far exceeds your insight. Even if the major had killed Paul, revenge would accomplish nothing."

She believed him. "But if you are not here to avenge Mr. Paul Bradnam, why did you come?"

"I had unfinished business with Falstone." Meeting her gaze, he said, "If Falstone were dead by some mischance, a new guardian would be appointed. As the children's remaining uncle, I would be the obvious choice and a far better one than their being made wards in Chancery."

"Did you kill the sheep?"

"Well…" He shrugged, discomfited. "I had to make sure my plan would succeed."

He saw her draw the obvious conclusion. An apparent fall from his horse causing Falstone a fatal head injury would be deemed an accident.

"Pray, do not faint, Mistress MacGavin, unless you have a vial of spirits of hartshorn in your pocket, which I take leave to doubt. Would a drop of brandy steady you?"

She forced herself to breath slowly, to steady her heart. "No. Does this mean you hold by your plan?"

"I do not. If I did kill him, you would make sure I hanged for his murder."

She did not speak.

"What do you take me for? I certainly could not retaliate against a woman." His irritation reassured her as a softer tone would not.

"And yet you would have the advantage of being able to loot the estate."

He frowned. "My family has not always shown to good advantage, but I protest I am not as expensive as Paul was or as Elizabeth is. My reason for securing the guardianship is no more, now she is married. I am in your debt for informing me of Elizabeth's decision." He went on, perhaps more to himself than to her, "From the date of her letter, she must have made her own plans and left Edinburgh within two or three days of my departure. As soon as I was gone, in fact. I wonder if she has sent a letter to the house to tell me she is now married and, by the bye, no longer wants custody of the girls as her husband does not wish to pay the costs of a suit in Chancery or raise another man's get."

"She does not phrase it so in the letter to Falstone."

"No, but I've no doubt that is why she now thinks it in their best interests to grow up at Scot Hall."

Margaret thought it best to not to respond to Harry Bradnam's interpretation of Lady Hawkslowe's letter as she herself had no very high opinion of her ladyship's devotion to her offspring. "Then there can be no further dispute between you and Major Falstone."

A slight, sad smile and a shake of his head. "Not now, ma'am. I admit I am glad of it. I have never been blind to my sister's and brother's weaknesses, although they were both rather lovable as children. I can't think how Corinna turned out so well."

"Then you will be returning to Scotland?"

"Ay, to pack up my belongings and arrange for the sale of the house we bought near Edinburgh. It's too big for me, and what would I do there? My sister will not need it. Her new husband has houses in Glasgow and London and a manor near Bristol."

"Do you mean to remove to London, then?"

"I suppose so. There or to Hades. This is a devilish coil. Do you know if Falstone is like to pursue me? I do not have a sense of him, our acquaintance having got off to a bad start."

Would he? "I think not. From the coachman's and Bessie's sworn statements, your brother is known to have abducted the girls, but the portion that implicated you and Lady Hawkslowe was not read at the inquest to avoid creating an even greater scandal. The maid, Bessie, swore she knew nothing of the abduction and only hid my boots as a prank at Ackerley's request. I believe Falstone will let the matter go, to avoid gossip. If you simply withdraw from here, no harm has been done but to the man who owned the sheep."

"Not much harm there. I've no doubt he found it while it was fresh and was able to make good use of the mutton and hide." He laughed without much humor. "I have lost my sister as well as my brother, now

Elizabeth has married a hard-headed Scot. If I have his measure, he'll pay his wife's bills but won't open his purse strings and let her dip her pretty fingers in. 'Drones hive not with me' is probably his motto." He grinned reluctantly. "And very wise of him, too. I would wager he'll break her of her habit of gambling—and losing—which I was never able to do."

She uttered a noncommittal *hmmm*. "Now I suppose you will be free to travel. Colin told me how much you enjoyed your time on the Continent."

"As you are not a goose, I've no doubt you understand something of my circumstances. Paul and I depended on Elizabeth to eke out the little income we were left, Paul more than I. I've been as economical as I could, but my sister's generosity allowed me to enjoy some of the elegancies of life."

Alasdair had told her both brothers were supported by Lady Hawkslowe with money and by housing them at Scot Hall part of the year. "I understood something of the sort," she admitted. "Have you considered marrying?"

"That is the common remedy for empty pockets. I should have taken it years ago. But I could not spare the time for courtship or marriage while I was responsible for Elizabeth and Paul. I would not be a very acceptable prospect to the papa of any lady with a decent dowry. I can get by. There's the income Paul and I were left, and now he is gone, I'll inherit his share. I'll have all the rent from our house in town. Our father's manor was sold years ago. And I'm clever with cards and dice."

She should leave it at that. The wind was blowing harder, and mounds of cloud puffed up over the hills like dough rising on a warm hearth. Besides, the afternoon was far advanced. They might soon be interrupted. She was not sure she liked Harry Bradnam, but she did feel some sympathy for him, purse-pinched and having spent years trying to help siblings for whom he had filled a parent's place.

"Colin told me you are skilled at a number of sporting and strenuous activities. I wonder if you would permit me to make a suggestion as to a possible career?"

"Please do, ma'am. I never scorn good advice." His eyebrows and the corners of his lips raised satirically.

"My late husband was accounted the best gunsmith in London. The government sometimes purchased guns from him."

"I would think a single gunsmith could hardly supply enough muskets to the army."

"He didn't. He sold pistols to an office in Somerset House. Small, accurate ones, for use by men engaged in delicate government work. He and the gentleman in charge were on excellent terms. I met him once myself, when he bought a ladies' pistol for his sister. MacGavin told me that department is always in need of men. I imagine there is a good deal of travel, and perhaps in time they come to want a more settled life." That would be the preferable reason for leaving the service. "I will give you his name if you think such work might suit you."

Harry Bradnam regarded her intently. "Would he not be surprised if I arrived to request a post without a letter of introduction?"

"His office is unconcerned about formalities. If he should want to know how you heard of him, give my name."

"Somerset House, you said. For whom am I to ask?"

"Sir John Fletcher. His title is so vague, he might be anything."

Bradnam rose from his seat on the wall. "That is unexpectedly kind of you, all things taken together. Thank you. Now it would be well if we went our ways before the storm commences, as seems likely. Pray make my apologies to Falstone both for my earlier actions and for trespassing on Scot Hall land recently. I'll assist you to mount."

When she was in her saddle, he sketched a bow. "Your servant, ma'am." He turned back toward the bothy.

Chapter 34

A roar of "Bradnam!" from the side of the cottage caused Athena to startle. Margaret steadied the mare and turned to see Alasdair Falstone frozen-faced as a mounted statue, leveling a long-barreled dragoon pistol at Bradnam. She clicked her tongue, giving Athena the signal to move forward between Harry Bradnam and the man she reluctantly admitted she still loved.

Using the calm voice she employed with horses and sometimes with tired, fractious children, she addressed the latter. "Major Falstone, Mr. Bradnam is leaving now he has heard of his sister's marriage. He means no one any harm." Bradnam's weapon was still lying on the wall where they had been sitting, not far from Bradnam. Neither one of them would harm her…intentionally.

There were many things she liked about men. Their tendency to take a miff at each other out of pique or misplaced pride was not one of them. Gideon had once observed that young bucks were like defective pistols, apt to go off at inconvenient times. Not that either Bradnam or Falstone was young enough to make it understandable.

"Margaret, take cover behind the house." He gave a slight jerk of his head toward the bothy's end wall.

"With all due respect, Major, I really cannot allow either of you to do something we will all regret. Only think of the scandal."

Bradnam gave a choke of laughter, quickly cut off. "Major, you have no reason to think well of my family. I came here under a misapprehension. Two, in fact, and Mistress MacGavin having explained matters to me, I have no further grievance against you."

Thank God Bradnam had kept a cool head. She leveled her governess gaze at Falstone. He had lowered his pistol, but his vexation was palpable. Margaret said gently, "Sometimes the fan is more useful than the sword."

The lines of tension eased. "Nevertheless, I would like you to remove yourself to a safe distance."

"Why should it be necessary unless one of you means to do something ill advised?"

Before he could frame a reply, Bradnam spoke. "Will it suit you if I move some distance from the bothy so that Mistress MacGavin can take charge of my flintlock? 'Tis on the wall," Bradnam added as if Alasdair might not have seen it, as Margaret was sure he had.

"Very well." He might not be quite easy, but he had had time to think of the consequences.

Bradnam walked away slowly, keeping his hands away from his pockets until he stopped and faced Falstone. Margaret rode forward without waiting for Alasdair to give his permission. Her lack of deference to his male authority might annoy him, but she was not some milk-and-water miss. She leaned down and possessed herself of the pistol. Good: not cocked. She held it pointed down on Athena's off side, all fingers around the butt.

At Alasdair's side, she murmured, "Don't you

think we should keep to our original plan?" He would recall they had agreed after the inquest not to take further action against Bradnam.

Between exasperation and amusement, he remarked, "You always were a rare handful," before raising his voice to carry. "Are we quits then, Bradnam?"

She sighed. He thought her headstrong and unwomanly. Well, and so she was.

"We are, Major. No one but my brother bears any responsibility for his death. I understand my sister now feels the children should grow up at Scot Hall, a decision with which I am in complete agreement." He grinned suddenly, and years and weariness fell away. "I mean to go to London and find some not-too-ungenteel work."

"Good luck to you."

"Thank you, sir. If I may collect my horse and my effects, I can be away before the storm breaks. Or at least to the nearest inn."

"You'll need to ride hard, as will we."

"I'll return your pistol to the wall, Mr. Bradnam."

He stood without moving, an eye on Falstone. "Thank you. 'Servant, Mistress MacGavin, Major. And my best wishes to you, ma'am."

Margaret trotted her mare to the wall and set the pistol back, before rejoining Alasdair. Harry Bradnam strode toward the bothy without hurry as the first, distant thunder rumbled like the wheels of some gigantic dray in the sky. She had a sudden, ridiculous fantasy of some nurse telling a frightened child, " 'Tis only God's traveling coach passing." She and Alasdair wheeled their horses with one mind, first cantering, then galloping.

****

They were wet to the skin when Campbell and one of the other grooms hurried to take their horses as they rode into the stable yard.

"Shall we run for the door as if we were as young as we used to be?" Alasdair inquired as he lifted her down from the saddle.

She grinned at him. He must have forgiven her unwomanly conduct.

The kitchen maids exclaimed at their condition, and Mistress Lindsay said she would send hot drinks up to their chambers.

"And I've set back supper, you not being home yet, so you've time to change and drink my posset down. Miss Isabelle and Master Matthew have had their supper, but Miss Janet and Lord Hawkslowe are waiting in the drawing room."

As they went upstairs, he said, "Let us talk after Janet and Colin have gone upstairs."

Her mind scurried in a dozen different directions. Talk about—?

The meal was set out, and Falstone dismissed the footman.

"Lord Hawkslowe and Janet insist on hearing what occurred today. We may as well tell them now so they will be free, curiosity satisfied, after supper." Something conspiratorial lurked in his eyes. Her heart leapt. Alasdair would give a military man's summary of the event and spare her having to talk. But she was permitted no opportunity to speculate or worry or hope, which was perhaps just as well.

"Mistress MacGavin, if I had known you meant to

use the map I drew, I would not have given it to you." Colin's reproach demanded an answer.

"I was sorry to deceive you, Lord Hawkslowe, but I thought it best not to involve you or Major Falstone or any other man."

"They do always keep all the adventures for themselves," Janet contributed.

Margaret would not have suspected her of a longing for excitement. Oh, fiddlesticks! Had her shooting of Paul Bradnam given it birth? Margaret had not intended to talk about her role today. Yet as a painstaking governess, she should try to encourage sensible conduct. There had been nothing really perilous about her meeting with Bradnam. Perhaps that was the best course to take.

"I did not rush into a dangerous situation, Janet. Based on my observations of Mr. Harry Bradnam, I believed he would not harm a female." Or on her intuition about him, far more difficult to explain.

From his eyes and a certain curl of his lips, she deduced Alasdair was not deceived.

"But still, ladies do not ride alone without even a groom in case of a riding mishap—"

Janet muttered, "Pooh," so softly only Margaret heard.

While the remark summed up her own feelings, she aimed a reproving glance at her charge. Janet blushed and lowered her eyes. Colin might have missed this little exchange, but Margaret thought Falstone had caught the second part at least. Perhaps he was as aware of her every word and action as she was of his.

"As a rule, I do not ride alone. In this one case, I felt it necessary."

"But why, ma'am? To confront our uncle alone seems contrary to common sense. Though I would wager on you against Uncle Harry in a pistol match." Colin contemplated the stewed celery without favor and helped himself to pickles instead.

She would not admit she had gone unarmed. The meeting would not have been improved by the presence of another weapon. "I considered it necessary to speak with him without introducing the threatening presence of a man. I have observed that when men expect violence, they tend to create trouble rather than prevent it."

"But…" Young Lord Hawkslowe either forgot what he had begun to say or thought better of it.

"They do, don't they," Janet remarked.

"Margaret, I hope you will not reveal all of our little foibles to Janet."

"Oh." Colin appeared to be deep in thought unless he was only deciding between the raspberry tarts and the almond cheese cakes.

"But knowing such things is far more useful than the ability to paint pretty watercolors, Uncle."

"Janet, I begin to fear you will be dangerous when you are older."

She smiled saucily. "Will you not tell us your part in the afternoon, sir?"

"I hardly did more than escort Mistress MacGavin home."

"What of Uncle Harry?" Colin asked.

Margaret and Falstone traded glances. He poured another glass of claret and sipped before replying. "We four agreed weeks ago not to pursue your uncle because it would cause talk. He was concerned about various aspects of the situation."

When he paused after this vague statement, evidently trying to decide what and how much to tell them, Margaret stepped into the breach.

"Your uncle was unaware of your mother's remarriage. Now that he does know, he understands you should not be uprooted by being moved between Lord Annan's estate and London when they go there. Mr. Bradnam agrees you will all do better to live here." She looked to Alasdair mutely.

Although the baron and his sister were not notably alike in face, they wore identical, pinched expressions. Neither spoke immediately.

Janet's voice was colorless when she observed, tight-lipped, "Mama would not deal well with widowhood. I suppose she and Lord Annan will live in London much of the year, which will please her."

If not Janet, Margaret reflected.

"Our mother's marriage might be for the best in spite of any talk it will cause," Colin said at last. "Without a husband, she has only her jointure to support her. I assume the Earl of Annan is not a purse-pinched Scottish peer, sir?"

"He has the advantage of owning or investing in shipbuilding and tobacco importation in addition to rents from his properties."

Colin Hawkslowe nodded briskly. "Then he can support her comfortably. As he married Mother on short acquaintance—"

"Eloped," his sister interrupted.

"—he must care for her."

Or be very foolish, though Alasdair had believed not.

While Janet considered her brother's conclusion, Colin addressed Falstone.

"As we need not worry about our mother trying to replace you as our guardian, matters appear to be settled."

Janet's thoughts followed a different path. "A Scottish peerage is not as desirable as an English one, of course, but she is a countess. I admit 'tis perhaps the best result Mama could hope for, and we must therefore be happy for her." Against their better judgement, her tone implied.

"Very true," Margaret agreed and leaned over to put an arm around the girl's shoulders.

"Janet, Colin, this has been a difficult day, and we all have much to think about. You may go upstairs now if you wish," Falstone suggested rather than ordered.

"Ma'am," Colin began, "and Uncle Alasdair, too…what are we to tell Isabelle and Matthew? Especially Matthew."

Margaret looked to Alasdair. She saw him debating with himself and wondered whether the stern soldier or the fond uncle would win.

"I think you need only say that Mistress MacGavin and I conferred with Mr. Bradnam and agreed that as your mother has now remarried, all parties think it best you live here."

"Matthew will want to know why Uncle Harry lied to him."

At Colin's question, Margaret beheld her love perplexed. She said, "Mr. Bradnam felt a little uncomfortable approaching Major Falstone directly. By lingering nearby, he hoped his presence would become known to the major—"

"And Mistress MacGavin."

She cast him a reproving glance. "And me, and that we would approach him so he could apologize for any misunderstandings and to discuss the matter. On neutral ground, you know."

Skeptical looks from Colin and Janet, though Colin said, "I think I can convince him."

"Will Uncle Harry visit?" Janet asked warily.

"I don't think—"

Margaret cut him off with an apologetic twitch of her lips. "I understand he means to take a post which may require a good deal of travel, some of it abroad, no doubt. We'll have to wait until he knows when he can come north."

"Thank you, ma'am. Uncle Alasdair, may Matthew and Isabelle apply to you or Mistress MacGavin if they have questions we cannot answer?"

"Certainly, Colin."

The pair took their leave, bowing or curtsying. As the door closed, Janet was saying, "I think we should not explain too much. When they are a little older—"

"Do you want to order a tea tray to the drawing room, Margaret? Or would you prefer something else?"

"I will take a glass of madeira. Bohea is insufficiently strong for today's alarms and excursions." Certainly, it was too weak for whatever subject Alasdair meant to address.

They left the servants to clear the table.

By unspoken agreement, they went to the family parlor rather than the drawing room. Falstone presented her a filled wine glass. In the evening light from the windows, the wine glowed. He poured brandy into a tumbler engraved like her own stemmed glass with the rose and brambles which were part of the family coat of arms. Leaving off the serpent and the stooping hawk had been a wise decision, Margaret judged.

She seated herself at one end of the sofa. Would he sit beside her or in an armchair? Her spirits sank when he took a chair facing her. He raised his glass in a toast, and she reciprocated. They drank, gazes locked. And Margaret waited.

His shoulders drooped so slightly she would not have noticed except that his posture was always ramrod-straight as befitted a military man. Exhaustion might account for it though he had shown no signs of it until this moment.

"I have been a soldier too long, with too few dealings with society. I have almost lost the habit of speaking without reserve."

She wanted to protest. His way with his nieces and nephews and the servants could not be faulted. Only her own foolishness made her yearn for more.

"I owe you an apology, Margaret. You would have made the perfect wife for a soldier. In spite of your father's advice, I should have married you. Not immediately, but if our attachment had lasted, Sir Percival and your father would probably have given their blessing. Like a hen-hearted fool, I resigned myself to having lost you."

"Your apology is unnecessary," she replied when she was able to speak around the lump in her throat. "I came to accept our marriage would have been a mistake. Would we be the people we are now if we had married? Perhaps you would not have reconciled with your brother. I only wish you had written to me instead of vanishing from my life as if you did not care."

"You were always in my thoughts. Sometimes I indulged in daydreams of Sebastian dying so I could return and make you a baroness. A boy's nonsense, and I realized it and prayed for forgiveness. I was never such a scoundrel as to wish my brother ill even when I was still furious with him. Nor such a fool as to expect or dare to hope you would wait for me, when I had no prospect of being able to support you in comfort. You were sure to receive an offer from some lucky man in better circumstances."

She willed her voice to be steady. "We've both made lives for ourselves."

"As we are old friends, will you permit me to say—"

Margaret sat frozen, clutching her glass.

"I am glad you married and were happy."

His face and words did not tell her how he felt about her marriage.

"He was considered a fine catch."

"But not for a gentlewoman."

"I was a dowerless fencing master's daughter, and my father and brothers approved of him."

This hardly seemed an adequate explanation. "I kept house for my father and brothers after moving to London. But Rupert married, and his wife took over that responsibility. I wanted a home of my own, and MacGavin did not demand I confine myself to managing his household. I knew something of firearms already, and when I showed an interest, he let me assist him."

"Forgive me, I should not have spoken."

"I don't mind." Did he understand?

Alasdair finally drank off his brandy. He had been

as slow to drink as she.

"There's a French saying about letting the water flow under the bridge, meaning to let go of the past. It may be good advice sometimes, but the river doesn't run dry, Margaret. I'm glad you found yourself able to go on with your life." He gazed at her steadily in the twilight's failing illumination.

If he had wanted her to continue to mourn his loss, she could have banished him from her heart though with regret. At the same time, his well-intentioned statement told her he had put his love for her behind him. She fought down bitterness and made her lips smile. "I did, as you have gone on with yours."

"But I haven't. I never found another love because I never stopped regretting I had given you up."

She stared at him, her mind a blank.

"I know early infatuations often die. You were younger than I. It's not surprising you recovered your spirits."

"Alasdair..." What can one say to something so mistaken?

"I would have felt guilty if you had not found someone to love. Although you lost MacGavin, perhaps eventually you will consider marrying again?"

"I liked and respected Gideon and was very fond of him, but I didn't love him, any more than he loved me. Our deepest affections had been given to others who could not be replaced."

He sat up straight. "Do you mean—? Tell me what you mean."

"I waited and waited for you, and if Rupert had not married, I might still be a spinster. Sybilla and I did not get along comfortably. Gideon MacGavin offered me marriage, and I accepted. We liked each other, and neither of us was lonely. Sometimes that is as much or more than one can expect."

"Margaret." He rose and moved to stand before her, bending to put his hands around hers where they were clenched at her waist. She opened them to clasp his and rose from the sofa, scarcely daring to hope. "You deserved so much more. Deserve so much more. Will you marry me, Margaret?"

Oh. "Yes." The word came out as a gasp. To save her soul she could not have said more although her heart was full of sentiments she ached to express.

He kissed her hands before drawing her into an embrace and pressing his lips to hers. The world disappeared around them. He broke the kiss off at last. Had he forgotten to breathe, too? She leaned against his chest, mindlessly glad to be wrapped in his arms. They stood entwined for long minutes, not speaking, her head against his shoulder, his cheek resting on the top of her head. The sheer comfort of it after so many tears and regrets was enough for the moment. Or was it? His arms and chest were hard with muscle. The aroma of smoldering peat from the hearth and the thyme, rosemary, and brandy scent of the Hungary Water he used on his handkerchiefs and perhaps his person blended intoxicatingly. She wanted—

But they were no longer hot-blooded young lovers. She wished they could recapture that passion, but those flames had burned down to embers. Her first marriage had been happy despite the lack of consuming love. The second could be at least as good.

With a deep breath, he released her.

"We could have the banns called beginning next

Sunday. Will you want to wait for your family to come for the wedding?"

Margaret found herself precipitated back to the workaday world. "While I wish they could be here, it's not practical. They can't leave the school and shop for as long as it would take to travel here and back. I will write them tomorrow. They will understand."

"Good. Having waited this long, I begrudge any further delay."

With regret, she recalled an impediment. "Should we be marrying so soon after Lord Hawkslowe's death?"

"We should. I believe my brother would be pleased for us to wed as soon as possible. My nieces and nephews need an aunt even more than they need a governess, and I need a wife and family." His smile was heartbreakingly sweet. "Besides, I love you. Let us not waste any more time."

He did love her.

Then he kissed her again, lingeringly. Passion blazed up like the flames in the game of snapdragon. Could she snatch the burning treasure without being burned and before the fire died down? Joy filled her: no need for haste. Their love had endured. Peat burns longer and hotter than wood. How delightful!

A word about the author…

Kathleen Buckley has loved writing ever since she learned to read. After a varied career, she began to write seriously, rather than as a hobby. Her first historical romance was penned (well, word-processed) after re-reading Georgette Heyer's Georgian/Regency romances. She is now the author of nine published Georgian romances: *An Unsuitable Duchess*, *Most Secret*, *Captain Easterday's Bargain*, *A Masked Earl*, *Portia & the Merchant of London*, *A Duke's Daughter*, *A Westminster Wedding*, and *A Peculiar Enchantment*. She is at work on the tenth and eleventh.

Warning: She writes traditional romances as true to their period as possible, with no explicit sex. There are occasional underhanded doings and some mild bad language, as the situations in which her characters find themselves sometimes call for an oath a little stronger than "Zounds!"

Visit Kathleen at

https://18thcenturyromance.com/

Thank you for purchasing
this publication of The Wild Rose Press, Inc.

For questions or more information
contact us at
info@thewildrosepress.com.

The Wild Rose Press, Inc.
www.thewildrosepress.com